I0818054

TANYSHA JANE

A Necessary Life

THE STORY OF MARY WOLLSTONECRAFT

Contents

Foreword

Mary Wollstonecraft was born on the 27th of April 1759 in Spitalfields, England. Her father's name was Edward John, and the name of her mother Elizabeth, of the family of Dixons of Ballyshannon in the kingdom of Ireland. Her paternal grandfather was a respectable manufacturer in Spitalfields, and is supposed to have left to his son a property of 10,000. She had three brothers and two sisters: Edward, James, Charles, Eliza, and Everina. Of these, Edward only was older than herself.

She was not the favourite either of her father or mother. Her father was a man of quick, impetuous disposition, subject to alternate fits of kindness and cruelty. In his family he was a despot, and his wife appears to have been the first, and most submissive of his subjects.

The unkindness or indifference from her father and family seemed to counteract the superiority of Mary's mind. From a person little considered in the family, she would eventually become its sort of director or umpire. For some reason or another, destiny did not intend for her to be a contented and unresisting subject of a despot.

The blows of her father, instead of humbling her, roused her indignation. Upon such occasions she felt her superiority and was apt to betray marks of contempt. The quickness of her father's temper led him sometimes to threaten similar violence towards his wife. In such situations, Mary would often position herself between her father and his wife, purposefully absorbing the blows that might be aimed at her mother. She laid whole nights upon the landing-place near their chamber-door, when, with reason or not, she apprehended her father might break out into paroxysms of violence. The conduct he held towards the members of his family, was of the same kind as that he observed towards animals. He was mostly extravagantly fond of them; but, when he was displeased, and this frequently happened, and for very trivial reasons, his anger was alarming.

The rustic situation in which Mary had spent her infancy, no doubt contributed to confirm the stamina of her constitution. She sported in the open air, and amidst the picturesque and refreshing scenes of nature, for which she always kept the most exquisite relish. Dolls and the other amusements usually appropriated to female children, she held in contempt; and felt a much greater propensity to join in the active and hardy sports of her brothers, than to confine herself to those of her own sex.

In 1765, he once more changed his residence, and occupied a convenient house behind the town of Barking in Essex, eight miles from London. In 1768, Mr. Wollstonecraft again removed the family to a farm near Beverly in Yorkshire. Here the family remained for six years. Mr. Wollstonecraft worked as a farmer, but the restlessness of his disposition would not suffer him to content himself with the occupation in which for some years he had been engaged, and the temptation of a commercial speculation of some sort being held out to him, he removed the family to a house in Queen's-Row, in Hoxton near London.

One of the acquaintances Mary formed at this time was a Mr. Clare, who inhabited the next house to that which was tenanted by her father, and to whom she was probably in some degree indebted for the early cultivation of her mind. But a connection more memorable originated about this time, between Mary and a person of her own sex, for whom she contracted a friendship so fervent, as for years to have constituted the ruling passion of her mind.

She was two years older than Mary. Her residence was at that time at Newington Butts, a village near the southern extremity of the metropolis; and the original instrument for bringing these two friends acquainted, was Mrs. Clare, wife of the gentleman already mentioned, who was on a footing of considerable intimacy with both parties. The acquaintance of Fanny, like that of Mr. Clare, contributed to ripen the immature talents of Mary. The name of this person was Frances Blood.

Before

Lisbon Portugal 29th November 1785

"Her breaths are shallow ma'am," the nurse dampened Frances' forehead with a towel.

"Fetch the doctor, I will wait here. Go! Hugh, come at once!" Hugh appeared in an instant.

"Where is the child?" he asked, kneeling beside Frances.

I pointed to the small cot a few steps away from her bed. "He is okay. The nurse washed him and he is fine."

"Frances? Frances? We are both here, my darling," said Hugh, resting his forehead on the bed. Frances' eyes would not open.

"Frances?" Her head turned to me. Small beads of sweat appeared at the corners of her brows and her face became pale. Similar to the dining room, the pungent odour of stagnant sweat and anguish filled her chamber. Frances coughed up more blood, each violent heave rattling her chest, and she rolled her head back to Hugh with a pained expression.

"My darling?" she whispered. "Everything hurts." I clutched her hand and rubbed her arm as her sweaty skin flushed between hot and cold.

"The doctor is on his way," said Hugh. I mustered a false sense of hope as Hugh's gaze wavered back and forth between Frances and me. "Just you wait on now, okay? He won't be long. Don't you go anywhere Frances. We need you." Consumption already destroyed half her body and pregnancy only prolonged the inevitable. My friend of ten years, disappearing before me like the early morning mists dispersing across a lifeless body of water.

"Mary?" she asked in her own gentle voice as a fit of coughing seized her. When her coughing stopped, she lay some minutes exhausted; then she whispered—"Mary, Hugh, lie down and cover yourselves with my quilt." I nestled close to her and closed my eyes.

As my thoughts darted from Earth to Heaven, I asked myself why I remain chained to life and its misery while my friend lay dying before me. Why is it the preservation of the species, not of individuals, which appears to be the design of the Deity throughout the whole of Nature?

Blossoms come forth only to be blighted; fish lay their spawn and are devoured; and what portion of humanity are born to be swept prematurely away. Does not this waste of budding life emphatically assert not men, but Man, whose preservation is so necessary to the completion of the grand plan of the universe? Children peep into existence, suffer, and die.

"What do we do?" tears pooled at the corner of Hugh's eyes and fell across his sun soaked cheeks as he nestled against her other side. As I turned my head to face them both, I could feel her warmth against me, and I pressed myself into her even tighter.

"Do remember what you told me all those years ago at the Clare's?" I sobbed as I held her hand. "And when I was ill, the beautiful little songs you'd sing to me. You've still those drawings to finish, Fanny, remember?" Hugh and I held her hands, and I kissed them as tears pooled at my eyes and flowed down my face.

She whispered. "You both must be sure and not grieve. William will be without a mother but he has you Hugh. We all must die one day, this day is mine." She released herself from my grip and pulled my chin towards her. "Promise me something, would you?"

"Anything."

"Do not diminish yourself to satisfy the world; the world is vast enough to live the life you deserve Mary."

"I love you better than all the world, Frances." I pressed her hand to my face as the warmth from her skin soaked into my cheeks. "All the world." My chest tightened, as if a heavy weight from above pressed down on me. Her fingers tremored in my grip and my wails echoed through the room. Take me instead.

Half an hour later, the doctor entered in a calm, authoritative manner and briefly attended to Frances. He muttered notations for himself, like a master adjusting a sculpture before him. After a few minutes, his mumbling stopped and he leaned in to whisper something to Hugh before departing.Tears streamed down Hugh's face as I held Frances tightly, afraid that if I let go, she would cease to exist. Hugh motioned to the door with his head, we both kissed her hands and spoke for a short while away from her bedside.

"What did the doctor say?"

He replied in a hushed tone. "He said her lungs are caving in on themselves and she'll simply stop breathing soon." Hugh looked to Frances and to their newborn baby in the cot. "What am I going to do Mary, do we tell her? Looking after him without any help is beyond my capabilities." We stepped forward and peered into the cot—their sleeping babe peacefully unaware his mother lay dying next to him.

"Her parents will be here soon from Ireland but we need to be with her now," I squeezed his hand and feigned a smile. "Return to her. I will inform the nurse we'll stay here through the night." I bowed my head. "And Hugh?"

"Yes?"

"Please, do not tell a dying man he'll be dead. Comfort her, she needs you," I said, and retreated to the sitting room. After arranging care of the infant and pouring ourselves two cups of tea, I returned to Frances' room to find Hugh cradling William. I paused at the doorway and tried to find a small slice of happiness in the painting before me I'd have to remember forever.

We attempted to give her tea, but she would not take it and after an hour, the nurse took William into his cot and I returned to lie by her side and hid my face in her neck.

"I want to sleep, but do not leave me, either of you. I would like to have you very much near me." Hugh kissed her forehead and I squeezed her hand.

I wiped her dampened hair from her face. "I'm not leaving Frances, I promise. Go to sleep and dream. I'll be here."

Hugh kissed her hand again. "I'm not leaving, you're—" Hugh caught my eye and I shook my head, bowing his head as more tears dripped from his eyes.

"Goodnight, Hugh. Mary."

"Goodnight, Frances," I kissed her hand again and closed my eyes.

Throughout the evening I waxed and waned in a delirium of sleep and restless life. I did not know how much time had past until the sunlight poked through a small gap in the curtains. I raised my head from her hand—my body dreary and heavy—and fixed my eyes on her chest and then to her eyes; her gaze fixed on the empty cot. Hugh lay asleep next to her, blissfully unaware she had already slipped into her eternal dream.

The weight of despair rendered me motionless and I collapsed to the floor, my chest searing with pain, as Hugh's world shattered in front of my eyes. As my body swayed back and forth, Hugh awoke within a moment and shook her body with force in an attempt to wake a lifeless husk. This extinction of my friend; the violent end of what I have termed domestic love.

I hope I shan't live long on this wretched earth.

Lisbon Portugal 1st December 1785

Death, in its stark finality, is the necessary end which punctuates the narrative of human existence. The ultimate equaliser, rendering irrelevant the distinctions of wealth, status or power. It strips away the veneer of earthly concerns, revealing the essence of what it means to be human.

Any moment might be our last. Everything is more beautiful because we're doomed. And fate? No one alive has ever escaped it. Not you, nor I; with us the day we are born. Death and fate await us; one day, our last sun will rise and we will descend to our death like nightfall.

This morning we buried Frances underneath a shady tree in the southwestern part of the British cemetery in Lisbon. I picked some flowers along our walk, whispered a prayer as her body entered the earth, and placed them on top of her earthly grave.

Frances was a woman of extraordinary talents. She would sing and dance. She drew with exquisite fidelity and neatness. When I first met her, I contemplated with a sentiment of inferiority and reverence. A girl, two years older than me at 18, spelt and wrote better than I. She inspired me to pay superficial attention to literature and when the wounds of childish inferiority wore off, I came to adore the inextinguishable thirst for knowledge she bestowed upon me.

As the priest said his last words, I leaned against Hugh, the warmth from his shoulder comforting me, and closed my eyes in a desperate attempt to escape from the terrible dream.

Lisbon Portugal 4th December 1785

To Eliza Bishop,

I'm almost afraid to see what lies ahead. So many things have happened in so short a time. My head grows light thinking of it.

After my arrival I could not write to tell you Fanny was ill. It seemed like signing her death warrant. I arrived last Monday, thirteen days at sea. Water and wind entered through cabin windows, while the ship dangerously rolled. By the time I arrived, Frances was already in labour and gave birth to a boy, William. By the next morning, she died. My spirits have forever flown, and I have lost all relish for pleasure.

I thought opening the school would be answer to my earthly problems.

Her brother George and Frances' parents arrived the day after her funeral, their ship held by opposing winds.

My head is stupid, and my heart is sick and exhausted. Soon I shall travel back to England, perhaps in a few weeks' time. I will care for her mother and father as George returned to Dublin. I have found a wet-nurse for the boy thank the heavens. I will share my last shilling with her parents to help them return to Ireland.

I don't know what I'm supposed to do.

M

Newington Green 27th February 1786

George Blood

I am indeed much distressed. My future prospects are still gloomy, moreover my debtors have a right to do what they please with me should I not be able to satisfy their demands.

My brother will not receive either of the girls, consequently Eliza in particular is helpless. Everina plans to venture into the world as a companion. However, I intend to stay on the Green and live without a servant; I am done with worldly pursuits and I rather think I have not much to hope for in life. Alas, if I can survive Frances' death, I can survive poverty and all the lesser ills of life. I feared this time, oh how I feared it.

My present plan would have made me shudder some years ago and now it does not terrify me. I cannot bear to think of bustling with the world forever in an extensive way. A little peace is all I desire.

As to your father and mother, I hope they are settled once again in Ireland. It weighs on me William did not live. I hope you can keep them from perishing. Often when I think of death as the only end of my sorrows and cares, I wish to them settled before I went to rest. Fate's decision should bring improvement, but it's the suspense and dread that troubles me.

In a dream the other night, poor Frances appeared to me and told me I should soon follow her. I am sick of the world, 'tis an unweeded garden. Weary of everything under the sun, I want a friend now I am alone.

Mary Wollstonecraft

Newington Green July 1786

George Blood

Thank you for your kind and affectionate letter. I must again repeat to you I am determined to earn my own substance, if not more, I hope to save money and pay my debts, which worry me beyond measure.

I have had two offers of being received as a governess in reputable families. One is in Wales, the other in Ireland. Lady Kingsborough in Ireland has offered forty pounds a year and half of that sum I could pay to discharge my debts and afterwards assist Eliza. I by no means like the idea of being a governess—consequently shut out from society and barred from pleasures of friendship.

Your letters my dear boy afford me great pleasure and I apologise if mine are not always written in an equal style of affection, for my lowness of spirits; I am often at war with myself. My heart sometimes overflows with kindness—at others seems exhausted and incapable of being interested about anyone.

Mary Wollstonecraft

Newington Green 23rd September 1786

My dear Eliza,

Yesterday I received a correspondence from Mrs Prior and I shall be in the employment of Lady Kingsborough within mere weeks.

Mrs Price died the other day and Dr Price intends on leaving the Green soon. He has been uncommonly friendly to me.

This is the last letter I shall write to you from this Island. Edward has behaved very rude to me and has not assisted me in the smallest degree—for it appears he is our father's son.

M

Henley Thursday 13th September 1787

To Joseph Johnson,

My dear sir,

Since I saw you, I have enjoyed solitude. Have you heard of a habituation for me? I often think of my new plan for life, and lest my sister prevail me to alter it— I have avoided mentioning it to her—I am determined!

Although your sex generally laugh at female determinations, I have never resolved to do anything of consequence that I did not adhere resolutely to it, till I had accomplished my purpose.

In the course of near nine and twenty years, I have gathered some experience and felt many severe disappointments. At last I long for peace and independence. Every obligation we receive from our fellow creatures is a new shackle, takes from our native freedom and debases the mind. Makes us mere earthworms. I am not fond of grovelling!

I hope to see you soon, when shall that be?

I am sir, yours.

Mary Wollstonecraft

London November 1787

Everina Wollstonecraft,

Presently my dear, I am once again thrown into the world. Last week I left Lord Kingsboroughs and they return in a few days to Mitchelstown. Hence, you can conceive how disagreeable pity and advice would be at this juncture.

However, Mr Johnson—whose uncommon kindness I believe has saved me from despair and vexations—assures me that if I exert my talents in writing, I may support myself comfortably. I tremble at the prospect. Should I succeed, my dear Girls, you shall have a home and a refuge for a few months a year where you can forget the cares that disturb the rest. In the meantime I shall strain every nerve in my body to procure a situation for Eliza nearer London.

You can scarcely perceive how delicately Mr Johnson is interested he is in my fate. He has now settled me in a little house at 49 George Street near Black-Friars Bridge. I have given him Mary, though I do not know when it shall be finished. Whenever I am tired of solitude I go to Mr Johnsons and there I meet the kind of company I find the most pleasure in. Despite everything, Charles writes angrily. I worry about the poor boy's fate.

Keep my plans from father and Edward. Only you and Eliza matter to me in the family and I wish to be a mother to you both. I wish to introduce you to Mr Johnson, you would respect him. And he has behaved so tenderly to me and shewn me humanity I have never known from anyone.

I am yours.

Mary

After

Number 72 St. Paul's Churchyard London
7th February 1809

The young Frances sat at my dining table and fiddled with her dark auburn hair between her fingers, twirling several strands until they wound no more.

"I know what plagues you. Why will you not accept my help?" She began breaking strands of her hair into smaller and smaller pieces, one by one and without a word.

"More soup, my dear one?" Anne called from the kitchen. Frances shook her head as a tear fell from one of her eyes. "She is okay, thank you, Anne." Her eyes averted my gaze as I stood from my chair opposite, posted myself in the seat beside her and placed an opened hand on the dining table.

"Joseph, why do you care for me so? I am not deserving of it. I am so wretchedly miserable," she said, her head still down.

"May I show you something?" I asked. At last, her eyes, now bloodshot and red, found mine.

After

December 27, St Paul's Churchyard, London
The year 1807

The young Frances sat at my dining table and fiddled with her dark auburn hair between her fingers, twirling several strands until they would no more.

"I know what plagues you. Why will you not accept my help?" She began breaking strands of her hair into smaller and smaller pieces, one by one and without a word.

"More soda, my dear one?" Anne called from the kitchen. Frances shook her head and a tear fell from one of her eyes. "She's okay, thank you, Anne." Her eyes averted my gaze as I stood from my chair opposite, perched myself in the seat beside her and placed an upturned hand on the dining table.

"Joseph, why do you care for me so? I am not deserving of it. I am so wretchedly miserable," she said, her head still down.

"May I show you something?" I asked. At last, her eyes, now bloodshot and red, found mine.

Act I

Number 72 St. Paul's Churchyard London 17th November 1791

"You are late," piqued Joseph. His familiar furrowed brow opened the door of his shop at Number 72 St Paul's Churchyard.

"Is he here?" I whispered loudly, entering his bookstore. The wooden scent of bookshelves reached my nose as I stepped inside.

"Godwin? Well, yes, of course. I told you—"

"Paine."

"Oh," he smiled. "Yes, he shall be here for a few weeks, months perhaps, one would assume," Joseph paused on the staircase, bent lower and whispered. "He is a quiet, odd sort of fellow. Still, I do admit I have an affinity with him."

As I entered the small, oddly shaped dining room, the antique floorboards bent under my step. Joseph never bothered the owner of his apartment to repair anything. A sullen-looking man, who I assumed to be William Godwin, glanced at me in mid-discussion with Thomas Paine, the latter of whom seated himself at the head of the long wooden table. The English-born American revolutionist reacquainted himself with England for the time being. The purpose of his travel was between himself and his God.

"Pray tell us your thoughts on everything in France—" said Thomas. "Oh, hello."

"How do you do?" I asked, as I set myself in a seat.

"My name is—"

"Ah!" someone thumped against Joseph's door. "He is here." In a matter of moments, Joseph's maid returned from downstairs and reemerged in the dining room with a man I did not recognise behind her.

"Madames and Monsieur's, this is Olaudah Equiano," said Joseph.

Thomas Paine rose and bowed. "The pleasure is mine, Mr Equiano. How do you do?"

"Well Sir indeed." Olaudah rounded the wooden table and posted himself in one of the empty chairs beside me.

"Anne's prepared us her delightful soup," Joseph's maid poured us each a small bowl of boiled vegetables and a glass of French wine. "By the way, this is Mary Wollstonecraft, from London. She works for our Analytical Review and writes. Mary is reaching the end of Vindication, which is quite thrilling."

"A pleasure." I raised my wine to Olaudah and adjusted my dress.

"Thomas Paine, a name synonymous with American nationalism, left an enduring mark on the nation's history. I am sure he is willing to share his rich trove of stories about the American Revolution, waiting to be unveiled and shared with us this evening. Olympe de Gouges, a playwright and philosopher from Paris. Helen Maria Williams, who has returned from Paris. And over here, William Godwin—another philosopher." Olaudah smiled at each of us as he made himself comfortable.

"Have you travelled far, Olaudah?" I asked, as each of us started our soup.

"Very, Mrs Wollstonecraft, I—"

"Mr Equiano, I now recalled where I remember your name," said Helen. "You are the writer of his own narrative? Mr Johnson here sold it a few years ago now." Olaudah nodded.

"My memoir, you are correct, Miss Williams. Though I believe those who publish their own memoirs cannot escape the imputation of vanity. It is also my misfortune what is extraordinary and uncommon is rarely, if ever, believed."

"I believe you," said Joseph. "A brilliant narrative we must share for our world to change," Joseph said, smiling before continuing to eat.

"Aye, Africa appeared quite curious indeed, but I too believe you sir," said Paine. Joseph removed himself from the table and disappeared down the stairs to his bookstore, returning with Olaudah's book. Despite the hardships he endured as a former slave, an air of quiet determination hung about him. His voice, rich and melodious, echoed the distant lands from whence he came from. His eyes, deep and expressive, sparkled with warmth and wisdom as he reflected on his triumph over past adversaries.

"Africa? Vhat vas it like?" asked Miss de Gouges as Joseph gave her Olaudah's narrative.

"Our pine apples, they are about the size of the largest sugar-loaf, and finely flavoured. We have pepper and various delicious fruits not seen in Europe. Honey is in abundance. Everyone contributes something to the common stock; and as we are unacquainted with idleness, we have no beggars. The West India planters prefer the slaves of Benin or Eboe to those of any other part of Guinea, for their hardiness, intelligence, integrity and zeal. I remember an instance or two when locusts visited us and destroyed our harvests for the year and produced famine."

"May I ask, how does one obtain slaves in Africa?" I asked. Joseph's intense gaze bore into me as he shot me a look.

"Of course. Why I wrote my story for questions such as yours, no? Seizing slaves in Africa is common, kidnapping is, more common than any other. When a trader wants slaves, he applies to a chief for them, you see, and tempts him with his wares. It is not uncommon, if on this occasion the chief yields to the temptation with as little firmness, and accepts the price of his fellow creatures liberty with as little reluctance as the enlightened merchant." Olaudah swirled his wineglass around and drank the remaining liquid before continuing.

"My mother named me Olaudah, which, in our language, signifies vicissitude or fortune also, one favoured, and having a loud voice and well spoken. As far as I can remember, we were totally unacquainted with swearing, and all those terms of abuse and reproach which find their way so readily and copiously into the languages of more civilised people. The only expressions I can remember were, 'may you rot, or may you swell'. My deep affection for my mother compelled me to always be near her during certain times. This led to us being confined in a designated house until we presented an offering for purification. Such is the imperfect sketch. My memory has furnished me with the manners and customs of a people among whom I first drew my breath." All six of us refrained from continuing to eat our soups. Instead, we lent forward over the table as Mr Olaudah recounted his tales.

"And you someone kidnapped you?" asked Godwin, whose eyes became widened with intensity with each sentence.

"Yes, sir. If I may?" Olaudah looked to Joseph, who smiled and gestured to his guests.

"One day, when all our people went out to their works as usual, and only I and my dear sister were left to mind the house, two men and a woman got over our walls, and in a moment seized us both, and, without giving us time to cry out, or make resistance, they stopped our mouths, and ran off with us into the nearest wood. They tied our hands and carried us until nightfall. We arrived at a small house where the robbers rested and spent the night. Unbound, but unable to take any food; and, being quite overpowered by fatigue and grief, our only relief was some sleep, which allayed our misfortune for a short time.

"Did you ever discover who they were?" asked Thomas.

Olaudah shook his head. "The next day proved a day of greater sorrow than I experienced; for my sister and I were then separated, while we lay clasped in each other's arms. From the time I left my own nation, I always found somebody who understood me till I came to the seacoast. I was sold. Three, maybe four times after I arrived. I was transported further along the coast and arrived at a town where I saw a slave ship anchored, waiting for its cargo."

"And den you vere, sent to America?" asked Olympe.

"Yes Madame, America. And through many trials and near-death experiences, I find myself here in this lovely apartment of yours, Joseph, eating dinner with you fine people." Olaudah finished swirling his wine and raised it to the group. "I say, we toast to liberty."

"And freedom." Olympe raised her glass. An aura of defiance and passion flowed into every part of her movement; unapologetic confidence, which commanded attention.

"To education," Helen and I said in unison.

"To resistance against oppression and slavery," added Olaudah.

"Here here," everyone raised their glass to Olaudah.

Olympe took a small sip from her wine. "If women have the right to mount the scaffold…"

"So we should have the right equally to mount the podium," I added, as both Olympe and Thomas' smiles grew larger as the air became thick with anticipation of philosophical debate.

"I shall add dat to my paper, Madame," raising her glass to me. Our worries, like an uninvited guest, occupied the empty chairs in quietness.

"How was the Federation Helen? I cannot believe you are back. I have not seen you in so long," I said.

"Ah, the Fête de la Fédération," said Thomas. "Spectacular. I resumed acquaintance with La Fayette. Did I tell you, Joseph?" Joseph smiled and shook his head.

Helen rested her spoon on the table. "I shall be able to give you a faint sketch, but your own imaginations must add colouring and spirit to it. If I may?" Each of us around the table nodded as Helen recounted her tale of Paris from the year previous.

"The celebrations started on the 13th of July, 1790, at the Notre Dame. The overture the musicians played was simple and majestic. Near the conclusion of the piece, the composer produced a melancholy emotion, affecting the audience."

"I had never heard anything such as it," said Olympe. "Dere vere zo many people in de streets."

"Neither," added Thomas.

"But what added to the effect was the sound of a loud bell which mixed itself with this awful concert, an imitation of the alarm bell which rung in every church and convent in Paris the day before the taking of the Bastille."

"It produced zo much eh, confusion in Paris vhen de bells rang," said Olympe. "Zo many people vere running about in terror. It 'ad never 'appened before dat night of de 13th of July in '89."

"The audience around me appeared to breathe with difficulty. Every heart, frozen with terror till the bell ceased. The music then changed its tone to a flourish of drums and trumpets."

"And then, the fete," said Thomas. "Whereabouts were you, Helen?"

"I seated myself on the right-hand side of the Champs de Mars. Two hundred thousand men walking in procession through arches. Half a million people assembled at the spectacle, which connected the enthusiasm of moral feelings with the solemn pomp of religious ceremonies. Twenty days of labour, enlivened by the enthusiasm of the people, accomplished what would require the toil of years. They worked the Champ de Mars into an immense amphitheatre, where forty rows of wooden seats, raised one above another with earth, enveloped the arena."

"And the distinctions of rank did not appear to matter," said Thomas. "I saw everyone in the crowd. Soldiers, women..."

"At the upper end of the amphitheatre, they built a Pavillion for the reception of the King, the Queen, their attendants and the National Assembly, covered with a striped tent-cloth of the national colours, and decorated with streamers of the same beloved tints, and a Fleur de Lys. They displayed the white flag above the King's seated spot. In the middle of the Champ de Mars, they placed the L'Autel de La Patrie, where priests dressed in long white robes burnt incense. They wrote several epitaphs on the altar, but the words La Nation, la Loi, et le Roi—The Nation, the law and the King—were visible from the greatest distance."

"De procession marched to de Champ de Mars, through de streets of Paris. It vas monumental, I have eh, never seen zomething zo spectacular in Paris," said Olympe.

"In the streets, at the windows, and on the roofs of the houses, the people, transported with joy, shouted and wept as the cortege passed. Old men kneeled in the streets, blessing God they had lived to witness the happy moment. The people ran to the doors of their houses armed with refreshments, which they offered to the troops; and crowds of women surrounded the soldiers, and holding up their infants in their arms, and melting into tears, promised to make their children attach themselves to the principles of the new constitution of France."

"And the King and the Queen were present?" asked Joseph. Helen, Olympe and Thomas all nodded.

"Of course," said Thomas.

"They had to be," added Olympe.

"The National Assembly walked towards the pavilion, where they placed themselves with the King, the Queen, the royal family. High mass was performed, after which Monsieur de La Fayette, who had been appointed by the King as Major General of the Federation, ascended the altar, gave the signal, and himself took the national oath. In an instant, every sword was drawn, and every arm lifted up. The King pronounced the oath, which the President of the National Assembly repeated, and six hundred thousand voices reechoed the solemn words."

"De Queen raised de Dauphin in her arms, shewing him to de people and de army," said Olympe. "De people I 'ad spoke to said only one subject of regret. Did you vind de same Helen?"

"Yes, some citizens I spoke to murmured the King took the national oath in the pavilion, instead of performing the ceremony at the foot of the altar."

"Monsieur de La Fayette, after de Federation, vent to the Chateau de La Muette. I vanted to see him but it vas impossible."

"The celebrations lasted for days," said Thomas. "The evening of the 14th of July was spectacular."

"Ah yes," said Helen. "The lights and celebrations illuminated the whole of Paris at night."

"And during de day, dey transformed de ruins of de Bastille as if it vere revived from de dead."

"They planted young trees in rows and covered the ground with fresh clods of grass. Illuminated with a blaze of light," said Helen.

"I wish to visit one day," I said.

"It fills me with horror even considering the possibility," said Godwin. I shrugged and grinned at Helen, inviting her to proceed.

"Once we arrived at the fortress and alighted from the

carriage, we descended with difficulty into the dungeons, too low to admit us standing upright. We visited the darkened rooms at noon with the light of a candle, for it would have been too dark otherwise. The sight of the chains and hooks used to restrain the prisoners, many of which being below the level of the water, left an enduring image in our minds. A noxious vapour promulgated from them, which more than once extinguished the candle, and the air so insufferable it required a deep spirit of curiosity to tempt one to enter."

"Good God!" said Joseph. My stomach squirmed.

"And to these regions of horror were human creatures dragged at the caprice of despotic power. What a melancholy consideration there appeared to be a greater number of these dungeons than I could have imagined."

"I heard there were tunnels," said Thomas.

"Me also Monsieur Paine. Zo many rumours of de Bastille vould circulate Paris every few months."

"You are both correct. Only the hard heart of tyranny itself would devise such an idea. Since the destruction of the building, many subterranean cells have been discovered underneath a piece of ground enclosed within the walls of the Bastille. It masqueraded as a bank of solid earth until the horrid secrets of this prison-house revealed themselves. A Frenchman told me they found some skeletons in the recesses, with irons still fastened on their decaying bones." Helen finished her story and silence enveloped the apartment for a few minutes, except for the clinking of spoons on bowls. Imagined horrors of the Bastille flooded my mind as Helen and Olympe whispered to each other about the Bastille in French, whilst Godwin and Paine began a small conversation about America.

"Miss de Gouges, the English nation is disposed towards your Revolution. Godwin here reminded me of my conversation with La Fayette several months ago."

"The English nation is disposed to the progress of liberty in the entire world, shall I say," said Godwin. Despite being considered a man of philosophical thought, he spoke few words.

"Aye," said Thomas. "This feeling will become more

general in England as the intrigues and artefacts of its government are better known, and the principles of the revolution better understood."

"It surprised me a nation so enlightened as the French submitted so long to the oppressions of their government," said Helen. "I reflected on the fact a despotic throne can only shine like the radiance of lightning, while everything around it is engulfed in darkness and horror. May no such strong contrast of light and shade again exist in the political system of France again. May the beams of liberty, like the beams of day, shed their benign influence on the cottage of the peasant, as well as on the palace of the monarch."

"Aye, well said Helen," said Thomas. "To liberty." He raised his glass to her and took a sip.

"We require a free press in England for any such thing to occur here," said Godwin. "I do not have an answer for how to achieve what we require, however."

"Nor I," I replied.

"I cannot say for certain, but I believe most English newspapers are on the pay of our government or at least, indirectly connected with it," said Joseph, who returned to reading one of his pamphlets.

"Truth will prevail, Joseph," said Thomas. "We cannot prevent the prevalence of truth. Daily falsehoods of those papers no longer have the desired effect. Anyhow, Miss de Gouges. The situation in Paris. The people are talking of war?" Olympe laid her spoon on the table and relaxed back in her chair, pausing for a moment as five pairs of eyes stared at her.

"Oui. Dere are er, how do you say, er..."

"Whispers?" asked Joseph, glancing up from his paper. "She will partake in war with us?"

"Again..." I said.

"Almost certainly, Monsieur. From vhat I 'ave been told."

"The Jacobins, they want this?" I asked.

"Mm, yes, Madame. And I believe dey will, how do you say, protest women voicing dere concerns about the war."

"You will still write?" asked Thomas. "Even though they can, well..." Remorse spread across his face as he traced the top of his wineglass with his finger.

"Précisément, Monsieur. Précisément. It does not matter to me. Dey cannot kill us all, eh?" Thomas continued to trace the wineglass with his finger as Godwin spoke first.

"And of the King?" asked Godwin.

"The King?" replied Paine. "Monarchy and succession have laid the world in blood and ashes. 'Tis a form of government which the word of God bears testimony against, and blood will attend it. They need to banish him, not kill him."

"You speak from the heart, Monsieur," said Olympe.

"France, she bleeds from the same vein as America once did," said Olaudah. "And I, too."

"Aye," said Paine. "And America will flourish, now the first twenty years of our lives are no more a precedent for the next twenty. As I hope you live yours in this new life you have made for yourself." The two nodded in recognition as we once again returned to our soups for a few moments.

"But your King Olympe," said Olaudah. "Your thoughts on the matter?" the table hushed once again as flickering candles illuminated Henry's Nightmare. One day, I shall have that painting torn down or ripped to shreds. "Louis is guilty as king, but once his title is eh, removed, he shall cease to be guilty in the eyes of our republic," she replied. "He might have been a virtuous king."

"Aye," Thomas nodded in reply.

"Louis made the great nobles pay deir debts and he alone, of all our tyrants, kept no courtesans. He vas weak," she continued. "His court deceived him; he deceived us and deceived himself."

"The Varennes plot is what did them in," said Helen. "Slipping into the night and attempting to flee? Only a fool would try."

"What will they do? Kill him?" I asked. The candles flickered upon the faces of my fellow guests as silence filled the room again. Thomas slumped into his chair in thought as the maid began tidying the soup bowls, replacing them with a small bowl of rice pudding.

"Oui, eh, most probably," replied Olympe. "But dere are many, many women and men who shall defend him not as King, but as Louis Capet. He does not deserve to die."

"No one deserves to die in the name of liberty," I replied. "No one."

"No one deserves to die in de name of justice and standing for vhat is right," added Olympe. "But, ah, here we are." Thomas and Godwin in thought and Joseph reading, Olaudah ignited conversation once again in a soft, solemn manner.

"There are whispers amongst my circle you are to print the Second Part of your epistle, Mr Paine." Joseph and Thomas glanced at one another as the pamphlet fell from Joseph's hands.

"The walls converse," said Joseph, in between small coughs and splutters. "You are correct but I shall not print it."

"Aye," said Thomas, covering a smile with his hands. "Maybe the walls whisper all the words Joseph mutters to himself when he is frustrated at our writing Mary." A mumble of laughter resounded from the table as the maid poured more wine. A smile almost appeared on Godwin's face, but I perceived it wouldn't form itself even if he wished it so.

"What say you then, Mr Paine?" I asked. "The newspapers near called for your head on the First Part."

"Aye," he replied. "Naturally they will try again."

"Will they follow France's edict and stop seditious publications here do you think?"

"Perhaps, though try as they might, I have far more friends and helpers than they realise."

"You must enjoy the notoriety, no?"

He laughed in reply. "And you Mrs Wollstonecraft? I quite enjoyed your first Vindication."

"Enjoy celebrity? Never. Whilst I quite enjoy the conversations and dining in regular fashion in the closeness of this fine gentleman and his guests," Joseph grinned, "I rather find obscurity enjoyable."

"But you are writing at the moment?" asked Thomas Paine. Joseph's smile grew even larger as his eyes widened.

"Yes," narrowing my eyes to Joseph who hid behind his pamphlet again. "The book is near completion and it—"

"It is quite the work," said Joseph, still hiding behind the pages.

"Thank you, Joseph, but your sentiments are not necessary. It is my truth and shall always be."

"Zo," said Olympe. "What are your most favourite parts?" I pondered my thoughts for a moment and scratched at the ageing wooden table beneath my fingers. Mere days ago the jumbled manuscript sat sprawled like a peppering of autumn leaves across this table.

"Well, I have come to learn, through many of my acquaintances, girls who have been weakly educated are often cruelly left by their parents without any provision; and, of course, are dependent on not only the reason, but the bounty of their brothers."

"Unlike you, Mary," said Joseph, flipping over a pamphlet page.

"You support your brothers?" asked William Godwin. The man speaks.

"Hmm? Oh. Well yes I—"

"And her two sisters," said Joseph, still behind his pamphlet. "You were telling us about these poor drudges, Mary?"

"Oh. Well, you see these brothers are usually, to view the fairest side of the question, good sort of men, and give as a favour, what children of the same parents had an equal right to." Olympe and Thomas made an attempt at their rice puddings and awaited the continuation of my story.

"In this equivocal humiliating situation, a docile female may remain some time, with a tolerable degree of comfort. But, when the brother marries, a probable circumstance, from being considered as the mistress of the family, she is viewed with averted looks as an intruder, an unnecessary burden on the benevolence of the master of the house, and his new partner."

Everyone around the table sat in thought for a while as they let my words stew in their minds like a bubbling pot of soup. "And the wife. A cold-hearted, narrow-minded woman, and this is not an unfair supposition; for the present mode of English education does not tend to enlarge the heart any more than the understanding, is jealous of the little kindness which her husband shows to his relations; and her sensibility not rising to humanity, she is displeased at seeing the property of her children lavished on a helpless sister."

Olympe raised her glass towards me. "My dear Mary, I have been telling this for years. Years!"

"One day, Olympe, we shall not be outsiders. Women, like us, will be educated. They will write and work and be free." Joseph placed his pamphlet on the table and rested his hands on his lap, nodding for me to continue.

"To prevent any misconstruction, I must add, I do not believe a private education can work wonders. Opinions and manners of society greatly influence the education of men and women."

"A type of public education, you could say?" asked Thomas.

"Acquiring education is not easy, and I doubt whether any knowledge can be attained without labour and sorrow; and those who wish to spare their children both, should not complain if they are neither wise nor virtuous." Paine let out a booming laugh, as Olympe and Olaudah joined in the commotion. A sort of smile appeared on William Godwin's face, though I do not think it a true one.

"You hold no prisoners in the fort of your mind Mary," said Thomas. "I enjoy it."

"It is truth though. They aim to make their children prudent; and prudence, early in life, is the cautious craft of ignorant self-love." Olympe spat out her wine.

"I am okay," she laughed a little as she wiped her green and white striped dress.

"Do you think we as a society shall ever achieve it?" asked Olaudah, as he finished his rice pudding.

"Once your people are free and girls have access to education, Mr Equino, we will have achieved what we have philosophised here tonight. She will stop the progress of knowledge if she is not prepared by education. Truth must be common to all. The fact is, however, men expect from education what education cannot give. The honey must be the reward of the individual's own industry. Trying to make youth wise through someone else's experience is as absurd as expecting the body to grow strong through mere talk or observation." Olaudah and I clinked our glasses and each took another sip of wine.

"One day," said Thomas, raising his glass to me and winking. "And may our friends build our path there." Olympe, Olaudah, William, Joseph and I smiled together at the mention of friends.

"The most holy band of society is friendship." I raised my glass and nodded to Joseph. "As rare as love is, true friendship is still rarer." He smiled from ear to ear and nodded in acknowledgement as each of us took a sip from our wines.

"Let us eat, drink, and love, for tomorrow we die." Joseph took another sip of his wine and winked at me. "I edited your book, you do not think I read what you write?" I giggled at his recital.

"Friendship is a serious affection, Joseph. The most sublime affection, rooted in principle and fortified by time."

"The reverse may be said of love," said Thomas with a glazed stare.

"Mary thinks the same," said Joseph.

"I do. Both cannot exist in the same heart; even when excited by different objects, they destroy each other. They can only be felt in succession-never at the same time."

"What is your opinion on love?" asked Godwin. I rubbed the base of my neck and swirled the remaining drops of wine in my glass.

"Why do you ask?"

"I am curious."

I rested back in my chair and paused to admire the scene of the six people around Joseph's table. A philosopher, an editor, a former slave, a Frenchwoman and writer, an Englishwoman and Thomas Paine, the man of many things and many titles. "It is better to be disappointed in love than never to love; to lose a husband's fondness, than forfeit his esteem. If it be the supreme good, let women be only educated to inspire it, and let every charm be polished to intoxicate the senses. But, if they are moral beings, let them have a chance to become intelligent; and let love to man be only a part of the glowing flame of universal love."

"And you are writing about this in your recent work?" asked Olaudah.

"Yes sir," I replied. "My reply to Talleyrand's proposal of

education."

"Does anyone require more soup before I dish the pastries?" asked Anne.

"No thank you," we countered. Joseph smiled and thanked Anne as she tidied the small bowls from the table and replaced them with small plates of pastries, jams and various creams.

"And what do you suppose women will do in society? If they are educated?" Godwin reached for a small pastry and began to tear it apart.

"What will they do? Well..."

"You must have some idea?" he said, raising his eyebrows and smiling at me.

I paused for a moment and studied his face in detail. "They might study the art of healing. Be physicians, nurses. Midwifery; though I am afraid the word midwife in our dictionaries will soon give place to accoucheur, and one proof of the former delicacy of the sex be effaced from the language."

"They could eh, study politics no?" asked Olympe.

I nodded and smiled. "And business of various kinds, if educated in a more orderly manner. Women would not marry then for support. I do wonder sometimes, how many women waste life away in the prey of discontent, who might have practised as physicians, regulated a farm, managed a shop, and stood erect, supported by their own industry, instead of hanging their heads surcharged with the dew of sensibility. Would men snap our chains and be content with rational fellowship, instead of slavish obedience, they would find us more observant daughters, more affectionate sisters, more faithful wives, more reasonable mothers—in a word, better citizens. We should then love them with true affection, because we should learn to respect ourselves; and the peace of mind of a worthy man would not be interrupted by the idle vanity of his wife, nor his babes sent to nestle in a strange bosom, having never found a home in their mother's."

"But how are women to exist, Mary?" asked Helen. "There is no trodden path to follow."

"Precisely my point Helen. How women are supposed to

exist in a state where there is to be neither marrying nor giving in marriage, we are not told. Moralists have agreed the tenor of life proves that man is prepared by various circumstances for a future state. They constantly concur in advising women only to provide for the present. Gentleness, docility, and a spaniel-like affection are consistently recommended as the cardinal virtues of our sex. I remember reading somewhere a writer declared it is masculine for a woman to be melancholy. It is not the government which is defective and unmindful of the happiness of one half of its members?"

"I like your sentiment," said Helen.

"That it does not provide for honest, independent women and encourage them to fill respectable stations? Let woman share the rights, and she will emulate the virtues of man; for she must grow more perfect when emancipated, or justify the authority which chains such a weak being to her duty."

"It angers me zo."

"You wrote your pamphlet also on this subject, did you not?" asked Helen. Olympe bit her bottom and attempted to stifle a smile.

"She did. I read every word." I smiled at Olympe who smile beamed. Her face, adorned with her bright blonde wispy hair bore the traces of both beauty and determination.

"What is your opinion? Do you agree with Mary?" Olympe nodded.

"Ignorance, neglect or contempt for de rights of woman are de sole causes ov public misfortunes and governmental corruption, in France at least. Woman is born free and remains equal to man in rights. Dese rights are liberty, property, security, and especially resistance to oppression. Nobody and no individual may exercise authority which does not emanate expressly from de nation. The laws ov nature and reason prohibit all actions which are injurious to society. No hindrance should be put in the way of anything not prohibited by dese wise and divine laws, nor may anyone be forced to do what dey do not require."

"And what about representation?" asked Thomas.

Olympe shrugged. "It must be de same for everyone; all citizenesses and citizens, being equal in the nation's eyes, should be equally admissible to all public dignities, offices and employments, according to their ability, and with no other distinction than their virtues and talents. No one should be disturbed for his fundamental opinions."

"I remember you wrote something in your declaration about thoughts and opinions of woman and I agree with you," I said.

"You mean my expression dat a woman can say freely, 'I am de mother of your child'?"

"Yes. So long as a woman does not lie about the paternity of her children, the liberty assures recognition by their fathers."

"What I do not understand is how are we supposed to make this so?" asked Helen. "We can talk about this forever."

"Public power," said Thomas.

"You mean institutional laws?" I asked.

"And any society in which de guarantee of rights is not assured or de separation ov powers not settled has no constitution," said Olympe.

"Like England," said Thomas.

"Precisement monsieur. The constitution is null and void if the majority of individuals composing de nation have not cooperated in its drafting. How is it fair and just? The torch ov truth in France's Revolution has not dispersed de clouds of folly and usurpation, though. Our sex has gained no advantages in the Revolution. Nothing." Olympe fiddled with her spoon on the table and flicked it between her fingers whilst she composed her breath. "For centuries of corruption, our sex has reigned over the weakness of men. Now our empire is destroyed. What is left for us? We 'ave nothing."

"They have to want to change Olympe," I said. "It is why I wrote to Talleyrand on the subject of education. If they are educated, at least their minds will be more free."

"I do not dink legislators will think sanely about the education of women in France Madame Mary."

Everyone around the table sat in silence momentarily, sharing in the small samplings of food from Anne. And then, as small conversations broke out between Olympe and Olaudah, as well as William and Thomas, Joseph and I sat in comfortable silence as Anne prepared dessert in the kitchen.

"Let us take a quick break, shall we?" said Joseph. "Anne is preparing some dessert, so best to wander for some air now."

*

Thomas, Olympe, Olaudah, Godwin and I exited to the street from number 72.

"Aye, the air is fresh," said Thomas, closing the door behind me. "I shall miss her," he said with a sigh.

"Do you intend to leave Monsieur Paine?" said Olympe.

Nodding in reply, Olympe and I linked arms and wandered along the cobblestone under the shadow of the golden dome. Joseph existed not in solitary in St Paul's Churchyard. Booksellers and small apartments lined its streets though, the buildings appeared small in stature compared to the church of St Paul. Men and women strolled past us, walking every which way, as the hive of activity bloomed near St. Paul's every afternoon and evening.

"Is it always like this?" asked Olympe.

"Mmm," I replied.

"It is, eh, a huge dome."

"It is rather grandiose, isn't it? Quite unnecessary, but it is quite easy to find your way here from anywhere in London, at least." We walked along its northern side and admired the intricate detail of the church's exterior. "Christopher Wren is the man who designed it." Olympe stopped for a moment and stared at the top of the church. Its cross stands proudly atop the dome.

"It is quite beautiful," she said, straining her neck to take in the view of the entire building.

"Come, let me show you my favourite view." We continued strolling a little west along St. Paul's Churchyard, leaving Olaudah, Godwin and Paine behind.

"Okay. Now. Close your eyes. This way, this way," I turned her around to face the church, some 300 metres away, glowing in the winter's afternoon light. "Now open."

She paused for a moment before opening her eyes.

She took a deep breath before speaking in her French-laden English accent I came to admire throughout the evening. “It is beautiful, Mary,” she said. “I appreciate it from dis distance rather than up close.” I nodded as I too soaked in the building’s view underneath the English sky. The buildings surrounding the church appeared infantile compared to the monstrosity before us.

“It is important to gain a perspective from whatever is in your view. It lets you appreciate it more.”

“Your writing?” she asked.

“I was more thinking of the church at this present moment,” I laughed. “But now you mention the situation, I guess you are perhaps right. I often take slight breaks between writing, otherwise my head is all jumbled.”

“Me also,” she said. “Otherwise, de words become de same.” We intertwined our arms again and started on our way back to number 72.

“Will you return to France soon?” I asked, making our way around small puddles of yesterday’s rain.

“Uh, soon.”

“You must visit when you are in London again, perhaps.” We both nodded at another pair of women walking arm in arm.

“Perhaps. I do not know when I vill come back.” Olympe’s eyes found the ground and mine returned to the dome. I fantasised what it would be like to view London from atop in the sky; view the chimneys poking their tall necks from buildings like reeds of grass along the Thames.

“Well, when you do, we shall make dinner at Joseph’s and discuss everything. You will have to tell me all about Paris.”

“Vhy you do not come to Paris?” We stopped short of the door of number 72.

“I do not...know. I haven’t considered it.”

“Hmm. Vell, you must visit,” Olympe’s eyes widened, and she smiled at the thought. “Come, de others I think are inside.” We returned to the dining room and sat down in the middle of a conversation, or more perhaps, a lecture from Paine.

“—The origin of the Government of England, so far as

relates to what is called its line of monarchy, being one of the latest, is perhaps the best recorded. Those bands of robbers parcelled out the world, and divided it into dominions." Joseph, William, Helen and Olaudah began eating their desserts as Thomas Paine continued.

"Where is the pudding?" a familiar voice called from the kitchen. Henry. My stomach sank like a ship crashing down from a wave.

"Ask Anne, I do not know," yelled Joseph, rolling his eyes. "Why is he regularly late? He practically lives here." Doesn't he just.

"—They so began, these robbers, as is typically the case, to quarrel with each other."

"Like all families," said Olaudah.

"Quite right," said Thomas. "People saw what was first acquired by violence as something they could lawfully take. Thus, like children taking small wooden toys from each other, they alternately invaded the dominions each assigned himself, and the brutality with which they treated each other explains the original character of European monarchy. Ruffian torturing ruffian. The conqueror considered the conquered not as his prisoner, but as his property. He led him in triumph, rattling in chains, and doomed him, at pleasure, to slavery or death. As time obliterated the history of their beginning, their successors assumed new appearances to cut off the entail of their disgrace, but their principles and objects remained the same. What at first was plunder assumed the softer name of revenue. And the power seized, they were destined to inherit."

"From such beginnings of governments, what could be expected but a continued system of war and extortion?" asked William. I sighed in agreement with him.

"Right, pudding acquired." Henry Fuseli waltzed into the darkened dining room, placed his small bowl of rice pudding on the table and began devouring it. Olympe and I stared in awe, mine an admiration of sorts—her expression resembled one more of disturbance.

"Why would the farmer," Thomas continued. "Lay aside his peaceful pursuit of the plough, and go to war with the farmer of another country? What inducement has the manufacturer? What is dominion to them, or to any class of men in a nation? Does it add an acre to any man's estate, or raise its value? Are not conquest and defeat each of the same price, and taxes the never-failing consequence?—Nevertheless, this reasoning may be good for a nation, it is not so for a government. War is the Pharo-table of governments, and nations, the dupes of the game."

"I do not follow," said Olaudah. "We have no government?"

"Dat would not work," added Olympe, half-looking at Henry. "There must be some form of government, no?"

"All hereditary government is in its nature tyranny. A heritable crown, or a heritable throne, or by what other fanciful name such things may be called, have no other significant explanation than mankind is heritable property. To inherit a government is to inherit the people as if they were flocks and herds. Mr Godwin?" Thomas turned to William, who was halfway through eating his rice pudding. "Can you explain the four forms of government for me?"

Stunned, Godwin struggled to find his voice. "Democratical, aristocratical, monarchical and..."

"The representative," I added.

"Thank you," he nodded. "What is called a republic is not any particular form of government. Res-Publica, the public affairs or the public good; or, literally translated, the public thing. It is a word of a good origin, referring to what ought to be the character and business of government; and in this sense, it is naturally opposed to the word monarchy, stemming from signification. It means arbitrary power in a person; in the exercise of which, himself, and not the res-publica, is the object. America, which is wholly on the system of representation, is the only real Republic, in character..."

The front door to Joseph's store burst open and a loud, booming voice shouted from down the stairs. "Joseph! They're coming!" In a flurry of movement, Joseph stashed his pamphlets under the table. Olympe seated herself upright and all our eyes fixed on Joseph.

"Oh for heaven's sake. Again?" Joseph pointed to the rear of the dining room. "Thomas, take the back lanes and..." Joseph could not find any more words to placate a frantic

Thomas.

"60 Shore Street," I said. "Tell my maid I sent you. She will let you in. They won't think to search my apartment. This is the first time I have met you." Thomas nodded and exited in a flurry. "Am I to go with him, sir?"

"No Mary," replied Joseph. "Wait here until our they go."

Thomas returned in a flurry and bumped into the table, and knocked over a candle. "Where the bloody hell is Shore Street?" Godwin and Olympe's eyes darted between Thomas, myself and Joseph as everyone fussed over the wax and small flame.

"Oh, sorry Joseph," said Thomas.

"Accidents happen. It's okay do not worry," said Joseph.

"Sir? Do I go with him?" Joseph shook his head in reply. "Thomas, once you reach the back lanes, wait for me. I will accompany you once they leave. Hide in the shadows or something." Thomas turned and dashed the way he escaped moments before.

"I just started my pudding." Joseph rolled his eyes and nudged Henry out of his chair.

"You," said Joseph, pointing to Henry. "Sit where Thomas sat." Henry took his bowl and, with his spoon in his mouth, made his way to the head of the table. "Sometime today Henry, for goodness' sake." He hummed a small tune as he waltzed around the table and sat down like a drunken king, right beneath his god awful painting.

"There is wax on the floor," said Henry.

"Olympe, Helen. Are you both okay to stay here a while?" I asked.

"Oui madame, I am okay." She straightened her dress and adjusted her golden hair as her eyes darted around the room. The next minute passed in a flurry as Anne cleaned Henry's small mess of pudding and removed any traces of Thomas Paine.

"Is there a Mr Joseph Johnson present?" a voice announced from downstairs.

"Yes."

"We have reports of a Mr Thomas Paine in your presence. May we enter?"

"Of course," said Joseph, readjusting himself in his wooden chair. Three men arose from downstairs, entering the dining room and with an air of palpable authority, and blocked the stairs with their backs.

"Paine. Is he here?" asked one of them.

"Is he in London?" asked Joseph, as one man gawked at Olympe.

"Madam," the bigger of the men asked. "Have you seen Mr Thomas Paine?"

"Non Monsieur, I have, er, not observed Monsieur Paine." Olaudah moved in his seat, as did Godwin.

"The last I heard, he was in America," I said. At the mention of the name, the shorter of the three spat onto the floor.

"We have on authority Mr Paine walked the streets this evenin' and entered this building," said the smaller of the three men.

"Your source must be misguided," said Joseph. "These fine people are dining with me here tonight, but Thomas Paine is not on the list." A small smile appeared at the corner of William Godwin's face. "If you see him, will you give him my regards? Now, can we return to our fine dinner this evening?"

The three men said nothing. Instead, they searched every crevice of the small upstairs rooms and in Anne's kitchen, opening up soup lids and throwing items about.

"He's a small man, but not that small," said Godwin. Olympe and I suppressed a laugh. Wafts of cigars and brandy drifted behind the three men as they trampled through Johnson's upstairs living quarters, thrusting things behind them in their aftermath.

"You," said the smaller one to Olaudah. "What are you doing here?"

"He is here on business," I said. "Who are you to ask questions?"

Joseph eased his jacket collar. "Mary—"

"You waltz in here and trash my employer's residence. Thomas Paine is not here, never was." I stood from my chair as a clang from the kitchen boomed into the silence. "Would you please do us a kind favour and leave? You have no business here." I pointed to the downstairs door as the smaller of the two, a young man only twenty or so, could not find the words to reply to me. "Well?" A saucepan lid circled a few times on the floor and stopped, breaking the room into complete silence.

"Come on boys, this one is in a right mood."

"Bet you're a right fit to keep 'round the house, 'ey miss." The older of the three bumped into Henry's head as the three descended downstairs and outside onto St Paul's Churchyard. We glanced at the kitchen as Olympe, Olaudah and I rushed to help Anne pick up any sharp pieces from the floor as silence befell upon the rest of the guests.

"Who were those men?" I called out to no one in particular.

"Joseph's friends," replied Henry. His smile floated through his words. "Oh, I am joking Joseph, come now."

"Pitt's dogs," said Joseph. "The Prime Minister must have received word he is preparing to print the Second Part, and I'd rather think they would not like it to occur." We retired to the dining room and each posted ourselves in our original seats. "They have visited me before."

"When?" I asked. "You have never mentioned anything of the sorts to me."

"I did not want you to worry. I am not printing it so they cannot do anything Mary, they want him. You heard what he was harping on about, tyranny and all the rest. He might as well call for Burke's head at this rate.." Joseph stood from his chair and paced around the table, picking up the strewn papers. "Anyway, Mary, wait a few moments, retrieve your coat, and leave. William, accompany Mary home, if you please. Helen, you stay here for a while."

"But—"

"It is for your safety and his. Olympe, you walk with Olaudah to your hotel." Everyone nodded in agreement. Godwin and I locked eyes. The man appeared indifferent to life. Heaven knows why he bothered.

We said goodbye to Henry, Helen, Joseph and Anne, and Godwin, Olaudah, Olympe and I scurried down the stairs and into the frigid air of a London evening.

"Au revoir Madame," said Olympe, bowing as she walked with Olaudah towards the church.

"Adieu." Godwin and I rounded Joseph's building and met Paine in the darkened laneway. With our agreement made in whispers, we travelled home west for over an hour; the usual route I would take being almost half the distance.

*

We entered my small apartment, and I placed myself on the chair and let my body relax. "Put your coats and things by the door. I'll see to it the fire is on soon. Anna?" Anna made her way downstairs and began lighting the fire.

"You okay Miss? asked Anna. "I was getting a little worried, madam."

"I am fine thank you dear. This is William and this is—"

"Edward. Pleasure to meet you." Thomas extended his hand to Anna, who stood and bowed in response, and then returned to lighting the fire.

"So," I said, "Joseph shall not publish it then?" Thomas and William placed themselves on the opposite sofa and sank into a slight rest.

"No," replied Thomas, sighing as he did. "Our mutual friend found the prospect of publishing my treasonous work a sort of brash idea. I do not blame him." Thomas half smiled and lent further back into his seat. "Some visitors of sorts came to remind Mr Johnson of his place. One would assume some printer-hand is spreading rumours as to what is contained in the Second Part."

"And what is in this Second Part?" asked William. The small flames cast a warm glow illuminating his eyes.

"An attack on the foundations of the English government. This government founded itself from an invasion and conquest of the country."

"You speak of William of Normandy?" I asked.

"Precisely," he replied. "And Magna Carta was only compelling the government to renounce a part of its assumptions." Godwin stood and began pacing back and forth behind his chair as Thomas Paine continued.

"Mr Burke, he is a stickler for monarchy, not altogether as a pensioner, if he is one, which I believe, but as a political man. His contemptible opinion of mankind, who, in their turn, are taking up the same of him."

Godwin appeared perturbed by the prospect of Thomas Paine in my dining room. "Will you speak at the Corresponding Society? On America and such things?" he asked.

"Aye, it is to be. Say, Mrs Wollstonecraft, are you or are you not publishing your book soon? You can come and speak. I shall much prefer it indeed."

"Whilst I am sure it would be quite the riveting spectacle, women do not speak at such things," said Godwin.

"I am most certain he was reading it at the table at supper." Thomas sunk further into the small armchair as though it moulded to his being. The small room, bar from a few items of furniture, was not equipped for parties larger than two, for my pecuniary measures would not allow.

"Mr Paine, women do not usually speak at these meetings. Have you not..." Godwin avoided my gaze and focused solely on Paine.

"Aye William, but I shall have you know Mrs Wollstonecraft here is particularly more articulate than I. What say you?" Thomas stared at me in expectation.

"Me?" I replied.

"Aye. Come, it shall be grand, shall it not?"

"And...speak?"

"Aye. I can not speak Mary, you saw what happened just now." Thomas' gaze moved to the flickering fire as did Godwin, who had altogether frozen in place.

"I—"

"Decide in the morning, then. I require sleep."

"They will not allow it," said Godwin, adding a small peppering of emotion to his words. He gestured to the small kitchen, as Thomas Paine began to drift away into a peaceful sleep.

"Mary," whispered Godwin. "It is madness. It is for men, not women, to speak."

"I care and consider your opinion with the weight of a feather. Have we not recently made acquaintance?"

He considered his reply for a moment. "Well yes. May I have this?" Godwin reached for a piece of bread strewn about the counter.

Nodding in reply, we leant against my small kitchen table

and stared at Thomas Paine only a few metres away. "What are we going to do with him?" I asked. Sighing, Godwin continued chewing his bread, still bereft of thought and emotion. "He won't be able to stay in London," I continued. "Any rational creature will recognise his face and I am persuaded there are spies in London crawling around every street."

"You are right there," said Godwin. "Which is why you should not speak at this, this thing."

"Did you not eat your soup?" I asked as he swallowed the last piece of bread.

"You have been to his dinners before tonight, haven't you?" his mouth half-full.

"Yes."

"Well, then you must have experienced how awful his soups are."

I let out a small giggle. "He does it on purpose."

"On purpose?"

"So his guests eat less, talk more." I tapped the side of my temples. For the second time this evening, a smile cracked from the corner of his lips.

"Genius. The man is a genius," Godwin continued eating small pieces of bread whilst we postulated thoughts in silence together. As Thomas Paine continued to drift off to sleep and the crackling fire filled the silence between us, I wagered for a moment whether continuing the conversation with the gentlemen was worth my vexation.

"Well, I should be off." Thank the heaven's. "Thank you for the bread." Godwin made way for the door and adjusted his coat.

"And Thomas?" We both held each other's gaze. "What do I do with him?"

"Send him round to his apartment in the morning, Mrs Wollstonecraft. Goodevening," he said as he exited into the night.

Number 72 St. Paul's Churchyard London 1st January 1792

"I have spoken to Henry and we have arranged a reading for this evening," said Joseph, clinking his spoon against the side of the bowl to eat the remaining meager soup.

"With whom?"

"Since you declined Thomas' invitation, albeit a sublime decision on your part, he would like you to read a few transcriptions from the book this evening. Olympe is still in London so she will attend. Olaudah cannot make it. Mary Hays may join. Our friend Henry and his wife Sophia will dine tonight with us as well." Joseph glanced at my face for a reaction I would feign to delight him in.

"What is the matter?" I couldn't help but half smile as I glimpsed at Henry's absurd painting hanging on the wall. "Do you think he intended to frighten people with it?"

"Do not make a fool of me, Mary. I am old. The expression you half-make on your face is as transparent as the air we breathe."

"A fool of you? Joseph, it is fine, we are friends. Nothing mo—"

"Do you desire to consistently repair your broken heart? It hurts me when you are downtrodden." He returned my book to his dining table and turned in his chair to face me.

I smiled and clenched his hands, cold from the morning chill, and held them in mine. "You care, but you fuss too much about my faculties. My intentions are pure I promise."

"Mary...he is married."

"Men and women can be friends, Joseph," I squeezed his hands.

"I only worry about you finding yourself with a broken heart and your sentiments destroyed. You feel with your heart." He let go of my hands, stood and made his way to the kitchen. "Do you remember when you wrote to me from Dublin?"

"I sent you many letters from Dublin." I fiddled with my hair and smiled at his justifications.

"You spoke of enjoying solitude, wandering around Henley, and you longed for peace and independence in London, did you not?" He returned to his dining table with a small cup of tea and reacquainted himself with the conversation.

I retrieved the book from in front of him and traced my fingers over its spine. "Perhaps I return then to be a humble companion to some rich old cousin instead of Mrs Dawson? Or return to being a governess in Ireland and destroy whatever remains of my faculties there with Lady Kingsborough? Perhaps, forgive me, live with Eliza and Everina? James even?"

"That is not what I mean, Mary," he said, sinking into his chair as his eyes widened at the surrounding room. His apartment, one usually bustling with customers, writers and printers, was now peaceful in the early morning. "I mean to say, you stretch every emotion in your heart when you love and sacrifice every part of your being. Your eyes do not lie whenever you speak about Frances."

"Joseph..."

"Mary...you say it yourself in there," he gestured to the book in my hands. "Platonic attachments are begun in false refinement, and frequently end in sorrow, if not in guilt."

"You are cruel..."

"I have known Henry for a long time. He is caring, but do not let your heart mistake his interest in you for love." I continued to ignore his gaze and flipped through the pages of the book.

"Have you any orders for this?" I wiped a small tear from my eye and traced over the words with my hands. Strange seeing one's own words appear in a book.

"You are holding the first of the few we printed last week, so no. Not yet." Silence resumed for a while as he returned to reading another book and Anne intermittently entered and exited the dining room, fussing over papers and organising the room for the evening.

The day lingered on like the morning. Several of Joseph's writers, including our friend Barbauld, joined for a quiet lunch and discussions about the prospect of 1792 and what it would bring for Joseph and Christie's Analytical Review. Thomas Christie, as per usual, appeared and said hello to whoever was present upstairs. Then he and Joseph disappeared downstairs to discuss business and politics.

Christie's trip to Paris in 1790 only surmounted his feelings towards the government's wretched stronghold on our country and every meeting with Joseph since seemed tied to France and its revolution.

"Join us for dinner this evening," said Joseph loudly. "Mary is reading some excerpts from her Vindication. I am sure she would be delighted at your presence." Christie murmured in reply and they returned to their conversation.

"I am full of soup Anne, thank you though," Anne half-attempted to pour another dish for myself. She nodded as much as her poor back would allow and returned to the kitchen.

I finished my critique of two plays by four o'clock and Joseph closed his store downstairs for the day. After sorting through papers he returned to the dining table, though it resembled less of a place for food and more of a writer's desk. He never complained.

"Meet Olympe at her hotel, I am sure she would be delighted to accompany you back here." I examined the piles of parchments before me; had I left his apartment today? I strained my mind but I could not remember. "Thomas will, as per usual, be befriending the coffee shop he is a frequent visitor of, perhaps you also collect him on your way." I nodded, placed several piles on top of other piles of parchments, collected my small satchel and made way for the Churchyard.

Olympe's apartment was a few streets away, north of St. Paul's and Thomas, if my summations were correct, would be amongst the remaining few coffee houses somewhere east.

"Mary?" Henry Fuseli appeared at my elbow without me noticing his approach. "Have you let yourself be cast down and you match the mood of this weather? Are you okay? I hear Joseph printed your book today?"

"Fuseli," I nodded. "Yes, it printed, but I'm off to find Olympe and Thomas and bring them back here for dinner." His expression turned from worry to curiosity. I glanced behind him and realised there was no one walking in his wake. "Is Sophia joining you this evening?"

"No, she is quite unwell, in bed the poor dear."

"Oh."

"Well, I shall see you when you return. Best keep him company," he bowed and disappeared through the front door of number 72. I walked north around the church and arrived soon after at Olympe's hotel. We greeted each other, reacquainted on the news of the day, and headed south-east to fetch Thomas.

"'ave you saw him madame?" asked Olympe, half-attempting to speak through her scarf. "It 'as been veeks vor me. Say, de last time I, eh, saw him vas at de dinner."

"I am surprised you are still in London. I thought you were returning to Paris? Oh goodness I cannot quite remember with what is occuring with everyone."

"Soon."

We weaved between horses, carts, boxes and goods whilst in conversation, which proved far more difficult than it needed to be. "You should join me in Paris, when I return or not?"

"Oh, I forgot to mention to you. We plan to travel soon, Joseph and I. Possibly Henry, as well."

"De Fuseli man? Gosh is he zo handsome," I could sense she was hiding a smile. "I vould however like to remove dat painting from de wall of your Joseph's room, it scares me zo!" I smiled at the thought of Olympe and I removing the painting in the early hours of the morning.

We entertained ourselves in conversation and before long, entered the small coffee house by the Thames. A select few gentlemen turned around from their chairs at our presence—a beautiful French woman and a woman who appeared in a perpetual state of exhaustion. "I am looking for Thomas Paine. Is he here?" One man pointed to the corner of the establishment where Olympe and I found him deep in conversation with several men around a small corner table.

"Oh, heavens, I am late for dinner, aren't I?" I approached the table and smiled, nodding in reply. "Well gentlemen, I will see you next week, same time?" A few of them raised their drinks to him and mumbled amongst themselves for a shot while as Thomas collected his things and thoughts.

"Of course, Thomas," replied one man. Thomas stood,

nodded to his friends and returned outside with Olympe and I.

"Aye. Did Joseph send you to retrieve me? Good Evening Miss de Gouges, by the way, apologies my head is well over the place. I somehow found myself at the coffee house."

"No matter, Monsieur Paine. It appeared as you vere 'aving fun no? How are you Monsieur? It 'as been quite some time eh." Olympe, Thomas and I made polite conversation as we returned to St. Paul's, meandering past lifeless trees frigid in their winter statue.

Dinner passed without event. Olympe and Thomas renewed acquaintance; Henry and I debated his painting once again and Joseph idled between our conversations. The proposed topic of my Vindication bare made a mention and I was thankful. I enjoyed the solitude of conversation not focused on me. By late evening we each said our goodbyes and vowed to see each other soon, at least before Olympe returned to Paris.

*

The early months of of 1792 passed idly. Between writing for Joseph's Analytical Review and reviewing every novel he gave me I became preoccupied with thoughts of France and the revolution. Olympe returned to Paris and every body anxiously waited for our eventual trip.

When we did attempt to travel, the weather delayed our departure for several days and it then became a rather stupid idea to continue. The five of us returned to London, and Joseph and I then continued north to acquire business opportunities for Thomas.

My mind fluctuated between enjoying independence and wishing to be necessary to someone. In every conversation with Henry I half-wished to suggest we could exist en tant que trois. It was an idle fantasy which would never see the light of day.

...ited to his friends, he returned outside with Olympe and I.

"Ah, Did Joseph send you to retrieve me? Good Evening, Madame de Gouges. By the way, my young friend is well over the place. I somehow found myself at the coffee house."

"No matter, Monsieur Paine. It appeared as you were waiting for me. How are you Monsieur? It has been quite some time since." Olympe, Thomas and I made polite conversation as we returned to St. Paul's and I... just unless the ... winter time.

Dinner passed without event. Olympe and Thomas renewed acquaintance, Henry and I debated his painting once again, and Joseph filled in between our conversations. The proposed topic of my Vindication book stayed unmentioned and I was thankful. I enjoyed the magnitude of conversation not focused on me. By late evening, we each said our goodbyes and vowed to see each other soon, at least before Olympe returned to Paris.

The early months of 1792 passed idly. Between writing for Joseph's Analytical Review and reviewing every novel he gave me, I became preoccupied with thoughts of France and the revolution. Olympe returned to Paris and even then, I anxiously waited for our eventual trip.

When we did attempt to travel, the weather delayed our departure for several days and the plan became a rather stupid idea to abandon. The three of us returned to London, and Joseph and I then continued north to acquire business opportunities for Thomas.

My mind fluctuated between enjoying independence and wishing to be necessary to someone. In every conversation with Henry I halfway had to suspect we could exist on that quest as though it was an idle fantasy which would never see the light of day.

Dover England mid-August 1792

The road to Dover, lined with past dreams and aspirations of English travellers, was this second time around welcoming of the four of us. Our first attempt was fraught with cruel winds and unforgiving seas. This time would be different we agreed.

Thomas contemplated the outside scene through the carriage window and I watched as the idle reflections of farm houses and trees glittered over his face.

"Burke again?" I asked.

"Hmm?" asked Joseph, whose nose appeared above the top of the pamphlet.

"Oh, not you," I gestured to Thomas. "Him." Thomas glanced from the window to me and appeared as though he was asleep with his eyes open, yet in reply handed a piece of parchment to me.

I skimmed over his scribbled notes which were in a mix of French and English. "Louis?"

"You worry about him too much," said Joseph. "Oof!" a bump under the carriage threw the bookseller into my sides. "We must be close," his nose still buried in his book. "Sea rocks."

Thomas returned to caressing outside with eyes as the air in the carriage reeked from my failed attempt at conversation. This was to be a joyous journey across the Channel. A near-mute, the painter's wife, an editor and a woman with a head full of questions and for the first time, men without the will or need to answer.

*

"The boat won't be sailing today Sir," said a young, boorish man of no more than twenty, upright against a pylon by the Channel's edge.

"What about this evening?" Paine asked.

"Perhaps—I mean. Perhaps Sir."

"Have you not heard from the harbour master?" I inquired. With a glance, the pilot shrugged and walked towards the boat, leaving us behind in his wake.

"That was—"

"Peculiar," remarked Paine, for a man recognises what he

is in the world.

"What a bottle-headed—"

"Well," remarked Joseph. "What do we do now?"

"Well?" asked Sophia. "We go home, this moment then."
Joseph sunk even further in stature which I thought improbable for his already small height in the world.

Joseph found a small harbour crate to perch on and postulated his brain's questions out loud. "Well, the three of you know my—uh—objections to the matter of returning. Mrs Fuseli and I–"

"Mrs Fuseli is capable of speaking for herself." I paced in front of them to and fro like a confused animal in a cage. "But this matter is the matter of Olympe." Sophia perched herself next to Joseph and folded her arms in an apparent display of remarked displeasure at the situation.

"You Mary, travel to France for Olympe. I travel for its, society. Its wealth, its grandeur. I shall travel to the markets, oh France has everything in the world there! One likes to see the people's things. And Mary, I have never met the woman, this Olympe you travel for. She is your friend." Sophia in truth. was innocent of heart. Married young, now the wife of one of the most coveted painters of our time.

"Our friend," Thomas interjected, somehow involving himself in the discussion from several metres away.

I looked a thousand ways to avoid her. "As I was saying," I continued. "France is...I mean our motivations are—" For the first time since leaving London, Thomas smiled at me.

"Perfectly well intended," said Thomas, lost in thought admiring the English Channel. "Do not be concerned Joseph."

"I'm well concerned for the both of you," Joseph quipped. Sophia's glaring eyes followed me with every pass.

"Well do not let our troubles become yours," I said.

"Do you know how many–" Joseph's coughing fit announced itself again. "How many–men I have–breathing down my–'

"Yes, do convey your plight, you rebellious bookseller. Why would Pitt's agents be breathing down your neck?" For the first time, humour made its mark on Thomas Paine's face.

"We find rooms then?" asked Sophia.

"I shall wait here for the post, whilst you and Joseph call on the taverns for rooms so we can sail tomorrow then. Mary, would you wait here with me?"

Sophia and Joseph left to find rooms whilst Paine and I strolled along the rocky shores of Dover. After several minutes of silence, for thoughts of France occupied my mind and seemingly of his, we returned to the pier.

"So. Expectation or worry?" Thomas shrugged and found comfort against a wooden railing on the pier. He paused for a moment and breathed in the salty air before replying.

"Both. And you?"

"Both."

"Mmm."

"I never asked you. Are you scared to travel to France?" A small smile crowned from the corner of his mouth.

"You are?" he asked. I considered my reply and joined him in a gaze across the empty sea, bar from an approaching mail ship.

"Sometimes I wish it were possible to re-establish my ignorance of the entirety of matters between France and England. Stroll on some foreign land somewhere and forget this land and its troubles. Reacquaint myself with the solitude of ignorance."

"Have you thought of America? I am sure a woman such as yourself would find life there quite respectable."

"Naturally." I smiled at the thought of the possibilities before me.

"At least the crown there is considered an absurdity," he replied. "Would you like me to write to Franklin for you? He helped me."

I shook my head. "I made a promise to a friend."

Thomas turned to face me, though I refrained from moving my eyes from the sea. "You forget I am with you in the matter of Olympe."

"Your celebrity is not foreign to me Tom and will not be unnoticed by them."

"You flatter me, Mary."

"Let me treat you with frankness for my nerves will be in a painful state of irritation if I do not speak."

Another smile appeared. "You, irritated nerves? Never." I brushed off his remark and met his gaze with a half smile. "Blake informed you of what happened to Johnson?"

"Yes. But Joseph has done no wrong. They cannot arrest him, he did not publish the Second Part. If I recall Joseph told to you not to suffer in your thoughts about his situation. You should not be concerned."

"It is every concern of mine," I said. "I shall not and will not suffer in silence whilst he is sent off to the gallows, you are executed either here or in Paris." I set in a pace to and fro along the pier, half against the wind; standing idle in thought vexed me.

"He will exhaust himself, Mary." His eyes followed my every move.

"Who, Johnson?" I paused in front of him. "The man knows not how to rest."

"No. Joseph will be fine. I repeat, he did not print the book, the government has nothing against him. And I meant Pitt. His tongue and pen let loose in a frenzy of passion will fatigue him." The sea air swirled around us in a fury only felt along the coasts of the isle, raging further as the conversation went on. "Burke, on the contrary, I do not know." He paused for a few moments as his arm reached for my shoulder. "You did the subject justice, Mary. Burke knows it."

"I am still dissatisfied with myself no matter what he knows or thinks. I dwell on my disappointments continuously. And, do not suspect me of false modesty Tom. If I allowed myself more time I could've–I could've written something better. Goodness, it is such as blur. The entirety of the work."

"I am convinced of the contrary." Thomas paused for a moment, adjusted his waistcoat and stood tall and proud. "Do you know of a place in America called Point-no-Point?"

"No...I cannot say I am familiar."

"As you proceed along the shore, gay and flowery as Mr Burke's language, it continually recedes and presents itself at a distance before you arrive at–"

"I don't see how–"

"But when you have got as far as you can go, there is

no point at all. Thus it is with Mr Edmund Burke's three hundred and sixty-six pages. Yours, on the contrary, Mrs Wollstonecraft," he bowed. "Is not full of paradoxes and difficulties." I bit my tongue and swallowed nothing but air. "On the topic of time, he had upwards of what was it, six, seven?"

"Eight—," I added.

"Eight months in hand, thank you. And extended a volume where he voluntarily declined to compare the English and French constitutions. As I am sure you are aware, we do not have one in England. Yet you, in a matter of weeks, might I add, became the first genus of a new writer." Thomas Paine smiled again.

I averted my eyes in search of something other than Thomas' face. "I should have written more to defend Dr Price."

"Mary, you found fallacy in Burke's reasoning. And your defence of Dr Price was honourable, as a true friend would write of him." He bowed and returned to the ocean in front of us.

"If Burke had but half as much reverence for the grey hairs of virtue as for the accidental distinctions of rank, he would not have treated Dr Price with such indecent familiarity and supercilious contempt." Thomas gripped one of my hands and squeezed it before letting it go and returning to the view in front of us. Together we admired the ocean before us. Somewhere, over the sea, lay France and all her troubles. I anticipated the future improvement of the world; of Europe. How much man still has left to improve upon it?

"Once I am in Paris and settled, Joseph suggested I continue writing on the Revolution." I said. "And thank you, Tom. It is pleasant not to find oneself mistaken in the nature of your character."

"What will you do when you arrive?" He breathed in the salty air and sighed. I hesitated to answer for in myself, I did not quite know. The thought of what awaited me in Paris frightened me so. But I felt it necessary to venture for I wanted to live and breathe the revolution. Soak in the thoughts and dreams of a country wishing to improve itself over again.

"Fillieatz has a house I can lodge for a while, though I do not know how long for. I shall join Olympe and attend some of the salons perhaps. I do not quite know though. Yourself?"

"Save the life of Louis Capet if I can. Though, I have a feeling it will not be successful. Try as I might to succeed in wishing it not so, my wish I do not think will become reality." Paine nodded towards the end of the pier behind me. A small crowd gathered as the small mail ship approached from continental Europe. The imaginary line between our two continents—which separated the imaginary rights of those in England from the imaginary rights of those in France—became more and more blurred every day.

"Do you think you can save him?" The sea spray caught my hair and he brushed it out of my face.

He shrugged in response. "I do not know. I can only try."

We walked along the Pier where Thomas received a few letters but nothing arrived for me from Mr Barlow. Opening letter after letter, we left the pier behind and continued walking along the beach to the small rocks on the shore whilst he kept reading.

"Oh, we shall be introduced to so many people Thomas! Oh, exciting is it not?" I leapt from rock to rock, avoiding the small splashes of the sea.

"Mary..."

"Oh, it shall be glorious!"

"Mary."

"Hmm?" Thomas stood on the sand as if a ghost crept inside his body and left him upright in death. "What is it? Thomas?"

Paine confirmed what everyone at Johnson's dining table feared. It was true. "Tuileries. They have stormed the Tuileries."

"They tried to escape again? Are they ma—?" He shook his head and collapsed, knees first into the sand. I glimpsed across the Channel towards France and my heart burned. Both heads of the French crown instil no affinity in my heart.

As I made my way to Paine, Johnson and Sophia's heads appeared from the cliffs behind us with the former almost toppling over himself.

"Tom," Johnson shouted. "Mary!" a small parchment in Johnson's hand flew in the wind like a flag in surrender. "Have you—"

Thomas raised the letter above him and a marked silence fell upon us as Johnson reached the edge closest to us, stopping for breath.

"Olympe, they have arrested her!"

"What?" Thomas and I both replied in unison. Johnson bent down, dropping the letter to me and I opened it. The ground might as well have swallowed me whole, for I'd rather acquaint myself with the sordid sorrows of death than have to–

"What is it? What does it say?" Thomas inquired.

"It says here she has been arrested. Who is Madame Roland?"

The colour of Paine's skin turned into a shade of verdant sea green. "The King's going to die."

"Thomas, what do we do? What if she is sent to the gallows?" Thomas began muttering to himself.

"They're not using the gallows anymore..." The wind grew in force, spraying sand and debris across the shore.

"What do you mean anymore?" I kneeled in front of Thomas on the sand and lifted his chin towards my face. "Thomas? I do not understand." A small wave ebbed against our legs" the water was warmer than I expected.

As Thomas tried to find words, Sophia and Joseph made their way to the beach and joined us on the sand. "Thomas?" asked Joseph. "Your letter. What does it say?" Wave upon wave washed into the side of Paine's motionless body as the letter from an unknown sender fell from his hands.

"Vive Le Revolution," said Paine.

As Thomas conveyed the scarce details of the Tuileries, myself, Joseph and Sophia agreed it would be better to turn back to London. Thomas decided, for his own safety and ours, it would be better for him to wait another day and attempt to cross the Channel to Calais. He would die here, either at the gallows or at the hands of Pitt's men, with a trial rumoured to begin within weeks.

Calais France 15th September 1792

Dearest Mary,

A collector of the customs approached me in our hotel in Calais, and had information against us, for he examined our baggage for prohibited articles. I was right. The Collector then called in several other officers and began first to search our pockets. He took from Mr A—— who then returned to the room, everything he found in his pocket, and laid it on the table. He then searched Mr F—— in the same manner and then did the same for me.

The Collector asked us to open our trunks, presenting us the keys which Mr A—— had on him. We declined the request unless he would produce his information, which he again refused. The Collector then opened the trunks himself and took out every paper and letter, sealed or unsealed. We assume he was acting under the direction of some other person or persons; he went several times out of the room for a few minutes and was also called out several times.

General Washington's inability to send me a private letter of friendship without it being subject to inspection by a custom-house officer was extraordinary.

Do not write to me about politics.

I shall be in Paris and will await your letter if you choose to join us here.

Thomas Paine.

Paris France 25th September 1792

To the people of France

Fellow Citizens,

I receive, with affectionate gratitude, the honour which the late National Assembly has conferred upon me, by adopting me a Citizen of France. As well as the additional honour of being elected by my fellow citizens as a Member of the National Convention.

The honours come accompanied by circumstances which allow me to commence my citizenship in the stormy hour of difficulties. I come not to enjoy repose. For I am convinced France and her liberty cannot be purchased by a wish, I gladly share with you the dangers and honours necessary to success.

I am well aware any moment of great change, such as the 10th of August, is unavoidably a moment of terror and confusion. The mind, highly agitated by hope, suspicion and apprehension, continues without rest till the change be accomplished. But let us now look calmly and confidently forward, and success is certain.

It is no longer the paltry cause of kings, or of this, or of that individual, which calls France and her armies into action. It is the great cause of ALL. It is the establishment of a new era, and it shall blot despotism from the earth, and fix, on the lasting principles of peace and citizenship, the great Republic of Man.

The success and events of the American Revolution are encouraging to us. The prosperity and happiness that have since flowed to that country, have amply rewarded her for all the hardships she endured and for all the dangers she encountered. The distance of America from all the other parts of the globe, did not admit of her carrying those principles beyond her own situation. It is to the peculiar honour of France, that she now raises the standard of liberty for all nations; and in fighting her own battles, contends for the rights of all mankind.

The same spirit of fortitude that insured success to America; will insure it to France, for it is impossible to conquer a nation determined to be free! Liberty and Equality are blessings too great to be the inheritance of France alone. It is an honour to her to be their first champion; and she may now say to her enemies, with a mighty voice. "O! ye Austrians, ye Prussians! ye who now turn your bayonets against us, it is for you, it is for all Europe, it is for all mankind, and not for France alone, that she raises the standard of Liberty and Equality!"

Your Fellow-Citizen,

Thomas Paine.

Paris France 11th November 1792

To the Attorney General of England, on the prosecution against the Second Part of the Rights of Man

Sir,

As there can be no personal resentment between two strangers, I write this letter to you, as to a man against whom I have no animosity.

You have, as Attorney General, commenced a prosecution against me, as the author of Rights of Man. Had not my duty, in consequence of my being elected a member of the National Convention of France, called me from England, I should have stayed to have contested the injustice of your prosecution; not upon my own account, for I cared not about the prosecution, but to have defended the principles I advanced in the work.

The duty I am now engaged in is of too much importance to permit me to trouble myself about your prosecution: When I have leisure, I shall have no objection to meet you on that ground; but, as I now stand, whether you go on with the prosecution, or whether you do not, or whether you obtain a verdict, or not, is a matter of the most perfect indifference to me as an individual.

If you obtain one, (which you are welcome to if you can get it,) it cannot affect me either in person, property or reputation, otherwise than to increase the latter; and with respect to yourself, it is as consistent you obtain a verdict against the Man in the Moon as against me; neither do I see how you can continue the prosecution against me as you would have done against one of your own people, who absented himself because he was prosecuted; what passed at Dover and Calais proves my departure from England was no secret.

My necessary absence from your country affords the opportunity of knowing whether the intended prosecution was against Thomas Paine, or against the Right of the People of England to investigate systems and principles of government; for as I cannot now be the object of the prosecution, the going on with the prosecution will shew something else was the object, which can be no other than the People of England. For it is against their Rights, and not against me, a verdict or sentence can operate, if it can operate at all. Be then so candid as to tell the Jury, (if you choose to continue the process,) whom it is you are prosecuting, and on whom it is the verdict is to fall.

The time, Sir, is becoming too serious to play with Court prosecutions, and sport with national rights. The terrible examples which have taken place here, upon men who, less than a year ago, thought themselves as secure as any prosecuting Judge, Jury or Attorney General, now can in England, ought to have some weight with men in your situation. The government of England is not the greatest, perfection of fraud and corruption that ever took place since governments began. You cannot be a stranger to the idea, unless the constant habit of seeing it blinds your senses; but though you may not chuse to see it, the people are seeing it and the progress is beyond what you may chuse to believe.

You cannot obtain a verdict (and if you do, it will signify nothing) without packing a Jury, (and we both know such tricks are practised,) is what I have reason to believe, I have gone into coffee houses, and places where I was unknown, on purpose to learn the currency of opinion, and I never yet saw any company of twelve men who condemned the book; but I have often found a greater number than twelve approving it, and this I think is a fair way of collecting the natural currency of opinion.

Do not then, Sir, be the instrument of drawing twelve men into a situation which may be injurious to them afterwards. I do not speak this from policy, but from benevolence; but if you chuse to go on with the process, I make it my request you read this letter in Court, after which the Judge and the Jury may do as they please.

As I do not consider myself the object of the prosecution, neither can I be affected by the issue, one way or the other, I shall, though a foreigner in your country, subscribe as much money as any other man towards supporting the right of the nation against the prosecution; and it is for this purpose only that I shall do it.

Thomas Paine

Paris France 20th November 1792

Citizen President,

As I do not know precisely what day the Convention will resume the discussion on the trial of Louis XVI., and, on account of my inability to express myself in French, I cannot speak at the tribune, I request permission to deposit in your hands the enclosed paper, which contains my opinion. I make this demand with so much more eagerness because circumstances will prove how much it imports to France, that Louis XVI. should continue to enjoy good health. I would be happy if the Convention would have the goodness to hear this paper read this morning, as I propose sending a copy of it to London, to be printed in the English journals.

I think it is necessary Louis XVI. should be tried; a spirit of vengeance does not suggest this advice, but because this measure appears to me just, lawful, and conformable to sound policy. If Louis is innocent, let us put him to prove his innocence; if he is guilty, let the national will determine whether he shall be pardoned or punished.

France is now a republic; she has completed her revolution; but she cannot earn all its advantages so long as despotic governments surround her. Their armies and their marine oblige her also to keep troops and ships in readiness. It is therefore her immediate interest that all nations shall be as free as herself; that revolutions shall be universal; and since the trial of Louis XVI. can serve to prove to the world the flagitiousness of governments in general, and the necessity of revolutions, she ought not to let slip so precious an opportunity

The despots of Europe have formed alliances to preserve their respective authority, and to perpetuate the oppression of peoples. This is the end they proposed to themselves in their invasion of

French territory. They dread the effect of the French revolution in the bosom of their own countries; and in hopes of preventing it, they come to attempt the destruction of this revolution before it should attain its perfect maturity. They have not succeeded in their attempt. France has already vanquished their armies; but it remains for her to sound the particulars of the conspiracy, to discover, to expose to the eyes of the world, those depots who had the infamy to take part in it; and the world expects from her that act of justice.

Yours,

Thomas Paine.

London England Saturday night late November 1792

To Joseph Johnson,

After some sleepless, wearisome nights, towards the morning I have grown delirious. Last Thursday, in particular, my suggestion caused considerable distress to Mr. and Mrs. Fuseli. I have suffered more than I can express. I acknowledge life is but a jest and an often frightful dream—yet catch myself every day searching for something serious. I am a strange compound of weakness, misery and resolution.

However, if I must suffer, then I will endeavour to suffer in silence. There is certainly a defect in my mind-my wayward heart creates its own misery. Why I am made this way, I cannot tell; and till I can form some idea of my existence, I must be content to weep and dance like a fairy around a fire.

My spirits sink on account of not saying goodbye, but I know you shall have prevented me from going for, though my employer, you are but the only fatherly figure I have. If any accident should happen to you whilst I am away, I should never forgive myself.

I shall write to you as soon as I arrive. I have been pursuing several strange thoughts since I began to write and have both wept and laughed.

Surely I am a fool.

Yours faithfully,

Mary

Dover England 9th December 1792

Dear Everina,

On Saturday I set out once more for Dover. I seem to strive against fate, for if I did not take my place I should have put off the journey again on account of the state of affairs at home, which are really rather alarming. My spirits sink, but I go. Yet if anything should happen to my dear friend Johnson in my absence, I shall never forgive myself.

I shall write to you when I am able. You tell me nothing of your health. You remember Dr Fordyce, I lately dined at his house and I have seldom been in company with more intelligent, pleasing women than his two daughters. Their education has been attended to and their father is now rewarded for their care.

You forgot to mention little Ann or George, be more explicit when you write next. By this time you have got my letter enclosing James' curious epistle and of course, you share my vexation, I hope I shall not see him again he tries my patience.

Mary

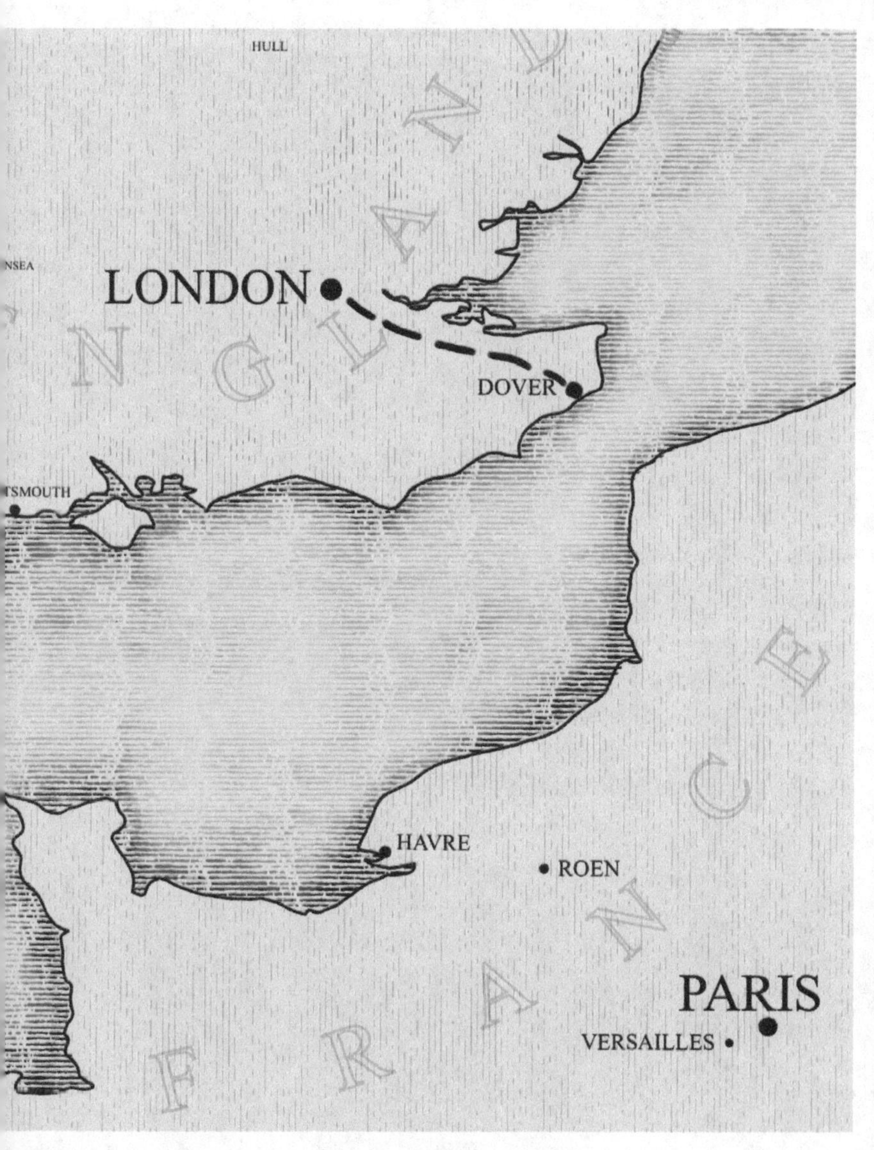

Mary's travels 1792

GENUINE EDITION

THE

TRIAL

OF

THOMAS PAINE

FOR A

LIBEL,

CONTAINED IN THE SECOND PART OF

RIGHTS OF MAN,

BEFORE

LORD KENYON,
AND A SPECIAL JURY,
AT GUILDHALL, DECEMBER 18

WITH THE SPEECHES OF THE

ATTORNEY GENERAL

AND

MR. ERSKINE

AT LARGE

LONDON

PRINTED FOR MR J. JOHNSON,
NUMBER 72 ST. PAUL'S CHURCHYARD

Guildhall London 18th December 1792

A Crown prosecutor named Arnold Percival stood, with all the solemnity befitting such a momentous occasion, and addressed the hundred or so men crowded within London's Guild Hall. The towering walls, steeped in centuries of history and tradition, and it's ornate hammer-beam ceiling had spied many trials in its life and the Trial of Thomas Paine was no different.

"Thank you and good morning," he said, too soft for the gentlemen towards the back to hear. "The wicked, malicious and seditious disposition contained in this here," he held high Thomas Paine's pamphlet for the twelve-man jury and the crowd to see. "Also wished to introduce disorder and—excuse me—confusion." His bellowing coughs echoed across the Hall.

"I stand here before you, in the very room Anne, Cranmer and Lady Jane Grey so acquainted themselves with. And it is here we shall try Thomas Paine." His blue eyes flashing restlessly from man-to-man. "This pamphlet, brought the government of this country into contempt—"

"Here, here," sounded the large audience of men.

"This pamphlet," he said louder, "endeavoured to cause it to be believed, that the Parliament of this country was openly corrupt in the face of day. In order to withdraw the affections of the people of this kingdom, against the law and constitution of this country, that the one Thomas Paine—"

The crowd leered. "Treason!"

"Liar!" said another.

"Traitor!"

"Quieten down please," said Lord Kenyon, seated behind his bench and peering down from behind his half-moon glasses.

"—wrote this pamphlet, and wishing and intending this mischief, did, on the sixteenth of February, 1791, wickedly, falsely, maliciously, scandalously, and seditiously published a certain book, called the 'Second Part of Rights of Man', signed Thomas Paine." Percival held the pamphlet even higher for the Hall to see, as though height made the signature easier to read. "It contained many false, wicked, scandalous, malicious, and seditious assertions." The jury clapped in unison.

As Percival returned to his seat, Lord Kenyon addressed Thomas Paine's representatives who whispered amongst themselves.

"The defendant had pleaded Not Guilty?"

"Yes, your Honour," the two men said in unison.

"Yes," the older of the two repeated.

"In absentia," Percival added, whose forehead now contained small beads of sweat. The judge surveyed the muted crowd and gestured to the Attorney General.

With several wads of paper in hand he crossed the floor to the judge, whispered something in his ear and turned once to face the expectant crowd. Clad in the austere robes of his office, his tall and imposing frame commanded attention as he strode purposefully across the chamber, every movement exuding an air of unwavering confidence and resolve. His countenance, stern and unyielding, bore the weight of his responsibilities as the chief legal officer of the crown.

"I want to thank all of you, all of you, every single one of you for joining us here, in this Hall of such, such significance, such importance." Pacing across the stone, his deep-set eyes, sharp and piercing, surveyed the proceedings and crowd with a keen intelligence that missed no detail.

"Gentlemen of the jury. Permit me to state, in my mind, my very clear, rational mind, there is not a cause more plain, more clear more certain, indisputable even, that has come before a court." The judge, seated high in the Hall raised his eyebrows.

"This was not the first of the kind which this defendant had thought it fit, fit to publish against our Government. When this one appeared—" Mr Percival held the pamphlet high again from his seat, "—printed on white brown paper and thrust, thrust in the hands of all persons, of all ages, sexes and conditions, we had to, had to take steps, Your Honour." The Attorney General's speech turned from an act of profession to an act of stage play in front of the court within seconds. The jury and the various men in the Hall drunk from his performance as though he were a publican pouring copious amounts of free ale.

"So many ready-made propositions, without regard to truth. It was well known that England had a powerful Democracy; but no—not a word of that-because it would not make the lower classes of the people discontented." As I wrote the Attorney's speech verbatim on the parchment in front of me, a man smelling of brandy tapped me on the shoulder from behind.

"You work for that ol' Johnson fellow do ya?" My stomach squirmed and I shook my head. "Well then, what do ya be doing there?" Ignoring him, I continued my inscriptions.

"Gentlemen, to whom are these poisons that are conveyed in this book addressed?" The Attorney's blue eyes waited for no answer. "They are addressed, gentlemen, to the ignorant, to the credulous, to the desperate; to those persons who are desperate to see that all government is irksome." As the words became louder and louder, several men in the crowd shifted in their seats. "With respect to the matter in my conscience, my clear, so well defined conscience, I call it treason."

"Traitor!" leered the crowd again.

"He should be hanged I say!" said another man, leaping out of his seat. Laughing, the Attorney placated the crowd, returning to a softer voice.

"Gentlemen. Gentlemen please. Permit me now to say a word or two on those passages I have selected for you." Percival arose once again from his chair and distributed twelve copies of a single page to the jury. The Attorney wandered over to the twelve men, removed his spectacles and begun cleaning them with his waistcoat.

"Good sir," he addressed a juror. "Will you read for me the inscription on page twenty-one?"

A few moments later, after several glances between them, a peculiar sort of man, with a thin frame and thin lips to match, spoke softly in reply. "This-this-this one?" the man asked, raising the parchment to the Attorney, who nodded.

As the man addressed the large Hall, his impercitable voice shook and quivered.

"All...hereditary..." the juror began shaking.

"Stand won't you? Let them hear you."

"...g-g-government is...in its nature..."

"Tyranny," finished the Attorney. "And what say you that? Mr..."

"Arnold, Sir."

"What say you to that? Mr Arnold. This, insidious statement so written by Thomas Paine?"

"Uh...not true? Sir? Yes—I mean, not true. Sir." The juror bowed and sat down in an instant.

"Not true exactly, exactly right, very good, very good." The Attorney quickly finished cleaning his glasses and picked up the paper inscription for himself. "An heritable crown," he continued. "Or an heritable throne, or by what other fanciful name such things may be called, have no other significant explanation, than mankind are heritable property. To inherit a government is to inherit the people, as if they were flocks and herds!" Lowering his glasses once again, he now addressed the crowd.

"Now, gentlemen. What is the tendency of this passage? That all hereditary government is in its nature tyranny?" he looked towards the jury. "So, stating it soundly, that in all circumstances whatever, hereditary government must in its nature, be tyranny?" the Attorney continued circling the floor and raising his voice as though professing great love for his wife, as the hammer-beam ceiling and stone floor reverberated his bellowing voice.

"Our King is noble!" a man shouted from two seats away. The crowd shouted profanities towards Paine's defendants.

"Quieten down, quieten down," said Lord Kenyon, too soft for anyone to hear. "Please."

"Now," the Attorney continued. "The king of this country inherits an office under the law—he inherits no persons—no," the Attorney circled back to stand in front of Lord Kenyon. "He inherits the office. As to any other inheritance, none else, as you know very well it belongs to him and I shall not stay to prove that one moment." He bowed and took seat again.

The Crown's assisting solicitor—a Mr Bearcroft of 72 Druid Lane, London—took hold of the stage in a less imposing way than that of the Attorney General. A former commoner, Bearcroft knew the less-expansive vocabulary of the good men in front of him. So, spoke very little.

"My Lord," he nodded. "Good men of this here jury," he nodded again. "And to the gentlemen of London and England. You—We—are not, ignorant?"

"No!" several men called back to him.

"You are not blind?" like the Attorney, he paced around the floor and took centre stage.

"No." they repeated back again.

"No! No you say. Well, we come now then, to this here inscription of the Crown itself on page 107." Bearcroft signified to the jury and one of them, with more confidence in his composure than the first, stood and read the inscription.

"How they going to hang old Paine anyway?" the brandy man

whispered in my ear, annoying some of the people around us whilst the juror continued to speak.

"How do you know they'll hang him?" I replied.

"Why he's guilty I'll say," he continued. Raising my eyebrows, I turned to face him. "Oi, I recognise ya. Where did ya say you were employed? Hardy is it not?"

I readjusted the coat around my neck and straightened my hair. "I didn't, now please—" Johnson, also readjusting himself and his appearance, winked at me before he turned to face the man.

"Would you two be quiet? I'm trying to bloody well listen." I gestured to my displeased neighbour as the man smelling of brandy leant back into his seat, and the juror rattled on about the well defined roles of monarchies and the dangers of citizens coming to their senses.

"And what is called the Crown, answers this purpose..." I fumbled for the letter in my coat. "...that fraud, hypocrisy and imposition of governments..."

Bearcroft once again, addressed the mumbling crowd. "Paine's intention appears here evidently, that the people of Great Britain have here no liberty nor a constitution. He says—and your Honour, I am sorry to utter here these words— their only possible means is to follow the French and topple down their present government." The crowd around me erupted in roar as men leapt from their seats and shouted towards the judge to hang Paine.

"Mr Paine," Bearcroft continued, though inaudible over the rambunctious crowd. "Should have explained to them the nature of their grief by which they are, apparently, oppressed. He should have pointed out to them a possible method for them to act in their original character, without the total dissolution of civil society like—"

"France!" a man shouted from the very back of the Hall, as one man in front of me spat to the ground.

The Attorney General joined Bearcroft on his stage. "Now, gentlemen. I also submit this evidence, this cold, scathing evidence that shows not only this man is the very writer of this book, but to show what his intention was." As he pulled another paper from his waistcoat, Bearcroft smiled to the crowd with a quiet satisfaction in his eyes.

"Now, where was I. Ah, here it is," continued the Attorney. "This is correspondence between Thomas Paine to a Mr Joseph Johnson who is his bookseller."

Mr Erskine, representing Paine, stood to address the court. "My Lord, as the Attorney General says, it is addressed to Mr Johnson, but Mr Johnson did not print the matter before the court." The two men, one Lord and the other a lawyer, stared intensely at each other; the room thickened with anticipation as no man nor mouse, uttered a word or a squeak. The man sitting next to me, who by name is the same, dug his hands into his waistcoat and adjusted his posture. After several seconds silence, Lord Kenyon broke away and gestured to the Attorney to resume his performance.

"Another letter, to a Mr Jordan of 166, Fleet-Street—"

"How did he acquire that letter?" whispered Johnson, underneath his breath.

"A spy, perhaps?" I said through my teeth.

"Find me once this sham is over." As the crowd erupted from their seats again, Johnson used his small frame to slip through the thick of people, out of the Hall and onto the streets of London.

"The letter is dated the 11th of November, the first year of the Republic," continued the Attorney.

"From Paris?"

"Potentially. My Lord, from Paris. However, if Mr Paine is, if any of his assassins are in London—and there is some reasonable ground to think there may be—if there are, I think for one, a man dying doing his duty is as good away of dying as of a raging fever or any other disorder." It was during this exchange I noticed a pigeon had wedged itself high upon the beams, right above the Attorney's head. In fact, it appeared as though a small army of pigeons had made camp in the rafters. Assassins of the sky keeping themselves a convenient distance from the commotion. I rather like pigeons.

"Now, gentlemen. I don't think I need trouble you any farther. Perhaps you will convict him, I have done my duty, my beautiful duty to this country and to his Lordship's court. I have brought before you, an offender. Now, Mr Bearcroft..." The Attorney gestured to the man who summoned a witness from the crowd, a Mr Thomas Champan. As the witness prepared to take his oath, Bearcroft and the Attorney whispered to each other in front of the jury as Paine's counsel confirmed with each other.

"What business are you?" asked the Attorney.

"A printer, Sir," replied Mr Chapman.

"Do you know the defendant, Thomas Paine?"

"I do Sir."

"Upon what occasion did you become acquainted with him?"

"Upon the recommendation of Mr Thomas Christie, sir," said Thomas. "I was introduced by Mr Christie to Mr Paine as a printer, to form a book he had."

"To form a book?" the Attorney had now made his way to stand in front of the witness, blocking the view of the Jury.

"Yes," replied Thomas.

"When?"

"1791, or thereabouts."

"What was the book?"

"The First Part of the Rights of Man." The crowd around me rose in their mumblings and the Attorney, addressing the question to the witness, looked over the crowd and smiled.

"Did you print the First Part of the Rights of Man?"

"Yes."

"Are you a publisher as well as a printer?"

"No Sir, that was a Mr Jordan of Fleet-Street." The Attorney retrieved the papers once again and held them high for the crowd to see, his voice becoming louder and louder.

"Had you any intercourse with Mr Paine, relative to printing this book, this very book, which I have in my hand?"

Chapman stayed silent for a few moments, looking to Erskine for support but, as per the rules, was met with silence. "The first edition of this book, I had sir, but I don't conceive I printed this edition. The first edition I did. The first part of the Rights of Man, I printed."

"And you printed the Second Part of the Rights of Man?"

"No. I printed a part of the Second Part." Mr Erskine stood as quickly as a man at attention and interrupted the Attorney.

"Do you mean that very book? Can you swear to it?" The Attorney's eyes shot round to Erskine, who looked completely pleased with himself.

"I cannot Sir," said Chapman.

"Then this Second Part of the Rights of Man," like a lion hunting its prey by the water's edge, the Attorney and circled around the witness. "Can you swear to that book?"

"A part of it."

"Well then," said the Attorney, smiling at the jury. "Will you inform my Lord and the jury what part you in fact did print then?"

"I printed, as far as I can remember, until page 112, signature H."

"You did this under the employment of Thomas Paine?"

"Yes Sir."

"Did you Mr Chapman," still circling. "Print the rest of the work from the letter H on page 112 to the conclusion of it?"

"No, Sir. I had a copy in my possession until 146. I stopped at page 112. I had the proof sheet and upon examining it, in my weak judgement, appeared of a dangerous tendency, therefore, immediately suspended printing and production." The Attorney circled back to position himself in front of the crowd once again. Nothing but smiles from the weary gentlemen greeted him.

"Have you, sir, seen Mr Paine write?" asked the Attorney.

"I have Sir."

"Do you know his handwriting?"

"I think I do-"

"Have you seen him write?" asked Mr Erskine, who had now wandered to face the witness, much to the displeasure of the Attorney.

"I have Sir," continued Chapman. "Several times."

"Be a good sir and look at this," said the Attorney, holding a letter from several meters away. "Is this, this here, Thomas Paine's writing?" he tapped the parchment with his fingers like a methodical clock passing seconds. Chapman lent forward as the crowd became all but silent once again.

"I think..."

"You think this is his handwriting?" Thomas Chapman held his breath for a few moments before letting out a large burst of air.

"Mr Chapman, please do continue," said Lord Kenyon.

Shifting in his seat as though on spikes, Chapman's eyes darted from Erskine to the Lord, to the Attorney. Repeatedly playing his part. "Yes, that is his handwriting now looking at it particularly," said Chapman.

"And this one?" Bearcroft passed several letters to the Attorney who, in quick succession, displayed them for several seconds for Chapman.

"Yes," he said.

"And this?"

"Yes."

"Look at this also."

"I believe it is."

"This one?"

"Hmm," said Chapman, leaning forward. "I cannot speak with any certainty to that one sir."

"Do you believe that to be his handwriting?" the Attorney, commanding both the words spoken and unspoken, waited for Chapman's reply.

After a moment of pause and another look towards the Attorney, he found his thought as though it appeared invisible around is head. "I rather think it is, but cannot speak with any certainty." The Attorney bowed and gestured to Lord Kenyon.

"Mr Erskine," said Lord Kenyon. "You may begin."

As Mr Erskine began interrogating the witness, the crowd and pigeons grew in an ever-increasing number. Men of all shapes, sizes, heights and gaits, packed the Great Hall to bear witness to the Trial of Thomas Paine. According to a famous author, the court is the perfect place for actors.

Placed neatly with Mr Bearcorft on one side and Lord Kenyon high-up on the other, the Attorney readjusted his court attire, smoothed his hair, and clasped his hands together like a steeple. The moment for the third and final act to commence had arrived.

"How often have you seen Mr Paine write, Mr Chapman?" asked Mr Erskine.

"A dozen times, perhaps."

"Did you look at him when writing? Observe him form his characters?"

"Why, decency would not suffer me to do it sir."

"I take it for granted that you did not suppose you should be called upon to prove his handwriting?"

"I did not Sir," replied Thomas.

"You did not take any notice of it?"

"I did not Sir." The Attorney arose with repidation from his seat, passing behind Lord Kenyon, who sat in the middle of the large wooden bench, and wandered over to the interrogation.

"Did you ever see any other writing than that you described?"

"No Sir."

"Then you are only inclined to believe that this one letter shown to you by the Attorney here is that of his handwriting."

"That is all sir."

The Attorney pulled one letter from his waist coat and held it for Mr Erskine to read. "This," he said. "Do you consider this last paper here is his handwriting?"

"I'm not on trial," Erskine replied.

"You may answer the question," piped Lord Kenyon.

"It...it doesn't appear to me to be the same. I never saw his handwriting in my life."

"What do you believe?" asked Lord Kenyon.

"Yes," said the Attorney. "What say you, Mr Erskine? Do you believe it is his handwriting?" The Attorney inched closer to Mr Erskine with every breath. The crowd to the left of him, Lord Kenyon to the right, and the jury behind, cornered Mr Erskine like a bull in a pen. Like a wave the crowd pressed forward with their chests. "Do you not know your client's handwriting Mr Erskine?"

"I believe it is," said Chapman, alarming both predator and prey.

"Do you mean to say you have a firmer belief than you expressed a moment ago?"

"Yes, Sir."

"What produced that belief?"

"The signature Sir. It struck me there was something more minute in the signature than when I noticed before."

"Mmm," said Erskine. "Peculiar."

The Attorney resumed. "Mr Chapman, may you read the contents of the letter for the jury and the gentlemen in the crowd?"

"What are you doing?" asked Erskine. The Attorney smiled, shrugged and handed Chapman the letter.

To Mr Jordan,

For your satisfaction and my own, I send you the inclosed, though I do not apprehend there will be any occasion to use it. If in case there should, you will immediately send a line to me, through Mr Johnson of St Paul's Churchyard, who will forward it to me. Upon receiving it, I shall come and answer personally for the work. Send also, for Horn Tooke.

The Attorney walked to the empty chair in place of Thomas Paine and turned to face the crowd.

"Now, Mr Erskine, can you read the second page?" a cunning smile, so large it appeared comical, appeared across the Attorney's face as he sat down on Thomas Paine's chair.

Shaking, Chapman handed the second page to Erskine who, after several moments, turned a white shade of green. "Mr Erskine, would you do us the pleasure of reading? Or shall I fetch a pigeon?" The Attorney turned his towards the rafters.

"My Lord, I object to this letter being read, how is this relevant to the matter at hand?" asked Mr Erskine.

"My Lord, it contains a libel of the most atrocious kind against his Majesty," said the Attorney.

"It cannot prove anything contained in the Second Part of the Rights of Man, nor will be evidence whether anything therein contained be libellous or not," Erskine's voice boomed. "As a matter of fact, the present information charges nothing respecting this letter and Mr Attorney General," pointing to the man smiling wickedly. "May as well read any other of Mr Paine as this pretended letter." Chapman sunk even further into his seat as though he entirely wished to disappear from view of the arguing lawyers altogether.

Lord Kenyon leaned forward over his bench as though he were about to scald a small child. "Mr Erskine. If the Attorney General had attempted to introduce the letter as either a matter of aggravation or inducement to the jury to find the defendant guilty on the present charge than I shall reject the letter."

"Thank you—"

"But," Lord Kenyon continued. "The letter contains an avowal that Mr Paine was the author of the book which is the subject of this trial." A smile more menacing than before appeared across the face of the Attorney. Erskine looked entirely bewildered. "And as the Attorney offered it only to prove this fact, then it should be read." The Attorney sauntered past Lord Kenyon and snatched the letter from Erskine's hands and read it aloud.

"You have, as Attorney General, commenced a prosecution against me as the author of 'Rights of Man'," the Attorney glanced at Erskine, who stared at the letter being read. "Had not my duty, in consequence of my being elected a member of the National Convention of France, called me from England, I should have stayed to have contested the injustice of that prosecution; not upon my own account, for I cared not about the prosecution, but to have defended the principles I had advanced in the work."

"He fled the country!" a man shouted from behind me.

"Traitor!"

"The duty I am now engaged in is of too much importance to permit me to trouble myself about your prosecution: when I have leisure, I shall have no objection to meet you on that ground. If you obtain a guilty verdict (which you are welcome to if you can get it), it cannot affect me otherwise than to increase my reputation; and with respect to yourself, it is as consistent that you obtain a verdict against the Man in the Moon as against me;

neither do I see how you can continue the prosecution against me as you would have done against one of your own people, who had absented himself because he was prosecuted; what passed at...My necessary absence-"

"Lord Kenyon, he left out a part just there," said Erskine.

"Continue," said Lord Kenyon.

"Ah, here is the part," said the Attorney, clearing his throat.

"The Government of England is as great, if not the greatest, perfection of fraud and corruption that ever took place since governments began, is what you cannot be a stranger to, unless the constant habit of seeing it has blinded your senses; but though you may not choose to see it, the people are seeing it very fast, and the progress is beyond what you may choose to believe. I speak to you as one man ought to speak to another; and I know also that I speak what other people are beginning to think. As I do not consider myself the object of the prosecution, neither can I be affected by the issue, one way or the other, I shall, though a foreigner in your country, subscribe as much money as any other man toward supporting the right of the nation against the prosecution; and it is for this purpose only that I shall do it. Signed, Thomas Paine." Erskine covered his hands over his face, took several long, deep breaths as the Attorney General resumed his seat.

"I'm beginning to like the ol' Paine now," said the brandied' breathed man behind me, loud enough for several people around us to hear.

"Me too," I replied. Another man seated a few people over lent forward and beamed from ear to ear.

"I stand here as the advocate for Thomas Paine," said Erskine. "What Mr Attorney General failed to mention and in fact, removed from his address to you, was that Mr Paine has had spies set upon him, for he was harassed at Dover and at Calais. You most undoubtedly wish to deal with every man that comes before you in judgment as you desire to be dealt with yourselves, if you should accidentally publish anything that might not be thought proper, and any man brings you to trial for it." Throwing Paine's letter on the ground, he openly faced the crowd like a lamb come to the slaughter.

"When a nation changes its opinion and habits of thinking, it is no longer to be governed as before; but it would not only be wrong, but bad policy, to attempt by force what ought to be accomplished by reason." His speaking voice conveyed a paternal tenderness I had yet to witness in a lawyer before.

He continued. "Rebellion consists in forcibly opposing the general will of a nation, whether by a party or by a government. There ought, therefore, to be in every nation a method of ascertaining the state of public opinion with respect to government. There is, therefore, no power but the voluntary will of the people that has a right to act in any matter respecting a general reform; and by the same right that two persons can confer on such a subject, a thousand may. The object, in all such preliminary proceedings, is to find out what the general sense of a nation is, and to be governed by it. If it prefer a bad or defective government to a reform, or choose to pay ten times more taxes than there is occasion for, it has a right so to do." Mr Erskine clasped his hands together behind his back and recited a paragraph from Paine's book aloud to the crowd.

"All hereditary government is in its nature tyranny. An heritable or unheritable throne, or by what other fanciful name such things may be called, have no other significant explanation than that mankind are heritable property. To inherit a government is to inherit the people, as if they were flocks and herds. Is it to be endured, says the Attorney General, the people are to be told they are like so many sheep and oxen? Certainly not. I am of opinion, a more dangerous doctrine cannot be instilled into the people of

England. Mr Paine is not doing that, when he states they are like flocks and herds; he is writing in answer to Mr Burke's book, that asserts the hereditary monarchy is fastened on the people, without any consent of their own. I hope, with confidence, that I am not transgressing those rules in doing the duties of my situation which are accidentally cast upon me." The murmurs changed from a low tone to one of small applause.

The Attorney General rose to reply, but Mr Campbell, the foreman of the jury, announced that his brother jurors had instructed him to say that the Attorney General could save himself the trouble of any observations, unless he had a different opinion himself, because they were satisfied.

The jury wasted no time in delivering their verdict: guilty.

Paris 25th December 1792

To Everina,

Tomorrow I expect to see Aline. During her absence the servants endeavoured to render the house, a most excellent one, comfortable to me, but as I wish to acquire the language as fast as I can, I was sorry to be obliged to remain so much alone. I devote myself so closely to the language and strive to understand what I hear that I never go to bed without a headache, and my spirits become fatigued from trying to form a just opinion of public affairs.

I have seen little of Paris; the streets are so dirty and I wait till I can make myself understood before I call on Madame Laurent, etc. Miss Williams is civil to me and I shall visit her frequently because I rather like her and I meet French company at her house. Her manners are affected, yet the simple goodness of her heart breaks through the varnish, so that one would be more inclined, at least I should, to love than admire her. Authorship is a heavyweight on female shoulders, especially in the sunshine of prosperity.

Mary

Paris 26th December 1792

To Joseph Johnson

On receipt of your letter, my dear friend, thank you for your punctuality, for it highly gratified me, had I not wished to wait till I could tell you that this day is not stained with blood. Indeed, the prudent precautions taken by the National Convention to prevent a tumult make me suppose that the dogs of faction would not dare to bark, much less bite, however true to their scent, and I was not mistaken. The citizens who were all called out are returning home with composed countenances, shouldering their arms.

I wish I could tell you that this day was not stained with blood but I would be wholeheartedly lying. About nine o'clock this morning their King passed by my window, silently bar the odd beat of a drum, rendering the stillness of the Parisian air more awful.

For the first time since I entered France, I bowed to the majesty of her people. I can scarcely tell you why, but tears flowed from my eyes. Louis XIV sat there with more dignity than I expected from his character, in a hackney coach, rolling onwards to captivity.

His pomp, glory and sunshine of prosperity overshadowed by gloom and misery.

There is blood on the hands of most inhabitants, and hurried footsteps pass by in the night. I wish I had the cat with me—I want to see something alive for death—with its writhing scythe, has in so many forms, taken hold of my imagination.

For the first time in my life, I cannot put out the candle; like the light of my heart, I fear the inevitable darkness if it were to ever go out.

Yours sincerely,

M. W

Paris early January 1793

"Thomas! Oh, you walk with such haste," I hurried between carts, animals and people meandering about their day. The winter sun, low in the sky, cast a soft golden hue over the frost-kissed landscape. Covered in scarves, the frigid Parisian air gnawed at my skin.

"Go home," he said, attempting to ignore me.

"I must come with you," I said, joining his quick pace across the cobblestone.

"Go home," he repeated, winding his way through small groups of people.

"You are positively frustrating." I said, attempting to keep up. "I do not care that you want me safe I—"

"Our countries are on the brink of war. Please Mary, please do not come with me. You are a British woman."

"What is that supposed to mean?" We stopped walking and Thomas turned to face me. His eyes, bloodshot and red, found mine.

"Everything has changed. Everything. This National Convention. Louis is on trial. Anyone who argues against Robespierre, Danton, Marat especially, any of the Jacobins, they die."

"Don't you dare."

"You're curious about what happens in those meetings, I understand. But I am protecting you from yourself," he said, with the finality of a father.

A small bout of laughter escaped from my chest. "You, of all men, think it fitting for me to need protection from the men whom you so associate yourself with? Tell me, father of the Revolutions, do you need protection?" I did not hold anger in my eyes, but the kindness he so often witnessed from me across the table at Johnson's dinners. I could not be angry at him. Disappointed, yes, but my father's blood does not live within me.

"You utter one word against their ideas, Thomas, and you shall march on towards the guillotine. Are you not standing in the spilled blood of last September?"

"You think me ignorant?" Thomas retreated a few steps towards the near-frozen Seine.

"You are a lettered soldier in their bloodied game against the crowned heads of Europe. Once they have finished with you, they shall discard you like a chamber pot out the window, throw you into the river for the rebels of the revolution to drink from." Thomas glanced behind him at the ghosts of floating bodies in the Seine and the haunting screams of September.

I stepped closer, mere inches away from his eyes. "Are you not going now, to stand for the head of King Louis?"

"Yes. I am but—"

"And if they disagree with your sentiments? What then? You throw your life away for the cause of their King?" Several passers-by on their way to a small market by the river slowed their pace past our conversation.

"My duty is to liberty," said Thomas. "Killing the French King is not the answer and they need to—"

"Will she save you when you're in prison?" I pulled my scarf tighter around my neck.

"Who?"

"Liberty. Is this not the essence of the Revolution? Is that not what your American Revolution was about?" Thomas pulled me away from the crowd to find quiet underneath a lifeless, frigid tree. Its leaves had all but wasted away into the cobblestone and mud.

"Someone is watching us," he gestured to a man piling bits of coal into a sack several metres away.

"How do you—"

"Mary," he whispered. "There was a twelve-man jury in England who engaged in a show trial that decided my fate which had already been decided. I have no home. I cannot return to England. I live here now. I must do what is right."

"You are not responsible for saving their King Tom," I whispered furiously in reply.

"Does he not deserve life? Who is responsible if not I?"

"We all deserve to live Tom." Thomas took a deep breath and his body let go of everything he was holding onto.

"Mary, we stand here to argue with one another but we both miss the point."

"The point?"

"Your reply to Burke, my reply to Burke, Olympe's pamphlets, Dr Price's sermon's, Olaudah's narrative...the whole point is that we all stand for what we believe in. Whether that is together or apart, the world is a far better place when people—"

"Challenge ideas?" I too let the frustration relax out of my body. Silence filled the air as the weight of Thomas' impending actions sank in. "I worry for you, Tom."

"I understand Mary," he held my hands and squeezed them gently. "But I will be okay, I promise. I have friends, though, if I understood half as much French as you do I would rather find my situation much further tipped in my favour." His weathered face smiled and laughter escaped from both of us. It was then I noticed in detail the marks of his tumultuous life on his skin, etched with lines that spoke of both hardship and determination.

"It is rare for people to be seen as who they are, Tom. But you wear your ideas on your shoulders like badges of honour. Whatever happens, always remember that won't you? You are a kindred spirit and though you worry me, I admire your steadfast commitment to the cause of liberty and your strength in the ongoing struggle for justice and equality." Thomas nodded, his smile faint this time. He glanced behind him in the direction of the Salle du Manège.

"I must go. They shall begin their debates soon."

"I know." I tried to smile again, but my chest burned and ached at thought of it all.

"I will see you soon." He removed himself from under the tree and began his long walk to the riding hall. I contemplated seeing his face one last time and my mind wandered.

"Thomas! Wait." I caught up to him within a few moments and he turned to face me.

"Yes?" I paused, not knowing what to say.

"Your coat, I remembered it needed adjusting. Here, let me."

"Oh," he spun around. Tailored for practicality rather than ostentation, his plain and patched, well-worn coat of darkened fabric was devoid of unnecessary adornments. Its simple lines and sturdy construction spoke to his no-nonsense approach to life. I fixed his cravat and retied it in a simple knot.

"May I?" He nodded and let me adjust his collar so it was neater and flatter. Though faded with age and use, his boots and waistcoat were respectable nontheless. I adjusted his sleeves and—

"Mary?" I lowered my eyes from his gaze. "I shall be okay. Go on would you, return to Olympe, I am sure she would do with your company." He bowed as his smiling eyes met mine, tipped his hat towards me and resumed his walk to the Riding Hall.

Sale De Manage Paris the same day

Thomas' secretary Bancal, who took his place amongst the six tiers of banquettes, gestured towards to the podium in the centre of the old Riding Hall. The Hall's high walls peel and the ceiling was severely damaged. Several parts and pieces of windows were either broken or missing.

"I say, there are quite the number of constituents here, are there not?" asked Thomas. His heart raced faster and faster. After an hour of speeches and many applauses the crowd settled down.

"Come, let us show France what they stand for." Nodding in agreement, Thomas walked to stand beside the platform as his secretary read his statement in French to the Assembly. Known to his friends as 'Bi-lingual Bancal', he coughed several times before embarking on Paine's speech.

"My hatred and abhorrence of monarchy are sufficiently known: they originate in principles of reason and conviction, nor, except with life, can they ever be extirpated; but my compassion for the unfortunate, whether friend or enemy, is equally lively and sincere." A small group of men applauded.

"I voted yesterday that Louis should be tried, because it was necessary to afford proofs to the world of the perfidy, corruption and abomination of the monarchical system. The infinity of evidence that has been produced exposes them in the most glaring and hideous colours; thence it results that monarchy, whatever form it may assume, arbitrary or otherwise, becomes a centre round which are united every species of corruption, and the kingly trade is no less destructive of all morality in the human breast, than the trade of an executioner destroys its sensibility. I remember, during my residence in another country, that I was struck with a sentence of M. Autheine, at the Jacobins, which corresponds with my idea,—"Make me a king today," said he.

"And I shall be a robber to-morrow."

"It is to France alone, I know, that the United States of America owe that support which enabled them to shake off the unjust and tyrannical yoke of Britain. The ardour and zeal which she displayed to provide both men and money, were the natural consequence of a thirst for liberty."

"Vive le Nation!" a man shouted.

"America!" said another, their voices echoing amongst the Hall.

"But as the nation restrained by the shackles of her own government, could only act by the means of a monarchical organ, this organ—whatever in other respects the object might be—performed a good, a great action."

"Let then those United States be the safeguard and asylum of Louis Capet. There, far removed from the miseries and crimes of royalty, he may learn, from the constant aspect of public prosperity, that the true system of government consists not in kings, but in equal, and honourable representation."

"In relating this circumstance, and in submitting this proposition, I consider myself as a citizen of both countries. I declare it as a representative of America, who feels the debt of gratitude which he owes to every Frenchman. I submit it also as a man, who, although the enemy of kings, cannot forget that they are subject to human frailties. I, in my role as a citizen of the French republic, support my proposition because I consider it to be the best and most politic measure that can be adopted.

"The French Nation carries her measures of government to a greater length. France is not satisfied with exposing the guilt of the monarch. She has penetrated into the vices and horrors of the monarchy. She has shown them clear as daylight, and forever crushed that system; and he, whoever he may be, that should ever dare to reclaim those rights would be regarded not as a pretender, but punished as a traitor."

"It has already been proposed to abolish the punishment of death, and it is with infinite satisfaction that I recollect the humane and excellent oration pronounced by Robespierre on that subject in the Constituent Assembly. This cause must find its advocates in every corner where enlightened politicians and lovers of humanity exist, and it ought above all to find them in this Assembly."

"Monarchical governments have trained humanity, and inured it to the sanguinary arts and refinements of punishment; and it is identical punishment which has so long shocked the sight and tormented the patience of the people, that now, in their turn, they practise in revenge upon their oppressors. But it becomes us to be on our guard against the abomination and perversity of monarchical examples: as France has been the first of European nations to abolish royalty, let her also be the first to abolish the punishment of death, and to find out a milder and more effectual substitute."

"In the particular case now under consideration, I submit the following propositions." Bancal gestured for him to stand next to him as he read Paine's final propositions.

"1st, That the National Convention shall pronounce sentence of banishment on Louis and his family," Thomas smiled at the crowd. "Secondly, we will keep Louis Capet imprisoned until the end of the war, and then we will carry out the sentence of banishment," Thomas smiled widely at the crowd. Sincerely do I regret the Convention's vote of yesterday for death—"

"Thomas Paine is incompetent to vote on this question. Because he is a Quaker, his religious principles oppose capital punishment!" said Marat, launching himself into the middle of the Hall and pointing towards Paine. Murmurs from the constituents begun to rise as a few men begun chanting 'Freedom of speech'. Thomas nodded to Bancal, who continued.

"I know that the public mind of France, and particularly that of

Paris, the dangers to which they have been exposed have heated and irritated its citizens. But if we were to project our thoughts into the future, when the dangers are ended and the irritations forgotten, what may seem like an act of justice today could then be perceived as an act of vengeance."

"My anxiety for the cause of France has become for the moment concern for her honour. If, on my return to America, I should employ myself on a history of the French Revolution, I had rather record a thousand errors on the side of mercy, than be obliged to tell one act of severe justice."

"I voted against an appeal to the people, because the Convention was wearied on that point; but I so voted hoping this Assembly would pronounce against death, and for the same punishment that the Nation would have voted, at least that is for reclusion during the war, and banishment thereafter." The complexion of Marat's face turned from red, to a warm shade of purple.

"France has but one ally—the United States of America. That is the only Nation that can furnish France with naval provisions, for the kingdoms of northern Europe are, or soon will be, at war with her. The person now under discussion is considered by the Americans as having been the friend of their Revolution. His execution will be an affliction to them, and it is in your power not to wound the feelings of your ally. Could I speak the French language I would descend to your bar, and in their name become your petitioner to respite the execution of the sentence on Louis."

"This is not the language of Thomas Paine," said a man called Thuriot. "This is not his words."

"I denounce the interpreter," Marat shouted. "I maintain it is not Thomas Paine's opinion. It is an untrue translation."

"I read the original I did," said another called Garan, standing proud from the third tier of seats. "I am fluent in French and English and the translation is correct it is."

An uproar broke into the stands. Men shouted obscenities at both Bancal and Thomas Paine in both French and English for several minutes. Realisation crept upon the face of Thomas Paine and after much quietening down, Bancal continued.

"Your Executive Committee will nominate an ambassador to Philadelphia; I sincerely hope that he may announce to America that the National Convention of France, out of pure friendship to America, has consented to respite Louis. That people, by my vote, ask you to delay the execution."

Marat began shouting in both languages. "Paine voted against the punishment of death because he is a Quaker!"

Thomas turned in a flurry and shouted from the podium. "I voted against the punishment of death from both moral motives and motives of public policy you imbécile." As the last word left Thomas Paine's mouth, Bancal sighed and threw the pages into the stunned and now silent crowd. Marat's face turned from shock to anger in mere seconds.

"He is guilty of treason!" Marat screamed at Paine. "L'arrêter!"

"Treason? Against who?"

"L'arrêter! Arrest him!"

The crowd's eyes fixed on Thomas Paine—now resigned to his seat in a mix of dismay and horror. A blank stare enveloped his face as dozens of hands pulled at his coat and dragged him out of the Riding Hall and into a carriage.

Rue Mesele Paris 1st February 1793

To Joseph Johnson,

The streets of Paris are certainly disagreeable; impossible to walk for air, and I always want air. I am endeavouring to acquire the language but I am exceedingly fatigued by constant attention to words.

Contradiction rests within me both physically and mentally. Yesterday a gentleman offered me a place in his carriage to return home back to England and I knew not how to say no. It would be foolish of me to return. I am, besides, writing a plan of education for the Committee appointed to consider that subject. You can thank Paine for that connection. The new constitution shall make its appearance, and Paris has been tranquil since the death of their King.

The Assembly arrested Paine, but he is free now. It went as well as I thought it would for him. I am grieved, sorely grieved when I think of the blood that stained the cause of freedom in Paris...I also hear the same live stream cry aloud from the highways through which the retreating armies pass with famine and death in their rear.

The perspective of the golden age, fading before the attentive eye of observation, almost eludes my sight, and losing thus in part my theory of a more perfect state, start not, my friend, if I bring forward an opinion which at the first glance is levelled against the existence of God! I am not become an atheist, I assure you, by residing at Paris; yet I begin to fear that vice, or if you will, evil, is the grand mobile of action and that when the passions are justly poised we become harmless, in the same proportion useless.

Mary

11.57pm

It appears France has declared war on England.

M

The house of Helen Maria Williams Paris 11th February 1793

"Ah, Mary, I see you are in—spirits," Olympe de Gouges continued sipping tea, surrounded by Helen and Charlotte Corday—whom I had not quite seen for several days—and several other gentlemen and women whom I made acquaintance with once or twice, perhaps. Adorned with paintings and small tapestries, the room we occupied was a quaint meeting spot for the foreign minds in Paris. An island amongst the treachrous waves, though how long it would prove safe nobody knew.

"They are not good spirits Olympe," said Miss Williams, half smiling at her. "Mary have you broken your fast this morning?" Nodding in reply, Helen stood to retrieve small pieces of bread from the table in the cosy sitting room. I had previously admired Helen's choice of rich fabrics that exuded a sense of calm and prosperity one could only imagine in England. I was glad she found a haven here.

"Madame, mesdemoiselles," an imposing figure, with an American accent, wandered to our table and bowed. His eyes, sharp and penetrating, seemed to take in the whole room. His coat, though worn from use, was of fine quality, its deep navy colour contrasting sharply with the paleness of his skin. Despite his outward confidence, as he stepped closer there appeared a vulnerability in his gaze with a hint of loneliness I had never noticed before in a man.

"Ah, Mr Imlay, a pleasure," said Helen, returning to our circle with her bread. "This is Mrs Wollstonecraft, the writer I mentioned not a mere few days ago." Imlay's eyes were a daring blue, ones I had never seen adorned on a man before. His jacket appeared new, the seams intact and unfrayed.

"Captain Imlay, but you may call me Gilbert please, a pleasure." I rose to meet his gaze and grabbing my hand, he kissed it, my skin burning at his touch.

"Mr Imlay here is from America," said Helen, interrupting the thickened air between us. "Fought in the Revolutionary War he did Mrs Wollstonecraft." Helen made a small glance in my direction. Pretending not to see her, I sat back down and reacquainted with my tea as Gilbert retrieved a chair from an adjoining table to join us.

"You reside in Paris Mrs Wollstonecraft?" asked Gilbert without averting his gaze from my own. "I'll say I am surprised you did not return home."

"Paris is her home for now is it not ma'dear?" said Helen, a half smile appearing on her lips. "Besides, the passage will no longer be safe." Olympe covered her own small smile with her tea cup as I widened my eyes at her.

"For now," I said. "Though I still have yet to compile my thoughts on the current matters at hand."

"Ah," said Gilbert. "Your thoughts on the—matter at hand. I shall say, an interesting matter we have is it not?" The manor we made acquaintance in was one of the last refuges for British subjects to discuss the now unfolding war between France and her contemporaries. Whoever orbited in and out of Helen's house, Madame Roland's and the Christie manor found themselves there by acquaintance.

"War is the adventure naturally pursued by the idle as we have all discovered," I said. "It requires something of this species, to excite the strong emotions necessary to rouse some inactive minds."

"Dat Marat will find himself..." Charlotte paused and inhaled the odour from the bread. "Washed in blood before de end of the year."

"Now now Charlotte," said Helen. As we discussed the ongoing politics and tumults of the day, Robespierre and the Jacobins, Gilbert Imlay couldn't avert his gaze from me. Men and women, in a hurry or not in a hurry, drifted in and out of the room like dancers ebbing and to and from a dance floor. Some would say hello to each other, others a slight nod or a raised brandy glass.

"And the King, what say you Mrs Wollstonecraft?" asked Gilbert. A waft of curiosity lingered from his body. I peered across the room in search of whose ears were listening.

"He was..."

"Go on—" he lent forward.

"Defective in judgement. Defective perhaps because he did not to see that he was surrounded with sycophants and no less, the overgrown influence of the nobility blinded his reason," I said, sitting up straighter.

"Dey should not have killed him," said Olympe.

"Agreed," said Gilbert. "But what else were they to do?" he pondered.

"Exile him, he would have brought back an army," said Helen as she rolled her third cigarette for the day, spilling some tobacco on her dress and wiping it away.

"Imprison him, but then the monarchists would have stormed any fortress to rescue him," I added.

"Bah, dis whole thing is worrisome," said Charlotte, continuing to section her pieces of bread like a jeweller taking apart polished diamonds from a ring.

"Vat?" asked Olympe.

"Everything," replied Charlotte with her mouth almost full. "I am positively frustrated at the state of the world."

"Now now, come come, it could be worse," said Helen, puffing a plume of smoke into Charlotte's face.

"Como?" said Charlotte coughing, as several men speaking at the adjoining table glanced in our direction through the thick smoke of cigars.

"Ve could be dead," said Olympe.

"We could be British," said Gilbert, his eyes fixated on my face for a reaction. Olympe and Charlotte giggled whilst Helen rolled her eyes in response. As Olympe, Charlotte and Helen discussed the now-beheaded King Louis in detail, Gilbert attempted further conversation with me, albeit unsuccessfully.

"Say, Mrs Wollstonecraft, you are a writer Helen tells me?" Gilbert's body inched even further towards me.

"You have been informed correctly," I replied.

"Are you, writing anything currently?" he asked.

"Yes," I said. "But I have not yet quite decided what it shall be, or whether it is worth publishing at all, really. I haven't been able to receive word from my publisher Jo—"

"Mr Johnson isn't it?"

"Yes, Joseph, a dear friend of mine. I do hope he is doing okay. The letters have stopped you see."

"I shall send word to check on him for you," he said. "The least I can do for a fellow writer," he added.

A writer. "You write." Someone had entered the room and everyone clapped. Thomas.

"Thomas! Over here!"

"I do write," replied Gilbert. "I shall leave a copy here for you at the manor."

"How lovely of you." I half smiled at Gilbert and turned my attention back to Thomas. "Thomas there is a chair over there, grab it and sit won't you."

"How vas prison Monsieur Paine?" asked Olympe.

"Aye, delightful madame."

"Who is this?" Just as he was about to sit, Thomas advanced his hand forward and shook Gilbert's.

"Captain. Captain Gilbert Imlay."

"Aye an American. You are far from home are you not?" Thomas" eyes narrowed as he took a seat and relaxed.

"The war and such things," replied Gilbert. "Business affairs."

"What type of business?" asked Thomas.

"Shipping and trade, mostly."

"Madame Roland?" a rather tallish man, with long silver hair appeared from behind one of the smaller doors that led to the kitchen.

"Over there," said Thomas, gesturing to a lady by the window. "Well now," he continued to Gilbert. "If I ever need something shipped back to America, I know who to send for." Thomas smiled and greeted the rest of us. Whilst he did not spend long in prison, he appeared deflated and less energetic compared to when we had met previously. The wind was out of his sails, one would say.

"How do you know Thomas? I presume you are friends?" asked Gilbert.

"Yes. Is there something wrong with the sentiment?" I said. Thomas poured a cup of tea and held it to his face to cover a smile. "Who was that man asking for Roland?"

"Jacques Pierre Brissot," replied Thomas.

"The Brissot?" I turned my head to the side as Brissot and Roland began conversing to the side of the room.

"And we met at a dinner hosted by a fine gentleman," said Thomas from behind his teacup. "And with you as well." He nodded to Olympe, and she smiled in return, brushing her blonde hair from her face.

"It vas lovely," she replied. "I must visit vhen everything iz finished with dis war." Olympe sighed and tapped the top of her teacup. "Vhen vill you return, madame?"

I pondered for a moment but my future appeared a blur. "I do not quite know. I am here to understand the truth of this Revolution like Helen. But the truth is sometimes not pleasant. If we turn from it, and doat on an illusion then we thicken the cloud, rather than dispel it. Therefore, I do not know how long I shall be here." Silence befell the group for a few moments until Gilbert broke it.

"Was anyone in Paris when they stormed the Hôtel de Ville?"

Olympe and Helen both nodded. "The Gardes Françaises, dey joined de people and took de Bastille."

"In the evening," added Helen, "The mob broke the windows of the hotel with stones. The troops around the mob did not budge an inch. They just, watched. It took them fifteen minutes to beat the door in pieces with iron crows. A shower of sashes, shutters, chairs, tables, sofas, books, papers and pictures rained incessantly from all the windows of the hotel."

"Den came de tiles, skirting boards, bannisters, framework and every part of de building dey could remove," said Olympe. "De troops, as Helen said, vere quiet spectators."

"Obviously the city guards realised what had happened and they placed themselves at the doors of the churches and all public buildings," said Helen. "It rained furniture, it was a curious scene absolutely. One of Madame Roland's friends said he saw a lad of about 14 be crushed to death by something as he was handing his plunder to a woman, his mother, it turned out. Crushed, right in front of her. It was not only common people there, there were reports of well-dressed men destroying archives and strewed the papers all around the streets of Paris." Thomas" body lent further and further forward as Olympe and Helen continued to recount their stories.

"Monsiuer Paine, you would 'ave heard of Marseille?" asked Charlotte.

"I have madame."

"Marseille, Rouen, Strasbourg, Nantes and the Loire Valley all fell within days," said Helen.

"I heard Grenoble did not fall?" asked Gilbert.

"You are correct," replied Helen. "As far as I can remember, in towns like Lyon and Bordeaux the power was shared between the people's administration and the royalists."

"Lille, Toulouse and Grenoble dey did not, succeed in, eh, taking over." Gilbert lent so his head was but the length of a feather from Helen.

"And I heard that the people's administrations were not, commoners," he said in a hushed voice. "But, les notables." Helen nodded and rested back in her chair.

"You are correct. Protection of the status quo."

"La Grande Peur," added Olympe. Gilbert's eyes glanced in my direction.

"Grand fear?" I glanced to Olympe who nodded.

"Nobody knew vhat vas, actually 'appening. And de people in Marseille, Rouen and zo on probably 'eard about Paris, de Bastille and Hotel and dought to demselves, pourquoi pas nous aussi?" Helen poured herself another cup of tea as Thomas sat back against his chair and rested his fingers against his chin. Everyone appeared to collect their thoughts for a while and nibble on small pieces of cheese from the table sat neatly between us all.

"Dere are zo many stories floating about Paris. Many beautiful chateaux 'ave been burnt. Destroyed. De seigneurs hunted like rabbits for sport whilst deir wives and daughters ravished. Unless ov course you wear de tricolour cocarde," said Charlotte.

"Which Mr Imlay, you should adorn on yourself if you like to not be set upon," said Helen. "And with you Mary, even if it is something small."

"Yes, Gouverneur Morris told me only last week that between the 14th and 22nd of July in '89, the Marquis de La Fayette and his men saved 17 people from Parisian lynch mobs," said Thomas. "How come you did not leave Paris Helen and return to England?"

"Yes, it was less a Grande Peur and more of a Grande Panique in Paris. And I need to be here. To bear witness to it all, just like Mary is." Helen smiled and raised her cup of tea towards me. I glanced towards the window and watched Parisians run about their daily lives. It seemed far-fetched that only a few years ago the entire city was enveloped in fear.

"And the King and Queen, they remained in Versailles throughout this ordeal?" asked Gilbert. Helen and Olympe murmured something to each other in French.

"How long 'ave you been in Paris Monsieur Imlay?" asked Olympe.

"I arrived here two months ago from America." Olympe raised her eyebrows and flicked shot me a wide-eyed look.

"The King and the Queen remained in Versailles, correct. Many of their family and aristocrats departed France I heard from Madame Roland." Roland had returned to her window seat and lifted her head towards our group at the sound of her name. "The Minister of War Victor-Francois de Broglie; Louis Joseph de Bourbon, Louis Joseph's son Louis Henri de Bourbon and his grandson Louis d'Enghien, all left Paris and Versailles."

"Then, the fourth of August," I added.

"La Déclaration des droits de l'homme et du citoyen est née à l'été 1789," said Olympe. "De precious rights of Man—"

"But not of woman," I said.

Olympe half smiled and lowered her head. "No. Not ov woman."

"And that is how the King and Queen found themselves, no longer residing at Versailles," said Helen. Olympe raised her teacup to the group and smiled and so did Thomas.

"Ah yes, a man I met on our ship from America mentioned this to me. The bread situation," said Gilbert.

"Since you know, vhy do you not explain?" Olympe rested in her chair and gestured for Gilbert to talk, though he appeared unable to form words. "Please, go on."

"The peasants were hungry and they stormed Versailles? They ran out of bread. At least that is what the man said."

"Mm, you are 'alf correct Monsieur," said Olympe.

"Well, you see, King Louis did not, accept or enact the laws that changed from the fourth of August. One could say he was un peu en colère," said Helen. "I was speaking to

Brissot a few months ago and the rumours of that September and October were that grain merchants were hoarding their supplies for fear of the mob—"

"I was told by Bancal it was to starve them," said Thomas.

"Either or," Helen shrugged. "Shops closed, for most of their workers were on the streets with muskets, or the merchants had no bread to sell."

"Zo, de peasants vere hungrier than before and vere angrier than before. "Les 5 et 6 Octobre 1789" vas vhen the tides of de Revolution changed Monsieur."

"Against their King?" I asked.

"Precisely," replied Olympe. "De women did not simply march to Versailles. Non. Virst, dey visited the Palace-Royal. In fact. Antoine! Pouvez-vous s'il vous plaît nous rejoindre ici. J'explique la nuit du 5 au 6 octobre à ces gens-là." A man in the far corner of the parlour turned to smile at Olympe and joined us after a few moments. "Mary, Gilbert, Thomas, dis is Antoine Gorsas. He publishes de Courrier de Versailles à Paris et de Paris a Versailles." Antoine retrieved a small chair from the nearest wall and posted himself next to Gilbert. His heavy-lidded eyes smiled as he greeted each of us. Combined with his large nose and wigged-hair, he exuded a sense of importance.

"Aye, you were at the trial of Louis?" asked Thomas as he nibbled on a small piece of cheese.

"Oui. I voted for Louis to be banished, not killed. I admire your courage, Monsieur Paine. Marat is simply dérangé."

Thomas nodded and shrugged. "They did not keep me long."

"Zo, Antoine, u 5 au 6 octobre."

"Oui Olympe. Zo, On the 4 au October I was at the Palace-Royal and in walks dis, group of women. Dey complain about de bread situation, de grain and how King Louis did not decide to pass de laws from August. I decided to, inform dis group of mainly women, that au 1 au October, Louis XVI allowed his regular Gardes du Corps to hold a huge banquet for some officers dat had arrived that day. Some, 240 officers in Versailles. Even dere was an orchestra there. They returned the next day, October 5 and gathered outside Hotel de Ville."

"But the King did not live at the Hotel?" asked Gilbert.

"Precisely Monsieur. In fact, de women first protested to the councillors of Paris. The Dames De La Salle who marched to Versailles vere simply going to the King because de councillors did nothing. Zo, de several thousand—"

"Several thousand?" I said.

"Oui, several thousand women marched to Versailles. About twenty or so made into the Assemble building, demanded bread and grain and by the next day, after some heads on pikes and some slashings, the King and Queen were made to return to Paris and moved themselves into the Tuileries."

Thomas held his teacup to Gilbert. "Revolution like this spreads like fire, it is why they persecuted me so and vowed for my head in England. Had the French Revolution confined itself to the destruction of flagrant despotism then Burke would have been silent."

"But it's gone too far for them," I added to his sentiment.

"Precisely. It will serve a lesson to the oppressor and an example to the oppressed."

"You are not vorried dey vill vind you here Tom?" asked Olympe.

"It is beyond the compass of his capacity to keep his arguments together in a logical order let alone organise an assassination attempt in Paris. They weren't successful in England and I shall like to see them try here." Thomas raised his cup to the group.

"Thomas Paine?" a man had entered the room and shouted. "You are hereby requested at the Assembly." Without a pause, he turned and exited the main room as all the guests' eyes turned to Thomas.

"Aye, well that is my cue." He half-bowed to each of us, smiled at me and I back at him. "I shall see you all soon." He said goodbye to a few other Americans and British present, waved goodbye to the room and left.

"He is quite the character is he not?" asked Gilbert. "Do tell me what you think of it when you read it."

"Read what sorry? I must have missed—"

"My book. I shall leave it here for you to read remember?"

"Oh, how lovely."

"Well, it was a pleasure. I must go and attend to some business affairs. Good day to you all." With the finality of his remark, Captain Gilbert Imlay stood, bowed to each of us and joined some gentlemen in the corner of the room.

"He fancies you," said Helen under her breath.

"Well then it is one sided. Such bufoonary."

"Mary!" said Olympe.

"Madames," Antoine stood, bowed and returned to the group of gentlemen he had left.

"Have you received letters from England of late Helen?" I asked.

"Do not change the subject," Helen insisted. "And no, I have not. Have you my dear?" I shook my head in reply. Letters from England haven't made an appearance since the previous month.

"It is a blessing for me in some ways," I said aloud with no real intention for anyone to hear, though Helen nodded in agreement.

"Your father?" she asked with a hint of trepidation.

"One of them, yes. He is unwell, or so I have been told by Eliza."

"And Everina?"

"The same as always I would imagine. I have not yet found a suitable prospect for her, but now the war has begun I do not think I shall find any amicable arrangement. Their domestic miseries do not bother me anymore."

As the afternoon passed, we treated ourselves to a small supper of bread, wine from various regions of France and a peculiar array of meats I could only dream of eating in England. Conversations danced between politics, poetry, Voltaire, Burke and Rosseau. One could only imagine the conversations on the streets of Paris as the air thickened with anticipation of what was to come. Whispers; rumours of the Assembly's plans spread like a vicious weed through the cracks of Parisian streets. The guillotine was erected not far from the mansions of Roland, Christie and Helen; a pointed example of the cruelness of humanity. How can one call themselves human when they take another's life?

"Ah, Mary, I vorgot to mention to you, I read your Vindication," said Olympe. "Zo beautifully written madame."

I smiled in reply and she took my hand and led me into a smaller sitting room that adjoined the main room of the mansion. If I was not mistaken, a small appearance of fear made its mark at the corner of her eyes. Her degree of simplicity, to uninterested observers, would almost appear weak. But that is the charm, the allure of most of us. Empathy lends itself to transparency of the human condition.

We sat down on the small wooden chairs by the marble fireplace, its mantle adorned with delicate porcelain figurines and gleaming silver candlesticks. Olympe sat as upright as fear itself.

"You brought me in here to tell me something?" she nodded in reply, though did not speak. "Are you afraid?" she paused for a moment considered her surroundings before she transfixed her gaze on the flickering flames of the fire.

"Dere is, rumour madame from when I was in prison for a few days," her lips trembled as the words left her mouth. "Dey will, how do you say, uh, arrest?"

"Arrest?"

"Oui. Arrest British subjects. It is not safe vor you. The guards and attendants vould not stop talking about it."

"I appreciate your concern Olympe I do," I gripped her delicate hands tightly between mine. "But I shall be safe, I promise you. They have nothing against me, I have not—"

"Dat does not matter madame," she replied. "I have vriends, in the Assembly as vell. Dey are talking, uh, discussing de arrest and—" she breathed and sighed into the fire as though it would suck away her anger.

"Olympe?" I asked.

"Mm madame?"

"You have a kind heart," I said, kissing the top of her hand. Her skin, soft underneath my lips. "But the world, this world, Paris! The Revolution" I gestured to the window. "It cannot be seen by an unmoved spectator, we must mix in the throng, and feel as men feel before we can judge their feelings and actions."

"You are not, vorried madame?"

I hesitated as my eyes drew to the fire. "If we want to live in the world, to grow wiser and better, and not merely to enjoy the good things of life, we must attain a knowledge of others at the same time that we become acquainted with ourselves. Knowledge acquired any other way only hardens the heart and perplexes the understanding."

"I do not quite follow madame."

"The politicians who sit in London and the House spew pamphlets on the Revolution yet, they are not present are they?"

"No, madame."

"Precisely. So how, then I ask, can they form an opinion on the matter on the vices and follies of the French when they sit in their chairs from across the Channel and postulate?"

"But madame, it is dangerous. Vat if dey arrest you?"

"Then they shall arrest me. I have done nothing wrong and neither have you." Her eyes understood my purpose.

"Mary?"

"Yes."

"How are you zo, zo brave? I write," a small tear fell from one of her eyes, the fire sparkling in it as it fell on her soft cheek. "But every time I speak to some amount of people I froze."

"You freeze?"

"Oui madame, my throat it burns and my hands, dey shake." I placed my hand on her chin and lifted her head so she could look at me.

"Do not hang your head by the dew of sensibility. Rise and write. Write for what you believe in dear Olympe. Do not tremble but speak, even though your voice may quiver in fear and eyes may pierce you from across the table, speak."

Olympe's alabaster skin appeared flushed for a moment as she smiled and returned her eyes to the fire.

"Whatever happens Olympe. Today, tomorrow, or the next..." I hesitated on my thoughts for a small while as Olympe pulled a small fire poker and brought it to life even more.

"Go on..."

"You are not alone," I said. "Not alone in your lust for equality. No matter what your friend Madame Roland says, your pursuit is honourable, just, loving. If she does not think women should write, do not let that stop you."

"Do you think ve vill endure this suffering?" she asked. The fire turned from a wavering flame to a small roar as Olympe added a short log to and kneeled next to the fire.

"Death consumes us in one way or another," I said without thinking. "But I'd sooner face a lion here in Paris than return to England and envelope myself in its continuous misery."

"It vas bad for you dere?" she asked.

"My entire family rely on me, yet they cannot see I am just as destitute as they. Their letters cannot reach me here and Olympe, it does not pain me. Am I guilty of wishing to not be necessary to them?"

"Not at all madame," Olympe smiled and invited me to join her on the rug near the fire. "You cannot be everything to your family all of de time. I vould sooner face a lion than be ov constant worry to my son."

"You have a son?"

"I do," she smiled. "He is vith his father. But Mary, you 'ave every right to pursue your own whims and wants. "Ow can you be necessary to others ven you do not care vor yourself?" She turned her head so she could see my face in the light.

"Dis Revolution. Vat is de end of it all? I do not, uh, see a good ending vor any ov us."

Paris Late February 1793

"Madame, a visitor for you awaits downstairs," called one of the manor's attendants.

"Who is it?" I said.

"A captain of sorts, I presume by the look of him," she said as she walked away from the door. Him again. As I entered the downstairs hallway Captain Gilbert Imlay bowed at my appearance.

"Mrs Wollstonecraft," he said with an air of obnoxious authority. 'you did not pick up your parcel." From behind his back he brought forth a small, wrapped package.

Nearing closer to him, I let a small smile loose from my lips.

"I apologise, I have yet to—"

"No need," he said. "I merely was passing by."

"Mr Imlay, do you not rent an apartment on the other side of Paris?" I asked.

"Yes, well, you see, I uh—happened to have, business—American business of sorts here. And I wanted to see Fillietaz house," gesturing to the grandiose staircase and the several doors behind us and the tiled floor that had not supported its owners footsteps in weeks.

"It is home, for now."

"For now," he added in a peculiar manner. "Your friends," he added. "They have informed me you are wanting to leave Paris?"

Helen. "I have a rather peculiar feeling it is not the safest to be here at the present moment. I am attempting to acquire lodgings but have yet—"

"I have secured you somewhere," he said, smiling. "Neuilly. Not far from here, just a few miles west. You will be safe there."

I retreated several inches until my dress acquainted itself with one of the lower stair railings.

"You have struck something in me, Mrs Wollstonecraft. I find you oddly fascinating. You are a writer and I agree with many of your ideas about the world, in your Vindication you—"

"You read my book?"

"Yes, I did quite mention it already," I rather think he failed to mention that. "Or perhaps I mentioned to Helen, anyhow, the point is, I am worried about you, we—" he gestured in the direction of the Christie manor. "Are worried for you."

"I do not need to be saved," I said, retreating onto the staircase. "I am independent and fine."

"It is clear you are independent Mrs Wollstonecraft but I shall be rather disappointed if I see your head rolling down the causeway of the square because you are British. Or dare I say, a woman," he added.

"They would not..."

"They would," he paused for a moment as we studied each other's expressions. His face had seen war and his eyes…I wonder how many women had stared into them just like I did. "And from what I can see on your face and at the manor just the other day, you have considered it have you not?" He inched closer with every word. "You write for liberty, for freedom and justice and education and right now, they will not have any of it."

"But—"

"Madame Roland, the Girdinon woman you met a few days ago, have you heard from her?"

"Well, no, we do not correspond exactly—"

"Her husband, Jean-Marie, resigned just a few weeks ago and just today, Marat and his conspirators have published that they are forbidden to leave Paris. It is beginning Mary."

"What is?" My knuckles turned white as I gripped the railing tighter and tighter. He was right and we both knew it would weeks, days even, before the British would be either arrested or removed from the city by either death or exile.

"The fall of Paris. It is why I have come to you. You need to leave. I shall be by here in the morning with horses and I shall take you myself."

"What about—"

"In the morning. Be waiting," he said with finality and with a short bow to the house's attendant and I, he disappeared into the Parisian evening.

"Madame?" the attendant rushed to close the door behind him. "Tomorrow?" I placed his book down on the entryway table and rushed to the window. The streets, near-deserted were a skeleton of what I imagined Paris to be. And as the evening's light spread through the city's buildings, there was something about Paris in this state which caused my mind to wonder what it had been like before. This was not the Paris I had imagined. No. This was the Paris of a nightmare. Death lingered like a smothering wall of smoke across the city. Everywhere I walked the odour of death impregnated each building.

The retreating figure of Gilbert, his tall stature recognisable amongst the Parisians, caused a small ache in my heart I found quite peculiar. I nodded to the attendant and returned upstairs and slept my last, solitary night in Paris.

*

"Hold your head high Mrs Wollstonecraft," said Gilbert. "Not quite far now." Though only a few miles away from the centre of Paris, Neuilly was far enough so we were in the true countryside. "A little way further up the way and we shall be there." Gilbert nodded to the sign in French.

"Have you visited the estate before?" I asked.

"No," he replied. "But the former residents are friends... of friends."

"Former?"

"They've left, did I not tell you? They are British and as the father, my friend's friend had dealings with the French which were, somewhat..." The horse's continual motion from side to side kept my heart in check. "Anyhow."

"Will it be—"

"You will be safe here, at least for the near future. Robespierre and his friends are much concerned with themselves in Paris. The gardener will look after you. You can pay him as little or as much as you see to it."

"Why are you treating me so?" I said, though whether he heard it or not, or chose to answer was unimportant. Gilbert, sensing my resignation to prcss, let the worlds swirl around his head and his unspoken words said enough. Was I enough?

"You are magnificent, Mrs Wollstonecraft," he said, though not to my face, but to the dirt road and whatever was at the end of the road held for me. "You inspire intelligence, your words mean something."

"They are words, I have done nothing."

"They are your words. Which reminds me, you should write whilst you are here. It will be quiet. You will have everything you need." As we continued in silence, a fire spread across my bosom, threatening to travel upwards and set fire my brain. The heaviness as though someone pressed their hand against my bosom, but not in malice. No. Not malice. The strangeness of it all was how could someone have the similar feelings for different people? Two alive and one who no longer walks this earth.

"Here we are."

As the horses came to a slow end what lay before us was magnificent. A three-storey chateau the size of ten, twenty of my apartments in London greeted us.

"And they are not here?" Gilbert began removing my bags from the horses and helped me down onto the gravel. It was the second time I had his skin touched mine. It was harder than what I imagined.

"Let me find the gardener," He disappeared through the trees beside the house and returned a few minutes later. "Mary, this is Joane. He speaks only French," I nodded and smiled at the old man, who gave an unforced smile in return.

"Bonjour Monsieur," I bowed a small pleasantry."

"Bonjour Madame Wollstonecraft," Joanne turned to Gilbert to assess whether he had pronounced my name correctly.

"C'est un plaisir de vous rencontre." His years had carved deep lines as he smiled and his eyes were kind, the ones which look for the beauty in everything and look for the good in things; look for the good in people. Oh I wonder what people see in mine.

Neuilly-sur-Seine France early March 1793

The days at Neuilly filled me with muted hope. Solitude. Alone, but never lonely. I had a companion in Joanne, who retrieved grapes from the vines along the road and who would leave them for me in the empty kitchen and would make small batches of meagre soup for the both of us. Writing was my only alternative, and I wrote some reflections and letters descriptive of the state of my mind; the events of my life oppressed me. When I looked out of my bedroom window, I saw a picturesque sight of the cottage's garden, complete with a charming shed. Vines twirled around the buildings; nature reclaiming them back into the Earth. The forest adjoining the cottage was often alive with the sound of trees swaying and rustling in the wind, their movements growing more vigorous with each gust. Day after day rolled away, passing in such an unvaried tenour. The cottage stood proudly, its elegant facade meticulously maintained—a haven amongst the horrors.

I did not allow any opportunity to slip of winning on the affections of Gilbert; though my strength of mind was clouded by the misanthropy of despair. He would visit when he could. Our long walks of friendship, discussing Paris, England and America, soon turned into discussions of our own lives. Mine, my father and family, his—business and the American War, which he still experienced when he closed his eyes at night. I found tender pleasure in his society.

"My father and mother were people of fashion; married by their parents. He was fond of the turf, she of the card-table," he said one afternoon on an idle walk along an empty road.

"My father was fond of the bottle and her incessant pleas for my father to marry her, as he had promised in the fervour of seduction, estranged him from her so completely, that her very person became distasteful to him; and he began to hate, as well as despise me, before I was born. My mother, grieved to the soul by his neglect, and unkind treatment, actually resolved to famish herself; and injured her health by the attempt."

"Are they, still alive?"

"No," I replied matter-of-factly. "My mother died a few years ago and my father is married to a bottle somewhere in the north of London. He is dead to me."

"Oh."

"I shudder with horror, when I recollect the treatment that woman had to endure at the hands of my father and—now I look back, I cannot help attributing the greater part of my misery, to the misfortune of having been thrown into the world without the grand support of life—a mother and father's affection."

"I will not disgust you with a recital of the vices of my youth Mary and I shall not trouble you with the details of a military life."

He endeavoured to soothe his mind, he told me, with writing, mistresses and travel. Continuous employment ensured the various phantoms of misery that made acquaintance with him each night did so for only a short while. Then, one idle afternoon of early March, the normal routine of dinner, soup and small pieces of bread was absent.

"Joanne?" I called, but only the empty house replied in creaks and flutters of small animals above the ceiling. "Joanne are yo—"

"Mrs Wollstonecraft," said a familiar voice behind me. Gilbert Imlay stood in expectation near the kitchen window. As I breeched the doorway, the flickering lantern lights caught my attention, emanating from underneath a large tree by the gardener's cottage.

"Gilbert what is—"

"He gestured to the lanterns and placed his hands in mine. "Come." He led me down the small path and onto a clearing covered in beautiful wild flowers. Joanne, with a smile on his face, leaned against his garden shed, enjoying a sip of wine and admiring his work.

"Depuis Bordeaux," he said as he raised a glass to the both of us. Gilbert smiled proudly in return. Joanne bid us farewell and retreated into the house, leaving us to find a comfortable spot among the wildflowers on a small jute rug. The fragrant scent of the flowers surrounded us, while the plate of cheese and various meats tempted our appetites.

"How did you...Why did—"

With a smile, he poured a second glass and asked, "Wine? The sky above us transformed from blue to a soft shade of purple, while the vibrant yellows and oranges of the sun disappeared into the depths of the dense forest. As time went on, a delicate hue of pink spread across the sky, casting a dreamy glow over everything around us. And as the sky grew darker, the air became a symphony of soothing bird songs, lulling the world to sleep.

"How can something so beautiful not be held, only admired from afar," I said aloud.

"The sky?" asked Gilbert.

"It is constantly changing. When we arise in the morning, a small part of us holds onto the belief that we will be granted the privilege of witnessing another spectacular sunset, despite the countless ones we have been fortunate to ponder in the past. But in the depths of darkness, we find ourselves tormented by our own demons."

As he sipped some wine, he confessed ruefully, "My demons certainly know where to find me. The debtors at least do, though I do think they are one and the same," he mused, his brow furrowed in contemplation.

"It is these thoughts that agitate my spirit Gilbert..."

"My debtors worry you?"

"Mine," I said, my voice filled with a mix of pride and guilt. "I do not believe I will ever escape the burden of my father's debt." My debt. I am burdened by the debts I owe to people. As you know, I write incessantly."

"I know," he said. "And it will be enough one day I am sure. But for now, do not let it worry you. We are here, amongst the forest..."

"Olympe remains in Paris. Thomas, Helen, all of them..."

"They are safe."

"For now, but what if—"

He kissed my hand, intertwining our fingers. A peculiar flutter inside my chest strummed its merry strings. He sighed and glanced at the sky again.

"I love you Mary." These words opened the tenderness of my heart; raw and exposed as the sun, the burning sensation filling every limb in my body.

“I love you too.” What would Frances think of this? Oh, my dear. The world would not be as vile if she were here; the silvery moon to Gilbert’s fiery sun. A comforting presence in my unknown. She is part of the earth now. One day, I shall join her. Not quite yet though.

“What occupies your thoughts? You have been absent for a while.”

My youth. A lifetime away.” His hands reached for my chin and his lips pressed against mine; smooth and warm. His presence ignited my heart as our foreheads touched, his auburn hair caressing my skin as we shared laughter.

“Kiss me again,” I felt myself say. And so he did.

The evening slipped away into dusk; dusk into dawn as we followed each other to my bedroom chamber. His hands and eyes undressed me. The fire consumed us; both of us were unwilling to put it out. His lips caressed my skin as he made love to me and I found myself a virgin no more. It was as unforgiving and raw as I had imagined it would be, not as painful as I had expected. Thoughts consumed me as we made love again before little sleep. My heart and body had found peace in his bosom.

On the morning of March 11th, 1793, we walked to the town’s edge together. Moura, his horse, became more friendly with each journey. She nudged me repeatedly that morning.

“Not now,” I laughed. “When he leaves,” I whispered to her. The barrier between the outskirts of Paris and Neuilly was our place. He kissed me on the forehead, exchanged few words between us, Moura received her grapes from my satchel and Gilbert returned to Paris. I walked back to the cottage, appreciating the open fields outside Paris. I returned by noon and sat with Joane at the head of the kitchen table.

“Madame,” Joane said while pouring a glass of wine. He motioned to the entranceway. “Letter.”

10 March, 1793

Dearest Mary,

Rumours suggest Paris is on the brink of civil war.

Vendee. The government. Here. North. South.
I inquired and learned that Gilbert had reached your lodgings. Stay there for a while, please. Neither of you will be safe here.

Wait for my next letter.

Yours,

Olympe de Gouges

As I waited for Olympe's following letter, I returned to my Reflections on France and dallied in the hopes it would one day soon see the light of day.

The house of Madame Roland later that afternoon

"Are you there, Miss de Gouges?" A loud knock at the front door.

Olympe opened the door to a dishevelled Captain Gilbert Imlay. "Oh no. Helen!" She yelled at the house. Gilbert stumbled into Roland's house with Helen and Olympe's assistance.

"Call vor Madame Roland," Helen reappeared at the entrance to the hallway and shouted at the attendant. "Olympe, this way dear, come." With Helen and Olympe either side of him, Gilbert and the two women retreated the parlour, Gilbert falling into the wooden chair and slumping into its embrace. His morning attire was in tatters; pants scuffed and marked with dirt, arms and face scratched with blotches of dried blood.

"I assume you did not receive dat letter I sent vor Mary?" Olympe smiled at Gilbert.

"Clearly," replied Gilbert. "Is she safe?"

"Dey are only in dis vicinity it appears at de moment, as you have discovered," Olympe pulled some threads from his shirt. The commotion died down, allowing Gilbert to rest, while Olympe and Helen resumed their post by the downstairs windows, keeping a watchful eye on the streets.

As the uprising of Paris grew and grew, Madame Roland and her associates worlds shrunk; suffocated by suspicion. Roland's house, similarly to the Christie house, became a refuge for enlightenment and a refuge for women and men who idealised a better world. But the sallonaire's world of lunches and political discussion had disappeared almost completely by March 1793.

"With their King gone, what else could the Convention possibly seek?" continued Helen.

"Pouvoir," replied Madame Roland. "Blood."

"Power?" replied Helen. "Guillotine anyone who stands against them? There will be no one left in Paris."

"Précisément," said Olympe.

"Pouvoir is like the rolling wheel of a carriage," continued

Madame Roland. "If dey stop the revolution, then the bloodthirsty will kill them instead. Zo," she continued. 'roll on it will." She shrugged her shoulders and retired to a small chair in her living room.

Gilbert, still dishevelled but less in pain moved himself to sit upright. "Thomas mentioned that there was a talk on separating Paris but—" the pain across his abdomen throbbed the more he spoke. "Jean-Marie, where is he?"

"Upstairs," replied Madame Roland. "Though I do not know how long we have left." Olympe rested her face against the window pane.

"Vill you leave?" asked Olympe. Pausing for a moment, Madame Roland turned to the few people in the parlour. Her sanctuary had diminished. Once a salon of free thought and hope and become a refuge for the weary. The former salonnaire had been reduced to a captive in her own city.

"No," she replied with finality. "They will have stations posted everywhere. What is the point of fleeing?"

"Your life madame," posed Olympe.

"Bah. My life means nothing if Paris is all but in ruins."

"Will he leave?" Gilbert nodded to upstairs. Madame hesitated to mouth the words, for if spoken, she thought to herself, they would be true.

"I..."

"The soup is ready," the attendant bowed to the group and returned to the kitchen.

"I must admit I am positively famished," said Gilbert, attempting to stand.

"You still have not told us vat happened to you Monsieur Imlay," said Olympe.

"I was set upon, by a group of Sans-culottes. I apparently was not wearing the tricolour clothing and I looked too wealthy." The four made their way to the small dining room, adjacent to the large kitchen. Paris, at least on the outside, was quiet. "But my

American accent stopped the punching and kicking and, eventually they let me on my way to you fine people." The four of them raised their glasses in the air, an admiration of life, of hope and justice. The fifth post, usually occupied by Mary, was set with a small bowl and a glass. Gilbert said a small prayer to himself under his breath and the soup was consumed in silence. The clinking of the bowls, the tolling of the bells and the small, now familiar murmurs of Parisians outside became the comforting backdrop of normality. Unsaid words thickened the air around them as though Robespierre and Marat were at the table with them.

"Charlotte," said Olympe. "I hear her." At the mention of her name, Charlotte Corday appeared from the hallway in a similar fashion to Gilbert.

"Hommes," she said, grabbing a spare chair from the edge of the room. "Good soup?" The others stared at the blood that had thickened on her brow. Her once long, flowing brown hair had been cut to her ears. It too stained with blood.

"It is as if see a ghost. What is wrong?" she said to no one in particular.

"Your brow," said Olympe. "Here let me..."

"I am fine," shouted Charlotte, brushing Olympe's hand away. "I am fine. I am..." Charlotte breathed in heavily and let out a long, resigned breath. 'Combien de temps cela va-t-il durer?" A small teared formed at the corner of Charlotte's eye and without hesitation, Olympe dotted it away with a small napkin.

"Ve do not know, but Charlotte?" said Olympe. "You are brave, and ve are here." Charlotte wiped small tears from her eyes.

"Where is Jean-Marie?" asked Charlotte.

"Upstairs," said Helen.

"Is he leaving?" asked Charlotte, as all eyes turned to Madame Roland.

"Not now," mouthed Helen in response.

"Would anyone like some bread?" Madame Roland rationed the meagre supply of bread to their plates and conversation reignited.

"Mary is writing a reflection on dis Revolution she told me," said Olympe, nodding to Mary's empty chair. "I am, uh, quite, uh, interested to read it. I hope de ending is zoon," she said, raising her glass to Madame Roland once again. At the mention of Mary's name, Jean-Marie Roland entered the room and whispered something in Madame Roland's ear. Standing at once to leave, Jean-Marie raised his hat to the group and the two left the dining without a word.

The remaining occupants of the table continued feasting on small pieces of bread and attempted to ignore the loud conversation from the kitchen.

"Si tu pars, nous ne nous reverrons plus jamais," shouted Madame Roland. Helen, not as well versed in French as her contemporaries, looked to Olympe.

"He is leaving for Roen," said Olympe resignedly.

"He will die," said Gilbert. "They will come looking for him here and when they cannot find him then..."

"Vat do we do?"

"Nothing," replied Gilbert. "There is nothing we can do." Helen and Olympe held hands across the dining table for several moments. Then, through the silence, a screeching wail emanated from the kitchen as the door to the servant's quarters slammed shut.

"Laissez-moi," said Olympe, rising from her seat.

"Who ordered the arrest?" asked Charlotte, breaking pieces of bread as she did so. "Robespierre?" Gilbert shook his head. "Marat." Charlotte's cheeks flushed with blood and the three remaining inhabitants of the dining room sat in silence once again.

As Olympe entered the kitchen, she found Madame Roland occupying the floor in front the exterior servant's door. Her face buried between her elbows and dress. As Olympe peered from the kitchen window, for the last time in her life she saw Jean-Marie as he disappeared behind a building.

"I..." Upon recognising whatever words she had were better left unsaid, Olympe joined Madame Roland on the tiled floor and rested her head against the door. In their silent acknowledgement, Madame Roland rested her head on Olympe's shoulder and tears began flowing not in sadness, but in anger.

"Our station created us enemies," Madame Roland sobbed through tears. "By those who have spoken the most ill of me, I have never been seen."

She continued. "Things are rarely what they appear to be, that the periods of my life in which I have tasted most pleasure, or experienced most vexation, were those which appeared to others the reverse." As she continued, Helen and Charlotte appeared in the doorway, the former's cheeks still flush with rage. In a silent gesture, the three women gathered around Madame Roland, embracing each other in pain. Knowing she was safe for a few moments, on the floor of a kitchen as her husband fled the city, a guttural scream bellowed from her body, collapsing even further into the arms of her friends.

As Jean-Marie Roland turned a corner, not far from his home, a faint scream echoed behind him. He paused for a moment on the side of a dirt road, his heartbeat became louder and louder. Unable to steady himself, he lent against a half-destroyed building.

To turn back, he would face certain death. To continue, his fate would be more uncertain. He felt for the pocket watch that Madame Roland bestowed upon him for their wedding, kissed it, holding it to his chest for a few moments and continued on his walk of refuge to Roen.

Neuilly-sur-Seine, France 5th April 1793

My dearest Joseph,

My thoughts are consumed by the storm raging in our beloved France. I write to you with a heavy heart, burdened by grave concerns for the fate of our dear friends and associates. No one is immune to the perils that beset us.

I have no capacity of mind to strengthen my convictions. Though I am agreeably situated here, peaceful days amongst the trees and winding paths of Neuilly, my thoughts rage, head burns. I often recollect with pleasure at the simplicity of life back home in London. Do I call it home? Though the air is pure, I am not well.

I have given misery all I have, a tear. I am low-spirited so of course my letter to you is dull. Oppressed by continual anxiety for which I can do nothing but write, for everything else is a labour to me.

The house of Madame Roland 31st May 1793

"Mary my dear," Charlotte ran to her in an embrace. "Are you well?"

"Quite. Though not the same for you all it appears. Good gracious it has been weeks."

"Months in fact," said Olympe.

"Yes you are quite right," I replied, making comfort on the chair. "Gilbert left?"

"Just yesterday," said Charlotte. "How come you are here?"

"He left a package for me at his apartment and I came to collect it. I do expect he wants me to live there."

"Return to Paris? Are you mad?"

"We're getting married Olympe."

"Married?"

"I cannot live in Neuilly forever. As much as I would like to of course."

"Mary—Madame Roland is—"

"Turning herself in," Charlotte finished what Olympe could not.

"Are you mad?"

"Yes," replied Madame Roland matter-of-factly, lighting another cigar. "But they cannot kill me for I have done no wrong." Silence, an all common friend of us all, ensued once again.

"Can we come with you?" asked Charlotte.

"No, no, my dear girl," replied Madame Roland. "You shall wait here and be of use to your friends. Mary will need accompaniment to Gilbert's apartment." Charlotte nodded and grabbed my hand.

Another knock boomed on the door. "Marie-Jeanne, open the door. We know you are there."

"Girls, upstairs quickly," Madame Roland's attendant, a Madame Sophie, flew from the kitchen and ushered the women upstairs.

"The letter said tomorrow," called Madame Roland to the strangers. "I do think you will find it is still May."

"Ouvrez la porte ou nous la renverserons avec nos piques. Ouvrez-le!"

"Save your pikes then," the sound of the door opened and a flurry of boots trampled into her home.

"Marie-Jeanne Roland, wife of Jean-Marie Roland and co-conspirator of the Girdions I hereby arrest you for conspiring against the republic of France."

"I am innocent. What are you—keep your hands off me. Je suis innocent!" she screamed.

After a few minutes of silence, the four us emerged from upstairs and tip-toed downstairs, hearts beating and breaths held. The front door, left open, allowed the coal-laden air into the house.

"Vat do we do, vat do we do?" Olympe turned to me but my brain refused to cooperate.

"Je me renseignerai demain. Nous avons des plans en place, ne vous inquiétez pas," said Sophie, who had lived with the Roland's for several years. Still not fluent in French, I turned to Olympe for an answer.

"Tomorrow, Madame er, Sophie, she vill inquire vor Madame." I fell into one of the parlour chairs as my mind burned again. As Charlotte paced the floor and Sophie returned to the kitchen, Olympe and I uttered not a single word.

"Bah," said Charlotte. "Dis is maddening. Sophie!"

"Oui?" calling from the kitchen.

"Où vont-ils l'emmener? Saint-Germain-des-Prés?"

"Oui, très probablement," replied Sophie.

"Dey vill most likely take Madame Roland to the prison in Saint-Germain," said Olympe, nodding in the direction of the church. "Où sont les papiers de Madame?"

"Madame à l'étage, dans son bureau. Dois-je les récupérer pour vous?"

"Non!" she replied.

"Olympe?" I asked. "What's going on? Paper?"

"Paper," she said, as she made her way upstairs and returned within moments. Olympe opened a small bottle of black ink and rushed to the desk of Madame Roland.

"What are you—"

"I need to write something. Anything. My head iz burning Madame Mary."

Neuilly-Sur-Seine June 1793

Gilbert,

I shall leave the key in the door, and hope to find you at my fire-side when I return, about eight o'clock.

Yours, Mary.

Neuilly-sur-Seine 13th June 1793

Eliza Bishop,

I have been convinced it is near impossible to obtain a passport. I have a plan in my head where you and Everina are included. I contemplate bringing us all together again. I have been endeavouring to obtain a passport for a long time.

I am now in the house of an old gardener writing a book. I am in better health and spirits than I have ever enjoyed since coming to France. I have lately received a letter from James, though dated two months ago.

It is indeed a long time since I have received a line from Mr Johnson. I write with reserve because all the letters I receive are opened.

In earnest I request you to write. I assure you that I am alive and most affectionately yours.

Mary.

Neuilly-sur-Seine 24th June 1793

My dearest Bess,

My endeavours to settle you here have been less fruitful than I had hoped. At present it would be madness to think of it occurring. Should peace and order be established in this distracted Land, then, perhaps? I have been hard at work writing this book of mine, for fear of returning to England and appearing idle.

I have not received letters from Everina, Charles, James, Edward or Johnson in such a while I am afraid they have been miscarried. If you receive any of my letters, please write to me. I feel quite lonely here now the communication is shut.

Do not touch on politics—

M

The American Embassy Paris 15th July 1793

"You are early for once," said Gilbert, kissing me on the forehead. "Come, let us go." Our rides to and from Paris were scarce but whenever we did it was under the cover of darkness.

"Are you nervous?" I asked him as I ruffled my dress over the foothold.

"No, are you?" We looked into each other's eyes, and he registered my expression. Hope, somehow, was the only glimmer I had left. As we made our way on horseback through the diagonal streets, we arrived at the American embassy my sunrise.

"Your papers?"

"Here," one of my small bags contained the current state of my life, along with several drafts, papers and odd ends and pieces.

"Say nothing unless asked."

"Understood," I said calmly. We approached the grandiose building, which stood stark against the smaller, poorer apartments surrounding it, making it appear even grander in scale. As Gilbert conversed with the man at the door, it opened to reveal a large hall, with clerks and attendants walking to and fro in hurried fashion.

"Must be something important," I whispered. Gilbert simply shrugged.

"Your names?" the attendant's eyes poured over each of us. I adjusted my dress and ordered everything just as I was told. Appearances matter, he said.

"Gilbert Everet Imlay."

"Mary Wollstonecraft, sir." Without acknowledging we had replied, the attendant scribed our names and passed us several pieces of parchment, shewing us away to a far corner of the room.

"Did I ask you, madame?" I gulped whatever wetness I could find in my throat. "Wait over there," he continued. Gilbert and I walked further on the grey, soulless tiles into the mouth of the embassy. Fitting.

"Do not let it worry you," whispered Gilbert. "I can see it on your face." I rubbed and picked at my fingers till they turned red.

"Why does one need to speak such as that to a woman?"

"I know my dear girl, I know. Now is not the time."

Eventually, though I knew not how much time had passed, a small man, no older than 40, peered from one of the various doors and shouted to the room. "A Captain Gilbert Everett Imlay and a Miss Mary Wollstonecraft, are you present?"

"Here sir," we said together.

"Well, come then, quickly." The man ushered us into a small room that contained an ornate wooden desk, a small window that let a sliver of light breach the room, and a small, unused bookcase which had a collection of dust rather than books.

"You are here to register her as your wife, correct sir?"

"Correct," replied Gilbert. "We were married several weeks ago but she—we—lived in Neuilly."

"It says here your address is in Paris. Is that correct?"

"Yes sir. We are moving into an apartment in the city."

"And you are aware of the current climate of Paris?"

"Yes sir," said Gilbert. "We understand."

The man let out a small groan as Gilbert handed him the rest of our papers.

"Your father is aware of this marriage?"

"Yes," I lied. "He is in London, sir."

"British?"

"Correct sir," I said.

The man, who had failed to inform us of his name, copied our papers for several minutes as Gilbert and I stood awkwardly as a child waiting for an ice cream. As each paper appeared it would be the last, he retrieved another from the ornate table drawer.

"Here, as filed, can you please sign on this parchment here?" Gilbert and I signed our names. "And this one here, Sir." After another few minutes of checking papers, thc unnamed man handed Gilbert our passports.

"Mr and Mrs Imlay, you are free to go." Filing the papers inside his drawers, the man stood and opened the door to the entrance hall. "Good day."

"Where shall we walk to, Mr Imaly?" I said, as he scooped

my arm around his. "The Seine? Perhaps Christie's?"

"I failed to mention this morning. I have to return north again."

"But—"

"But," he paused, "I shall return when I can. You can be quite sure of that, Mrs Imlay." My eyes widened. "You know of our plans," he continued.

"Yes," I said, hesitating for a moment. "But they do change"

"My dear girl, it is business. You said yourself you are quite willing to help. The man I mentioned to you? Noah? The one near Gothenburg. He shall be in contact with you over the next few months. So will Ellefsen."

"The captain?" I said as my eyes drew to several people making haste towards the direction of the city.

"The captain correct. I think it shall be a prime business opportunity, I can feel it Mary can you?" People pushed and ran faster and faster in succession.

"Mary?"

"Hmm?"

"I said you are quite willing to help, are you not?" Gilbert looked toward my gaze as more and people hurried past us.

"Monsieur?" I called after a stranger. "Monsieur, uhhh, pouvez-vous s'il vous plaît me...dire quel est le, uhh, problème avec tout le monde? Pourquoi courent-ils?"

"Marat. Quelqu'un l'a tué," the man replied and continued running. My heart pounded.

"Mary, what is it?" demanded Gilbert. "Mary answer me. What did the man say?"

"Marat." I said. "He's dead."

Paris 17th July 1793

Dearest Joseph,

I know this letter may not find you, but circumstances have shifted with such swiftness that I find myself driven to convey the developments that have befallen me.

Charlotte Corday met her fate at the guillotine and the echoes of her execution reverberate through the city. She assassinated The Friend of the People in his bathtub and yesterday she was judged at the Place De Greve wearing that awful red blouse of a traitor. The Jacobins rolled her out in a tumbril alone. The summer's evening, warm and embracing of life, drenched the crowd in a summer rain as soon as she appeared.

After the execution, the most indignant and shameful acts occurred, and I have spent the last evenings trying to erase it from my burning mind. One of the men hoisted her head from the basket and slapped her across the cheek. And this morning, I discovered from one of the maids they performed examinations of her to see if she was of pure faith.

Olympe's brain burns akin to mine. We write and we can not stop and I worry the fire which burns inside her will be put out by the same men who killed Charlotte. But that is mere idle worries at the present moment.

In these moments of solitude, I am left to ponder the complexities of my own life. Gilbert has gone north on business and I find no solace amidst the tempest that surrounds me. I have faith that you will comprehend the depths of my sentiments.

Yours always,

Mary

Paris 19th July 1793

"You are sure?" I asked Olympe, finishing her last few lines with her ink.

"I am sure madame," she replied. "I shall publish it anonymously, post it on every street corner for citizens to read." She took another sip of her wine and scrawled the last few words. "There, it is done. Eh, Voila!" Olympe rested her head against the chair and sighed. "Eh, dat vas exhausting! Eh, madame."

"I cannot believe Charlotte," I said, rubbing my fingers all across my face. It was soothing, though I could never quite make sense of why.

"I know madame," replied Olympe. "It iz awful, awful. I spoke to her, a few days ago now, and she mentioned dis, Marat fellow. I did not zink she vas going to kill him."

"You knew?" My eyes shot to her face. Her golden hair, which usually adorned the sides of her pale-white face hadn't been brushed, let alone made, in weeks.

"Yes, but–'

"Why did you not say anything Olympe?"

"Because she iz, was, an adult. I did not zink anyone would be dat stupid. It iz only going to make tings worse is it not?" Olympe shrugged and lent back into her chair. "Dere waz nothing we could 'ave done, madame. Her mind waz decided so."

I collected the few pages from her wooden desk and rolled them tightly in a scroll. "Shall we walk together to the printer then?" Olympe collected herself at the mention of the printer. She tidied her small desk, collected more of her papers and idle thoughts, and gathered her things into a small satchel.

The Three Urns

Citizens,

I have roamed the four Corners of the World, more in a reverie than in reality, for life is but a dream. Everywhere I found the same men, idiots and aggressors, dupes and scoundrels; a world full of crime and error, so to speak.

But because extremes are so similar and because excessive evil always gives birth to good, revolutions essentially regenerate governments through their excessive depravity. French people stop; read; I have many things to tell you. I very much doubt that the world began with Adam and Eve, or that it must end with the French Revolution.

These are tales used by the corrupt priests of the Ancien Régime to stupefy our credulous females. However it is reasonable to assume, as ancient and modern history shows, that no peoples have ever died out at the moment of their regeneration. Meanwhile France, divided by three governmental parties, seems to be close to dissolution. But the supreme desire of an invisible being, who presides over the great destinies of empires, acts as a brake on the patricidal furies of the villains of all factions who only want to tear apart the republic and share out the remains. If we are really worthy of being republicans then what can they achieve? "What can a crashing wave do against a rock? Did Hercules succumb to the exertions of the Pygmy?"

Oh French, what has caused your dissension? The death of the tyrant? Well, he is dead! All factions must fall with his head and, despite myself, your extravagant criminality recalls to my mind the panoply of great revolutions: I place it before your eyes; dare to observe it. The Syracusans having dethroned their tyrant told him to flee far from their shores, or stay and become their equal; they allowed him to be master of his fate, the chap obeyed his sovereign and became a schoolteacher. The Roman republic chased out the Tarquins: in vain did they attempt to arm their tyrannical friends against a people who wanted freedom; they died itinerant vagabonds.

The English, whom you try so hard to mimic, sent Charles I to the scaffold. This historic act of justice could not free them from tyranny for the dying Charles perpetuated royalty in England. Alas, oh French, such is our actual state: Louis Capet is dead, yet Louis Capet still reigns among us. Stop pretending it is not so, it is time for the mask to fall and for each of you to freely pronounce, openly, if you do or do not want a republic. It is time to put a stop to this cruel war that has only swallowed up your treasure and harvested the most brilliant of your young men. Blood, alas, has flowed far too freely!

Spouting republicanism with hearts full of royalism you arm region against region little caring about the denouement of this bloody drama. Despite seeing the thoughtlessness and imprudence of your horrible dissimulation I still want to serve you and save you. And you talk of God? Crime has broken his patience: struck these sacrilegious hordes; he has put men back where they belong. He started in France; and will go around the world and finish in the antipodes. He wants to skim the Revolution like a liqueur that, having soaked for a long while all the detritus of ideas that made up its body, becomes a nectar as healthful as it is sweet. Crime to fight crime, one attacking the other; make sacrifices of the great, that is the secret. Find a prompt and efficient solution. The divided French, you are fighting for three opposing governments; like warring brothers you rush to your downfall and, if faith does not halt you, you will soon imitate the Thebans and end up slitting each others throats to the last man standing. Can we not live in more auspicious times?

I do not want foreigners, jealous of your glory, greedy for your treasures, to come and invade our territory. It is neither the death of Louis Capet, nor the nobles" slighted pride, nor the upturned altars that caused the coalition of tyrants to arm their slaves: it is to divide up France and eclipse her splendour; it is to strengthen their own crown that they want to place on the throne, not a king of spades but a king of diamonds.

Oh tyrants of the world, tremble; God is not on your side! If the fate of a divided people is, at last, to understand the necessity of definitively choosing a form of government, one which must, unchallenged, quieten all opinions, then the French, at the very least, shall be masters of their choice so that they offer themselves the government that best suits their character, their customs and their climate in order that their revolution forever serves as a lesson to tyrants and not to peoples. The French can no longer procrastinate: the day of reckoning has arrived.

Now is the time to establish a decent government whose energy comes from the strength of its laws; now is the time to put a stop to assassinations, and the suffering they cause, for merely holding opposing views. Let everyone examine their consciences; let them see the incalculable harm caused by such a long lasting division (the total upheaval of the motherland) and then everyone can pronounce freely on the government of their choice. The majority must prevail. It is time for death to repose and anarchy to return to the Underworld. Several départements are rising up in favour of federalism; the royalists are strong both in and out of the country; the constitutional government, one and indivisible, is in a courageous minority. Blood flows everywhere, this struggle is appalling and dreadful in my view. It is time for the combat to cease. I would like the Convention to express the spirit of the Decree that I will dictate to you.

The Convention, deeply upset so see France divided by opinions and beliefs on the form of government that must save her Motherland, proposes, in the name of humanity, that for an entire month the rebels be denied arms, even those abroad, in order that the entire nation has the time to pronounce on the three forms of government dividing it. All the départements must be enjoined to convoke primary assemblies: three urns must be placed on the President of the assembly's table, each one labelled with one of the following inscriptions: republican Government, one and indivisible; federal Government; monarchic Government.

The President will proclaim, in the name of the endangered Motherland, the free and individual choice of one of three governments. All voters will have three ballot papers in hand, their choice will be written on one of them: it will not be possible to make a mistake, either on the urn or on the paper, that the voters" probity dictates. They will place a ballot paper in each urn. The government that obtains the majority of votes will be sworn in by a solemn and universal oath of allegiance; this oath will be renewed on the urn for every citizen, individually. A civic celebration will accompany this solemnity; this sensitive and decisive act will calm passions and destroy factions...the rebels will disperse themselves; the enemy powers will ask for peace; the universe, as surprised in its admiration as it was attentive, for so long, to the dissension in France, will cry out: the French are invincible!"

Remember that I am an aerial voyager coming from the land of lunacy, I can therefore discuss with you; yes, like you, by saying foolish things in the name of humanity, I can achieve good things; like you, I love the Motherland and Equality; I would be delighted to live under a republican government, but this government, as you know, has to be led by virtuous and disinterested men.

Examine without trembling, if you can, the suffering of France. Do you see those arms ripped from this fertile soil;

see the cultivators, in their thousands, fall on the battle field. See our finances, all our means, used up; see the entire dissolution of France. See those perfidious men, thirsty for blood, sell us to the enemy Powers; swearing on the Republic but awaiting the height of disorder in order to proclaim a king. A prompt remedy is needed for so much hardship. The national wish must, finally, be solemnly pronounced, and the choice no longer put into question, so that neither the rebels nor the foreign powers can any longer say that the majority of French want a monarch, or some other form of government.

I will remain anonymous for now but, if I can save my Motherland from the abyss I can see her about to fall into, I will name myself as I rush to be by her side.

*

"Non," the printer shook his head defiantly. "Non, are you mad mademoiselle?" Olympe snatched the parchments from the printer.

"Non Monsieur, j'ai besoin de votre aide pour imprimer ceci, s'il vous plaît." Olympe hesitated a few moments before the elderly man turned and shooed her away with his hands as though we were a small flock of birds.

"Va-t'en, femme. Vous me ferez tuer. Loin avec vous!"

"Olympe, let us go." I opened the door to Paris and waited, but she refused to move.

"Monsieur, s'il vous plaît, je—"

"Je vous signalerai si vous êtes encore là à mon retour de presse. Loin!"

"Olympe leave him be. We shall find another." Olympe huffed and left the printer's shop, bumping into his wares, small books and baskets as she left, quickening her pace as her feet touched the cobblestone.

"Mary, this is not, uh, how do you say, going to plan?" Olympe hastened her pace even more as she weaved between people on the street. "Ah dat printer, vat am I to do now?"

"Where are you? Olympe stop, where—" she approached the end of a small street, took several steps and found herself in the middle of an intersection of three much larger roads. "Olympe!" I pointed towards a carriage that thankfully veered around her, missing her by a feather. "Are you trying to have yourself killed?" Olympe dropped her small satchel on the street and collapsed onto the ground. As I reached her, I outstretched my hand and a defeated, forlorn Olympe looked up at me.

"Vat do I do?"

"At this moment, madame? Remove yourself from the middle of the street," I whispered. "Come, let us—" my eyes shot to a slow stream of red water behind her on the road. "Olympe, retrieve your satchel and—" Blood. My eyes followed it to its source. Small groups of Parisians were talking in small murmurs near a scaffold with a guillotine high atop it.

"I—oh madame!" Olympe screamed as I pulled her from the street, weaving between carriages, horses and people.

"Madame, you must breathe. Breathe." I placed my hands on her shoulders, as Frances once did for me all those years ago and breathed with her. After a few minutes of calming her down, we found ourselves underneath a small canopy of a bakery.

"This had bread once," said Olympe still breathing heavily. 'may I have my satchel?" her hands were empty.

"You had your satchel with you madame, it fell with you. I told you to retrieve—" We looked towards the middle of the street and a boy, no more than fifteen, hunched over it and appeared as though he were already inspecting its contents.

"My—"

We walked a few paces forward, both staring at the boy intently.

"Qu'est-ce qu'on fait? Mary!" The boy seemed to ignore the world around him as he read Olympe's letter to the citizens of France. After a few minutes of waiting, he folded the paper in half, placed it into the satchel and began to walk towards the river.

"Wc can detain ourselves on the street or follow him Olympe." I looked into her eyes. Her face moulded itself from desperation into curiosity. "I am attentive to your current state of mind, so it is your choice." Olympe turned her head from me to the boy already disappearing into the crowd.

"Laisse nous partir!" said Olympe. We followed the boy for several minutes, weaving in between people, horses, carts, trees and buildings until the boy approached a small apartment. He knocked on it twice, said a few words to the occupant who pulled the young boy inside and slammed the door.

"Where are we?" I whispered to Olympe, both pretending to peruse a small store-front. She looked along the narrow street as her eyes hunted for any distinguishing features or signs.

"I dink madame, that is a printer. This one was, uh, how you say, also on my list?"

"The boy made his way to a printer?" She spent a few seconds counting the houses from the corner and then nodded.

"It appears, madame."

"Either the anonymous writer is about to become famous or hated."

"Or both," she said shrugging as she bit into a small piece of bread.

Neuilly-sur-Seine Past Twelve o'clock Monday night
August 1793

Gilbert,

I wish you thee, my love, goodnight! Before I go to rest, with more tenderness than I can to-morrow. You can scarcely imagine with what pleasure I anticipate the day, when we are to begin almost to live together; and you would smile to hear how many plans of employment I have in my head, now that I am confident my heart has found peace in your bosom.

Cherish me with that dignified tenderness, which I have only found in you; and your own dear girl will try to keep under a quickness of feeling, that has sometimes given you pain.

I may deserve to be happy; and whilst you love me, I cannot again fall into the miserable state, which rendered life a burden almost too heavy to be bear.

Mary.

I will be at the barrier a little after ten o'clock to-morrow.

Paris Wednesday morning August 1793

My love,

You have often called me, dear girl and I like to see your eyes praise me; and Milton insinuates, that, during such recitals, there are interruptions, not ungrateful to the heart, when the honey that drops from the lips is not merely words.

I shall probably not be able to return to Saint Germains to-morrow; but it is no matter, because I must take a carriage, I have so many books, that I immediately want, to take with me.

On Friday then I shall expect you to dine with me—and, if you come a little before dinner, it is so long since I have seen you.

Mary.

Paris Friday morning September 1793

A man called here yesterday for the payment of a draft. I have since seen him, and he tells me that the business is settled.

So much for business! May I venture to talk about less weighty affairs? How are you? I have been following you all along the road in this comfortless weather. When I am absent from those I love, my imagination is as lively, as if their presence had never gratified my senses. To make a woman piquant, it often requires a touch of foolishness, as ninety-nine out of a hundred men would agree. One reason I wish my whole sex to become wiser, is, that the foolish ones may not, by their pretty folly, rob those whose sensibility keeps down their vanity, of the few roses that afford them some solace in the thorny road of life.

Of late, we are always separating. Crack, crack and away you go. This joke wears the sallow cast of thought. Though I write cheerfully, some melancholy tears have found their way into my eyes; they linger there, as a glow of tenderness in my heart whispers that you are one of the best creatures in the world. When we are settled in the country, or America together, more duties will open before me, and my heart, which now, trembling into peace will learn to rest on yours, with that dignity your character, not to talk of my own, demands.

Take care of yourself, and write soon to your own girl (you may add dear, if you please) who sincerely loves you, and will try to convince you of it, by becoming happier.

Mary

Paris 30th October 1793

Dearest Joseph,

Olympe's predictions were correct. The Committee of Public Safety banned women's clubs and societies this morning and several days ago Helen and her British contemporaries were arrested. My present circumstances do not allow me to write to you and they have run in my head ever since I arrived in Paris all those months ago. I can assure you I am safe. Gilbert's name and nationality afforded me protection and I beg of you to receive him gracefully for I most probably am alive from our situation.

Yours always,

Mary

Paris Sunday evening October, 1793

Gilbert

I have just received your letter, and feel as if I could not go to bed tranquilly without saying a few words in reply—merely to tell you, that my mind is serene and my heart affectionate.

Ever since you last saw me inclined to faint, I have felt some gentle twitches, which make me begin to think, that I am nourishing a creature who will soon be sensible of my care.—This thought has not only produced an overflowing of tenderness to you, but made me attentive to calm my mind and take exercise, lest I should destroy an object, in whom we are to have a mutual interest, you know. Yesterday—do not smile!—finding that I had hurt myself by lifting precipitately a large log of wood, I sat down in an agony, till I felt those said twitches again.

Are you busy?

****

So you may reckon on its being finished soon, though not before you come home, unless you are detained longer than I now allow myself to believe you will.—

Be that as it may, write to me, my best love, and bid me be patient—kindly—and the expressions of kindness will again beguile the time, as sweetly as they have done tonight. Tell me also over and over again, that your happiness (and you deserve to be happy!) is closely connected with mine, and I will try to dissipate, as they rise, the fumes of former discontent, that have too often clouded the sunshine, which you have endeavoured to diffuse through my mind. God bless you! Take care of yourself and remember with tenderness your affectionate Mary.

I am going to rest very happy, and you have made me so.

This is the kindest goodnight I can utter.

Paris 12th November 1793

A public prosecutor by the name of Antoine-Quentin Fouquier-Tinville, stood to address the citizens in the smoke-laden room. Sitting opposite him from the stand, at a distance of about ten metres, was Marie Olympe de Gouges; with a cloth in her mouth and fastened behind her head. Her dress, once pristine, now bore the signs of wear and tear, with its hems frayed and stained. Her hair, once a radiant blonde, was frazzled and torn.

"Marie Olympe de Gouges, widow of Aubry, age thirty-eight, femme de lettres, a native of Montauban, living in Paris, Rue du Harlay, Section Pont-Neuf—you are hereby charged with having composed a work contrary to the expressed desire of the entire French Nation." Olympe did not raise her head from the ground.

"They took you to the prison called l'Abbaye, and they sent your documents to the public prosecutor of the Revolutionary Tribunal. Is that correct?" Olympe did not move.

"In your writing, entitled Les Trois Urnes, ou le Salut de la patrie, there can be found the project of the liberty-killing faction. You composed and had printed words which can only be considered as an attack on the sovereignty of the people." A few of the men who sat beside Antoine stomped their feet on the ground in unison.

"The author of this work, you," Antoine looked from the parchment to see Olympe now gazing at him. "Approbated the judgement of the tyrant condemned by the people. You openly provoked civil war and sought to arm citizens against one another by proposing the meeting of primary assemblies to deliberate and express their desire concerning either monarchical government." He continued, his voice louder and louder.

"There can be no mistaking the perfidious intentions of this criminal woman, and her hidden motives, when one observes her in all the works to which, at the very least, she lends her name, calumniating and spewing out bile in doses against the warmest friends of the people, their most intrepid defender." Antoine lowered the parchment to the bench in front of him, removed his glasses and rounded the podium to speak to Olympe.

"Madame, do you have anything to say on these accusations?" She fidgeted with her hands tied in front of her. "No?" Antoine gestured to her prison guard, who stood guard beside her, and he forced her chin upwards to face him. Antoine removed himself from behind the bench and moved towards Olympe with every word. "You posted your work to your son, employed in the army of the Vendée as officer de l'état major, and in a poster entitled Olympe de Gouges au Tribunal Révolutionnaire, sought to degrade the constituted authorities, calumniate the friends and defenders of the people and of liberty, and spread defiance among the representatives and the represented, which is contrary to the laws, and notably to that of last December 4th." Now mere inches from Olympe's face, he lowered himself so that he was eye-to-eye with her. "What say you to that?" he asked, smiling.

Olympe let out a muffled scream.

"You have nothing to say?" Antoine smiled as men behind him stomped their feet once again. "Pity," he said, turning to face the mean seated beside his empty chair.

"Shall we hear from witnesses?" Antoine pointed to the wooden door at the end of the room, as a hunched, elderly man walked into the room and made to stand in front of Olympe to face the men at the bench. As Antoine returned to his seat, the crowd murmured.

"Monsieur," said Antoine. "You are a bill-poster in Paris, correct?" the man nodded.

"Oui."

"And you refused to post copies of Les Trois urnes?"

"Oui Monsieur."

"Why?"

"De material, in the poster Monsieur."

"The material? The principles you read in this?" Antoine held the poster in question high for the room to see. Olympe peered behind the elderly gentlemen.

"Oui."

"You may go, merci." A guard walked with the elderly man towards the spilling crowd in the room and sat him down. A few men tapped him on the shoulder and clapped as he sat down. Antoine and his six male contemporaries murmured between themselves as another witness walked into the room, but instead of placing him at the front, they posted him next to Olympe. His weary eyes appeared swollen, puffy, and bloodshot. His face bore bruises, marring his once smooth complexion.

"Monsieur, you have seen the document in question?" Antoine held several papers for the young boy to see. "Answer my question. Have you seen this document?

"Oui," said the boy. The moment Olympe turned towards him, she felt her heart skip a beat. The boy who found her satchel.

"And how do you know this document?"

"I found it, mMonsieur."

"You found it. Where did you find it?"

"On the road Monsieur, in a satchel."

"You lie. You collude with this turncoat and delivered this document into your employer's hands. We possess a signed word from your printer, attesting to the fact that you were the one who encouraged him to print it." With one hand, Antoine raised another parchment above his head, keeping it out of reach for both the boy and Olympe to read.

"That is not—" The guard standing behind Olympe and the boy slapped him on the head, cutting off his protest.

"You and she share the same level of responsibility for this treasonous work." The crowd began to shout and leer for their heads.

"Now, now," said Antoine to the crowd. "Let us continue." He nodded to her guard and the man untied the cloth from her head. "Madame, you will speak only when spoken to or we shall resume your previous situation." Olympe said nothing.

"Now, Miss de Gouges," Antoine demanded. "Explain the basis for your treasonous actions." He threw the documents onto the floor. As Olympe gazed at the printed parchments, her heart swelled with a mixture of pride and anticipation. Glancing at them for a moment, she then lifted her head and uttered her words with conviction.

"My intention was pure. I wanted to show our citizens my love of liberty and my hatred of every kind of tyranny." The crowd leered at her.

"You authored these pamphlets?" Antoine nodded to the pamphlets strewn across the floor.

"Oui, of course."

"You authored La France sauvée ou le Tyran détrôné?" Olympe rolled her eyes as she read from the manuscript in question.

"It clearly says, BY OLYMPE DE GOUGES, are you daft?" the crowd shouted louder and louder.

"And you sent twenty-four copies of your letter to the Capet woman to the Committee of Public Safety?"

"Oui, I did not want there to be any confusion, Monsieur," she smiled.

A man screamed at Antoine from the crowd. "I shall give you 20 francs for Olympe's head right now! This woman is a traitor!"

"I shall give you thirty francs, sir!" replied Olympe. The crowd stunned itself into silence. Shock spread across the faces of Antoine and his men at the high bench. Olympe's eyes widened as she noticed, causing her to lean back in her chair. Her hands, still bound, tingled with anticipation. With a sly grin, she spread her legs under her dress and lent back in her chair. The crowd's eyes shifted back to Antoine, watching as his face transformed from a ghostly white to a flushed shade of crimson.

"Your sentiments to the representatives you insulted and calumniated in your writings, they are the same? Antoine clasped his hands together and leaned forward, his eyes focused on Olympe and the boy.

"Oui," she said again. "My sentiments to Robespierre and Marat are the same." Antoine fixed several papers in front of him and whispered something to the men seated next to him. Upon hearing the following judgement, Olympe's smirk lingered on her face as she revelled in the atmosphere of the circus unfolding around her.

"The Tribunal, based on the unanimous declaration of the jury, states that, one, it is a fact that there exists in the case writings tending towards the reestablishment of a power attacking the sovereignty of the people." Antoine spoke louder and louder as the crowd leered towards her.

"Secondly, that Marie Olympe de Gouges, calling herself widow Aubry, is proven guilty of being the author of these writings, and admitting the conclusions of the public prosecutor, condemns the aforementioned Marie Olympe de Gouges, widow Aubry, to the punishment of death in conformity with Article One of the law of last March 29th." Antoine lowered the parchment and gestured to the clerk. "Monsieur, read please the law."

The man seated next Antoine coughed and spluttered a few times, patted his chest and spoke to the crowd. "Whoever is convicted of having composed or printed works or writings which provoke the dissolution of the national representation, the reestablishment of royalty, or of any other power attacking the sovereignty of the people, will be brought before the Revolutionary Tribunal and punished by death," and declares the goods of the aforementioned Marie Olympe de Gouges seized for the benefit of the republic."

"Merci Monsieur," said Antoine. "Restrain her please."

"What about the boy?" asked Olympe. Antoine paused for a moment as he spoke to the surrounding persons.

"Same sentence," he said with a mischievous grin. As the crowd jeered at them, they assaulted them with spit, yanked Olympe's hair, and tore her dress even more. The boy winced with each kick and punch from the crowd; the guard did nothing. Olympe's composure remained intact as they led them through the doorway; her smile a silent defiance in the face of her return to the prison.

Paris 3rd November 1793

"Mrs Imlay, wake up," said my maid. "It is your friend Olympe, madame."

I blinked in a daze and to find her posted at the end of the bed. She handed me a small piece of parchment and my heart skipped its trace-like state a few times as I could not find words within my being. "I...today?"

"It is in an 'our madame," her eyes wandered to the small clock on the mantlepiece. "Are you rested?" I nodded and sat further up in bed. "The monster ails you, madame." I ran my hands over my stomach and smiled. "I can leave you to—"

"No, no," I said, I reached for her hands and held them between mine. "I shall regret it if I do not go. But we must be careful."

"I understand," she said, cleaning the top of her apron. In silence, she wrapped me in a nondescript cloak. I let my hair down, allowing it to flow across my shoulders as we embarked on our journey through the streets of Paris.

We did not reach the Place de Revolution until 3.50pm; the square swarming with hundreds of people. I endeavoured to look for Olympe, but she had yet to be brought to face the public. A few minutes went by and a decrepit wooden cart approached from the Tuileries Palace side of the square and a dishevelled Olympe exited the cart with her hands tied in front of her; a shadow of herself. As she stepped to the side, the heart-rending sigh of melancholy sunk into my soul; the boy who found her satchel. My heart sunk into one state, after being fatigued by another.

As Olympe stood at the base of the scaffold, the surrounding crowd chanted. "Vive la République!" They stamped on the ground, clapped and cheered.

"Mary!" I left her behind me in the safety of two other women and rushed to the front of the crowd; the all-consuming want for her head igniting my brain as I did so.

Olympe ascended the stairs with grace, the mute boy following behind her. She paused at the threshold of the last stair and looked to the crowd; and the moment I hoped for revealed itself. Olympe's eyes locked themselves with mine and as the surrounding crowd threw themselves at each other; shouting and cursing at her. I lowered my body to the ground, bowed my head and closed my eyes. As I opened them, she smiled at me in silent acknowledgement; of words unsaid, thoughts unwritten, dreams unlived. She bowed her head, turned to face the scaffold and resumed the last few steps of her life.

As she approached the guillotine, a wigged-man holding a parchment opened it and addressed the crowd. "Madames and Monsieur's, citizens of the Republic. You are hereby witness to the execution of one Marie Olympe de Gouges and Jean-Du Pont." At the mention of her name, a hand touched mind.

I spun to see Thomas Paine holding a finger to his lips. He nodded his head and turned towards Olympe. The crowd became louder, more violent in their torment to her and as Olympe looked saw Thomas and half smiled at his presence. With a deep reverence, Tom bowed his head towards her.

With her eyes transfixed on us, she raised her voice and shouted to the eager crowd. "Children of the Fatherland, you will avenge my death" The executioner untied both their hands and retied them behind their backs. He placed a white cloth over her eyes, and the crowd became louder and louder until she knelt at the base of the guillotine. And then, silence.

As I gripped Thomas' forearm, my heart pounded in my chest. I closed my eyes, whispered a silent prayer, and when I opened them, the executioner's hand grip the rope, raised the guillotine high and paused as the end of Olympe's life lingered in the air.

"I am sorry," I murmured, as the deafening thud of the guillotine's blade met her flesh, causing my body to jolt. Thomas gripped my arm and we held each other as the crowd waved their hats and cheered.

"Vive la République!" My eyes darted from her headless body to the sky. I closed my eyes and wondered how a god could watch as man mercilessly kill his fellow man. Another living death I would endure without a friend in the world.

and as the surrounding crowd threw themselves at each other, shouting and cursing at her, I gave all my body to the ground, bowed my head and closed my eyes. As I opened them, she smiled at me in silent acknowledgement of words unsaid, thoughts unwritten, dreams unlived. She bowed her head, turned to face the scaffold and resumed the last few steps of her life.

As she approached the guillotine, a wizened man holding a parchment stepped up and addressed the crowd. "Madame and Monsieurs, citizens of the Republic. You are hereby witness to the execution of one Marie Olympe de Gouges and Jean Du Pont." At the mention of her name, a hand touched mine.

I spun round. Thomas Paine holding a finger to his lips. He nodded his head and turned towards Olympe. The crowd became louder, more violent in their hatred to her, and as Olympe looked at Thomas and I, she smiled at his presence. With a deep reverence, Tom bowed his head towards her.

With her eyes transfixed on us, she raised her voice and shouted to the angry crowd, "Children of the Fatherland, you will avenge my death!" The executioner grabbed both their hands and tied them behind their backs. He placed a white cloth over her eyes, and the crowd became louder and louder until she knelt at the base of the guillotine. And then, silence.

As I grasped Thomas' forearm, my heart pounded in my chest. I closed my eyes, whispered a silent prayer, and when I opened them, the executioner's hand gripped the rope, raised the guillotine high and paused as the end of Olympe's life lingered in the air.

"I am sorry," I murmured, as the deafening thud of the guillotine's blade met her flesh, causing my body to fold. Thomas gripped my arm and we held each other as the crowd waved their hats and cheered.

"Vive la Republique!" My eyes darted from her needless death to the sky. I closed my eyes and wondered how a good God could watch as man mercilessly kill his fellow man. Another living death I would endure without a friend in the world.

After

Number 72, St. Paul's Churchyard London,
February 7th, 1809

"Come, my dear child, they are downstairs." Frances placed her soft hand with mine and we walked step-by-step down to the store. As I trifled through several boxes, looking for one in particular, the she traced piles of books with her fingertips.

"Ah, here...for when you were ready." I placed the ornate box on the counter. Her eyes widened and curiosity half-replaced the sadness lingering within her. "Open it." Her fingers fumbled on the latch. Dust and small debris dropped onto the counter with each unsuccessful pull. "Do you have your pocket watch with you?" I asked.

She hastened herself upstairs and returned almost within an instant. "In my satchel, as always," she said. "But, what do I do with it?" The small golden watch shone in the moonlight. I hadn't seen it in years, but its beauty was just as vivid as the one she entrusted to me. I reached into my coat pocket and showed Frances my pocket watch.

"She gave it to me, it is the brother to the one you have." I placed her delicate fingers against the small indentation and turned the ornate box to its side and gestured to her watch. As she placed it into the mechanism, a small click echoed through the room. Pausing briefly, the author took a slight step back, her eyes widening at the contents of the box.

"How...Why do you have this?"

"She trusted it to me—the box, I mean. My suspicions were right." A coughing fit took hold of my chest as she opened the box and a tear fell from her eyes.

Mary had wrapped multiple pieces of parchment and a book in soft cotton and placed a small lock of her auburn hair inside.

"I cannot...I cannot do this..."

With a nod, I said, "You can, I know you can. I am right here." Frances retrieved the parchments from the box and held the small lock of hair in one hand.

"These are," she untied the parchments from the cotton and peered at the first one, "her letters?" she asked.

"Most of them," I said, walking to the front door to ensure it was locked. "Some of them are missing or destroyed. Gilbert demanded his back and he returned hers. Her letters to her sisters, some of them survive because of her copying a few of them. Whilst you can read all of them if you like, there are several of them that have been plaguing me for years."

She furrowed her brow and asked, "What do you mean?" I returned to the parchments and we unwrapped them together, spreading them across the bookstore's counters.

"There are over two, if not three, hundred letters here. We both have a watch in case something happened to either of us. I have read as much as I could, but since you started asking questions a few months ago and the more and more I pondered the idea, I thought it was high time you read them." I pointed to several pages of Mary's letters to Gilbert. "When she was in Paris, late 1793, all of 1794 and during her travels in 1795, something is off about them." I pointed to several lines of dashes scattered throughout her letters.

"Here...and here...and here. From late '73 and stopped in '75. If you read the sentences in context, the dashes are inserted instead of names. See here?"

Paris, December 31, 1793

Though I have just sent a letter off, yet, as —— offers to take one, I am not willing to let him go without a kind greeting, because trifles of this sort, without having any effect on my mind, damp my spirit.

"I am not quite sure I understand. Who is she talking about?" I retrieved one of Mary's letters from Scandinavia. "Here," I handed her another of her letters.

Tonsberg, July 18, 1795

Gilbert,

I have begun Letters Written During a Short Residence in Sweden, Norway and Denmark, which I hope will discharge all of my monetary obligations. I am lowered in my own eyes on account I should have started it sooner.

I am here in Tonsberg, separated from my child—and I must remain here for a month or I might as well never have come.

"She travelled to Scandinavia?" I smiled and nodded. "I have neared heard of this."

"If you want to understand what occurred in that brilliant mind of hers, you will need to ascertain whatever it was she was looking for in Scandinavia."

"She was…looking for something?"

"We did not communicate much at all whilst she travelled there. I spoke to her after her incident, and she—" her expression turned blank. "Her mind burned from Gilbert's treatment of her—"

"Oh."

"She didn't go to Scandinavia with Marguerite to write a travel memoir. Assuming she acted as Gilbert's emissary for his sordid business, meeting people would have been necessary." She retrieved several letters and parchments from the counter and spread them further on the floor.

"What about Marguerite? She would have known something? I could ask her?"

"She was a dear. I tried to divulge some information, but from what she told me, she stayed in Gothenburg whilst Mary travelled further north. Do you know where she is?"

She shook her head. "Not since she was removed. Do you have the travel memoir printed somewhere here?" I nodded and pointed to one of the wooden bookshelves in the far corner of the shop.

"Middle shelf, on the left." Frances stood and wandered past the high bookshelves, tracing their bound spines with her fingers as she did. "What am I looking for?"

"Letters Written During a Short Residence in Sweden, Norway and Denmark." I smiled, remembering the conversation Mary and I had about the title. It was days of correspondence. "Did you find it?"

"This is the travel memoir and these are her letters?" She returned to the floor amongst the scattered letters, opened the book, and placed it next to the scattered parchments.

"Correct." I retrieved a small chair from behind one of the larger bookshelves and sat opposite her whilst she began reading the letters in more detail. Her laugh, her smile, even her mannerisms - everything about her reminded me of Mary.

Pausing, her eyes shifted from the book to the Scandinavian letters. "What if I read the letters to Gilbert and the memoir concurrently?" I smiled at her again. Another brilliant mind in the world. "You have already thought of that though, haven't you?" I nodded and relaxed into the chair and marvelled at her mind.

"Will you go to Scandinavia with me Joseph?" she asked. "People might remember her? I could follow her trail and talk to anyone she mentions. Maybe some of the merchants Joseph?"

"No my dear," I said, coughing a little more than usual. Honestly, I don't think I have much time left on earth my dear. These lungs, but I can arrange for someone else to accompany you if you need. It is no minor feat to conduct it on your own at your age."

"Joseph," she said. "Did you love her?" I blinked at her, pausing as our friendship flashed in my mind.

"In mid-August 1792, we attempted to cross to Paris but were unsuccessful. We returned to London and travelled north for a few days on business to source another writer for the Analytical Review. When we returned, everyone assumed we had been married. Oh, the rumours!" I laughed. "We found it quite amusing. But no my dear, I think I loved her as a friend and she did me. Our relationship lacked a name, as we are not blood relatives, but I did my best to care for her. Though I was stupidly cruel to her once."

"Cruel?" Resting on her knees, she eased onto the floor. "How could you be cruel?" I covered my lips and considered her question.

"I thought Mary may endeavour to find someone to marry. I was stupid. Completely and utterly stupid. I sent a potential suitor to her apartment one evening, and she was extremely cross with me. She eventually forgave me, but I worried about her. I didn't want her alone when her heart didn't understand solitude."

"Why couldn't she find contentment in solitude?" She gathered a few of Mary's letters that had slipped from her grasp.

"Besides Jane, one of her childhood friends and Frances Blood, your namesake, Mary didn't have anyone to care for her. She was alone in the world and she was responsible for all of your aunties and uncles when her mother and eventually her father died. Her heart was so desperately alone. My assumption is she clung onto affection like bees drawn to sweet nectar. Only it made her heart sick and not better."

Frances returned to the letters in front of her. "If the dead tell no tales, she sure kept a lot of secrets."

MARY WOLLSTONECRAFT BY JOHN OPIE

THOMAS PAINE

OLAUDAH EQUINO

JOSEPH JOHNSON

WILLIAM GODWIN

HENRY FUESLI

OLYMPE DE GOUGES

HELEN MARIA WILLIAMS

MADAME ROLAND

ANTOINE JOSPEH GORSAS

JEAN-MARIE ROLAND

BRISSOT

THE DEATH OF MARAT

JEAN-PAUL MARAT

MAXIMILIEN ROBESPIERRE

THE PEOPLE OF PARIS ENTERING THE PALAIS OF THE TUILERIES, 20. JUNE 1792

STORMING OF THE BASTILLE

THE FÊTE DE LA FÉDÉRATION ON 14 JULY 1790 CELEBRATED THE ESTABLISHMENT OF THE CONSTITUTIONAL MONARCHY.

THE STORMING OF THE TUILERIES PALACE, 10 AUGUST 1792

LE SERMENT DU JEU DE PAUME BY JACQUES-LOUIS DAVID (C. 1791), DEPICTING THE TENNIS COURT OATH

EXECUTION OF LOUIS XVI IN THE PLACE DE LA CONCORDE, FACING THE EMPTY PEDESTAL WHERE THE STATUE OF HIS GRANDFATHER, LOUIS XV PREVIOUSLY

THE EXECUTION OF ROBESPIERRE ON 28 JULY 1794
MARKED THE END OF THE REIGN OF TERROR

Act 2

Paris 8th November 1793

Dearest Joseph,

These letters shall never reach you but I write to you in earnest for my burning mind will not soften. Each day I wake and I receive word of another execution. Armies confine themselves to slaughter in battle; it is not so with parties and this Convention, the Committee, who, under violent circumstances, fearing to see the combat renewed, have so secured themselves from new attacks by inexorable rigour. Robespierre and his order make their preservation a matter of right. He and those around him regard those who attack their ideologies as enemies when they fight, and conspirators when they are defeated. They shall destroy them alike by means of war and of law.

People thinking for themselves have more energy in their voice than any government, which it is possible for human wisdom to invent; and every government not aware of this sacred truth will, at some period, be suddenly overturned. Olympe paid the price for her attempt to bring reason to France's citizens. Olympe was Robespierre's vengeance, his terror and self-preservation; for she took interest in the business of her fellow sex as you recall from dinner all those months ago. She contemplated the comfort, misery and happiness of her nation to which she belonged and her spirit of passion and reason were beheaded along with her body. So too with Madame Roland, though their reasoning was not of her voice but her company. She died by her association, it so appears.

Lyon warred against their liberty; Lyon exists no more.

Caen, Marseilles and Bordeaux a near similar fate. The condemnation against their French Queen was directed at Europe and she faced the guillotine on the 16th of October. Twenty-one Girondist were executed on the 31st of October; Brissot, Vergniaud, Gensonné, Fonfrède, Ducos, Valazé, Lasource, Sillery, Gardien, Carra, Duperret, Duprat, Fauchet, Beauvais, Duchâtel, Mainvielle, Lacaze, Boileau, Lehardy, Antiboul and Vigée. Displaying all the stoicism of our times I am told they sang the Marseilles on the march to their execution.

I do not know how I fell into these reflections, Joseph; this continual separation weighs heavy on my mind.

Paris Monday night 30th December 1793

Gilbert,

A melancholy letter from my sister Everina has harassed my mind—that from my brother would have given me sincere pleasure. There is a spirit of independence in his letter, that will please you; and you shall see it, when we are once more over the fire together.

I think that you would hail him as a brother, with one of your tender looks, when your heart not only gives a lustre to your eye, but a dance of playfulness, that he would meet with a glow half made up of bashfulness, and a desire to please.

Where shall I find a word to express the relationship which subsists between us?—Shall I ask the little twitcher?—But I have dropt half the sentence that was to tell you how much he would be inclined to love the man loved by his sister. I have been fancying myself sitting between you, ever since I began to write, and my heart has leaped at the thought!

I did not receive your letter till I came home; and I did not expect it, for the post came in much later than usual. It was a cordial to me—and I wanted one.

There was so much considerate tenderness in your epistle tonight, that, if it has not made you dearer to me, it has made me forcibly feel how very dear you are to me, by charming away half my cares.

Yours affectionately.

Mary.

Paris 31st December 1793

Though I have just sent a letter off, yet, as ——— offers to take one, I am not willing to let him go without a kind greeting, because trifles of this sort, without having any effect on my mind, damp my spirit. You, with all your struggles to be manly, have some of his same sensibility. Do not bid it begone, for I love to see it striving to master your features; besides, these kind of sympathies are the life of affection: and why, in cultivating our understandings, should we try to dry up these springs of pleasure, which gush out to give a freshness to days browned by care!

The books sent to me are such as we may read together; so I shall not look into them till you return; when you shall read, whilst I mend my stockings.

Yours truly,

Mary

Paris 1st January 1794

I hate commerce. How differently must E———'s head and heart be organised from mine! You will tell me, that exertions are necessary: I am weary of them! The face of things, public and private, vexes me. The "peace" and clemency which seemed to be dawning a few days ago, disappear again. "I am fallen," as Milton said, "on evil days;" for I believe that Europe will be in a state of convulsion, for half a century at least. Life is but a labour of patience: it is always rolling a great stone up a hill; for, before a person can find a resting place, imagining it is lodged, down it comes again, and all the work is to be done over anew! Should I attempt to write anymore, I could not change the strain. My head aches, and my heart is heavy. The world appears an unweeded garden where things rank and vile flourish best.

You now tell me, that, if it were not for me, you would be laughing away with some honest fellows in London. The casual exercise of social sympathy would not be sufficient for me—I should not think such a heartless life worth preserving.

It is necessary to be in good humour with you, to be pleased with the world. I was low-spirited last night, ready to quarrel with your cheerful temper.

I do not want to be loved like a goddess; but I wish to be necessary to you.

Paris Monday night 6th January 1794

Love,

I have just received your kind and rational letter, and would fain hide my face, glowing with shame for my folly.

I would hide it in your bosom, if you would again open it to me, and nestle closely till you bade my fluttering heart be still, by saying that you forgave me. With eyes overflowing with tears, and in the humblest attitude, I entreat you.

Do not turn from me, for indeed I love you fondly, and have been wretched, since the night I was so cruelly hurt by thinking that you had no confidence in me.

It is time for me to grow more reasonable, a few more of these caprices of sensibility would destroy me. I have, in fact, been much indisposed for a few days past. Do you think that the creature goes regularly to sleep?

E——— did not write to you, I suppose because he talked of going to Havre. Hearing that I was ill, he called kindly on me, not dreaming that it was some words that he incautiously let fall, which rendered me so

Paris Wednesday morning January 1794

I know the quickness of your feelings—and let me, in the sincerity of my heart, assure you, there is nothing I would not suffer to make you happy.

My own happiness depends on you—and, knowing you, when my reason is not clouded, I look forward to a rational prospect of as much felicity as the earth affords—with a little dash of rapture into the bargain, if you will look at me, when we work again as you have sometimes greeted your humbled, yet most affectionate Mary.

Paris Thursday morning January 1794

I have been unwell, and would not, now I am recovering, take a journey, because I have been alarmed and angry with myself, dreading the fatal consequence of my folly. But, should you think it right to remain at Havre, I shall find some opportunity, in the course of a fortnight, or less perhaps, to come to you, and before then I shall be strong again.

The girl has come to warm my bed—so I will tenderly say, goodnight and write a line or two in the morning.

Paris February 1794

I seize this opportunity to inform you, that I am to set out on Thursday with E———, and hope to tell you soon (on your lips) how glad I shall be to see you.

I have just got my passport, for I do not foresee any impediment to my reaching Havre, to bid you goodnight next Friday in my new apartment—where I am to meet you and love, despite care, to smile me to sleep—for I have not caught much rest since we parted.

Le Havre 12th March 1794

Gilbert,

We are such creatures of habit, my love, that, though I cannot say I was sorry, childishly so, for your going, when I knew that you were to stay such a short time, and I had a plan of employment; yet I could not sleep.

I turned to your side of the bed, and tried to make the most of the comfort of the pillow, which you used to tell me I was churlish about; but all would not do. Nevertheless, I took my walk before breakfast, though the weather was not inviting. And here I am, wishing you a finer day, and seeing you peep over my shoulder, as I write, with one of your kindest looks, when your eyes glisten, and a suffusion creeps over your relaxing features.

But I do not mean to dally with you this morning. So God bless you! Take care of yourself and sometimes fold to your heart your affectionate Mary.

Paris 28th July 1794

The guillotine stood tall, its blade gleaming in the pale light of Parisian dawn, ready to claim yet another victim in the name of revolution. Yet this time, it was not an ordinary soul condemned to its unrelenting hold—it was Robespierre, the embodiment of tyranny and oppression.

After the Convention authorised his arrest, he and dozens of his supporters sought refuge in the Hotel de Ville. Helen informed me that units loyal to the Convention later stormed the building the same evening and detained Robespierre, who severely injured himself attempting suicide.

My thoughts flew back to conversations at Helen's where we had dared to challenge the prevailing order of our society and we wondered if this day would come. Madame Roland and the ministers, Charlotte Corday. Olympe de Gouges, my courageous friend who spoke truth to power—her ideals crushed under the weight of tyranny.

As I witnessed Robespierre's downfall, I could not help but feel a sense of grim satisfaction—my mind calmer. In his demise, justice was served as a reckoning for the lives he had extinguished in pursuit of his distorted vision of revolution. Madame Roland, Charlotte Corday and Olympe de Gouges, though gone from this world, were vindicated in this moment, their sacrifices not in vain.

Yet even as I watched Robespierre meet his end, I could not shake the sense of sorrow and worry that enveloped me. Robespierre, though a prominent figurehead of the Reign of Terror, was not the sole architect of its horrors. And a nagging worry gnawed at the depths of my soul.

While his demise may bring a momentary sense of catharsis, I feared that it was but a superficial remedy for the deeper malaise that afflicted the revolution. Were we truly striking at the root of tyranny, or were we merely pruning its branches? Would his death herald a new era of liberty and justice, or would it merely pave the way for another despot to rise in his place? For he was but an actor in a play of power struggles and ideological fervour that had consumed the French nation. These questions weighed heavily on my mind as I watched the events unfold before me, the wheel of the revolution rolled on.

The French Revolution is a strong proof how far things will govern men, when simple principles begin to act with one powerful spring against the complicated wheels of ignorance. War is the adventure naturally pursued by the idle, and it requires something of this species, to excite the strong emotions necessary to rouse inactive minds.

In the pursuit of revolution, France unleashed forces beyond its control—forces which had consumed the very ideals it had sought to uphold. For true revolution cannot be achieved through the mere removal of figureheads; it requires a fundamental reordering of society, a dismantling of oppressive structures, and a commitment to the principles of equality and justice for men and women. For periods of revolution draw into action the worst as well as the best of men.

From implicitly obeying their sovereigns, the French became suddenly all sovereigns; yet, because it is natural for men to run out of one extreme into another, we should guard against inferring that the spirit of the moment will not evaporate, and leave the disturbed water more clear for the fermentation. Men without principle rise like foam during a storm sparkling on the top of the billow, in which it is soon absorbed when the commotion dies away.

Robespierre, Danton, Marat and their supporters took every precaution to divide the nation, and prevent any ties of affection. Equality could have been the device to consolidate their ideals in search of liberty. One lesson from America that I have reflected on lately, is that men determined to be free are always superiour to mercenary battalions even of veterans. Even the palace guards in Paris could not amply defend themselves from the Parisians willing liberation.

And as I stared at the headless body of Robespierre, he reminds me that the complication of laws in every country has tended to bewilder the understanding of man in the science and mechanisms of government. Artful politicians, like the headless one before me, take advantage of the ignorance or credulity of their fellow citizens. They make laws by ambition rather than reason and treat with contempt the sacred equality of man, for they are anxious only to aggrandize, first the state and afterwards often their fellow individuals. In all civil wars, personal vengeance mixes with public and takes advantage of it. Because, when fear induces a man to smother his just resentment, the festering wound is only to be cured by revenge.

The French people had long been groaning under the lash of a thousand oppressions; they were the hewers of wood, and drawers of water, for the chosen few. Once they threw off the imprinted hateful fears of servitude, it should have been apprehended they would expect the most unbridled freedom, and detest all wholesome restraints, no longer bound by reins of tyranny.

Robespierre stood with selfishness at the dawn of French liberty, for pay and plunder were his motives. He and his supporters saw a nation, having shaken off the prejudices of ages ripe for picking. Few, like the Girdonists, attempted with reason to trace out the road which one would suppose lead to virtue, glory, and happiness.

But will the world learn from the mistakes of the past, or will it continue down the path of violence and oppression? For the swell of the sea continues once the storm subsides. The answer, I fear, lay in the hands of those who would come after us, in their willingness to heed the lessons of history and strive for a better world. For the first inventor of any instrument has scarcely ever been able to bring it to a tolerable degree of perfection and the discoveries of every man of genius, the optics of Newton excepted, have been improved, if not extended, by their followers.

Can it then be expected, that the science of politics and finance, the most important, and most difficult of all human improvements; a science which involves the passions, tempers, and manners of men and nations, that estimates their wants, maladies, comforts, happiness, and misery, and computes the sum of good or evil flowing from social institutions; will not require the same gradations, and advance by steps equally slow to that state of perfection necessary to secure the sacred rights of every human creature?

A slow march to build a society founded not on the cult of personality, but on the principles of reason, compassion and human dignity. For then and only then could we truly claim to have achieved the lofty ideals for which we had so ardently fought.

But for now, as the crowd roared its approval at Robespierre's demise, I could only hope that justice had been served, and that the sacrifices of Madame Roland, Olympe de Gouges, and countless others would not be forgotten in the annals of history.

*

After witnessing Robespierre's execution, my girl and I returned to Le Havre to reacquaint ourselves with Gilbert and once again press my bosom so tenderly to his heart.

We spent several days together, before he returned to Paris on business once again.

Le Havre Sunday 17th August 1794

Gilbert

I have promised Mr Wheatcroft to go with him to his country house, where he is now permitted to dine—I, and the little darling, to be sure—whom I cannot help kissing with more fondness, since you left us. I think I shall enjoy the fine prospect, and that it will rather enliven than satiate my imagination.

Le Havre Tuesday 19th August 1794

My love,

I write in a hurry, because the little one, who sleeps for a long time, begins to call for me. Poor thing! When I am sad, I lament that all my affections grow on me, till they become too strong for my peace, though they all afford me snatches of exquisite enjoyment.

This for our little girl was at first very reasonable, more the effect of reason, a sense of duty, than feeling. Now, she is in my heart and imagination, and when I walk out without her, her little figure is ever dancing before me in my mind.

I will witness the ———————— leave tomorrow and be sure to retain your receipts as promised.

Le Havre Havre Wednesday 20th August 1794

It is done ——————— will write to you when they arrive.

Pray ask some questions about Tallien whilst you are in Paris, I am still pleased with the dignity of his conduct. The other day, in the cause of humanity, he made use of a degree of address, which I admire, and mean to point out to you, as one of the few instances of address which do credit to the abilities of the man, without taking away from that confidence in his openness of heart, which is the true basis of both public and private friendship.

But I have left poor Tallien. I wanted you to enquire likewise whether, as a member declared in the convention, Robespierre maintained several mistresses. Should it prove so, I suspect that they rather flattered his vanity than his senses.

Here is a chatting, desultory epistle! But do not suppose that I mean to close it without mentioning the little damsel, who has been almost springing out of my arm, she looks like you, but I do not love her the less for that, whether I am angry or pleased with you.

Yours affectionately, Mary.

*

The following days at Le Havre Frances and I spent in solitude, quiet and at peace. The return journey to Paris would be within days and once again we would be thrust into the light of the revolution and uncertainty. Paris was on the horizon and I would once again press my heart to Gilbert, for distance and time had separated us for so long.

Paris 12th September 1794

"My darling girls," Gilbert kissed us both on the forehead. "Come, come, I have something I need to show you." Gilbert placed our bags on the floor and led Frances and I to adjoining parlour and stood in front of a writing desk which had a view of the window. "What do you think?"

"Is it? Is it for me?" Gilbert stood aside and nodded.

"I thought you might like a proper space to write, it even overlooks the street you see, here," he drew the curtains back further and opened the window. "You see, air, window, it is perfect."

"Why did you..." Gilbert's expression turned almost at an instant. "Do not tell me you are leaving again."

"Mary—" I handed Frances to the maid and as they disappeared into the other room, I closed the doors.

"Gilbert this is unfair." My heart began to pound and beat the edge of my body. "Why do you treat me so poorly? I have not—we have not seen you for months. And now you disappear again? Where are you going?" I paced back and forth in front of the desk.

"London. I—"

"London? You return to London?"

"It is to secure our comforts Mary, our future. What we spoke about, remember? America?"

"Was Le Havre and ———— not that future? Your business transactions with Mr ———— and Mr ———— were, I thought, the entire plan Gilbert? That is what you told me some six months ago." Gilbert stepped closer and held my hands.

"I did Mary, I did, but there is business that needs attending to in London. The trade is beginning to become larger again and I need to be there to secure our agreements. It does not work if I am here in Paris, it will not work. You must understand Mary please, please." His eyes pleaded with me.

"When will you return?"

"January," he said. "No later than January, I promise you. By then, the profit from our situation will flow through in coins and then we can begin our journey to America.

Purchase that little farm of ours, away from all this, all this wretched world. Just you and I and Frances." He rested his forehead against mine and smiled. "I love you Mary. But you need to trust me. I need to go."

"But I shall miss you terribly. My heart aches when we are apart."

"Mine too, but it is for the best."

"When do you leave?"

"Tomorrow..."

Paris 22nd September 1794

Gilbert,

Apart from looking at me, three other things bring her delight:

—to ride in a coach, to look at a scarlet waistcoat, and hear loud music.

—yesterday, at the fête, she enjoyed the two latter; but, to honour J. J. Rousseau, I intend to give her a sash, the first she has ever had around her—and why not?—for I have always been half in love with him.

Well, this you will say is trifling—shall I talk about alum or soap? There is nothing picturesque in your present pursuits; my imagination then rather chuses to ramble back to the barrier with you, or to see you coming to meet me, and my basket of grapes. With what pleasure do I recollect your looks and words?

Paris 23rd September 1794

I have been playing and laughing with the little girl so long, that I cannot take up my pen to address you without emotion. Pressing her to my bosom, she looked so like you (entre nous, your best looks, for I do not admire your commercial face) every nerve vibrated to the touch.

Public affairs I do not descant on, except to tell you that they write now with great freedom and truth; and this liberty of the press will overthrow the Jacobins, I plainly perceive. Robespierre be damned.

Have I anything more to say to you? No; not for the present—the rest is all flown away; and, indulging tenderness for you.

Paris 28th September 1794

I have written to you three or four letters; but different causes have prevented my sending them by the persons who promised to take or forward them.

I cannot help being eager to hear from you; but I shall not harass you with accounts of inquietudes, or of cares that arise from peculiar circumstances. I have had so many little plagues here that I have almost lamented that I left Le Havre. I slept at St. Germain's, in the room (if you have not forgotten) where you held me lovingly against your heart. I did not forget to fold my darling to mine, with sensations that are almost too sacred to be alluded to.

Adieu, my love! Take care of yourself, if you wish to be the protector of your child and the comfort of her mother.

I have received, for you, letters from Coleman. I want to hear how that affair finishes, though I do not know whether I have the most contempt for his folly or knavery.

Your own Mary.

Paris 1st October 1794

I just now stumbled on one of the kind letters, which you wrote during your last absence. You are then a dear affectionate creature, and I will not plague you. The letter which you chance to receive, when the absence is so long, ought to bring only tears of tenderness, without any bitter alloy, into your eyes.

After your return from England I hope indeed, that you will not be so immersed in business, as during the last three or four months past—for even money, taking into the account all the future comforts it is to procure, may be gained at too dear a rate, if painful impressions are left on the mind.

My little darling grows every day more dear to me—and

she often kisses me, when we are alone together, which I give her for you, with all my heart. Marguerite, the new maid is vivacious, which is better for the child.

Paris 26th October 1794

My dear love, I wished so earnestly to hear from you, that the sight of your letters occasioned such pleasurable emotions, I was obliged to throw them aside till the little girl and I were alone together; and this said little girl, our darling, is the most intelligent little creature. I once told you, that the sensations before she was born, and when she is sucking, were pleasant; but they do not deserve to be compared to the emotions I feel, when she stops to smile upon me, or laughs outright on meeting me unexpectedly in the street, or after a short absence.

My heart longs for your return, my love, and only looks for, and seeks happiness with you; yet do not imagine that I childishly wish you to come back, before you have arranged things in such a manner, that it will not be necessary for you to leave us soon again.

Paris 26th December 1794

I have been, my love, for some days tormented by fears. I had been expecting you daily and I heard that many vessels had been driven on shore during the late gale. Well, I now see your letter—and find that you are safe; I will not regret then that your exertions have hitherto been so unavailing.

Come to me, my dearest friend, husband, father of my child! All these fond ties glow at my heart at this moment, and dim my eyes. With you an independence is desirable; and it is always within our reach, if affluence escapes us—without you the world again appears empty to me. But I am recurring to some of the melancholy thoughts that have flitted across my mind for some days past, and haunted my dreams.

My little darling is indeed a sweet child; and I am sorry that you are not here to see her little mind unfold itself. Her eyes follow me everywhere. She is all vivacity of softness and I love her more than I thought I should.

Yours most truly and tenderly

Mary.

Paris 28th December 1794

I know John urges you to stay, and is continually branching out into new projects, because he has the idle desire to amass an enormous fortune, rather an immense one, merely to have the credit of having made it. But he, who is governed by other motives, should not lead us on.

Stay in London, my friend, for as long as it is necessary. I do not consent to you taking any other journey, or the little woman and I will be off. The Lord knows where. Do not be surprised if, having suffered so much in life, I sometimes grow gloomy and suppose, when left to myself, that it was all a dream and that my happiness is not to last. I say happiness, because remembrance shrinks all the dark shades of the picture.

Paris 29th December 1794

How I hate this crooked business! This intercourse with the world, which obliges one to see the worst side of human nature! Why cannot you be content with the object you had first in view, when you entered this tiresome labyrinth? If you do not soon return, the little girl and I will take care of ourselves; we will accept none of your cold kindness—your distant civilities—no; not we.

I grow sad, very often when I am playing with her, that you are not here to observe with me how her mind unfolds, and her little heart becomes attached! I do not like this life of continual agitation and I am determined to try to earn some money here myself, in order to convince you that, if you choose to run about the world to get a fortune, it is for yourself. The little girl and I will live without your assistance. I will never abandon certain principles of action.

I consider fidelity and loyalty as two distinct things; yet the former is necessary, to give life to the other and such a degree of respect do I think due to myself, that, if only honesty is a good in its place, brings you back, never return!

If a wandering of the heart, or even a caprice of the imagination detains you—there is an end of all my hopes of happiness—I could not forgive it, if I would.

I have got into a melancholy mood. You know my opinion of men in general; you know I think them systematic tyrants, and that it is the rarest thing in the world, to meet with a man with sufficient refinement of feeling to control their desire. When I am thus sad, I lament that my little darling, fondly as I doat on her, is a girl. I am sorry to have a tie to a world that for me is ever sown with thorns.

You have always known my opinion that I have always declared. Two people, who mean to live together, should not be long separated. If certain things are more necessary to you than me—search for them—Say but one word, and you shall never hear of me more.

If not, let us struggle with poverty—with any evil, but these continual troubles of business, which I have been told were to last but a few months, though every day the end appears more distant!

Paris 9th January 1795

I just now received one of your hasty notes; for business so entirely occupies you, that you have not time, or sufficient command of thought, to write letters. I am really unable to bear the continual inquietude which your and ———— never-ending plans produce.

Paris 30th January 1795

From the purport of your last letters, I should suppose that this will not reach you; and I have already written so many letters, that you have either not received, or neglected to acknowledge. I do not find it pleasant, or rather I have no inclination, to go over the same ground again. If you have received the letters, and are still detained by new projects, it is useless for me to say any more on the subject. I have done with it forever; yet I ought to remind you that your pecuniary interest suffers by your absence.

Paris 9th February 1795

The melancholy presentiment has for some time hung on my spirits, that we were parted forever; and the letters I received this day, by Mr ——, convince me it was not without foundation. You allude to some other letters, which I suppose have miscarried; for most of those I have got, were only a few hasty lines, calculated to wound the tenderness the sight of the superscriptions excited.

Indeed, my head turns giddy when I think that all the confidence I have had in the affection of others is come to this. I did not expect this blow from you. I have done my duty to you and my child; and if I am not to have any return of affection to reward me, I have the sad consolation of knowing that I deserved a better fate. My soul is weary—I am sick at heart; and, but for this little darling, I would cease to care about a life which is now stripped of every charm.

I know what I look for to found my happiness on. It is not money. With you I wished for sufficient to procure the comforts of life—as it is, less will do. I can still exert myself to obtain the necessaries of life for my child, and she does not want more at present. I have two or three plans in my head to earn our subsistence.

Do not insult me by saying that "our being together is paramount to every other consideration!" Were it, you would not be running after a bubble, at the expense of my peace of mind.

Paris 10th February 1795

You talk of "permanent views and future comfort". Not for me, for I am dead to hope. The inquietudes of the last winter have concluded the business, and they have not only broken my heart but also destroyed my constitution.

I conceive myself in a galloping consumption, and the continual anxiety I feel at the thought of leaving my child feeds the fever that nightly devours me. It is on her account that I again write to you, to conjure you, by all that you hold sacred, to leave her here with the German lady you may have heard me mention. She has a child of the same age, and they may be brought up together, as I wish her to be brought up. I shall write more fully on the subject. To facilitate this, I shall give up my present lodgings, and go into the same house. I can live much cheaper there, which is now become an object.

I've had 3000 livres from Joseph, and I shall take one more, to pay my servant's wages and then I shall endeavour to procure what I want by my own exertions. I shall give up the acquaintance of the Americans in full.

When you first entered these plans, you bounded your views to the gaining of a thousand pounds. It was sufficient to have procured a farm in America, which would have been an independence. You find now that you did not know yourself, and that a certain situation in life is more necessary to you than you imagined—more necessary than an uncorrupted heart. For a year or two, you may procure yourself what you call pleasure; eating, drinking and women; but in the solitude of declining life, I shall be remembered with regret—I was going to say with remorse, but checked my pen.

As I have never concealed the nature of my connection with you, your reputation will not suffer. This has been such a period of barbarity and misery, I ought not to complain about having my share. Surely I had suffered enough in life, not to be cursed with a fondness that burns up the vital stream I am imparting.You will think me mad: I would. I wish I could forget my misery—so that my head or heart would be still.

Paris 19th February 1795

When I first received your letter, putting off your return to an indefinite time, I felt so hurt that I know not what I wrote. I am now calmer, though it was not the kind of wound over which time has the quickest effect; on the contrary, the more I think, the sadder I grow.

Society fatigues me inexpressibly. So much so, that finding fault with everyone, I have only reasoned enough to discover that the fault is in myself. My child alone interests me, and, but for her, I should not take any pains to recover my health.

What is our life then only to comprise separations? Am I only to return to a country that has not merely lost all charms for me, but for which I feel a repugnance that almost amounts to horror, only to be left there a prey to it?

Why is it so necessary that I should return? Brought up here, my girl would be freer. Indeed, expecting you to join us, I had formed some plans of usefulness that have now vanished with my hopes of happiness.

London 2nd April 1795

Mary

Business alone has kept me from you.

Come to any port and I will fly down to my two dear girls with a heart all their own.

Gilbert.

Le Havre 7th April 1795

Gilbert,

Here I am at Havre, on the wing towards you, and I write now, only to tell you, that you may expect me in the course of three or four days. I sit, lost in thought, looking at the sea—and tears rush into my eyes, when I find that I am cherishing any fond expectations.—I have indeed been so unhappy this winter, I find it as difficult to acquire fresh hopes, as to regain tranquillity. Foolish heart, I could almost wish that it should cease to beat, to be no more alive to the anguish of disappointment.

I deprived myself of my only pleasure, when I weaned her, about ten days ago. I am however glad I conquered my repugnance.

It was necessary it should be done soon, and I did not wish to embitter the renewal of your acquaintance with her, by putting it off till we met.

Mary

Brighthelmstone Saturday 11th April 1795

Gilbert,

Here we are, my love, and mean to set out early in the morning; and, if I can find you, I hope to dine with you to-morrow.

I shall drive to the hotel where Joseph tells me you have been and I hope you will take care to be there to receive us.

Are we not to meet soon? What does your heart say?

Yours truly Mary.

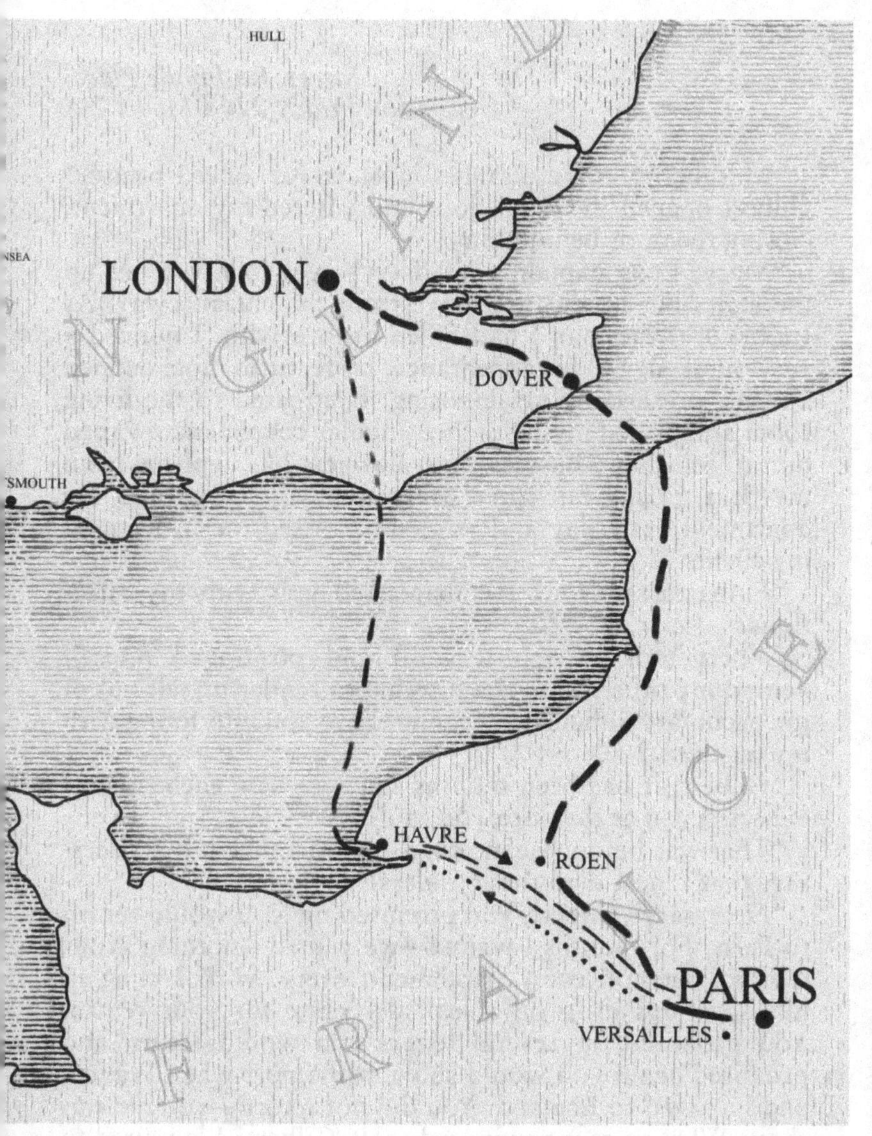

Mary's travels 1794-1795

26 Charlotte Street, Rathbone Place,
London Friday 22nd May 1795

"Marguerite, take Frances upstairs at once, please." Gilbert opened the front door and entered my apartment, closing the door behind him.

"Mary, I can explain—" Gilbert's eyes followed her up the stairs but he did not move from the entranceway. As I looked at the man I had fallen in love with, I noticed a newfound edge to his appearance, his features more defined and his presence more imposing. I retreated to the living room and placed myself on my singular couch, and awaited him to join me. "Business has. Business has kept me from my dear girls. I am sorry Mary, but you barge into my apartment yesterday and you embarrassed me in front of my clients."

"Embarrassed you? I embarrassed you with my affections?"

Gilbert took a step forward and positioned himself behind my other sofa. "I am trying to render myself out of my pecuniary difficulties. I cannot have you interfering with my business."

"Gilbert, it has been months since we saw each other. I expected you at the port, you said—"

"That was before the meetings were arranged. It is necessary that I meet with these traders—"

"Necessary? Gilbert, you promised me you would return to Paris. For months I waited—we waited—nothing. Your words linger on every parchment, every word I cling to like some raindrop on a leaf, desperate for your return. You promised, in several letters you would return and promised again you would show at the port when Frances and I arrived to England. You did not return—you did not show. What were we supposed to do Gilbert? I laboured to calm my mind at the hotel and you were not there." Gilbert resigned himself to sit on the small sofa and took several deep breaths before collapsing his head into his hands. His attire worn and dishevelled, a shadowy figure of the man I had met in Paris. "What is it that you require, Gilbert? If you tell me I won't be indignant, nor will I utter another complaint, but please just tell me what you need from me."

"I need time," said Gilbert. "I need time to rid myself of this Norway business." His eyes glanced towards as he stood, made his way to the extinct fireplace, rested his hands against the mantlepiece, and lowered his head to the ground. "It sunk." My chest tightened and hands tensed.

"Tell me frankly what you mean? Noah said everything was perfectly in order for it to arrive?" I rose from my chair and reached my hand to Gilbert's back. He did not flinch or move a muscle, his head still resigned to the floor.

"The last letter I received from Noah was in February. Ellefsen's last letter was in January. It sunk off the coast of Norway in November and Ellefsen will not respond to any of my letters and I want reparation."

I took a step back as my thoughts scrambled to remember Le Havre. "I do not understand." I grasped the sofa for support and relinquished myself to the seat. "The ship—the ship is in Ellefsen's name, Gilbert. You directed me to write his name as the holder." Gilbert grasped the mantlepiece until his knuckles turned white, then took a candelabra and hurled it across the room.

"My money Mary. He has sunk my ship, my business, and he hides in the shadows from my associates. I shall find him, with every last breath." My hands shook as I watched Gilbert pace around the room. "I have been so angry, Mary. So outraged." Gilbert turned and knelt in front of me. "Forgive me for my silence, my betrayal of your graces. My head has been so full since November." His eyes met mine again, and he clasped my hands in his and kissed the top of them.

"What shall you have me do?"

After

Number 72, St. Paul's Churchyard, London May 2nd, 1809

"My dear. It is so good to see you again. How was she Anne?" Anne and Frances entered the dining room with their travel bags.

"Oh, she were alright Joseph," said Anne, smiling at Frances. "No, she were brilliant I tell you, that young'n mind o' hers."

"I found Noah, the contact they had in Gothenburg that she removed from her letters," said Frances. "I met him I did Joseph. He was positively delighted to see me. And we spoke about her in such great detail I have to recount to you every part of it. Oh you would have loved it there Joseph."

"I am sure I would have. Tell me, did you solve the mystery?" Frances posted herself at my dining table and retrieved several stacks of parchment from one of her bags on the floor.

"Here, here and here. This is everything I found." She laid every piece of parchment she could retrieve in a single scoop of her hands and presented them for my inspection.

"And?" I lent over the table. "Was I correct?"

"You were," her face lit up with a beaming smile. In Mary's happier days, she had the same spark in her eyes. "My father was involved in trade business. All thc dashed lines in those letters of hers, mostly they are business associates of Gilbert's. Probably why he asked her for his letters back. It's also why I think she never mentioned any of this to you Joseph. They appear dangerous people."

"And what else did you find?"

"Well, we visited Tonsberg and—"

"Joseph it was magnificent I tell you, so charming!" Anne called from the kitchen. "The little 'ouses by the water's edge."

Frances giggled. "We found a judge there, Wulfsberg. He was quite confused as to why I was visiting. However, once I explained who my mother was and what I was looking for, he gave me this." She handed me a parchment from across the table. "Mary wrote a letter addressed to a Count Bernstorf."

I glanced over at the letter. "This is why she went to Copenhagen then?" She nodded in reply and pointed to the bottom of the parchment. Frances returned to the kitchen to help Anne as I read the letter and accompanying parchments. When she returned a half hour later with Anne, cups of tea in had, we placed Mary's letters in order, removed several pages from her travel memoir and paired them with various letters and parchments she collected on her travels.

"Shall I surmise what I think happened?" Frances and I stood side by side as Anne sat opposite and relaxed into her chair, marvelling at the sight of hundreds of letters before her."Together," said Frances."After she witnessed Robespierre's execution in late July 1794, she travelled to Le Havre in early August. There, a ship set sail from Le Havre to Norway called—""The Liberte," Frances nodded to Anne."The ship disappeared without a trace, or that is what Imlay thought." I pointed to several letters from Paris, Le Havre and London which contained several omitted lines. "For some reason, Imlay moved back to Paris that month so it was in fact Mary who witnessed the ship leave from Le Havre.""The judge we acquainted ourselves with provided no details about what was on the ship," Frances placed both her hands on the table and lent over the letters."Were you able to ascertain anything?""He mentioned a highly influential family in the area was eager to bury the whole incident. And that man there, Count Bernstorf, I think mama pleaded with him in this letter to help her because, well, she needed help from someone with authority maybe to aid her in her attempt to restore justice for Imlay." I would have done the same thing.Frances and I glanced over the letter from Mary to the Count again together. "Judge Wulfsberg is convinced that Mary discovered the ship, but said there wasn't enough proof at the time of the entire ordeal. The ship was in Peter's name apparently so she had no proof it was in fact the Liberte."

"A sordid ordeal Mr Joseph!" said Anne.

"Now I understand why she was so upset. It partly clarifies the events of May and November '95." I handed Mary's letters to Frances. "Here. She was so distraught. Originally, I thought it was solely because of Imlay abandoning her in Paris late 1794 and early 1795. One evening in May, Imlay knocked at the door downstairs until I answered it. I had little to do with the wretched man. Anyhow, he explained that he visited her apartment, and the maid did not answer the door and neither did Mary. He assumed I had a key, which I did, so together we caught a coach back to Rathbone and found Mary in her bed in quite a state."

"By 'state' you mean—"

"We found a Laudanum bottle nearest her bedside and, well, we called for the doctor at once. She was not well. And from what you told me, I now think she probably blamed herself for the missing ship. Her mind was in such a state of despair, she probably blamed herself for the entire thing. It was not her fault of course, the poor woman blamed herself for everything. Did I ever tell you Mary once rescued her sister from her cruel husband because she blamed herself for arranging the marriage in the first place?"

"I do not think so. You meant Aunt Everina?" I posted myself in the chair and gestured for Frances to do the same. I shook my head and let a small laugh escape. "Eliza. She found herself in Ireland, pregnant and at the behest of a fool of a man. She wrote to Mary and over the course of several months Eliza, Mary and Everina planned Eliza's escape. One evening, Mary arrived in a carriage with Everina, whisked Eliza away and flew off to London. Mary said Eliza was half-biting at her wedding ring the whole trip."

"I never knew that."

"She also once saved a French vessel from sinking. When Frances passed away in November of 1785, she stayed a few weeks in Lisbon and decided to return to London on or about the 20th of December. According to Mary, though she told the story wildly different to how I will now tell you, while the ship made passage to London, they fell in with a French vessel, in great distress."

"She saved a ship from sinking?" Frances' eyes widened as she reclined into her chair. "So the story goes, the vessel was almost destitute of provisions and half-sinking. The Frenchman hailed them and entreated the English captain, in consideration of his melancholy situation, to take him and his crew on board. The Englishman replied that his stock of provisions was by no means adequate to such an additional number of mouths, and refused compliance. Mary, shocked at his apparent insensibility, took up the cause of the sufferers, and threatened the captain to have him called to a severe account, when he arrived in England. She finally prevailed, and had the satisfaction to reflect, that the persons in question possibly owed their lives to her interposition."

Frances smiled but bit her lip as she gazed across the letters again. "So Imlay never told you why she was so distraught in May?"

"No. Once the doctor arrived, he left. At least he had the decency to retrieve me, I guess." I shrugged my shoulders as Anne refilled our cups of tea.

"Why did she did she travel to Scandinavia if she was distraught and blamed herself? Why did she not she not stay here in London and why didn't Imlay go instead?"

"In her book, 'Letters from Sweden and Norway', the 'affectionate friend' whom she writes to is Imlay—a somewhat romanticised tale of him anyhow. I suppose you shall have to study the letters anew now you have learned about the ship. Now I believe it was to redeem herself for something she was not responsible for. And to prove to him that she loved him." Frances scoured her eyes over the dining table. She fiddled through several papers and found Mary's letters from May and the one she wrote in November 1795. Reading them in silence once again, her eyes welled with tears.

"He never loved her, did he?" I took a deep breath and rested my hand on the table and traced a faint burn mark on the table, remembering the evening before everything changed. I bit my lip, attempting to form words that wouldn't harm her, but it proved futile. Our eyes finally met and with a sigh, I shook my head.

Act 3

I dread to unfold her mind, lest it should render her unfit for the world she is to inhabit—Hapless woman! What a fate is thine!

Somewhere off the coast of Denmark and Sweden, 21st June 1795

"Ma'am?"

"Yes Marguerite?"

"Do you think..." She gestured with her hand to a small lighthouse, the only human structure on the otherwise barren island, both in foliage and with not a mortal soul in sight. "I know, you wanted to travel to Gothenburg today. Shall we not ask him, ma'lady?" The captain—a common and good natured man—but men with common minds seldom break through general rules.

"I inquired this morning upon waking," I grabbed at the shoal beneath my legs. "And apparently he's a man of principle, or his word. Scantily paid mind you. Alas, it would require to quit their hovels and that, he would not do."

"What about that one?"

"Which one?"

"That one!" She pointed at a sailor who was knotting small pieces of rope at the end of the hull. In my attempt to emancipate myself from the dreary wreck of a boat not fit for passengers, I had not yet requested the assistance of his sailors. Hmm.

"Give him a guinea or two and they vill row us out, I am sure of it, madame. Or..." she gestured with her head towards the idle rowboat hoisted on the side of the boat.

"No, we can not row, we shall sink!"

"Como?" she said, grinning.

I pulled my coat on, wrapped my scarf tighter around my neck, fixed the bottom of my dress and made my way to the small sailor, traversing crates, rope and bloodied fish entrails to reach him.

"Excuse me sir?" The sailor continued securing rope. "Sir?"

"Ah. Ja?" His eyes widened in surprise as he caught sight of me.

"I wish, well, we wish," I gestured to Marguerite, "to rid ourselves from this, boat. Can you help?" Another sailor, who I failed to see prior to my engagement with the smaller one, appeared in haste from behind a wide crate.

"Leave?" The other sailor interjected. "You?"

"Yes." He had a weathered appearance to his frame, as if winter had took hold of his body and spat him back out at its end. "We wish to leave in that," I pointed to the rowboat tied near Marguerite. "The captain has declined us service. I was wondering if you might help?" The sailor halted himself from securing the rope and turned to his crew mate. In an unintelligible mumble and, appearing in accord with each other, they spun round and faced me.

"Four?" The weathered sailor said.

"Four? Four what? Four guineas? Are you making a fool of me?" They both shook their heads in unison. I rattled around for my coins inside my satchel and held them in my open my hands. "Two. Would you assist us both and my little girl for two guineas?"

Several minutes later and much to the captain's frequent looks of disapproval, the upbeat sailors had hoisted the rowboat onto the sea and had transferred Marguerite and Frances. Knowing it is better to leave a friend than an enemy, I thanked the captain with a courtesy and clambered into the rowboat. Marguerite appeared pleased with herself.

As the weather calmed both the water and the occupants of the rowboat, we arrived on a small shore. I wondered at our not seeing any inhabitants. Marguerite, timid and not accustomed to adventuring, stayed in the small boat whilst both sailors and I scoured the shoreline for any sign of life.

As we traversed some of the hills, two men appeared further down the shore, heading towards us from a wretched primitive hut on the horizon. I stood behind the two sailors as the strangers approached. After apparent small pleasantries, the two sailors pointed to the rowboat in the ship in the distance. The two strangers" clothes were in tatters; dirt cemented on their skin, hair unkept and knotted; solitude conspired to consume them. After the sailors assessed the situation, our smaller sailor stepped to the side and gestured for me to converse with the strangers. The five of us conversed in a mix of English and Swedish. As we translated to and fro between the languages, we learned that 8-10 miles up the north side of the coast lay, a small pilot's dwelling. We thanked the men, who were unable to provide neither hospitality or a larger boat and returned to the North Sea.

"Row, there?" The smaller sailor, whose aquamarine eyes smiled with his face, pointed in the direction of what I assumed to be north.

"Yes, we need to travel to Gothenburg."

"No, no, no," the weathered sailor interjected. "No Gothenburg. Too far. Sink." He pointed towards the open bay which occupied the space between Sweden and Norway. "Boat. Ship. No this." The smaller of the two banged on the tired old row boat, now with its tail-end in water.

I pulled more coins from my satchel handed the to the sailors. "For your troubles and his displeasure." Following my gaze to the far off boat, the small sailor took a breath, smiled and begun readying the small boat for departure. As the weather had calmed, the open bay appeared more hospitable than before. The poor captain.

*

The shore appeared grand as we sailed north, I should have enjoyed the two hours it took to reach it, but the fatigue which was visible in the countenances of the sailors. Instead of uttering a complaint, the two laughed about the possibility of the captain's taking advantage of a slight westerly breeze, to sail without them. Despite their good humour, I could not help growing uneasy when the shore promised no end to their toil. As Frances lay asleep in Marguerite's arms, and our luggage tucked beneath the nip of the boat, I closed my eyes and let my body rock forth and so with the lull and wisps of the smooth waters.

"Dose men," piped Marguerite, breaking the few minutes

of silence. “Said eight or zo miles madame?” I nodded in response and continued my search of the shoreline. The weathered sailor, who must have sensed our anxiety, hastened his speed in which he turned the oars.

Before I could determine what step to take in such a dilemma (for I could not bear to think of returning to the ship), the sight of a barge relieved me, and the sailors quickened towards it for information. Upon arriving, another stranger ordered us to pass some jutting rocks, where we should see a pilot’s hut.

Huge dark rocks, like the rude materials of creation formed a barrier of unwrought space between the sea and the shore. As we passed the darkened rocks and rounded the corner, a small hut appeared just shy of the shoreline. The sailors landed the boat, gestured for Marguerite and I to wait and they quickened their step to reach the cottage.

“‘Tis much different from France madame, don’t you think?” With the ashes of Paris burned into my skin, I shuddered at the thought of returning. The lack of both women and children on our current journey disconcerted me, but it was all in the mind. As I reflected on Frances’ first few months in this world, one sailor waved me over. I kissed Frances on the head and made my way towards the hut, traversing the sandy shoreline as I went.

“M’Lady,” said one sailor.

“Ma’am.” Two men, both taller in stature and in breadth than our sailors bowed their heads.

“Sir,” I curtsied to both of them—a formal but wasteful gesture.

“Your sailors have been, telling us about your directions. They say you want to travel to Gothenburg and Arundel?” The older of the two gestured to the north.

“Your English is convenient?” I smiled, thankful for not having to repeat our prior engagement.

“Of course ma’am. Under the direction of the lieutenant, our station requires us to, converse with travellers like yourselves from every part of Europe it seems and—”

“English is the common tongue,” the other pilot chimed in.

“Right. Yes you are right Olle. So, north?” said the first

man.

"Yes. North. We were making passage on the boat where these sailors make livings but the wind withheld us yesterday." The two sailors, one fixing a stone or a shell from his shoe, smiled in unison. "Their captain," I continued. "A principled and respectable man, hindered my maid's and I's attempt to emancipate ourselves from the boat. So we asked these lovely sailors to assist us."

"I see. Well," said the older of the two. "We cannot help you much. Without our lieutenant's orders we cannot abandon our posts," appearing to be a common theme in these areas, bar our two sailors. "But we can point you to his lodgings around those rocks."

"I don't want to trouble these sailors any more than we have, I do not suppose you could take us yourselves could you?" I imagined their captain sailing south without them. "If it's not too much trouble I'd appreciate the hospit—"

"I'm afraid not," said Olle. "Without the lieutenant's orders we cannot—"

"Two guineas?" Two more would not hurt to ensure safe passage for our emancipators. "Please."

"Ma'am. You see there?" He pulled on my shoulder and turned me so I could see the bay and our rowboat. "Past those jagged rocks you'll find the lieutenant's hut. He speaks English and he will help you on your journey, I am sure." As I examined the horizon for any signs of life, France's cries echoed across the bay causing my chest to tighten.

"We best be leaving, thank you," I turned back towards Olle and his companion, half curtsied, and flew down some wooden steps to the shoreline. The sailors said their thank you's to the pilots and followed my trail back down to the rowboat.

"Safe travels!" Olle shouted from their residence. Holding my hand up in reply, I started pushing the boat back out to sea, soaking my day dress and the bottom of my coat in salty water. Although warmer than I had expected, once inside the row boat the cool air reminded me that I was much farther north than I had been before. Smiling, the two sailors joined us and started to row towards the jagged rocks the sailors described.

As we neared the protuberance of rocks and manoeuvred around the cliff, a small boat approached us.

"The Lieutenant," said one of the sailors.

Wanting nothing more than our continued passage and for the sailors to return, I reassured Marguerite that we would be okay and had our baggage removed into the lieutenant's boat. As he could speak English, a previous parley was not necessary. Marguerite's respect for me could seldom keep her from expressing the fear on her face as I put ourselves into the power of a strange man. I thanked the sailors for their troubles and we sailed from each other in the opposite direction. The lieutenant, whose name eluded me, gestured towards his cottage and as I neared it, I was glad to spot a female figure. Unlike Marguerite, I hadn't been consumed with thoughts of theft, murder or other misfortunes that trouble a woman's mind, as sailors would say.

"Madame, Miss Marguerite, Frances," the lieutenant gestured towards my babe in Marguerite's arms. "My wife, Kajsa," she curtsied. "My grandson," he waved, "visiting from Denmark. My youngest daughter, Anna and her husband Jonas." The lieutenant's wife and his family stood in expectation as Marguerite, Frances and I exited his boat and entered the house. In what one would call rural elegance, little sprigs of juniper adorned the wooden floor (the custom of the country, as I later discovered) and the drawn curtains produced an agreeable sensation of freshness, softening the ardour of noon. "They do not speak a speck of English but I will translate as much as I can," the lieutenant, who had now removed some of his external wear, hurried into the small kitchen with his daughter.

Kajsa fixated on the fussing of Frances, smiling and cooing at the babe as is so traditional amongst our species - apparently transcending cultures. Within several minutes Kajsa, the lieutenant and his daughter spread all that the house afforded onto the whitest linen atop their table.

With the sensation of the waves flowing through my still body, I relaxed into a small sitting chair as the family fussed around the dining room. I had never quite seen a man so excited about dinner as they spread fish, milk, butter and cheese across the table to prepare for supper.

"Sit, my dear, sit here." The lieutenant pulled a chair from underneath the table and gestured towards it. I walked, though with a small sway in my step, and sat down.

"I know those legs too well my lady. I have lived many years here, seen many travellers, though two ladies are not our usual guests, I must say," at the comment, Marguerite, sans Frances, returned from upstairs and retreated to the sitting chair I had occupied. Though, before she sat down comfortably, I beckoned Marguerite to sit next to me. As Kajsa and Anna continued to fuss over the table and the lieutenant preoccupied in the kitchen, I took my chance.

"I'm in need of a favour from you," I said.

"Anything, madame," replied Marguerite. "Why are we whispering?"

"The lieutenant's name. He told me on the boat and I missed it somehow. May you ask?" Marguerite's shoulders softened and she giggled under her breath.

"You are too prideful madame," she said, still whispering. "It is okay not to know somezing. I know ze feeling wiz all your talks of politics and France. I know not even 'alf of what you say sometimes madame," Marguerite placed her hand on my shoulder and smiled again. Her eyes appeared a little older than I remember, a little less blue. "For you I vould do anything," I nodded and smiled in reply. Seasons were ever changing but Marguerite, her timid and kind soul, was now a constant in my life.

"Jonas!" The still-unknown-named lieutenant shouted and once Jonas returned from the upper level, the family joined Marguerite and I and the now full table. "So," said the lieutenant. "Please tell me more about your travels."

"Where does Miss Mary start?" said Marguerite, acknowledging the current state of affairs our lives had so found. "Pari, Ireland, Portugal with that, king of theirs!"

"France, well, Paris - one city I'd rather not be reacquainted with for a while," I said as Marguerite poured milk in both our glasses, a stark difference to the entrails of Fish we had acquainted ourselves prior.

"France?" The lieutenant and his family waited for both Marguerite and I to take our portions of cheese.

"Yes, in fact, in Paris," a shiver travelled down my spine.

"It was not an adventurous time. In fact it was quite the opposite."

"You do, uh, like, foreign?" the lieutenant looked towards his wife for reassurance. Her eyes widened and she shrugged. "Foreign lands?" he continued.

"Yes," I smiled and laughed under my breath. I too am accustomed to the intricacies of learning a new language. "This time it is business for my husband. He ha arranged a meeting of sorts in Gothenburg," Marguerite's feet brushed against mine. "But I know not the details of what we're here for, just that.."

"You have a beautiful home here...?" asked Marguerite.

"Noah," he replied. My eyes widened and Marguerite transfixed her eyes on me.

"Noah? Sir, is Gilbert Imlay your business acquaintance?" Noah shuffled back in his chair and his gaze fixed between myself and Marguerite.

"Mary? As in Mary Imlay?" I nodded. "My word. I have not received a letter for some time from you or Gilbert in some time. The last letter I received from him was in February. I have sent three since and none have been returned by reply."

"Curious," I said, looking at Marguerite. "When did Gilbert say he received the letter last? February was it not?"

"Yes madame," she replied.

"I have made my own inquiries. Gilbert did not inform me of your journey here?"

Noah looked to his wife and she shook her head. "Gilbert has not written in over a month." The inside of my stomach churned.

"The letters must have been lost," I said, placing a small piece of cheese on my plate.

"They must have," said Noah, whose eyes turned from inquiry to curiosity. "It is a pleasure to meet you Mary. Come now, let us all eat before we expire." As the family began their portions we bonded over shared adventures, though, Noah had explored more of Scandinavia than I could imagine being able to in a lifetime.

As we finished our lunch making talk of foreign lands and its inhabitants, Marguerite offered to help tidy and I retired upstairs to their guest apartment to change into something swarmer. As I was about done sorting through my clothes, the lieutenant and his wife knocked and at my call, entered the room.

"Madame, if you so wish to try our...delicacy," Noah pointed to a pot filled with some black liquid. "You are most welcome to." Kajsa placed a small holder, equivalent to a teacup on the dresser and poured the liquid into it.

"Oh thank you," I said and inhaled the odour; burnt earth. "Is it, coffee[1]?"

"Something of the sorts madam, we hope you like it," with an air of mystery they both left the room as quietly as they entered.

I returned downstairs, with the mysterious liquid in hand and the man of the house apologised for chatting, but declared he was so glad to speak English he could not stay out of conversation. He need not have apologised; I was equally glad of his company. I could only exchange smiles with the wife, as she was busy observing the make of our clothes. My hands, I found, had first led her to discover that I was the lady. Amongst the peasantry there is, however, so much of the simplicity of the golden age in this land of flint—so much overflowing of heart and fellow-feeling, that only benevolence and the honest sympathy of nature diffused smiles over my countenance when they kept me standing, regardless of my fatigue, whilst they dropped courtesy after courtesy.

The situation of their house was beautiful, though chosen for convenience. The master being the officer who commanded all the pilots on the coast, and the person appointed to guard wrecks, it was necessary for him to fix on a spot that would overlook the whole bay. As he had seen some service, he wore, not without a pride I thought becoming, a badge to prove that he had merited well of his country. He told me he had been paid in honour, for the stipend he received was little more than twelve pounds a year.

I was eager to climb the rocks nearest the house to view the country, and see whether the honest sailors had regained their ship. With the help of the lieutenant's telescope, I saw the vessel under way with a fair though gentle gale. The sea lay still and calm, its surface mirroring serenity, not a hint of disturbance in sight. My conductors had arrived and joined their captain. Resting ourselves on the earth's heavy rocks, the lieutenant and I watched over his keep.

"Do you like it here, lieutenant?" Noah, fixated with something on the ground, mumbled in reply.

"Ah.. yes it is, quite beautiful. It is open enough for travellers to regain supplies and protect the bay. My favourite place are by those rocks, you can obtain a view of the hills if you ascend high enough." He pointed to the giant, protruding rocks we had made acquaintance with earlier. They formed a suitable bulwark to the ocean. Come no further, they emphatically said, turning their dark sides to the waves to augment their idle roar. The view was desolate; still little patches of earth of the most exquisite verdure, enamelled with the sweetest wild flowers, promised the goats and a few straggling cows comfortable herbage.

"It is peaceful here," as we spoke, Noah closed his eyes and breathed in the salty air. "And I can see why you chose to stay here, even though some of your family moved away." I gazed around with rapture, and felt more of that spontaneous desire which gives credibility to our prospect of happiness than I had for a long, long time before. I forgot the terrors I had witnessed in France, which had cast gloom within my bones and suffocated the enthusiasm of my character. Too often damped by the tears of disappointed affection to be lighted up afresh, this simple fellow-feeling of nature enlarged my heart.

"Will you stay another day? Jonas wishes to show you the river." He gestured down to the idle house by the sea, where Jonas and Marguerite were seated outside in its small, overgrown garden.

"I cannot impose any longer than we already have lieutenant. Gothenburg calls and—"

"Oh nonsense," he said. "We can pay a visit to a family who live not far from here. The master of the house speaks English and will enjoy conversations like these as much as I do. He's the drollest dog in the country," he said as he laughed. I contemplated the idea as I brushed the earthen soil off my dress and walked a little further on towards the protective rocks, delighted with the beauty of the scene. After an hour or so relishing in the small warmth and calm wind, I rejoined the house and the lieutenant who, upon my arrival, informed me we were all to visit the other family who lived not far if I would like to accompany them.

Past the river, small streams and meadows, the largest country abode I had ever seen greeted us. I was introduced to a numerous family; but the father, from whom I was led to expect so much entertainment, was absent. The lieutenant consequently was obliged to be the interpreter of our reciprocal compliments. The phrases were awkwardly transmitted, it is true; but looks and gestures were sufficient to make them intelligible and interesting. They were overflowing with civility; but, to prevent their almost killing my babe with kindness, I was obliged to shorten my visit; and two or three of the girls accompanied us, bringing with them a part of whatever the house afforded to contribute towards rendering my supper more plentiful; and plentiful in fact it was, though I with difficulty did honour to some of the dishes, not relishing the quantity of sugar and spices put into everything. At supper my host told me bluntly that I was a woman of observation, for I asked him men's questions. It was at supper we made arrangements for our journey onwards the next day, unfortunately missing out on Jonas' river expeditions.

I could only have a car with post-horses, as I did not choose to wait till a carriage could be sent for to Gothenburg. The expense of my journey (about one or two and twenty English miles) I found would not amount to more than eleven or twelve shillings, paying, Noah assured me, generously. I gave him a guinea and a half. But it was with the greatest difficulty that I could make him take so much—indeed anything—for my lodging and fare. He declared that it was next to robbing me, explaining how much I ought to pay on the road. However, as I was positive, he took the guinea for himself; but, as a condition, insisted on accompanying me, to prevent my meeting with any trouble or imposition on the way.

After our dishes and supper, I retired to my apartment with regret. The night was so fine that I would gladly have rambled about much longer, yet, recollecting that I must rise very early, I reluctantly went to bed; but my senses had been so awake, and my imagination still continued so busy, that I sought for rest in vain.

Rising before six, I scented the sweet morning air; I had long before heard the birds twittering to hail the dawning day, though it could scarcely have been allowed to have departed. Nothing, in fact, can equal the beauty of the northern summer's evening and night, if night it may be called that only wants the glare of day, the full light which frequently seems so impertinent, for I could write at midnight well without a candle.

I contemplated all Nature at rest; the rocks, even grown darker in their appearance, looked as if they partook of the general repose, and reclined more heavily on their foundation. After our coffee and milk—for the mistress of the house had been roused long before us by her hospitality—my baggage was taken forward in a boat by my host, who rode along in the carriage with us, because the car could not safely have been brought to the house.

However, walking to join the carriage I fell without any warning onto the rocks, leaving my brain half confused. How I escaped with life I can scarcely guess.

1. I later found out coffee was prohibited in Sweden.

July 1st, 1795

My affectionate friend,

I labour in vain to calm my mind—my soul has been overwhelmed by sorrow and disappointment. Every thing fatigues me—this is a life that cannot last long. It is you who must determine with respect to futurity—and when you have, I will act accordingly—I mean, we must either resolve to live together, or part forever, I cannot bear these continual struggles.

But I wish you to examine carefully your own heart and mind; and, if you perceive the least chance of being happier without me than with me, or if your inclination leans capriciously to that side, do not dissemble; but tell me frankly that you will never see me more. I will then adopt the plan I mentioned to you—for we must either live together, or I will be independent forever.

My heart is so oppressed, I cannot write with precision—You know however that what I so imperfectly express, are not the crude sentiments of the moment—You can only contribute to my comfort (it is the consolation I am in need of) by being with me—and, if the tenderest friendship is of any value, why will you not look to me for a degree of satisfaction that heartless affections cannot bestow?

Tell me then, will you determine to meet me at Basle? I shall, I should imagine, be at——before the close of August; and, after you settle your affairs at Paris, could we not meet there?

God bless you!

Yours truly Mary.

Poor Fanny has suffered during the journey with her teeth.

July 3, 1795

Believe me (and my eyes fill with tears of tenderness as I assure you) there is nothing I would not endure in the way of privation, rather than disturb your tranquillity.—If I am fated to be unhappy, I will labour to hide my sorrows in my own bosom; and you shall always find me a faithful, affectionate friend.

I grow more and more attached to my little girl—and I cherish this affection without fear, because it must be a long time before it can become bitterness of soul. She is an interesting creature. On ship-board, how often as I gazed at the sea, have I longed to bury my troubled bosom in the less troubled deep; asserting with Brutus, "that the virtue I had followed too far, was merely an empty name!" and nothing but the sight of her—her playful smiles, which seemed to cling and twine round my heart—could have stopped me.

Love is a want of my heart. I have examined myself lately with more care than formerly, and find, that to deaden is not to calm the mind—aiming at tranquillity, I have almost destroyed all the energy of my soul—almost rooted out what renders it estimable.

Despair, since the birth of my child, has rendered me stupid—soul and body fading away.

I am now endeavouring to recover myself—and such is the elasticity of my constitution, and the purity of the atmosphere here, that health unsought for, begins to reanimate my countenance.

I have the sincerest esteem and affection for you—but the desire of regaining peace, (do you understand me?) has made me forget the respect due to my own emotions—sacred emotions, that are the sure harbingers of the delights I was formed to enjoy—and shall enjoy, for nothing can extinguish the heavenly spark.

Gothenburg July 1795

"If a woman is not prepared through education, she will cease to progress in her pursuit of knowledge," I rested my head against the carriage door, frustrated by the indifference and anxious solicitude of it all. Marguerite dismissed my gaze and instead focused on Frances, engrossed in her thumb sucking.

"I do not understand Madame, how de men vould accept women into their schools," said Marguerite.

"Denying woman her civil and political rights to education forces a woman to be a convenient slave for a tyrant of every denomination. Including that of our fathers." Small houses in rows appeared before us with their oil lanterns illuminating the small carriage. Gothenburg.

Built by the Dutch, Gothenburg appeared on all accounts, a clean and airy town. Built on swampy marshland with canals akin to Amsterdam, with Dutch architects and builders, it is said Gothenburg was a Dutch colony on Swedish soil. With the ability to fish opened by the canals, sailors once ruled its seas. Now, the opportunity to make a shilling from a sale was too good to ignore. Fishing made way for merchants, now the ones with the largest fortunes. We passed by inn after inn, with every merchant, man or both paying due respect to the bottle. Wafts of fish drifted along the intolerably bad streets, apparently still a concoction for their hearty meals.

The carriage driver sped down the road and arrived at the inn on the outskirts of the town. Eager to please, the inn-keeper awaited our arrival with two maids in waiting behind him.

"Mrs Imlay. I received word from your lieutenant you would be arriving, along with your servant." I had no capacity left in me to be entirely civil to the man.

"This is Marguerite. And she shall accompany me to my room and I will not hear another word of it."

"Ma'am, our guest rooms are equipped for one guest per room only." he looked Marguerite up and down as if she were a lamb come to slaughter. Both a woman and a maid, she was at the bottom of the list of nobility. "It can sleep downstairs with the rest of the maids." The two maids bowed their heads and bit their lips.

"Marguerite's employment is for my babe. I do not see it fitting she has to sleep downstairs. She will stay with me. I do not care if you need to arrange a bed on the floor." I brushed past his shoulder with Marguerite and Frances in tow, smiled at the two maids, and retreated to the inn. The inn-keeper muttered something in reply, but I did not care to listen.

We sought refuge from the other guests and retired to the drawing room. Marguerite, with Frances on her lap, mouthed the words, "Thank you' to me. We shared our common smile. In every state of life, we are the slaves of men. As Marguerite and I continued our conversation from the carriage, a rather well-dressed man appeared before me with Noah in tow.

"Ma'am," Noah stepped awkwardly in front of the man. "This—," he glanced sideways at the stranger, "man here is asking for your passport." My heart dropped to the bottom of my chest. I stared at Marguerite who had Frances now tied to her bosom, and she shook her head.

"Tror du att du bara kan gå in till min stad utan att betala? Du och dina," the stranger began shouting and raising his fists towards Marguerite, looking her up and down. "Kvinnlig slav." Noah stood between us and the man effacing his national character.

"Tillräckligt," said Noah. "Enough! Vi kan tillhandahålla hennes dokument imorgon. För nu, var iväg med dig." Noah took several steps towards us and guarded us from the man's arms. After several seconds, the man turned and walked away and Noah, both out of breath and in shock, slumped into the chair next to me.

"That—" Noah held his chest, "was the custom-house officer on the hunt for his money."

"You mean the town's money? How did he catch word of our arrival?"

Noah snorted. "I believe he thinks they are one and the same. They would have eyes and ears everywhere Mary."

I smiled and gestured to Marguerite to hand me Frances. Upon kissing her cheek, Noah explained our course of action.

"We shall make our way into the town centre tomorrow and produce whatever documents you have. When there, we can sort out the man and his mission to siphon money from all of your pockets."

"I, I mean—we—were not provided with a passport. We haven't entered any great town since arriving from England. I was told I could obtain one in Gothenburg." Noah smiled at Frances playing with the small damp curls dangling around my face. "But thank you for helping us." Noah nodded.

"I promised I would protect you both," he said, his smile widening as Frances looked up at him and mirrored his expression. The wind had whipped through her hair, leaving it windblown and untamed from the carriage journey. I brushed it out of her face and kissed her on the forehead. "From highway men an imposition."

"That man is one and the same," Marguerite interjected. We laughed together and let our bodies relax into the chairs, now safe from all custom-house officers and untoward men in our immediate vicinity. Dust lined every crevice and crack, with the small candles illuminating far too little to see the drawing room's darkened corners. The iron hearth was half-filled with soon to be expired logs, teetering on the edge of life in both size and energy.

As the evening wore on, we conversed about Gothenburg and Noah educated on some of its history. By later evening, the town bell in the distance struck nine, Noah stood up, tipped his lieutenant's hat towards us and retired to his room down the hallway.

*

"Ma'am?" Marguerite pointed towards an enormous pile of fish on one stall. I touched the scaly head of the market fish as contempt and disgust befriended Marguerite's soft face. One of the market sellers leaning against a railing piqued up at our presence.

"Have other wares if one is interested. Sugar. Spices. Trinkets and—"

"Trinkets?" asked Marguerite. ""What kind of trinkets?"

"This and that. I even have some of the ship dat sunk off de coast," my eyes widened. I leaned in closer towards him.

"What was the name of the ship?" The seller stepped closer to us and pointed at a small piece of wood.

"Maria, she was called madam," the market seller tipped his hat towards us. "Does that interest you? We have other items if that does not—"

"And when did it sink?"

"You ask a lot of questions for a lady."

"When did it sink?"

"November," he replied. "Here." The seller fumbled around several pieces of wood and handed one to me. It was weathered, as though it had settled for years beneath the water. "Did you hear?" he whispered. "The Maria is said to have had silver on it, from France! I could not believe my ears when we were told she had sunk." He held up some smaller items of what appeared to be small white shards. "Parts of her cargo." I moved closer, inspecting the small jagged pieces further. "Porcelain, true as the sky is blue." Marguerite looked up at the sky above us. A few seconds later it started speckling with rain. I pulled Marguerite's arm and stepped away from the seller.

"Madame?" We left the seller before Marguerite could ask more questions and made our way towards a small cobblestone street, far quieter than the general market. Marguerite lent around the corner and took another glimpse at the man selling the items.

"I thought the Liberte sunk in November?" asked Marguerite. "And the seller said the ship's name was Maria."

"Apparently," I replied. I joined Marguerite and looked at the seller, who had resumed rearranging his piles of trinkets, items and his separate stand of fresh fish. The odour seemed to penetrate every piece of fresh air along the docks.

Marguerite pulled Frances closer to her chest as we left the markets behind us and made our way along the cobblestone street into the main part of Gothenburg.

"You are braver than I," she patted Frances to lull her asleep who, in the course of our small conversation, began closing her eyes to the world.

"Let us explore the town before we leave." Cod and haddock, salmon and trout, glistened and silently called to passers-by. Vendors and merchant's men extolled the virtues of their particular catch and haggled over prices. The marketplaces themselves, a riot of activity, with merchants and shoppers alike jostling for space and bargaining over goods. Barrels of salted fish, wooden crates of shellfish, and stacks of drying cod hanging from hooks overhead each stall. Gutting knives and the sounds of fish flapped on wooden tables filled the air, along with the unintelligible chatter in their foreign accents.

Despite the frenetic energy of the markets, there is a certain sense of order to the proceedings. The vendors are proud of their wares, and take care to present them in the best possible light. And the customers, for their part, relish the opportunity to select the finest fish for their meals and families. Rows of fish continued throughout the canal, of which was filled with barges and small boats transporting goods to and from the city's port.

"Was your bread sweet this morning, madame?" said Marguerite. The sugar from this morning's bread had not yet left my mouth. "Last night the leftover salmon from their supper permeated the kitchen this morning," we giggled together as neither I nor Marguerite genuinely enjoyed fish, dried and smothered in salt or half-alive.

"I did it find it sweet, true. Far sweeter than the bakeries of London and Paris," I said. "Salmon though, is for the merchants and dare I say, nobility. What about the poor?" I grabbed her arm and pointed towards a bakery nestled in amongst a row of log houses. "I was told by an acquaintance from St. Paul's that most of this northern population eat rye bread. Baked only once per year."

"Once per year?" I nodded in reply.

A small group of children from one of the cobblestone alleys rounded the corner and almost tumbled us over. "Wages are low," I said, trying to remain upright whilst traversing between the small humans. "Necessity must teach them to pilfer, whilst servility renders them false and boorish." Marguerite's gaze fixed on the locals who gathered beneath the charming, multi-coloured two-storey houses.

"They look so thin," she whispered in my ear. "I feel sorry for them, madame." I nodded again in reply and stared once again at Frances. Gothenburg was separated into small, but distinct, commercial districts. Scotch, French and Swedish, but the Scotch, I believe, were the most successful.

"The commerce business with France since the war appears lucrative, and has enriched the merchants, I am afraid, at the expense of the other inhabitants, by raising the price of the necessaries of life."

Shortly after observing the locals, we found a secluded part of the dock that offered a clear view of the city, canals and the distant North Sea.

"Still," I said. "The men stand up for the dignity of man by oppressing the women." I leaned back against the railing, taking in the view of Gothenburg common. Frances, still asleep in Marguerite's free arm, looked at peace with her situation.

"I was talking to one maid from our first evening and I asked 'er what it was like to live 'ere as a maid at ze inn," joining me in admiring the city, Marguerite took a deep breath before speaking. "She said zat, err, during winter zey 'ave to take ze linen down to ze river to wash it in ze cold water. Their 'ands end up cut by ze ice, crack and bleed." I winced at the thought.

"One would assume this is a labour left solely to those poor drudges," I said. Marguerite looked down at Frances, nodding.

"The men wouldn't disgrace themselves by carrying a tub to lighten their burden I can assure you. It'd be their labour and theirs alone." I kissed France's forehead, knowing fullwell of the world I had brought her into. Understanding my intent, Marguerite grabbed my hand and squeezed it.

"Are you happy?" she asked me. "Here?" I paused for a moment and once again my eyes returned to Frances.

"Happiness is illusive," Marguerite's smile faded. "Banishing pleasure does not exclude pain, I know, and for her," I gestured towards Frances. "My little frolicker brings me a strange, natural feeling within." Marguerite's smile returned at the mention of the babe in which she held.

"And England?" We both looked towards what we

assumed was South West. Pondering for a moment, she held her words in her throat before softly letting them exist in the space between us. She nodded in the direction of my home. "Will ze Révolution Française spread M? To England?" If I was correct in my assumption of her manner of speaking, there was a hint of hopefulness.

"Uneasy lies the head that wears the crown," I observed once more the happenings of the surrounding dock. "And respect for nobility has decreased, except amongst themselves," Marguerite sniggered at my sentiment, as I looked past Marguerite's shoulder watched a poor woman carry a load of wares along the street far heavier than she ought to. Two small girls played with each other on the corner of the street.

"Madame?" Marguerite followed my gaze towards the young woman, whose full skirt brushed against the dirty ground.

"But I for one have no interest in, George," I looked back at Marguerite as Frances stirred against the cool wind. Standing side by side, both enamoured by the docks and the small fortress that occupied the mouth of the city's water entrance, Marguerite placed her head on my shoulder and nestled Frances in between us.

"I'm 'appy, madame," I rested my head against hers. "Admittedly," she continued, sighing. "I miss Paris but I 'ave you and Frances," I wrapped my arm around her shoulder, pulling her and Frances closer. I had never noticed it before, but she smelled of fresh cotton and flowers. "Come now ma'am, Noah is expecting you." Marguerite let go of our embrace and walked towards the intolerable inn we were compelled to call home for another evening. We bid farewell to the docks and canals and continued our journey through the vibrant streets.

"Madam," Noah tipped his hate once more to me. "Miss Marguerite, Mary and I will be back a little later." I glanced at Marguerite and nodded, who then proceeded several paces in front of us towards the inn.

"It is preferable for Miss Marguerite to stay here in town," said Noah.

"She can—"

“Trust me,” he said with more finality than I had heard him use. “I need to talk to you about the Liberte and I would rather not trouble her mind. She can remain in the inn for the afternoon with Frances.” Noah rested against the inn’s wooden fence, which had long overstayed its welcome in the garden. “Frances appears content with her.” Noah’s weathered appearance shown through even more in the sunlight. In cloud he was at one with the landscape, blending in with Sweden’s frigid environment. In the presence of sunlight, his disposition transformed. A visible sense of lightness and joy radiated from him. It was akin to the contentment of an aging hound, taking delight in the simple pleasures of walking on freshly cut grass and feeling the comforting warmth of the earth. I watched through the window as Marguerite and Frances ascended the stairs and disappeared into the building’s heart.

“I have frequently, with indignation, heard gentlemen declare that they would never allow a servant to answer them; and ladies of the most exquisite sensibility have in my presence forgotten that their attendants had human feelings and forms,” I said. “If you are so wondering why I have a fondness for her.” I smiled at Noah who was rustling through his coat for something.

“Is she family? A cousin, perhaps?”

“No, but the closest I have to me at this moment. Shall we?” We walked a few paces towards his carriage and climbed inside. “I do not know a more agreeable sight than to see servants part of a family,” I continued. Noah grinned as the carriage moved onward. “By taking an interest in their concerns, you inspire them with one for yours. Lately, she’s taken an interest in the goings on of her home. France.”

“In your letters you never spoke about France,” the window from the carriage gave view to the winding canals, meandering their way through Gothenburg. “Your papers and passports were arranged this morning, if you were postulating on the matter,” Noah joined my gaze to the landscape.

“I assumed you were reacquainted with our evening friend then?” I replied, laughing slightly as the carriage shook us too and fro.

"Though, he seemed less intoxicated this morning and dare I say friendly," we laughed together as the driver hastened his speed out of the airy town.

*

The house in which we so arrived by foot, after leaving the carriage and its driver an hour down the hill, had improved land about it. Nestled amongst pine-clad rocks, a blue lake surrounded the northern side. The rolling meadows from the south swirled around the house as though the ground itself spawned it naturally. Nothing appeared forced or out place. One recess, particularly grand and solemn amongst the towering cliffs, had a rude stone table and seat placed in it, that might have served for a Druid's haunt, whilst a placid stream below enlivened the flowers on its edges, where light-footed elves would gladly have danced their airy rounds. The beauties of nature appear to me now even more alluring than in my youth.

As Noah and I walked together towards the cliff's edge, the solitary house behind us - the icy northern sea before us, I allowed my body to relax its muscles against the air, frigid and tense like the sea below it. I rarely let myself calm like an ocean on a summer's morning.

"I must implore you to be safe on your journey north," the hour's silence had been broken. Although it was nearing late evening, the northern sky still shone, illuminating the cliffs and rocks around us. Noah furrowed his face.

"Safe?" My eyes scanned the surrounding environment. Barren. "I am always safe." I scratched at my neck slightly and loosened my dress so I could breathe easier.

"Yes," he said. "But I fear for Marguerite and Frances. The northern countryside is a cold and barren place, not fit for a babe and your timid servant. May I, with respect ma'am, implore that Frances and Marguerite stay at the inn and remain in Gothenburg whilst you attend to the ship business alone. I can arrange a weekly rate at the inn for her and another servant to accompany you further north." I smiled at his care and kindness. Knowing the current happenings of France and the business I was here to attend to, I agreed that it most probably was the safest option for us all.

"I am no stranger to travelling alone," again interrupting his thoughts and worries. "I shall be okay." I touched his shoulder and he smiled in return, as he continued to battle the raging current of anxiousness inside his head. "Another servant won't be necessary," I nodded. "I shall be fine." Noah walked a few metres towards a brutish boulder that overshadowed its smaller counterparts that littered the cliffs. Come no further the boulder implored.

"Something bothers you, or am I mistaken?" Noah begun to kick small stones under his feet and refused a reply. "Whatever it is, you can tell me. I have an idea that you did not bring me this way to look at a house one would presume." I made comfort on the shivering earth; the northern summer made small attempt to curtail winter's icy grip on the land.

"May I—" he kicked a stone underneath his shoe again, I half expected him to announce his affection for me, for what else would leave a man so unwilling to speak? "May I impose a thought on you?"

I half smiled, though still unsure of the direction of his conversation. "Spare the pleasantries Noah, do go on." He hesitated on his words as though they were caught in his throat like Marguerite had done earlier with me.

"Whilst you and Marguerite explored the markets this morning I made more inquiries as to the whereabouts of the Liberte and—" he turned from my gaze to the vast ocean. "All I could discover is that a ship made port in Stromstad called the Maria. I spoke to someone from the north, someone from the town."

"Stromstad?"

"North of here, though I could not tell you how far in a coach. But, Mary, he informed me there is a ship making repairs there, a ship called the Maria."

I folded my arms and looked towards the ocean with Noah. "And when did the ship arrive in Stromstad?"

"January of this year and it has been there ever since."

"And does it have–"

"Three masts? Yes, three masts." With a relentless fury, a wave crashed into the rocks below us and sent plumes of salty mist high into the evening air as the meaning of our conversation became clear. The solitude of the place around us was palpable, with only the mournful cries of seabirds and the crashing of the waves to break the silence.

Here, one can feel the weight of their own insignificance, standing alone against the elements and the vast expanse of the sea, as if the whole world were nothing but a fleeting moment. The cold, unyielding rocks and the wild, untamed sea mock any attempts at human control or mastery, reminding us of our own fragility.

"She is a cold an unyielding beast that has swallowed far many sailors than you or I would be capable of reasoning with," said Noah, gesturing to the ocean. "Mary may I ask," he breathed deeply and approached me in a fatherly manner, as if to soothe a child. "Gilbert dispatched you with no letters, no information and left you to your wares?" Noah fixed me with his gaze and awaited my reply. My chest burned and my eyes began to sting like a raging flame. "Mary?"

I pushed against the bottom of my throat in an attempt to stop the burning sensation. "Can we return to the carriage? I am finding it quite—"

"Mary, answer my question. Did Gilbert supply you with any information to hunt down his ship? Did he tell you where I live?" I pushed further into my neck to focus my thoughts. My chest became heavy and my shoulders felt like as if they were trying to separate themselves from my neck. I shook my head and a bead of a tear formed in one my eyes. "You travelled here, to Scandinavia, with no information, other than you are looking for the Liberte. He has not accompanied you to do his business and he did not inform me that you were arriving, let alone would require assistance?"

My mouth turned dry. "He is busy in London and..." I could not find any more words. He loved me and that was all that mattered.

"Let us return to the carriage." We walked the hour back to the carriage and upon our arrival, opened its door and gestured for me to join him on our return to Gothenburg.

On our return journey, Noah recounted the tale of how

he had first encountered Gilbert several years prior, during the American's tour of the Scandinavian lands for commercial purposes. Noah himself was a solitary man, possessing an inquisitive mind and an eye for profit, and as such he traded in illicit goods and commodities on occasion from his pilot's hut. It was through these underground dealings that he had initially come into contact with Gilbert, who proved to be a shrewd businessman with a keen eye for a profitable enterprise.

Together, Noah and Gilbert had formed a lucrative partnership, with Noah procuring black market wares and selling them to Gilbert for transport and subsequent sale in England and France. The partnership proved to be highly advantageous for both parties, and their dealings had remained successful and profitable for some time.

"I was raised a poor man and I can assure you I have no intention dying the same way," he said.

As murmurs of revolution in France spread northward, merchants grew increasingly anxious, and for good reason. With the outbreak of war between France and England, the once-lucrative trade routes that France had established with their northern counterparts were blockaded by the British. Flying under the neutral Norwegian flag that we chose in Le Havre, the ship, armed with small French cargo made its way north where Noah claimed he was responsible for receiving this vessel in Gothenburg.

"But as you know, or maybe assumed, Liberte and its two commanders in Peter Ellefsen and Coleman, never showed here in Gothenburg."

"Gilbert never mentioned to me any of this, only that it never reached Gothenburg as you mentioned." I said between his stories.

"And now my dear Mary, you are here to find the ship, find the captain and find the cargo. For Gilbert?"

"Well, yes," I replied. "The plan is to use any of the money we can recover to go to America."

"The money you recover? To America?" he asked.

"Yes, Gilbert said he has some land there he wants to build a small house on. Fanniken would love it there, far from England and this mess of Europe." The carriage came to slow stop and the driver opened our door.

"Let me," said Noah, as he exited the carriage and helped me down onto the street. We bid the driver a goodbye and made the short walk to the inn by foot, glowing in the distance. The town was alight with both flame and fiddle as music hummed along its streets. A crescent hung in the darkened sky above us, wooing me to stray abroad. It was not a silvery reflection of the sun, but glowed with all its golden orange splendour. It reminded me of leftover oils that Henry would be covered in.

"I will talk to another acquaintance of mine then, they can take you north in the morning," he said as he slowed his pace further. "It shall be easier to join a carriage north rather than go alone. I'll see to it that is arranged also," he tipped his hat towards me and dashed past the gate to retrieve his wares from the inn.

As I waited for Noah, I stared at some of the inn's inhabitants through a small window pane and noticed Marguerite tidying the small supper room. Few like to be seen as they really are, like Thomas, but Marguerite, with her undisguised confidence, which, to uninterested observers, would almost border on weakness, is the charm, nay the essence of our friendship; all the bewitching graces of childhood again appearing. Though timid often in unfamiliar occasions, such as the possibility of brutish pirates and occasions of strange men, she was fierce with her love and tenderness of my Frances, my Fannikin. She occupies her mind not with frivolous thoughts like dress and embroidery but converses in politics and so alike. When melancholy takes possession of me, when the world has disgusted me, and friends have proved unkind, she is a bulwark against idle thoughts and loneliness. Words are easy, like the wind; faithful friends are hard to find. It is with her I...

"Ah, here it is," Noah walked out of the inn and handed me a small parchment paper. "Open this when you arrive. It is assurance from me to whoever you need that your intensions are honourable." I scrunched the paper into a small section of my dress and nodded. "Someone will be here for you in the morning. Goodbye Mary," I nodded again and he flew past me into a parked transport carriage and closed the door as it pulled away into the evening.

"Thank you!" I shouted, the sound of my voice reverberating in the silence. Leaning out of the carriage window, Noah glanced at me with the same eyes that Joseph did when I left. He tipped his hat towards the air and nodded. Everything will be okay.

On the road to Stromstad July 1795

The following morning I left Frances and Marguerite behind me in Gothenburg and travelled in the company of two gentlemen, one of whom was Noah's acquaintance, the other was his German servant. Not intending to make a long stay, I gave Marguerite several coins and wares for the followingf week and so departed.

As the roads were barren, even at the height of day, Noah sent a courier the night before to requisition horses for every post along our journey. Unlike the road towards Gothenburg and the inn I first made acquaintance with, our route towards Stromstad was good and pleasant.

The first night of our travels forced us to retire at an inn in Stenungsund. The beds, although they appeared to be well endowed with down, felt as though I was sinking into a grave when I entered one. Placed in a sort of box, I expected to be suffocated before morning. Even in summer I am told that residents here sleep in down. How would one bare it in the heat?

I postulate that Sweden's inhabitants are afraid of the outside air, nay, never feel the warmth of it; for every building I enter has shut its windows not wanting the frigid air to impregnate the unfelt warmth inside. I couldn't exist in rooms this boarded in winter. Noah's acquaintance, in limited English, explained that rooms are only heated by a stove, with wood fed to the fiery monster twice a day.

The following morning, upon joining my carriage company for a breakfast serving of spiced rye bread, we were so informed that we'd not find a tolerable inn past Kvistrom, our destination for the second day of our travels. I partook in the custom of separating the dry bread and swallowed the pieces and attempted to hold back my disgust. One of the gentlemen in company, passed me a small travel jar from his coat pocket and attempted to hide a smile from appearing on his face. Motioning with his hands, he instructed me to open the jar.

"Ata," he paused for a few moments as though he was reading an invisible book behind me. "Ata...no," he paused again.

"Eat?" I asked.

He smiled and nodded. "Ja," I held the jar up to the early morning window light and found small dried herrings inside. I could not quite decide what would be worse. Ingesting herring that most probably died months before or suffer the humiliation of rejecting a kind stranger's offer to help. I decided the former was the most polite thing I could do.

Suffering from my affliction of kindness towards strangers my stomach became a sister to the raging North Sea that beat against the cliffs on the western side of our carriage. Consequences of politeness that my sex adheres to, too I shall suffer.

The road on which we travelled was on the declivity of a rocky mountain. At the bottom of it, a river hastened forward to reach the ocean, whilst on the right of us a thickly wooded forest rose towards the sky. The loveliest banks of wild flowers variegated the scene before us and promised to exhale odours to add to the sweetness of the air. But promise is all it was, for I was soon informed by the English-speaking of the two in my carriage that farmers used herrings as manure after the oil had been extracted.

As the two gentlemen continued to converse between themselves, my stomach suddenly lurched against the cliffs of my abdomen and I beckoned the carriage driver to stop. "Ma'am?" I shoved the door open and half-knocked the driver over in his attempt to open the door from the outside. Within seconds, I tasted herring for the second time and the road became a plate for my insides.

After I regained my wits and sensibility and the ocean inside me calmed, we continued on towards Tanumshede and by sunset we reached a charming retreat nestled by a stream. With great difficulty and with limited privacy, I performed my daily ablutions and later retired to my bed, full of a tolerable supper which replaced the former home of dried herrings, now reacquainting themselves with the earth by the roadside somewhere. Alas, at least the birds had a hearty meal if they were to happen across it. I shuddered at the thought.

We continued further north the following day, and the sea and nature consequently appeared ruder and ruder, the bones of our world exposed against the icy northern air. Still it was sublime. Another day passed and the sun appeared afraid to shine. The wild flowers disappeared in the meadows entirely. The farm houses, all but made of the woods around them, kept the icy cold out. The absence of children was noted, as such the absence of any vegetable growing in their farms.

Advancing towards Quistram, as the sun was beginning to decline, I was particularly impressed by the beauty of the situation. A mossy herbage and vagrant firs covered the road and at the bottom, a river straggled amongst the recesses of stone. As we drew nearest to the town, the loveliest banks of wild flowers variegated the prospect, and promised to exhale odours to add to the sweetness of the air, the purity of which you could almost see, but alas, not smell. The aforementioned herrings spread over the patches of earth destroyed every other deligh in the air.

A combination of bleak wind, grey rocks and icy breeze fought the idea that it was indeed supposed to be towards the end of summer. If the sun ever shone here, the stones would hardly warm. If the first dwelling of man happened to be in a spot like the one before our eyes, it is no wonder he was tempted to run for the sun in the south. We arrived early the second evening at a little village called Quistram, where we determined to pass the night.

After a tolerable supper—for it is not easy to attain fresh provisions on the road—I retired, to be lulled to sleep by the murmuring of a stream, of which I with great difficulty obtained sufficient to perform my daily ablutions.

The last battle between the Danes and Swedes, which gave new life to their ancient enmity, was fought at this place 1788; only seventeen or eighteen were killed, for the great superiority of the Danes and Norwegians obliged the Swedes to submit; but sickness, and a scarcity of provision, proved fatal to their opponents on their return.

It would be easy to search for the particulars of this engagement in the publications of the day; but as this manner of filling my pages does not come within my plan, I probably should not have remarked that the battle was fought here, were it not to relate an anecdote which I had from good authority.

The sun appeared afraid to shine, the birds ceased to sing, and the flowers to bloom; but the eagle fixed his nest high amongst the rocks, and the vulture hovered over this abode of desolation. The farm houses, in which only poverty resided, were formed of logs which attempted to keep off the cold and drifting snow: out of them the inhabitants seldom peeped, and the sports or prattling of children was neither seen or heard. The current of life seemed congealed at the source: all were not frozen, for it was summer, you remember; but everything appeared so dull that I waited to see ice, in order to reconcile me to the absence of gaiety.

As the verdure meadows slowly turned into fields of rock it appeared as though we had reached the frontier town of Sweden. Stromstad.

*

The town of Stromstad, built on or under large rocks, was absent of trees, grass and other various forms of nature. A steeple (for what is a church without a steeple), towered amongst the collection of small houses. With our carriage parked and the horses fed, we were most hospitably welcomed into the home of a local merchant, the little sovereign of the place, because he was by far the richest, though not the mayor. The two gentlemen and myself were introduced to a very fine family. Women of youth stared at me as we entered their living room.

"Hallå," I smiled and hastened my way towards the edge of the room of their house. "Talar du Franska? Svenska?" I asked, towards the merchant of the house.

"Je peux parler Français," the three young women, perplexed with the exchange between their father and I, sat in amusement.

"Je voyage en Norvège. Ces deux messieurs," I pointed towards my two companions. "Séjournent ici à Stromstad." His family smiled at our continued exchange though bereft of understanding.

"Merci de nous laisser rester Monsieur. J'irai demain en boat et je vous quitterai alors." The merchant pointed towards the small stairs behind me.

"Votre chambre est là-haut. Les deux messieurs avec

qui je parlerai bientôt," he said. One of the young women grabbed one of my hands and begun walking me up the stairs towards my room.

"De rien." Exhausted from the road, I nestled comfortably into the small bed with the sound of the sea lulling me to sleep.

Arriving at Gothenberg from Hull

Gothenberg to Stromstad

July 14, 1795

Gilbert.

When you first met me, I was not this lost. I could still confide, for I opened my heart to you, of this only comfort you have deprived me. Whilst my happiness, you tell me, was your first object. Strange want from you. Your not writing is cruel and my reason is perhaps disturbed by constant wretchedness.

You haven't written to me in Gothenburg. Very well, act as you wish. There is nothing I fear nor care for. When I see whether I can obtain the money I came here about, I will not trouble you with letters you do not reply to. I am convinced, if you give yourself leave to reflect, you will also feel, that your conduct to me, so far from being generous, has not been just. I mean not to allude to factitious principles of morality; but to the simple basis of all rectitude. However I did not intend to argue.

Stromstad Sweden 15th July 1795

I arose for breakfast with the two gentlemen and the English-speaking of the two, who had overheard my discussion with the carriage driver yesterday, suggested we should "Peep into Norway," as the distance was only three Swedish miles.

"I need to visit the port before I leave, there is something I need to see there."

"We shall wait then," replied the gentleman. "This is what Noah mentioned?" I nodded in reply and tidied myself of breakfast crumbs. "We can come with you if you like?"

"No not, it won't be necessary," I replied. "No one knows I am here, I think I shall be safe for now. If I do not return in ten minutes, go on to Norway without me." I thanked the family, left the house and made the short walk to Stromstad's port, located on the western side of the commerce town.

To my utter surprise, a three-mast ship stood tall in grandeur at the far side of the port, though it appeared as though it had several injuries to one of her sides as well as a damaged mast. As I approached the lapping water's edge, a tall, rather brutish man made way in my direction. I paced for a few moments until he approached.

"Ja? Vad är det du vill ha?" he said.

"Do you speak English, perhaps? Or French? Franska?" I said, gripping my elbows with my hands for support.

"Yes. Little. I help?" he asked.

"Are you the harbour master here?"

He made himself appear taller and looked up and down the port. "Yes. Who's asking?"

"Mary," I said. "I am heading to Norway tomorrow on business. But I am inquiring about the ship you have there."

"Yes?"

Gripping my elbows harder, I swallowed and found some strength and composure. "Is it," I paused. "For sale? Is it for sale?"

"For sale? Sell? The ship?" He turned towards its bow and scratched his eyebrow. After a few moments of silence, he shook his head and his tired-brown eyes narrowed into mine. "No. No sale. Repairs. Was, uh, damaged by rocks."

"Is the owner here? Or his representative? I would like to inquire as to the..." waiting for his answer I took a few steps and let the water lap the bottom of my dress.

"The Maria Margrethe." He answered.

"Ah yes, the Maria's potential for sale," I said. "She is a beauty, though I'm sure the damage will be repaired by those good people in good time." He smiled at the mention of his workers, who, by observation, continued to work even though their master was absent.

"Yes," he nodded. "But no. Ellefsen. Not here." In my attempt to not arouse suspicion I stared at the bluish-grey water for if it were possible, my stomach would have otherwise lurched itself out of my body. Ellefsen.

"Ah," I said still inspecting its bow. "A shame. It looks as though this ship has been at war no?" I said.

"Rocks, yes," he said as a small smile appeared at the corner of his lips. "But she makes, uh, good repairs now," he pointed to a small group of men working on one of its sides. "They are good fixers and strong." He gave a little hearty laugh, tapped his biceps and nodded.

"How long will she be making repairs for?"

"Three months more," he replied. I retreated from the water, thanked the harbour master for my inquiries and made my way towards the small path next to the water. The ship before me appeared weathered and damaged and several planks of wood missing from its side. The sails were in tatters and several of its windows were smashed. The starboard side appeared to be in the worst condition, as though it had come in contact with some type of stationary object. Bereft of a plan, I decided the best course of action was to join the gentlemen in Norway by road and ferry for a day adventure until I could formulate one myself.

Upon returning to the merchant's house, I discovered that they had awaited my return. I had never travelled through Sweden, but one of my companions assured me that I should not there find anything superior, if equal, to the wild grandeur of the views I would encounter on our way. Verdantly green meadows and beautiful lakes surrounded us in every part of our journey. We scaled mountainous cliffs and traversed around rivers covered in pines. By late noon, after waiting an hour for horses to arrive at our post, we had arrived at the ferry.

The difference in manners between the two sides of the river was almost noticeable as soon as we arrived. Norwegians seemed more industrious—wealthier. The Swedes (for neighbours are seldom the best friends) accuse the Norwegians of dishonesty, and they retaliate by bringing a charge of hypocrisy against the Swedes. The proximity of the two countries and their previous circumstances rendered both unjust, speaking from their feelings rather than reason.

Travellers who require that every nation should resemble their native country had better stay at home. It is absurd to blame a people for not having that degree of personal cleanliness and elegance of manners which only refinement of taste produces. Inquiry and discussion. This spirit of inquiry is a characteristic of the present century.

Fredericshall, where Charles XII of Sweden joined the mortal coil from the trenches of warfare, stood as protector from the Swedish in the South and the East. Fredriksten Fort, where the city became hostage to several sieges, sat proudly on the southern side of the river and overlooked the two islands and commodious bay. I was told by the English gentlemen, that upon the last siege by Charles in the earlier years of our century they set fire to their houses to prevent occupation, like the self-degradation that some of those of our sex attend to when met with unwanted mal-intention of the opposite sex. Uninhabitable is their intention, and so too was the intent of the some 4000 residents of Fredericshall.

As my companions wandered about the town I made fruitless inquiries at the harbour as to the whereabouts of Ellefsen, it was as though I were attempting to grasp smoke rising from an evening fire.

As the White Queen of the Night reigned in small splendour, we made our return journey to Stromstad. The darkness competed for the sky against the sun that loitered just below the horizon, which illuminated the cliffs that shaded her. The balmy air freshened into morning, with the chirping birds who sensed rather than saw the advancing day. The light grey sky ushered in purples, pinks and orange hues and I was sorry to lose the soft watery clouds which preceded them, which excited a kind of expectation that made me almost afraid to breathe, lest I should break the charm.

I saw the sun—and sighed. At the morning glare, one of my companions awoke and realised the carriage had mistaken the road for Stromstad. We backtracked and reached the small port by no less than five in the morning.

A dish of coffee and fresh linen recruited my spirits, and I set out again for Norway, leaving the ship for its repairs. This time I I'd attempt to land much higher up the coast than our expedition the previous day. Shrouded in thick morning mist, the boat I was to travel in seemed too small to cross the Northern Sea. But, I was assured safe passage by both the pilot of the vessel and another English passenger, who had both sensed my worry. Wrapping my great coat round me, I found some old sails at the bottom of the boat and laid down, its motion rocking me to rest. Discourteous waves interrupted my slumber now and then and obliged me to rise and feel a solitariness that was not so soothing as that of the past night. By midday, the pilot beckoned me to join him at the helm, and so began instructing me on what I should have occupied my time with whilst visiting Stromstad.

"Lejonkällan? You did not visit?" I shook my head. "De vater dere is a cure for your ails," he winked at me and continued explaining Stromstad in depth.

As I listened to the pilot tell extraordinary tales of previous voyages, I noticed the absence of tides and, what appeared to be a consequence; no sandy beach on the distance shores. Perhaps this observation has been made before; but it did not occur to me till I saw the waves beating against the bare rocks, without ever receding to leave a sediment to harden. By four o'clock, and now learned in northern Swedish history, we had made shore in a town called Laurvik, situated on the southwestern coast of Norway.

As the Norwegians not often saw travellers I became a fixation for foreign eyes. So curious they were, I was half tempted to write on a paper, for public inspection, my name, from where I came, where I was going, and what was my business. Some acted as though they approached nobility - for though they'd be horribly mistaken - and offered to assist me with my wares. Others, less timid, inquired after my wants.

Not having brought a carriage with me, as I assumed I'd meet one once landed, I was detained whilst good people of a local inn set about to their acquaintances in an attempt to procure me a carriage. After a small supper of fish was prepared on my account, I attempted small pleasantries and touched a small sliver of food. Only a few were brave enough to attempt English.

Not an hour or so later, a rude sort of cabriole was at last found accompanied by a driver, half drunk. A Danish sea captain and his mate would also be joining our journey north. As there wasn't enough room for two in the cabriole, the former of the two was to ride on horseback, at which he was not very expert, whilst his mate joined me in the cabriole.

"Have you travelled to Tonsberg before?" I attempted to ask my young mate, who sat the furthest away from my rump as he could be. A blank stare replied and the realisation set in that it would be a pleasant and quiet journey ahead. As the driver mounted behind to guide our horses, he prepared to flourish the whip behind us over our shoulders. There was something so peculiar about our appearance; a foreign woman, a small hunched man, a half drunk driver and a Danish sea captain who couldn't straighten his horse, that a crowd started to form behind us as we mustered up the energy to move forward. Women and children joined and within a minute the commotion drew upwards of 30 or so people. Jerking forward, the driver addressed the crowd and horses.

"Vekk med deg!" he cracked his whip to the ground and instilled joy across the children's faces. I burst into laugh and away we flew and entered a full gallop once we had reached the edge of the town. As we were no longer in view of the village, not wanting to offend friend nor foe, I reached into a crevice I had Marguerite sew into my dress and threw to the birds, the fish my stomach was to entertain for supper. At least the fish would make acquaintance with the ground on my terms this time.

As we made our way north to Tonsberg, we passed over what appeared to be fertile land; the roads in good repair and the country the most improved I had seen since leaving England. Rolling hills and jutting rocks still littered, if one could say, the landscape. The icy North Sea to my right, was a peaceful ever-present reminder that I was not in France or England. As the Danish captain took strong command of his good and patient horse, we made good pace and reached Tonsberg by late evening.

Tonsberg Norway 17th July 1795

As I broke fast at the inn, a post-boy arrived at the inn's door, made inquiries for my whereabouts and handed me a fresh letter.

"Excuse me, who is this..." the post-boy ignored my question and had already left by the time I had turned the letter over. Peculiar.

> July 17th, Tonsberg
>
> Mrs Imlay
>
> It is my greatest pleasure to welcome you to Tonsberg. Your associate Noah informed me a few days ago of your plans and I am glad to find that you have made it in safety. I have not heard from your husband Gilbert for some weeks ago and I presumed he did not want to proceed with the charges.
>
> You can find me in the local chambers, waterside. We have much to discuss.
>
> The Mayor.

*

The mayor lived almost at the waterfront, a current hive of activity. Tønsberg, one of Norway's oldest towns, has been a significant hub for trade and commerce since the Viking Age and by all appearances, a bustling maritime centre. Rows of steeply pitched timber-framed houses, similar to Gothenburg, interweaved with shops, taverns and warehouses; its narrow cobblestone streets connecting them. The smell of saltwater and fish made my insides turn again.

As I approached the foothold of the doorway, it opened as if the mayor had stood behind the door in expectation. A short, plump man (though what he lacked in stature he made up for in energy), invited me in a sort of hurry only seen by post-boys in London.

"Mrs Imlay. A pleasure, please sit," he led me through a grand parlour furnished with elegant, sturdy furniture. We passed an intricate tapestry on the wall, most likely from a far off land and entered his drawing room. Filled to the brim with various papers, books and nautical instruments, a desk sat in the middle, though in stark contrast to its surroundings, was devoid of papers. I dropped my satchel on the floor next to the small guest chair whilst the mayor resumed his seat.

"You've travelled well I take it?" he asked.

Nodding, I replied. "The captains of this area seem sound and good natured except—"

"The person in question." The mayor sat back into his chair which overshadowed the rest of the room. His maid appeared and poured coffee into his small porcelain mug as I reached for Noah's letter in my satchel and handed it to the mayor.

After a few minutes of reading the mayor clasped his hands together and smiled at me.

"Why does Gilbert send his wife?" I pinched my skin until the pain numbed my thoughts. The mayor let out a small laugh and muttered something to himself in Danish.

"Oh. He is very busy and he thought it would be better for me to visit here," I lied. I retrieved Gilbert's letter and placed it back where it belonged. "He travels for business. As you know, it is hard to keep up," I fixed the satchel and returned to the mayor, whose pointedness had transitioned to small curiosity. "I take it you would rather do business with Gilbert then?"

"Dat's not vat I said," he paused and assessed my expression. "Vhy did you come here? Not him?"

"Well—" I love him. "I witnessed the loaded cargo of silver. It is I who gave the orders to Ellefsen to leave Le Havre with his crew and I watched him sign the receipt." I half relaxed my chest and began to breathe again.

"And vhere was Mr Imlay?"

"Paris," I replied. "He had to leave the day the sh—"

"Zo," he paused for a moment. His eyes met mine again but anger nor contempt formed their expression; it was the same expression I adorned when watching the poor drudges hauling their washing to the water with their icy hands. "Gilbert," he gestured to my satchel on the floor. "Was in

Paris and you, Mrs Imlay, vere in Le Havre?" I volunteered to stay. "You, zaw vith your own eyes de silver cargo make its way on to the Liberte and," he paused and took a sip from the mug of burnt liquid earth that had now impregnated its scent into the stale room. "You gave de orders for de ship to leave?"

"Correct," I said.

"What vere Ellefsen's instructions?" asked the Mayor.

"Pass through the British blockade and make way for Gothenburg where Gilbert's associate was awaiting the silver."

"Ah yes, dis Coleman fellow?" he asked.

"No, a Swedish pilot named Noah," I gestured to Noah's letter on the table. "But the ship never arrived in Gothenburg and—"

"So not, uh, dis—Coleman?" asked the Mayor.

"No sir. Coleman was Ellefsen's right-hand man. An American fellow."

"I vas told Coleman vas de one waiting for the silver in Gothenburg, dat he vas de one who vas supposed to receive de silver."

"By who?" I asked.

The mayor laughed. "Ellefsen. I 'av also been told dat de ship is somewhere off de coast of our Norway, maybe Arendal," he said, as he grabbed a small piece of blank parchment from the floor. "Do you believe dat to be true Mrs Imlay?" he retrieved a small pen from the other side of the floor and began writing hastily on the parchment. "Mrs Imlay?" he paused writing and awaited my reply.

"Oh," I said. "No, I think the ship is in Stromstad." He wrote several lines on the paper, scrawled what I assume to be his signature, bent over to find his stamp and within moments, stamped the parchment, folded it and handed it to me.

"You saw it there?"

"A ship is currently being repaired in the port of Stromstad. I inquired as to the owner and I was told by the harbour master the owner was none other than Peter Ellefsen."

"Did you inquire de name of de ship?"

"Maria Margurethe," I replied matter-of-factly. "I do not

see why it would be named that."

"Maria Margurethe? Vhere have I…hmm, no matter. I have here de shipping records from de last months," he rose from his chair and made way for a small pile of papers located in a dusty corner of his apartment. "Hvor la jeg de sprengte tingene" he muttered to himself. "Ah," he said now bent over a pile of waist-high papers. "Here."

"Take dem, take dem, please read," he said, returning to his chair. I flicked through several pieces of parchment and bewildered, placed them back on his desk.

"These won't be much use to me sir," I said. "But thank you all the same." He leaned over his desk and pointed to several inscriptions.

"Sølv is de verd you are looking vor," he said, pointing to each record. "Dough," he continued, slumping back into his chair and pausing for a moment. "I don't dink dat—"

"Ellefsen would not have unloaded the silver lawfully sir," I said, interrupting him. Winking at me, he rose from his chair. "Dat is vhere I have heard the name before."

"The name? Sir?" He disappeared from the room in a sort of frantic way.

"Margrethe," he called from another room.

"I do not follow Sir," I called back. The maid shrugged her shoulders and offered me a coffee.

"No thank you," we both turned to the mayor who returned with a book half the size of himself.

"Here," he said, dropping the weighty book onto the desk. Dust and small debris pillowed away from the book in a small cloud as the three of us coughed and tried to remove the dust from the air. "Records. If you can, vind Risor in dere."

"What exactly am I looking for sir?" I opened the enormous ledger to a random page. The maid could sense my immediate frustration and rounded the small desk with a small coffee pot in one hand and traced the bottom of the page with her fingers from the other.

"Ah. The town name, bottom of the page," said the mayor. "It is in, how do you say, order?"

"Alphabetical order?"

"Ja!" the mayor clapped and swayed his hands. "Risor,

Risor." The mayor, his maid and I proceeded to turn page after page until we reached East Risor. "Now, de terms of sale. These are deeds records. If I am not mistaken, we need to look for Egeland Jernverk."

"Egeland? Jernverk?" The mayor nodded.

"Iron works," he smiled and winked. After another few moments of scouring the page, the maid pointed to the words Egelands Jernverk. "The second list is de owner." The mayor pointed to the names next to Egelands. Ellef Thommesen, Margurethe.

"I still do not follow. These are, the owners? But what—" I asked. The mayor sat down in his chair, clasped his hands together and smiled wider than before.

"Mrs Imlay, do you know how our names are formed in this country?" I shook my head. "Vell, here," he pointed to the two names. "Ellef, was the owner and you see here, purchased in 1723. Now, vhy I looked here is dat only a few months ago I vas speaking to a merchant from Risor, who mentioned de owner of the ironworks, Margurethe, a formidable woman, paid for his crew to Gothenburg."

"Ah uh," I said.

"I have suspicions, dat dis Ellefsen fellow, Peter, or we pronounce it Peder, is the son of this fellow Ellef and his wife Margurethe."

"And if you are correct then..."

"Den Mrs Imlay, you are fighting against one of the wealthiest families in Norway."

"And if I had a spare 36 silver platters with the Bourbon crest and 32 silver bars and needed somewhere or someone to offload and store them and my family happened to be in the business of melting iron then—"

"Nettopp," he said. "Precise." The mayor closed the ledger and stood, gesturing for me to do the same. "Come," he continued. "Bring your letter, you can write to Gilbert and inform him dat ve shall be underway with de trial within a month."

"A month?" Marguerite.

"We must make for—" The three of us stopped and turned towards the exterior door which had resounded three separate knocks.

"Did you speak to anyone of our meeting Mayor? Who would have–" The post-boy. But the letter was sealed.

"Ja, hvem er det?" the mayor called out, gesturing to me to stand behind him.

"Apne opp. It is Ellefsen," a familiar male voice replied from the other side. The mayor whispered something to the servant, who upon instruction, pulled me into the kitchen towards the back of the house.

"Jeg hørte at en Mary Imlay er I byen," his familiar voice enraged my blood as it drew closer. "Jeg må snakke med henne." The mayor and Ellefsen conversed back and forth in a mix of Danish and Norweigan. To and fro, now familiar words like Sølv, Maria and Stromstad intermingled in their conversation.

"Mrs Imlay, it is okay to come out now." His maid gripped my arm. "Mrs Imlay, he vill not hurt you, I promise." Though I had only met the woman this morning, our eyes met and there was a shared feeling of fear.

"What do I do?" I asked her, but with no reply and a confused expression, my heart began to beat like the drums of war. Heat spread around my arms and my chest felt heavy again. She brushed off her apron, retrieved a small tray from storage, stood at the doorway and awaited me to join her. The fire from the hearth made my body even hotter as I looked around for a window as my means to an end, but there was no way out. She waited for me to decide but gestured with her head in the direction of the mayor and smiled.

I rounded the doorway, walked through a smaller, more quaint room than the others and reached the doorway to the drawing room. The maid entered, greeted both of them but only silence replied. I took a deep breath, pinched my wrist again and entered the study. Ellefsen.

"I vas telling Peter dat de trial vill probably be in Christiana," said the mayor. "The letter I did give you vas for Judge Wolfsberg who vill oversee the trial." My heart inside my bosom slowed to a pace almost indistinguishable from death as I stared into the cold, darkened eyes of Peter Ellefsen.

"Why?" I asked. "Why did you steal the silver?" Peter

averted my gaze. "I saw you load the ship at Le Havre. You signed the paper in front of me and I watched you as your mate Coleman and your crew sailed from the French coast." He continued to ignore me and attempted to return to his conversation with the mayor.

"Sir ik—"

"Self-preservation is, literally speaking, the first law of nature and I understand your attempt now to defend yourself at the trial but you can not even look at me?" One step at a time, I moved closer until we were separated only by the desk. "I know it has not sunk."

"I will see you at the trial," said Peter to the mayor and returned the way he came in silence, slamming the door shut behind him.

Tonsberg Norway 18th July 1795

Gilbert.

I have begun *Letters Written During a Short Residence in Sweden, Norway and Denmark*, which I hope will discharge all of my monetary obligations. I am lowered in my own eyes on account I should have started it sooner.

I am here in Tonsberg, separated from my child—and I must remain a month at least for the trial, or I might as well never have come.

I shall make no further comments on your silence.

God bless you!

Adieu.

Tonsberg 19th July 1795

The mayor had sent a young woman to me just after lunch, who spoke a little English, and she agreed to call on me twice a day to receive my orders and translate them to my hostess. I lamented that I had not brought my child with me as I would have to settle debt for Marguerite and France's now extended stay.

I spent my mid-afternoon meandering by the tideless water and, in sight of no one, let my hair free in the soft western breeze. It is here I realised the timing of the day and looked towards where I imagined the land of Portugal would be. The rosy tint of afternoon, her smile that will never again charm my senses, unless it reappears on the cheeks of my child; still too young to ask why the tears start so near to pleasure and pain. Her namesake I yearn for.

*

In the following days, I seldom met another human creature. The often calm ocean, lulled me to sleep as it lapped against the earth's grey pebbles. Fisherman spent their days casting nets over the ocean surface searching for supper. Gulls hovered against the slight western breeze during the day and retired to their cliffy rocks at night. The temperament of my soul renewed itself and increased my sensibility along with it. One late evening, two women—one of whom was my Danish translator—hastened their way to me as I returned from one of my walks.

"Miss Mary!" she called out to me and beckoned her following company to further increase her strides. In the distance I could see the door swing open from the inn.

"Anna! Sofie!" a woman stranger called to the two, stepped out into the evening and followed after them. Within a minute all three women, with only one of them my acquaintance, stood exasperated in front of me.

"Miss Sofie," I said, smiling at the other two. "How are you?" she replied with a smile, though hers was breathless.

"Hills," she said, struggling to form her words. "Zo many hills." With a hand above her ribs and the other on who I presumed to be Anna, Sofie made our introductions.

"Dis here is Anna," Sofie squeezed Anna's shoulder, who lent against her and smiled at her introduction. "Dis here is Maia," now closer, I realised was one of the servants at the inn, though her bright blue eyes and fair hair were not an uncommon sight in this area.

"Are you well?" I said and we all laughed, for both Sofie and Anna were still out of breath for they had, by my reasoning, walked from their farms on the opposite side of Tonsberg.

"Yes," Sofie nodded and gestured to the ground. "Please, can ve sit?" all in agreement, we moved our dresses and sat together on the cooling ground and all turned to gaze at the Northern sea lapping at their continent's feet in the near distance. Today, unlike most days, was their day of rest and were graced with another fine late summer's starry evening.

"Ve find you for ve bod had idea vor today," Sofie looked at Anna who again, smiled. "Have you svum in—" Sofie turned to Anna again and whispered.

"Hva er 'hav på Engelsk?" Anna shrugged but looked at me and pointed towards the ocean.

"Hav," Anna awaited for a reply. Confused, Anna made swimming motions with her hands and we laughed again.

"Sea?" I said. "Ocean perhaps?" Sofie's face lit up and both Maia and Anna clapped.

"Sea! Dat is it. Have you svum in de sea before?" Thinking for a moment, I realised I hadn't. I shook my head and Anna's face beamed in excitement.

"Har hun aldri svømt I havet før?" Maia whispered to Sofie and looked at me with inquisitive eyes as though I were a small animal. "Hvor bader hun?" Maia's head turned and smiled at me.

"Shhht," said Sofie, who slapped Maia's knee. "Ask her yourself." Sofie revealed her plan for my day. Maia had a foreign curious mind, as do I.

"Ve vould like to take you to de, sea, to svim or "Bathe" as you say, in Engelsk." Sofie then begun to explain that in the Norwegian summer, some of the Tonsberg women would often row to a small sheltered cove away from village eyes and bathe in the water.

We retrieved some of my garments from the inn and borrowed a small rowboat that had been upturned on the mossy rocks. I insisted on taking the oars and learning to row and I soon became expert. The persistent timing required by the oars lulled me into a sort of indulgence of forgetfulness of everything but the ocean.

Not soon after feeling a sort of warmth in my arms, we reacquainted with the rocky outskirts of Norway's coast and moored our boat. The three women and I removed our outer-garments, ensured the coast was free and together entered the cool water. We splashed, played and attempted to communicate our joy in whatever way we could. Laughter was universal; for that I am thankful.

As the three conversed in their language at times, I swam about and came across an abundance of star fish in a small decline of rocky shore. I had never observed them before, for they had no hard shell like the ones I had seen on the seashore. They appeared as though they were thickened water with a white edge and four purple circles, with an incredible number of fibres or white lines. As I touched them, the cloudy substance would close, first on one side, then on the other. But when I took one out of the water and into the air, it appeared only a colourless jelly. As I watched the small ripples fade into the water, the joyous laughter from the girls turned into screams of terror within my brain.

Death. Her headless body, bereft of life, slumped onto the platform. Vive Le Republique. The boy's headless body.

"Sofie. Är Mary okej?"

My name is Mary Wollstonecraft, and I am alive.

"Mary vhat's wrong?" asked Sofie. I tore some of my undergarments and used the pieces to scrub my skin. I am the one who helped her to the printers. My fault. "Mary?"

"Hon måste sluta, hon kommer att skada sig själv," said Anna.

"Mary. Stop," Sofie grabbed my shoulders like a lioness approaching her cub. 'stop, stop, stop, you vill hurt yourself." I focused on my arms. Sofie let go of Anna and knelt beside me in the water. "Listen to me," she pulled my chin up towards her. "You are safe," she said with more assurance than anyone had ever said before.

"Marguerite, I need her here, I—"
"Look at me," Sofie parted the wet hair from my face. "You are safe. Anna is here, Maia is here. I'm here," she said.

I released my breath and we knelt in the water together in a warm embrace, the waves pushed and pulled me. Let me go. The wind brushed my face like the small, intimate caresses of a mother. Nature, in all her god-like glory, more a mother to me than the hateful womb I came from.

"Mary?"

The mind is its lonesome place, and in itself can make a heaven of hell, a hell of heaven.

"Mary?" As I opened my eyes, the white light of the moon no longer embraced the northern sky above us, instead gave way to an aura I had only ever dreamt of.

"Sofie," I said. Her head now on Anna's shoulder. "Hmm?"

I turned my face up towards the sky. "Look."

"Nordlys," said Anna, her voice quiet against the rolling waves. "De Nordern lights," she said.

"It's..." The words lodged themselves in my throat as the green fire immolated itself in a continuous rage of dancing lights.

"Vakker," said Sofie. "Beautiful."

"Vakker," I repeated. Let me go. The dancing fire reminded me I shall cease to exist and this active restless spirit of mine, equally alive both in joy and sorrow, will be organised dust; food for worms. Or food for flowers, perhaps; unnecessary to the continual advancement of time in its infinite onward march.

It seemed as impossible to stop the current of my thoughts, as of the always varying, still the same, torrent before me; I stretched out my hand to eternity, bounding over the dark speck of life to come. No, surely something resides in this heart that will be untouched in death; this life is more than a dream—one that will not disappear into an everlasting eternity of nothingness when one sleeps forever.

Journey to East Risør late July 1795

The Mayor of Tonsberg summoned me to visit East Risør, where Ellefsen lived, to discuss the whole affair with him and to make my own, final inquiries before the trial. If a reconciliation should, in consequence, take place, it is to be registered, and we are not allowed to retract.

The fear of censure undermines all energy of character; and, labouring to be prudent, they lose sight of rectitude. Besides, nothing is left to their conscience, or sagacity; they must be governed by evidence, though internally convinced that it is false. As I passed through Lauvig to East Risør, I found myself walking amongst a pack of lawyers; the locusts of society, discussing follies and vices of the townsfolk.

What little I have seen of the manners of the people does not please me so well as those of Tonsberg. I was forewarned that I would find them still more cunning and fraudulent as I advanced west, in proportion as traffic takes place of agriculture. Their towns are built on naked rocks, the streets are narrow bridges, and the inhabitants are all seafaring men, or owners of ships, who keep shops.

I was informed that we might still advance a mile and a quarter in our cabrioles; afterwards there was no choice, but of a single horse and wretched path, or a boat, the usual mode of travelling. We therefore sent our baggage forward in the boat, and followed rather at a slow pace, for the road was rocky and sandy.

I was surprised, at approaching the water, to find a little cluster of houses pleasantly situated, and an excellent inn. I could have wished to have remained there all night; but as the wind was fair, and the evening fine, I was afraid to trust to the uncertain wind. We therefore left Helgeraac with the declining sun.

Though we were in the open sea, we sailed more amongst the rocks and islands than in my passage from Stromstad; and they often forced very picturesque combinations. Few of the high ridges were entirely bare; the seeds of some pines or firs had been wafted by the winds or waves, and they stood to brave the elements. I sat in a little boat on the ocean, amidst strangers, with sorrow and care pressing hard against my brain. Oh how I missed my child.

As the rain poured on and the night growing ever darker, the pilot declared that it would be dangerous for us to attempt to go to the place of our destination—East Risør—a Norwegian mile and a half further; and we determined to stop for the night at a little haven, some half-dozen houses scattered under the curve of a rock. Though it became darker and darker, our pilot avoided the blind rocks with great dexterity.

Light slumbers in a small hut produced dreams, where Paradise was before me. My little cherub was again hiding her face in my bosom. I heard her sweet cooing beat on my heart from the cliffs and saw her tiny footsteps on the sands. Newborn hopes, like the rainbow, to appear in the clouds of sorrow, faint, yet sufficient to amuse away despair.

The following morning we hung about for a considerable time entering amongst the islands, before we saw about two hundred houses crowded together under a very high rock—still higher appearing above. Talk not of Bastilles! To be born here was to be bastilled by nature—shut out from all that opens the understanding, or enlarges the heart. Huddled one behind another, not more than a quarter of the dwellings even had a prospect of the sea. A few planks formed passages from house to house; mounting steps like a ladder to enter.

The only road across the rocks leads to a habitation sterile enough, you may suppose, when I tell you that the little earth on the adjacent ones was carried there by the late inhabitant. A path, almost impracticable for a horse, goes on to Arendal, still further to the westward.

As we landed, I inquired for a walk and climbed near two hundred steps, eventually graced by a view of the sea. The ocean and these tremendous bulwarks enclosed me on every side. I simply wished for wings to reach still loftier cliffs near the boundless waste of water. Wandering there alone, I found the solitude desirable. I shuddered at the thought of remaining here in the solitude of ignorance and I shudder at the thought of leaving this world of which I have seen so little.

When I returned I found my baggage at a small inn and awaited the meeting with Ellefsen the following day.

Journey to Risor

East Risør Norway 21st July 1795

"I am looking for Peter or Peder Ellefsen?" I entered a small, nondescript office in the middle of East Risør. The attendant gestured to a door located at the end of a small hallway without lifting their eyes from their paper.

"Thank you," I said. By the time I reached the door and went to knock, the door swung open in a frenzy to reveal Peter Ellefsen, who placed himself in front of the near-closed door. My neck flashed hot and my body froze in its place.

"Mrs Imlay," he said, as voices continued to talk behind him. "How are you?"

"We need to talk," he said. "Would you?" he gestured to a door to the left of the hallway and opened it. "They know I want to talk to you," he pointed to the door. "They have permitted me." I tried to peer into the room but Ellefsen closed it and then opened the door next room. "Please?" The air became stale and thick. I clutched my satchel to my chest and turned to see the attendant still face down in whatever so preoccupied them. The voice of who I assumed to be Judge Wulfsberg spoke in hushed tones and a familiar voice, the Mayor of Tonsberg, replied in the same manner. "I will only need a few minutes."

"You want to talk? Speak then."

"Yes," replied Peter. "In here, if you will Mary."

"It's Mrs Imlay to you." He nodded and opened the door and waited for me to enter. All that occupied the solitary and lonesome space was a small desk, three wooden chairs and piles of parchments stacked on top of each other in bookshelves. I posted myself on the chair facing the door and kept my satchel to my chest.

"Leave it," I said. "The door stays open."

Peter raised his hands and smiled. "You found your voice have you?" posting himself in the chair opposite.

"What is it to you?" Peter took a long breath in, placed his hands in front of him on the table and did not look at me.

"I wish this entire affair did not happen. All of it. Everything."

"You admit it then? Everything?"

"Yes, and I...I apologise, I am sorry. Please, you have to understand." He lent forward in earnest. "I have spent months in gaol for this."

"Are you sorry they caught you out or sorry that you did it Peter?" His eyes lowered from mine and became transfixed on his hands. "You play about with people's livelihoods and like a moth about a candle, you're going to get burnt. In your case end up in gaol."

"I did it for our children...Margrethe, the oldest one. Besides, you will never bring proofs forward enough to convict me. I cannot return the money, 'tis all gone."

"Gone? I am sorry, what do you mean gone Peter? And you have children? You never mentioned it."

"Melted, mostly. Yes, my wife and I, Maria." I almost choked on my breath.

"I have been told your family own the ironworks, is that correct? If so, I came here to settle the business that you have so created Peter. Inquire of your relations what they can advance on your behalf and I will endeavour to compromise on the matter."

"I—"

"Oh, I forgot to mention, I spoke to the harbour master in Stromstad." Peter's eyes widened and met mine in a near-instant. "He does send his warm regards, the ship is making good repairs have you heard?" I stood at once, collected my things and approached the door way. "Meet me here tomorrow at noon with your offer." I left the small office and knocked on the door.

"Come in," replied a voice. The Mayor of Tonsberg and a man I presumed to be Judge Wolfsberg greeted me with smiles and gestured me to join them in their discussion. The room was cold and damp and the air reeked of salt. The ocean permeated into every crevice and crook it could weave itself into.

"Vhere is Peter?" asked the Mayor, looking behind me.

"I've insisted he speak to his family to sort out this situation and we can save a trial," I smiled at the judge who had posted himself behind a desk, not unlike the one he owned in his apartment. Only this time the room we was albeit somewhat larger and more fitting for a judge. His eyes appeared weary, curious even.

"Mrs Imlay," said Wolfsberg as he extended his hand with an air of the most profound respect. His aged eyes sparkled with kindness and intelligence, he reminded me of Joseph.

"A pleasure." I nodded in reply as the Mayor smiled at the introduction of his acquaintances. "Count Bernstoff writes highly ov you." Noah.

"My intention is to visit him in Copenhagen on way home whenever that shall occur. Soon, one hopes." An echo of a slamming door reverberated around the office.

"Ah yes, the trial. if Peter does not make an offer." Judge Wulfsberg began to explain, at length, the process of what would occur if Peter's family did not want to compromise. It would involve countless witnesses, the crew mostly, as well as several merchants from East Risør. He also disclosed that they arrested Peter in Arendal in December, following the alarm raised in a letter from Gilbert and several of the crew. "We set him free against a caution of 10,000 rdl, which his stepfather, Major von Holfeldt, posted."

"The ship, the Liberte, is in Stromstad, I can say with some degree of certainty by the countenance of Peter's expression when I mentioned the harbour master." The Mayor's smile widened.

'"Tis true then? The ship in the port?" asked the mayor. I nodded in reply and he smiled like a small child about to receive something sweet.

"I do love a good mystery," said the mayor.

"He also mentioned the silver has been melted," the mayor and the judge glanced at each other. "It could be as far as England or back to France by now." I buried my head in my hands and waited for either of them to reply.

"Vell, ve wait to see vhat they say," said the mayor. "You 'ave come this far Mrs Imlay, do not despair."

"I suggest you go home, rest, find some supper and wait till tomorrow. What did you ask of him?"

"Return to me with an offer tomorrow at noon."

"Good, good," replied the judge. "I shall return here tomorrow with the mayor here and we shall await what they say." I thanked them both for their time, exited the office and returned to the inn.

The most genial and humane characters I have met with in life were alive to the tranquil country scenes around them. The people here in East Risør, who rest shut up (for they seldom even open their windows), smoking, drinking brandy, and driving bargains, appear less human. I have been almost stifled by these smokers. They begin in the morning and are rarely without their pipe till they go to bed. Nothing can be more disgusting than the rooms and men towards the evening—breath, teeth, clothes and furniture, all are spoilt.

I could do nothing but wait. No books; and to pace up and down a small room at the inn, looking at tiles overhung by rocks, soon becomes wearisome. I cannot mount two hundred steps to walk a hundred yards many times in the day. Besides, the rocks, retaining the heat of the sun, are intolerably warm. The shrewdness in the character of these people kept me from entertaining myself with them.

My present journey gave fresh force to my opinion that no place is so unimproving as a country town. I should one day like to divide my time between the town and country; in a lone house, with the business of farming and planting, where my mind would gain strength by solitary musing, and in a metropolis to rub off the rust of thought, and polish the contemplation of nature rendered it just. But chance does more to gratify a desire of knowledge than our best laid plans, perhaps.

"Mrs Imlay?" The Mayor of Tonsberg knocked at entered my small room at the inn. "I apologise for the intrusion. Have you dined already? The English vice-consul requests you for his evening's dinner. Shall we?" He paced around the room, the floor creaking as he did and begun to inspect the various items and wares on the wooden shelves.

"I...I haven't finished writing for today, I actually—"

"Come...his house is grand, a view of de sea! I vill wait for you downstairs." The mayor bowed, exited the room and shut the door behind him.

Ten minutes or so later I joined him on his walk to the grand house he spoke of. By the time we reached the situation the afternoon begun its daily ritual of darkening its sky. As we approached what one in France would call a chateau, the servant of the house opened the door and brought us inside to the parlour, a mix of quaint English style with Norwegian influence.

"Mrs Imlay, this is the English Vice-Consul Mr Hoskins. Mr Hoskins, Mrs Imlay—"

"Mrs Wollstonecraft actually." I nodded and together the mayor and I followed Mr Hoskins and his servant to the even larger dining room. I expected to meet some company, yet was a little disconcerted at being ushered into an apartment full of well-dressed people, and glancing my eyes round they rested on several very pretty faces. Rosy cheeks, sparkling eyes, and light brown or golden locks; for I never saw so much hair with a yellow cast, and, with their fine complexions, it looked very becoming and out of place from the people at the inn.

"Friends from far and wide it is my pleasure to have you here with us this evening," Mr Hoskins gestured to the table and everyone posted themselves in the empty chairs. Large bowls of various meats and fish adorned his table, their odours permeating the air around me.

"Why does he live in East Risør?" I whispered loudly to the mayor. "These people seem too well-mannered for this town."

The mayor let out a small laugh as he began to carve a small section of meat. "Guest house. He lives in Christiania, he knows Wulfsberg very well." I did not recognise Wulfsberg, seated next to Mr Hoskins. The mayor attention'd a small cough and nodded in the direction of my companion posted behind me.

"Mrs Wollstonecraft is it?" a polite woman, more a lady, introduced herself and her English companion to me, who seemed disinterested in the entire affair taking place before her. "Clara."

"A pleasure," I said. "Do you know Mr Hoskins well?"

"Of sorts, I married his son," she too began to carve pieces of meat to her plate, the odours of flesh piercing the room as everyone did so. "Once a week is quite enough to dine with one's own relations and you have joined us on our particular dinner."

"Oh, I did not realise."

"No matter at all to me dear, it saves me from dining with

my sister's family," she winked at me and smiled.

"Your family live here?"

"England, but my sister lives here. The Ellefsen's, you may have heard of them, they own the big ironworks in the town. Wretched old thing of course. I like to be more or less ignorant of what they do. Ignorance is like a delicate exotic fruit; touch it and the bloom is gone." My eyes darted between everyone, searching for anyone who resembled Peter. "Charles wanted to visit his papa this summer and so, here we are. You're not involved in it all are you?"

I gulped. "Do they attend these dinners often?" the mayor placed food on my plate though my appetite had disappeared.

"Who, my sister and her family?" she asked. "No. Relations are simply a tedious pack of people, who haven't got the remotest knowledge of how to live, nor the smallest instinct about when to die. I haven't seen her in years, I find myself at these dinners and always have a ready excuse not to dine with them. What brings you to East Risør? Wretched place. Have you been to Italy? It is the sweetest thing you ever saw in your life." I gulped and I could sense the mayor's eyes glaring at the back of my head.

I feigned a cough and attempted to act civil. "Business, of sorts. Passing through. And no, I have never visited Italy."

"Oh how lovely. It is god awful here and I try to leave it as soon as we arrive. Put me out on one of the farmer's fields and let me lie down amongst the daises. It smells awful around here. You should acquaint yourself with Italy, by the way, simply marvellous place."

"Do you know much about your sister's family? I have heard they are quite prominent around Norway?"

"I would say one of the richest. If I remember correctly, they own business in Arendal too, further south than you would probably like to venture, but, most of the cargo from Europe is most likely touched by an Ellefsen business in some form I would guess." My throat burned at the thought. "You cannot appreciate how much I despise that wretched trade and wish it would disappear. And if all women become like their mothers then my sister has it coming for her."

I paused for a moment and soaked in the situation occurring before me. "The greatest disappointment we can meet with is the gratification of our fondest wishes," I shook away the tear that began to form in one of my eyes and toasted with the mayor.

"To good fortunate and grace," said the mayor.

"Good fortunate and grace." Everyone raised their tumblers. As the conversation between Clara and I ended abruptly, the guests began to read translations of some of the most useful German productions lately published, and one of our party sung a song ridiculing the powers coalesced against France, and the company drank confusion to those who had dismembered Poland. The men were generally captains of ships. Several spoke English very tolerably, but they were merely matter of fact men, confined to a very narrow circle of observation. I found it difficult to obtain from them any information respecting their own country, when the fumes of tobacco did not keep me at a distance.

The evening was extremely calm and beautiful. I thanked the mayor and Mr Hoskins, said goodbye to Clara and the Judge and not being able to walk, I requested a boat as the only means of enjoying free air.

The view of the town was extremely fine. A huge rocky mountain stood up behind it, and a vast cliff stretched on each side, forming a semicircle. In a recess of the rocks was a clump of pines, amongst which a steeple rose picturesquely beautiful. The churchyard is almost the only verdant spot in the place. Here, indeed, friendship extends beyond the grave, and to grant a sod of earth is to accord a favour.

I should rather choose, did it admit of a choice, to sleep in some of the caves of the rocks, for I am become better reconciled to them since I climbed their craggy sides last night, listening to the finest echoes I ever heard. Someone in the distance blew a French horn, and there was an enchanting wildness in the dying away of the reverberation.

Spirits unseen walk abroad, and flit from cliff to cliff to soothe my soul to peace. I reluctantly returned to be shut up in a warm room, only to view the vast shadows of the rocks extending on the slumbering waves. I stood at the window some time before a buzz filled the drawing room, and now and then the dashing of a solitary oar rendered the scene still more solemn.

*

"You have no proof of what happened." Peter stood with his arms crossed against one of the small room's walls. "My family won't settle with you and you can go to trial."

"You admitted yourself yesterday that you're sorry it happened. Please Peter." He kicked a small stone from underneath his shoe and sunk his body further onto the wall.

"Take us to trial, but you won't win. There's no silver left. We won't agree to anything."

"Did you unload the ship at Arendal?" his eyes shot up and widened again. "Ah, so I am right then."

"Where did you—"

"Country towns Peter. They are small and all-knowing." I winked at him and stood. "If you won't agree to a compromise, I shall inform the judge of your decision. Good day to you and what a sorry business you turned out to be." I left the room once and returned to Judge Wulfsberg and the mayor.

"Can we depart? Please, I want to leave this town." I slumped into the chair next to the mayor and the two shared a knowing look between them.

"I already thought that was to be the case. I've written these letters to our witnesses. The trial will begin at once in Tonsberg upon our return. You do not need to attend, but I do need you to write exactly your interaction with Peter in France." I nodded and, upon handing me ink and a quill, began writing the description of events in Le Havre, Paris and August 1794.

"I will come to the trial though," I said to the judge, who nodded and gestured for me to keep writing. The two continued to converse in their language whilst I described every detail I could remember. The cargo from Paris, Le Havre and witnessing the silver loading onto the ship, it sailing away into the distance under the Norwegian flag.

"You need to address your name at the bottom when

you are done," the judge pointed to the space underneath the last line. My heart began to burn and pound faster and without another thought, signed it.

Mary Wollstonecraft

Tonsberg Norway 30th July 1795

Gilbert

I have just received two of your letters dated 26th and 30th of June and you must have received several from me. I will try to write with a degree of composure. I wish for us to live together, because I want you to acquire a habitual tenderness for my poor girl. I cannot bear to think of leaving her alone in the world, or that she only be protected by your sense of duty. Preserving her is my most earnest sense wish.

When we meet again, you will see that I have more resolution that you give me credit for. I will not torment you. If I am destined to be tormented and unhappy, then I will conceal my anguish, so the tightened cord of life or reason will at last snap and set me free. Tonsberg has invigorated life in me I had thought lost forever. I walk, I ride on horseback, I row, bathe and even sleep in the fields. My health is consequently improved.

Tonsberg, August 5th, 1795

My mind is calmer, yet still the same in many ways. I have come to the realisation that I simply cannot live without passion. I feel the want of it very much so in society rather than solitude.

Writing you, whenever an affectionate epithet occurs, my eyes fill with tears. The trembling hand of mine stops. If I am doomed to be unhappy, I will confine my anguish to my own heart. Tenderness rather than passion has often made me overlook delicacy. The same tenderness will in future restrain me.

Tonsberg Norway 7th August 1795

I cannot tell you that my mind is any calmer. Though I stroll through the woods and rest on the rocks. This state of suspense, my friend, is intolerable; we must determine on something and soon we must meet shortly or part forever. I acted foolishly when I was with you, I expected too much and let pleasure slip from me. I cannot live with you, I ought not-if you find another attachment.

There is little reason for me to expect a shadow of happiness. After the cruel disappointments that have made a home in my heart. Our child depends on our being together.

Still, I do not wish you to sacrifice a chance of enjoyment for an uncertain good. I feel certain that I can provide for her - it shall be my object, if we are indeed to part to meet no more. Her affection must not be divided. She must be a comfort to me, if I am to have no other. And only know me as her support. I feel that I cannot endure the anguish of corresponding with you, if we are to only correspond. If you seek for happiness elsewhere, then my letter shall not interrupt your repose.

I will be dead to you.

I cannot express to you what pain it gives me to write about an eternal separation. You must determine, examine yourself. But for God's sake! spare me the anxiety of uncertainty.

Adieu. I scarcely know what new form of misery I have to dread. I ought to beg your pardon for having sometimes written peevishly. But you will impute it to affection, if you understand anything of my heat.

Yours truly

Mary

Tonsberg, August 9, 1795

Five of your letters were sent after me. One dated 14th of July was written in a style I did not expect from you. I then can assure you that you shall not be tormented with anymore complaints. I am disgusted with myself for having so long importuned you with my affection.

My child is very well. We shall soon meet, to part no more. I hope, I mean, I and my girl, I shall wait with some degree of anxiety until I hear how your affairs terminate.

Yours sincerely,

Mary

Tonsberg Norway 20th August 1795

The mayor greeted me with his friendly smile as I entered the last day of the trial. "You can sit anywhere you like Mrs Imlay," the mayor gestured to his large wooden dining table in the front part of the house. "I will nod at you ven is it in its final parts."

Peter sat with his attorney towards the end of the table nearest the window and I posted myself as far as I could away from the brute. Conversations soon settled amongst the twenty or so people in the room as the Judge returned to his seat. As the proceedings began, I found myself torn between the desire for justice and the need for mercy.

Peter Ellefsen, though he stood accused of a grave crime, was not without his supporters among the townsfolk, who appeared to whisper of his desperate circumstances and the injustices he had faced. Judge Wulfsberg, his brow furrowed in thought, called forth witness after witness, each offering their testimony in turn.

Several people in the room spoke when requested and the mayor sat quietly in his seat next to the judge. By noon, everyone broke for lunch and as I waited by the water in the warm air, a familiar voice sung my name.

"Mrs Wollstonecraft, Mary!" Clara sung from behind. "Oh I am simply so glad to see you."

"Clara, what are you—where is Charles?"

"Oh I left him behind. I wanted to see this trial for myself."

"You were at the trial just now?"

"Oh of course. You did not tell me you were here for this whole wretched thing. Oh my goodness Mary you simply should have said something, I could have helped you! I would have simply died with vexation and not seeing this. Never mind, never mind, come now darling we shall go for a stroll and admire this town from afar before it resumes. How are you darling anyway? Oh, Charles mentioned to me that you are a writer! A writer Mary, simply magnificent. You write on education?"

As the seabirds circled overhead, their cries mingling with the gentle lapping of the waves against the shore, we strolled arm in arm along the water's edge. "Yes, mostly the notion that girls and women should be educated."

"The whole theory of modern education is radically unsound. Fortunately, in England at any rate, education produces no effect whatsoever. If it did, it would prove a serious danger to the upper classes don't you think?" I laughed at the unseriousness of Clara. As I gazed out across the fjord, I couldn't help but marvel at the sheer magnificence of nature's handiwork. The water, so clear and pristine, seemed to hold within its depths a thousand untold secrets, whispered tales of voyages undertaken and adventures yet to come.

"It is an old, but a very true observation, that the human mind must ever be employed," I continued. "A relish for reading, or any of the fine arts, should be cultivated very early in life for the mind to have some resource in itself, and not to be entirely dependant on the senses for employment and amusement."

"And what of a young girl's temper? I would rather say temper is the manifestation of all the follies in our world," asked Clara.

"I agree," I laughed. "Half the miseries of life arise from peevishness or a tyrannical domineering temper. Governing our temper is truly the business of our whole lives; but surely it would very much assist us if we were early put into the right road?" Clara stopped to pick up a grey rock from the shore and studied it closely.

"I would rather think few people look into their own hearts Mary, or think of their tempers, though they severely censure others, on whose side they say the fault always lies."

"This trial—"

"Yes?"

"I don't suppose you are able to relay to me what occurred this morning?" Clara turned to view the water and threw the small rock into the water.

"I do not know much Danish I am sorry Mary. But come sit with me after lunch and we shall ponder the outcome together. I would rather like to see Ellefsen brought to justice for you at any rate." We strolled further along the water for half an hour or so and returned the town as the trial recommenced. Clara and I posted ourselves towards the end of the room and awaited Wulfsberg.

As the judge reentered the room, his countenance was different, poised even. An hour passed by and I could do nothing but sit and listen to the Danish words fly around me. Clara made small noises at words she recognised and pointed to several witnesses she knew or at least, had heard of.

Then, the mayor looked in my direction and nodded as the judge switched to English.

"I hereby, dismiss the trial of Peder Ellefsen brought forward by the one Gilbert Imlay and his emissary Mrs Imlay acting on his behalf," the judge gestured to me as Peter and several people clapped at the announcement. As everyone gradually left the room, Clara and I stayed seated, reluctant to join the dispersing crowd.

"I am sorry Mary," the judge lent forward across the table to Clara and I. As tears flowed down my face, a rush of warmth flooded through me. Noah, Gothenberg, my sleepless nights. All for nothing. What would Gilbert think of this?

"I do not...I do not understand—" Clara squeezed my hand tightly and stood to address the judge.

"On what grounds was it dismissed? Mary said she saw the ship in Stromstad."

"Dere vas not enough evidence, only rumour," the judge bowed his head.

"You have my statement," I said between tears. "The ship is in Stromstad...I don't—"

"I questioned the harbour master a few days ago, summoned from Stromstad and he said the owner of the ship was Ellefsen and it was not The Liberte but the Maria."

"Yes it may be on paper, but that is the ship! Gilbert's ship!"

"Mary, you have no proof." I placed my head on the table and attempted to restrain tears from falling. "He has not been found innocent or guilty, remember that, just dismissed."

"What am I going to do?" I raised my head from the table as the judge stared at me. "Gilbert sent me here to collect the money and now I leave with nothing? This is my only hope...my one chance to—"

"Go to Copenhagen and speak to Count Bernstoff, he may be able to help you further quite possibly," the mayor had returned to the room. "Oh and there are a few more things I have written," the mayor reached into his pocket and pulled out a piece of parchment. "One of the crew mentioned he heard de silver may have been taken to Flensburg by a skipper Søren Ploung. The judge here could not find him or the silver but it might be worth making inquiries there if you visit."

"Near Hamburg?"

"Correct," replied the mayor. "Mary, I know dis is not vhat you wanted...but the Ellefsen's, dey know people."

"Thank you Mrs Imlay, I need to return to my chambers. I will be seeing you." The judge stood from his chair and left without a reply. The mayor sighed and wandered over to Clara and I and posted himself in the seat beside us.

"People, sir?"

"Yes, people. Judges, lawyers, merchant-folk," he lent in and whispered. "I am surprised dis even vent to trial."

"You're saying the Ellefsen's may have influenced the trial?" the mayor nodded and lent back in his seat.

"But, it vould be no good to try to prove dat Mary, but I 'ave my suspicions."

"They probably could have," said Clara. "They are a big family here and I know his mother and father paid a lot of money to bail him out of the arrest in the first place."

"What do I do then?" The mayor resigned himself to the seat and clasped his hands together.

"Hamburg, like I mentioned. Visit there and see if you can find anything. If not, you have your Count. Now, I must return to the townsfolk and see to it they return to their homes and do not cause a ruckus in my town 'ey. I'll be seeing you Mrs Imlay. Do visit before you leave won't you?" I considered the idea but thought it better to leave a friend than an enemy, so I nodded in reply.

Till trials by jury are established, little justice can be expected in Norway. Judges who cannot be bribed are often timid, and afraid of offending bold knaves, lest they should raise a set of hornets about themselves. The fear of censure undermines all energy of character; and, labouring to be prudent, they lose sight of rectitude. Besides, nothing is left to their conscience, or sagacity; they must be governed by evidence, though internally convinced that it is false.

Return to Gothenburg 22nd August 1795

I said goodbye to the mayor and left Tonsberg, wearied and exhausted. On entering Moss I was struck by the animation which seemed to result from industry. Here I met with an intelligent literary man, who was anxious to gather information from me relative to the past and present situation of France.

The newspapers printed at Copenhagen, as well as those in England, give the most exaggerated accounts of their atrocities and distresses, but the former without any apparent comments or inferences. Still the Norwegians, though more connected with the English, speaking their language and copying their manners, wish well to the Republican cause, and follow with the most lively interest the successes of the French arms. So determined were they, in fact, to excuse everything, disgracing the struggle of freedom, by admitting the tyrant's plea, necessity, that I could not persuade them that Robespierre was a monster.

Approaching, or rather descending, to Christiania, though the weather continued a little cloudy, my eyes were charmed with the view of an extensive undulated valley, stretching out under the shelter of a noble amphitheatre of pine-covered mountains.

The situation of Christiania is fine, and I never saw a bay that so gave me an idea of a place of safety from the storms of the ocean; all the surrounding objects were beautiful and even grand. But neither the rocky mountains, nor the woods that graced them, could be compared with the sublime prospects I had seen to the westward

I can scarcely say why, but in this city thoughtfulness slides into melancholy or rather dulness. I felt like a bird fluttering on the ground unable to mount, yet unwilling to crawl tranquilly like a reptile, whilst still conscious it had wings.

I walked out, for the open air is always my remedy when an aching head proceeds from an oppressed heart. Chance directed my steps towards the fortress, and the sight of the slaves, working with chains on their legs, only served to embitter me still. The greater number of the slaves I saw here were not confined for life. Their labour is not hard; and they work in the open air, which prevents their constitutions from suffering by imprisonment.

The Norwegians are extravagantly fond of courtly distinction, and of titles, though they have no immunities annexed to them, and are easily purchased. Christiania is a clean, neat city, but it has none of the graces of architecture, which ought to keep pace with the refining manners of a people. Square wooden houses offend the eye, displaying more than Gothic barbarism.

As I have been most delighted with the country parts of Norway, I was sorry to leave Christiania without going farther to the north, though the advancing season admonished me to depart, as well as the calls of business and affection.

June and July are the months to make a tour through Norway; for then the evenings and nights are the finest I have ever seen; but towards the middle or latter end of August the clouds begin to gather, and summer disappears almost before it has ripened the fruit of autumn—even, as it were, slips from your embraces, whilst the satisfied senses seem to rest in enjoyment.

As I made my way to Gothenburg, my body became altered by disappointment. When going to Lisbon, the elasticity of my mind was sufficient to ward off weariness, and my imagination still could dip her brush in the rainbow of fancy, and sketch futurity in glowing colours. But now, nothing.

I passed by beauty and elegance, the spiry tops of pines are loaded with ripening seed. The sun gives a glow to their light-green tinge, which is changing into purple, one tree more or less advanced contrasted with another. The paths in the woods are not entangled with fallen leaves, which are only interesting whilst they are fluttering between life and death.

The grey cobweb-like appearance of the aged pines is a much finer image of decay; the fibres whitening as they lose their moisture, imprisoned life seems to be stealing away. I cannot tell why, but death, under every form, appears to me like something getting free to expand in I know not what element—nay, I feel that this conscious being must be as unfettered, have the wings of thought, before it can be happy.

Return to Gothenburg

Gothenburg August 26th 1795

I arrived here last night and with the most exquisite delight, once more pressed my babe to my heart. We shall part no more. The pleasure it gave to me, to see her run about. I have promised her that I will fulfil my duty to her, and nothing in future shall make me forget it. I will also exert myself to obtain an independence for her, but I will not be too anxious on this head.

I have already told you. I have recovered my health, vigour and even vivacity of mind. As for peace, we will not talk of it. I was not made, perhaps, to enjoy the calm contentment so termed.

You tell me that my letters torture you. I will not describe the effect yours have on me. Certainly you are right, I received three of yours just now. Our minds are not congenial. I have lived in an ideal world and fostered sentiments that you do not comprehend - or you would not treat me thus. I am not and will not be an object of compassion.

Something whispers me to put an end to these struggles. Be free - I will not torment when I cannot please. I can take care of my child. You need not continually tell me that our fortune is inseparable, that you will try to cherish tenderness for me.

Do no violence to yourself.

When we are separated, our interest, since you give so much consideration to pecuniary considerations, will be entirely divided. I want not protection without affection and support I need not. I had a dislike to living in England, but painful feelings must give way to superior considerations. I may not be able to obtain the sum necessary to maintain my child and self elsewhere. It's too late to go to Switzerland and I shall not return to France. I shall not force myself on you anymore.

Adieu! I am agitated, my whole frame is convulsed and my lips tremble as if shaken by cold, though fire circulates in my veins.

God bless you.

Mary

Copenhagen Denmark September 5th 1795

To Count Berntstoff,

When I arrived at East Risør, Ellefsen waited on me, and, as we were alone, behaved in the humblest manner, wished that the affair had never happened, though he assured me that I never should be able to bring the proofs forward sufficient to convict him.

He enlarged on the expense we must run into - appealed to my humanity and assured me that he could not now return the money. Willing to settle the business I desired him to inquire of his relations, who are people of property, what they would advance, and come to me in the evening when I would endeavour to compromise the matter.

He came and was almost impertinent. He had been spurred on by his attorneys, the pest of the country, their plan, I perceive, is to weary us out by procrastination.

To you, Sir, as a known lover of justice, I appeal, and I am supported by the most worthy Norwegians who wished by the respect they paid me to disavow the conduct of their countryman.

I am Sir yours

Respectfully

Mary Wollstonecraft, femme Imlay

Copenhagen Denmark 6th September 1795

Gilbert

I received just now your letter of the 20th. I had written you a letter last night, into which slipped some of my bitterness of soul. I will copy the part relative to the business in which you endeavoured for me to obtain here. I am not sufficiently vain to imagine that I can, for a moment, cloud your enjoyment of life you so desire to enjoy.

Gracious God! It is impossible for me to stifle something like resentment, when I receive fresh proofs of your indifference. What I have suffered this year is not to be forgotten. I have not the lively sympathies and the happy substitute for wisdom—insensibility. My agonies are of a broken heart—pleasure and I have shaken hands.

I see here nothing but heaps of ruins and only converse with people immersed in trade and sensuality.

I am weary of travelling - yet seem to have no home, no resting place to look to. I am strangely cast off. How often, passing through rocks, I have thought. "But for this child, I would lay my head on one of them and never open my eyes again!" I meet with families continually, bound together by affection or principle—and when I am conscious that I have fulfilled the duties you set me forth—almost to a forgetfulness of myself—I am ready to demand of Heaven. Why am I thus abandoned?

You say now you have some confused affection for me. That you wish to see me when we return to England.

I do not understand you. It is necessary for you to write and determine some mode of conduct. I cannot endure this suspense. Decide. We live together or eternally apart. I shall not write to you again till I receive an answer to this. I must compose my tortured soul.

I travel to Hamburg soon, to finish business and demand the silver aforementioned. I will say nothing more of that.

You say you will meet us there?

I do not know whether I write intelligibly for my head burns and my heart aches. You write I suppose back in London and after dinner when your head is not the clearest and as for your heart—if you have one—I see nothing of affection, unless a glimpse when you mention the child.

Adieu.

Copenhagen to Hamburg September 1795

What a farce is life. I have everywhere been struck by one characteristic difference in the conduct of the two sexes; women, in general, are seduced by their superiors, and men jilted by their inferiors: rank and manners awe the one, and cunning and wantonness subjugate the other; ambition creeping into the woman's passion, and tyranny giving force to the man's, for most men treat their mistresses as kings do their favourites, ergo is not man then the tyrant of the creation?

How can I avoid it, when most of the struggles of an eventful life have been occasioned by the oppressed state of my sex? We delve into reason when we feel forcibly.

But to return to the straight road of observation. The sensuality so prevalent appears to me to arise rather from indolence of mind and dull senses, than from an exuberance of life, which often fructifies the whole character when the vivacity of youthful spirits subsides into strength of mind.

*

The road from Copenhagen was very good, through an open, flat country that had little to recommend it to notice except for the cultivation, which gratified my heart more than my eye. I took a barge with a German baron who was hastening back from a tour into Denmark, alarmed by the intelligence of the French having passed the Rhine.

His conversation beguiled the time, and gave a sort of stimulus to my spirits, which had been growing more and more languid ever since my return to Gothenburg. Marguerite and the child often fell asleep, and when they were awake, I might still reckon myself alone, as our train of thoughts had nothing in common.

Marguerite is much amused by the costume of the women; the pannier which adorned both their heads and tails, and with great glee recounted to me the stories she had treasured up for her family when once more within the barriers of dear Paris. She reminded me of the importance she should assume when she informs her friends of all her journeys by sea and land, showing the pieces of money she had collected, and stammering out a few foreign phrases, which she repeated to me in a true Parisian accent.

The man I had hired at Copenhagen advised me to go round about twenty miles to avoid passing the Little Belt except by a ferry, as the wind was contrary. But the gentlemen overruled his arguments, which we were all very sorry for afterwards, when we found ourselves becalmed on the Little Belt ten hours, tacking about without ceasing, to gain the shore.

I then supped with my companions, with whom I was soon after to part for ever—always a most melancholy death-like idea—a sort of separation of soul; for all the regret which follows those from whom fate separates us seems to be something torn from ourselves.

These were strangers I remember; yet when there is any originality in a countenance, it takes its place in our memory, and we are sorry to lose an acquaintance the moment he begins to interest us, though picked up on the highway. There was, in fact, a degree of intelligence, and still more sensibility, in the features and conversation of one of the gentlemen, that made me regret the loss of his society during the rest of the journey; for he was compelled to travel post, by his desire to reach his estate before the arrival of the French.

Arriving at Sleswick, the residence of Prince Charles of Hesse-Cassel, the sight of the soldiers recalled all the unpleasing ideas of German despotism, which imperceptibly vanished as I advanced into the country. I viewed these beings' training to be sold to slaughter or be slaughtered with a mixture of pity and horror.

Despite the heavy and gloomy castle, the grounds surrounding it were tastefully arranged. A walk, winding under the shade of lofty trees, led to a regularly built and animated town. I crossed the drawbridge, and entered to see this shell of a court in miniature, mounting ponderous stairs—it would be a solecism to say a flight—up which a regiment of men might have marched, shouldering their firelocks to exercise in vast galleries, where all the generations of the Princes of Hesse-Cassel might have been mustered rank and file, though not the phantoms of all the wretched they had bartered to support their state, unless these airy substances could shrink and expand, like Milton's devils, to suit the occasion.

From what I have seen throughout my journey, I do not think the situation of the poor in England is much, if at all, superior to that of the same class in different parts of the world; and in Ireland I am sure it is much inferior. I allude to the former state of England; for at present the accumulation of national wealth only increases the cares of the poor and hardens the hearts of the rich.

After leaving Sleswick, we passed through several pretty towns; Itzchol particularly pleased me; and the country, still wearing the same aspect, was improved by the appearance of more trees and enclosures. But what gratified me most was the population. I was weary of travelling four or five hours, never meeting a carriage, and scarcely a peasant; and then to stop at such wretched huts as I had seen in Sweden was surely sufficient to chill any heart awake to sympathy, and throw a gloom over my favourite subject of contemplation, the future improvement of the world.

The prospect of Hamburg at a distance, as well as the fine road shaded with trees, led me to expect to see a much pleasanter city than I found.

I was aware of the difficulty of obtaining lodgings, even at the inns, on account of the concourse of strangers at present resorting to such a central situation, and determined to go to Altona the next day to seek for an abode, wanting now only rest. But even for a single night we were sent from house to house, and found at last a vacant room to sleep in, which I should have turned from with disgust had there been a choice.

Hamburg 1795

Hamburg gates close early in winter and slightly later in summer to discourage outsiders from settling there. Immense fortunes have been acquired by the secret manoeuvres of trade. The hospitality of Hamburg is confined to Sunday invitations to the country houses I have mentioned, when dish after dish smokes upon the board, and the conversation ever flowing in the muddy channel of business, it is not easy to obtain any appropriate information.

During my present journey, and whilst residing in France, I took opportunity to peep behind the scenes of what are vulgarly termed great affairs, only to discover the mean machinery which direct the many transactions of business. The sword is kinder than the contractors and locusts who have preyed on human life.

These men, like the owners of slave ships, never acknowledge the blood by which their money has been gained, but sleep in their beds in peace, terming such occupations lawful.

Hamburg 1795

Gilbert

I have just finished a letter.

Three mails arrive without one for me. I am labouring to write but your silence is an act of cruelty. Had the captain remained a few days more I would have returned to England. What have I to do here?

You do not appear in Hamburg on the date you put forth some weeks ago. You do not write.

I have inquired as to the silver. Nothing. No mention of it and no one knows of Peter or Coleman.

I have written to you extensively.

Informed of my intentions to meet you here in Hamburg, I have waited. Do not leave me in suspense. I have not deserved this of you. I did what you asked. You said this was a necessary venture for me to expedite on yet am I necessary to you?

I cannot write my mind is so distressed.

Adieu.

Hamburg 27th September 1795

Gilbert

When you receive this, I shall either have landed or be hovering on the British coast. Your letter on the 18th that arrived yesterday decided me so. By what criterion of principle or affection you term my questions extraordinary and unnecessary I cannot determine.

Your whereabouts and promise of meeting me—us—in Hamburg goes unfulfilled. You had perpetually recurred your promise of meeting me in the Autumn—was it extraordinary that I should demand a yes or no?

Your letter is written with extreme harshness, coldness I am accustomed to. I find no tenderness or humanity, only a desire to lighten your burden.

I am above disputing words, it matters not what terms you decide.

To the fiat of fate I submit. I am content to be wretched—but I will not be contemptible. Of me you have no cause to complain, but for having too much regard for you—for having expected a degree of permanent happiness, when you only sought momentary gratification.

I am strangely deficient in sagacity. Uniting myself to you, your tenderness seemed to make amends for all my former misfortunes. On this tenderness and confidence did I rest. But I leaned on a spear that has pierced me to the heart.

Preparing myself for the worst, if your next letter be like the last, then I shall write to Mr Johnson to procure me a lodging and not to inform anybody of my arrival. There I will endeavour to obtain a sum necessary to take me to France, from you I will not receive anymore.

Some people, whom my unhappiness has interested, though they know not the extent of it, will assist me to obtain the object I have in view - the independence of my child. Should a peace take place, any ready money will go a great way in France, and I will borrow a sum, which my industry will enable me to pay at my leisure, to purchase a small estate for my girl.

She shall complete her education and then I can introduce her to a society she'll like—for securing her happiness depends on me. Finally, when she is happy, I shall die in peace.

I shall not remain on the vessel the whole way, because I have no place to go to. Therefore, if you enquire of my whereabouts, post it to the Captain. I wish to see you, though it be for the last time.

Return to England

Journey to Risor

London Sunday 4th October 1795

"You found someone else? One does not find something unless they are looking." Gilbert turned his head away from me and tried to stiffen his shaking leg.

"You were away, you were..."

"Away? You sent me away." The collar on my dress became tighter. Pulling at it to loosen it did nothing but frustrate me. "When the tumult of business in Norway was over I was hoping you to repose in the society of an affectionate friend, and be together with Frances." Gilbert lowered his head back down to his lap. "You have formed some new attachment and left me in extreme anguish at landing without having any friend to receive me."

"I-"

"Tell me that you wish it and I will sever this Gordian knot that binds us."

"I do not want...I only...I do not," Gilbert still could not raise his head and meet my gaze. I paced behind the small chairs of the parlour as my chest became heavier and heavier.

"Do not keep me in suspense Gilbert, I expect nothing from you, or any human being." I gazed out the window at the people returning home from their days. Oh to have a simple life, a life without duty. "I have fortitude enough to determine to do my duty yet I cannot raise my depressed spirits or calm my trembling heart if you do not say what you want."

"I can assist you," said Gilbert, I could tell he was looking at me. The feeling of someone's gaze upon one's own back. "But I cannot be with you. It is this business, this sordid business I involve myself in." The pain in my heart surged deeper and deeper until I felt something crack inside me

"You told me you had no attachment," I said, without turning to face him. "You told me you had no attachment, and you lied. God gave you one face, and you make yourself another. You do not meet us in Hamburg, give no reason but now here I find you with that actress. You throw off a faithful friend only to pursue the caprices of the moment."

"I did not think it would hurt you. How did you find

out?"

"The cook," I said, turning to face him. "Do not mention the confession which I forced from her. Nothing but my extreme stupidity could have rendered me blind so long. And your issue is with me discovering you had an attachment is that it?"

"I did not think…'

I paused and clenched my fist and with a few breaths, released the tightness of my body, and sunk into the feeling of which ignited my every limb. "May you never know by experience what you have made me endure." I could not tell whether shame or contempt held a place in the eyes of the man that stared into mine, but it does not matter now.

"Good evening to you." I lowered my head, turned and left the parlour, returning to London's evening.

London early evening 10th October 1795

Gilbert.

I write you now on my knees; imploring you to send my child and the maid to Paris, to be consigned to the care of Madame Fillieatz.

Also, let the maid have all my clothes without distinction.

Soon, very soon shall I be at peace. When you receive this, my burning head will be cold. I would encounter a thousand deaths, rather than a night like the last. Your treatment has thrown my mind into a state of chaos; yet I am serene. I go to find comfort, and my only fear is, that my poor body will be insulted by an endeavour to recall my hated existence. But I shall plunge into the Thames where there is the least chance of my being snatched from the death I seek.

Should your sensibility ever awake, remorse will find its way to your heart; and, amid business and sensual pleasure, I shall appear before you, the victim of your deviation from rectitude.

Mary

"Miss Mary?" I looked up from my letter to Gilbert and folded it into its envelope as Marguerite entered my small bedroom with Frances. "Mmm?"

"De little one, she asks for her mamma." Marguerite placed Frances on my lap. "Do you require anything, madame?" Frances' delicate fingers played with my hair as I pressed the envelope harder and harder.

I shook my head and kissed Frances on the top of her head. "Only this little one and the whole world shall be right again, won't it?" Frances rested her head underneath my chin and words I had heard an old friend sing in a church in London formed inside my mouth.

"Amazing grace, how sweet the sound, that saved a wretch like me...I once was lost, but now am found; was blind, but now I see. 'Twas grace that taught my heart to fear, And grace my fears relieved; how precious did that grace appear, the hour I first believed?" Marguerite placed herself in a chair next to Frances and I, rested her head on my shoulder and she hummed along to the rest of the tune in her beautiful French accent."When this flesh and heart shall fail, and mortal life shall cease, I shall possess, within the veil, a life of joy and peace." Several tears formed at the corner of my eyes and fell onto Frances' auburn hair. Marguerite held one of my hands as we rocked side to side together as Frances turned her head towards us.

"Mumma? Walk. Tomorrow?" My heart burned.

"Marg..." I choked at the words in their futile attempt to leave my throat. "Marg..."

"I shall take you, my dear one," said Marguerite, rubbing Frances' shoulder. I closed my eyes and the three of us held each other until exhaustion took hold of us and rest upright would not suffice our weary bodies.

"I shall take her to sleep Madame. I shall see you in the morning." She lifted a sleeping Frances from my lap and placed her against her shoulders.

"Marguerite?" She paused at the door and turned towards me at my desk. "Thank you. For everything you have done. We would not have endured Scandinavia if it were not for you," I gestured to Frances, who I hoped was dreaming of wildflowers and better days than the one she would wake up to tomorrow.

"You are...velcome, Madame," she said, smiling as her eyes immediately shot to the letter on my desk. "You are seeing Monsieur Johnson tomorrow, at his shop before lunch madame. Shall I wake you in the morning?"

"Oh yes—right, thank you. I forgot."

"Good evening Madame Mary." She turned to ascend the apartment stairs with Frances and as soon as I heard the door close, I tidied my desk, returned Gilbert's letter to its place and retrieved two of my winter coats. As I made my way past the stairs, I paused at the threshold as a small beam of moonlight peeped through Frances' door.

"Mama?" Frances peered from behind the wall near the top of the stairs. "Where going?"

"Nowhere, my sweet girl. Let us get you back to bed." I placed my things at the bottom of the stairs and ascended to take Frances to her bedroom.

"Mama?" her golden brown eyes shone in the moonlight from the window and another tear formed.

"Yes little one?" I ascended the stairs, returned her to her cot, closed the curtains and knelt down beside her. Coughing to stifle another tear, I kissed her hand as memories of France burned in front of my eyes. Neuilly. The sunset and the stars. Our barrier girl. "Sleep my love," I kissed her on her forehead, helped her into sheets and held her hand; my unfortunate girl.

I could not be the mother she needed. I stroked her hair until she drifted to sleep, collected my coats and ventured to Battersea Bridge.

When I arrived it was overcrowded with people—I did not want anyone to rescue me. No one needed to save this wretched life of misery and pain. And so I walked to Putney in the pouring rain. Despite the cold and misery, there was at least a sense of calmness.

And so I stood on the edge of Putney Bridge and I closed my eyes; putting a period on this wretched and unnecessary life.

After

Number 72, St. Paul's Churchyard London, 7th May 1809

"Did you know she wanted to end her life?" asked Frances.

"I knew she was struggling dear. Her maid Marguerite mentioned something to me the week prior. It pains me that I never said anything to her, I thought she was to be okay."

"Joseph dear, I'm going to put another log on the fire for you," Anne yelled from the kitchen.

"Thank you." Frances smiled and hugged her knees to her chest as she looked again at all the letters on the floor.

After contemplating the scene before her, she reached for a smile pile of letters, much smaller than the other years of Mary's life. "What happened after November?"

"She existed in a state of anguish. Several of her friends and I kept a regular watch on her for the following weeks and when we knew she was on the mend, she was transferred to Mrs Christie's house. I offered to secure her lodgings again but she wouldn't bear to take it let alone even consider it. Speaking of, why will you not stay here? There is room for you upstairs."

"I cannot—"

"Your father and his wife will be perfectly fine on their own. It is not your responsibility to care for all their children."

"But I love papa," she said, hugging her chest tighter. "And Jane and Mary."

"What would she want for you?" I gestured to all the letters on the floor. "She loved you so dearly."

Frances wiped another tear from her face and poured over the letters again. "After November. Is when she met papa?"

"Correct," I nodded.

"Did she ever see Imlay again?"

"I think she saw him twice. Once at Mary Hays' house and the last time on a road walking out of London somewhere, I was told. Then she met William in January in 1796 and in March 1797 they were married at St. Pancras, as you know. And well, the rest they say, is history."

Act IV

London Sunday morning October

"Mary? Mary wake up would you," a familiar voice shouted at me from somewhere in the darkened room. Joseph. "Mary please wake up." I opened my eyes and felt softness underneath my fingers. My own bed. A doctor was fussing about the room with Marguerite and a nurse in tow. "What in the devil were you doing?" asked Joseph, pacing back and forth at the end of my bed.

"I am…alive?"

Joseph paused his frantic pacing and placed his hands on my feet. "Two boatmen, rowing through the fog, saw you in the water. They rescued you Mary. And Marguerite found your note, called for Gilbert who then called for me." My head raged and burned. "She is quite warm, see to it please," said Joseph to the nurse. The temperature of my body did not match the coldness I felt. I did not want to be here.

"Leave me be," I said. Joseph posted himself next to my bed and coughed a few times into his handkerchief. "I am not letting you do that again. Why did you not come to me?"

"I don't want to be a burden to you. You have already preoccupied yourself with so much of my life Joseph." He lowered his head as I burrowed mine into my pillow

."It is your duty to live, not only for your friends' sake, not only because you are gifted, talented and have much more to give to the world, but for the sake of your child."

"But—"

"I won't hear anymore of it. You told me the other week you are planning the second part to Vindication are you not? Whilst I had women in the store asking for Rights of Woman just the other day. And I nearly went to mention there shall be a part two," he lent forward and smiled. "But we'll keep that between us."

London Monday morning October 1795

Gilbert

Yesterday morning, someone inhumanly brought me back to life and misery. In my mind it was one of the calmest acts of reason. In this respect, I am only accountable to myself. Did I care for what is termed reputation, it is by other circumstances I should be dishonoured. You say you know not how to extricate ourselves out of the wretchedness into which we have been plunged. You are extricated long since—But I forbear to comment—If I am condemned to live, it is a living death.

I think, that you lay much more stress on delicacy, than on principle; but I am unable to discover what sentiment of delicacy would have been violated, by your visiting a wretched friend—if indeed you have any friendship for me. But since your new attachment is the only thing sacred in your eyes, I am silent. Be happy! My complaints shall never more damp your enjoyment—perhaps I am mistaken in supposing that even my death could, for more than a moment.

You asserted you will do all in your power to contribute to my comfort (when you only allude to pecuniary assistance), appears to me a flagrant breach of delicacy—I want not such vulgar comfort, nor will I accept it. I never wanted but your heart—That gone, you have nothing more to give. Had I only poverty to fear, I should not shrink from life.

Forgive me then, if I say, that I shall consider any direct or indirect attempt to supply my necessities, as an insult which I have not merited—and as rather done out of tenderness for your own reputation, than for me. Do not mistake me; I do not think that you value money (therefore I will not accept what you do not care for) though I do much less, because certain privations are not painful to me. When I am dead, respect for yourself will make you take care of the child.

Since your new attachment is the only sacred thing in your eyes I am silent—Be happy. My complaints shall never damp your enjoyment. Perhaps I am mistaken in supposing that even my death could for more than a moment...I never wanted but your heart. That gone, you've nothing more to give, for if I had only poverty to fear I should not shrink from life. I write with difficulty.

I have to request you to let Marguerite bring them to me. I shall go this evening to the lodgings, so you need not be restrained from coming here to transact your business. And, whatever I may think or feel, you need not fear that I shall complain to public ears. No! If I have any criterion to judge of right or wrong, I have been most ungenerously treated, but wishing now only to hide myself, I shall be silent as the grave in which I long to forget myself. For sweetest things turn sourest by their deeds; lilies that fester smell far worse than weeds.

I shall protect and provide for my child. I only mean by this to say that you have nothing to fear from my desperation. Farewell.

The letter, without an address, which you have put up with the letters you returned, did not meet my eyes till just now. I have thrown the letters aside. I did not wish to look over a register of sorrow. My not having seen it will account for my having written to you with anger under the impression your departure, without even a line left for me, made on me, even after your late conduct which could not lead me to expect much attention to my suffering.

My mind is broken.

I seldom know where I am or what I do. The grief I cannot conquer (for some cruel recollection never quits me, banishing almost every other), I labour to conceal in total solitude. My life therefore is but an exercise of fortitude, continually on the stretch and hope never gleams in this tomb.

I am buried alive. I meant to reason with you and not to complain. You tell me I shall judge more coolly of your mode of action some time hence. Is it possible that passion clouds your reason as much as it does mine? My heart is rooted in my desire for you. I know that you are not what you appear to be now, and you will not always act and feel the way you do now, even though I may never be relieved by the change.

Even at Paris my image will haunt you, you will see my pale face, and sometimes the tears of anguish will drop on your heart which you have forced from mine. I cannot write. I thought I could quickly refute all your ingenious arguments, but my head is confused. Right or wrong, I am miserable...I have loved with my whole soul, only to discover that I have no chance of a return and that existence is a burden without it. I do not understand you. If by the offer of your friendship you will only mean pecuniary support I must again reject it. Trifling are the ills of poverty in the scale of my misfortunes. God bless you!

P.S I have been treated ungenerously. You seem to me only to have been anxious to shake me off, regardless of whether you dashed me to atoms by the fall. In truth, I have been rudely handled.

London 1796

I languished in bed for several weeks. One morning in early January I did not arise until eleven o'clock. The following week, Johnson sent a man to call for me, a superficial puppy who I wish to never see again. First I thought it a joke, a stranger, a mere acquaintance knocking at my door. I shall not mince matters, he was rude and cruel.

I found myself poor and destitute but I will not condescend myself or bend my spirits. If it was necessary to act contrary to my principles to support Frances the struggle would soon be over. I would never prostitute myself for maintenance which his proposal of marriage appears to be. I am poor but I can live without his benevolent exertions.

By mid-January, Mary Hays invited me to dine with Johnson after he made his unnecessary apology. It was there, one cold January evening I reacquainted with William Godwin, the expressionless philosopher, or so I thought.

*

"I read the last volume of Heloise you sent me," said Godwin, our hands intertwined as we comforted together on the sofa. I glanced around my sitting room for William's book and smiled at the sight of it by the door. "You haven't finished mine yet have you?" I rested my head into his neck and sighed.

"This evening, I promise. Or will you dine with me?"

"I am dining with Elizabeth remember?" my heart fluttered at her name as I closed my eyes, wishing Mrs Perfection would disappear entirely.

"I did not wish to see you anyway," I lied behind a smile. As he recounted his week's affairs and matter of acquaintances he would be dining with the following week I gazed at his eyes, round and prominent, more distinguished than the ones I found frustrating in December of '91.

As we recounted our lives back and forth and stories of our youth, I kept my childhood friend close to my heart. I did not want to share her with the world, entwine her memory with the man accompanying me on my sofa. How many times would my heart be split into pieces?

*

As the following months slipped away, I struggled to attain peace of mind, yet I could not trace the emotions to their source. If a dream or a wish could whisk Frances and I to France or Italy, I would be off in a twinkle. Though, I am convinced it is my mind not the place which requires changing. My imagination betrays me continuously, a fresh misery every day. William talks of roses that grow on every path of life, I encounter only thorns.

He would send letters. Which soon turned to love letters, if I may call them. They would sometimes calm my mind, my painfully active mind haunted by old sorrows which come forward with new force every time I remember them. I spent many mornings walking with Frances—she would run about and chase floating butterflies and falling leaves. By the end of August the weather turned foul and barely permitted us our evening walks.

Number 72, St. Paul's Churchyard, London 14th September 1796

"Frances! Oh my dear how are you?" Joseph opened the door to Number 72 and looked behind my legs for the usual hand-holder attached to me.

"She has the chicken-pox," I said as I stepped inside his bookstore. "Thankfully I am sort of glad now I know what is wrong with her, the poor girl. I cannot stay for long as I like to be near her when she is sick."

"I shall come by your apartment tomorrow then." He smiled and we ascended the stairs to the dining room together.

"Hello Anne. No tea for me this morning thank you, a short visit." Joseph and I relaxed into his dining chairs and began our usual routine of conversations on politics, current essays and upcoming reviews.

"Have you heard from Paine recently?" I shook my head. "I haven't received a line from him in months, almost a year probably." I glanced at the painting again and remembered the dinners in December of '91 and January of '92. Things were much simpler back then.

"Have you heard from Olaudah?" Joseph shook his head. I peered at the empty chairs at the end of the table and the one once occupied by Thomas and Olympe. I coughed to mute a tear from forming.

"Hm? Oh the dinners. Quite some time ago now. Everything has changed." Joseph followed my gaze to the painting and sighed. "Henry is not returning your letters is he?" I scratched a small mark into the dining table. "You must let it go. You have William now do you not?"

"I told you the promise I made to myself at fifteen. I resolved myself to never marry for dependence or interested motives. And now I find myself near destitute again and I don't wan't to repeat the same mistake I made with Imlay. The brute can't even pay what he promised."

"I thought Imlay was to pay you monies for Frances?" Joseph retrieved a pamphlet from the pile nearest to him and began reading silently to himself.

"Yes well he alluded to the fact he would. My entire confidence in him plunged me into an eternal difficulty. I understand it is a consequence of what some would call my own folly Joseph. Such a stupid woman I was."

"That is not true. And I have told you repeatedly there is enough writing to keep you employed as much or as little as you need." I could barely look at him. Besides his attempt at marrying me off to some poor soul of a man, nothing but kindness and care coursed through Joseph's veins; protection of a father, care of a friend.

"I am out of patience with myself than you can form any idea of—"

"Mary," Joseph rested the pamphlet on the table and took in a large sigh. "I know your mind is active but you need to be content with yourself. You are a mother and you are raising Frances on your own. What else could the world expect of you?" I bit my lip and half smiled. "You have written more words in your life than the common man would think. On that you also appear tired, are you sleeping?"

I retorted with a sniff. "Frances has been tearing herself to pieces from scratching, I have barely slept." I rubbed at my eyes as he handed me the pamphlet and retrieved another one to read.

"Return it by next week. If you must work whilst she is sick, see to it that you get fresh air at least." He tapped the dining table a few times and furrowed his brow at my expression. "Are you in love with William? If I may be cruel to ask."

"I find myself wanting to express an increasing affection for him, but I do not know whether it is love. I think my mind is confused as to the property of love considering I do not think I have ever experienced it before. Is love even real? I do not quite know," I half-mused to myself. Joseph threw the new pamphlet back on its pile, took my hands in his grasp and smiled.

"If it so be, do not bastille your heart because of him. Live in the present moment. Though that mind of yours tends to live in the past and future." He patted my hands and nodded to the door. "Go, you best be off to see your Frances. Give her my well wishes when you see her won't you? Tell her her 'seph will be around tomorrow." I nodded and stashed the pamphlet in my satchel.

I said goodbye to Anne and Joseph and returned to St. Paul's Churchyard, the September wind blowing the leaves amongst the cobblestone. I breathed in every smell I passed and on my walk home. Small raindrops pattered the streets as summer hath too short a lease in London. It was as if nature had decided it would make a continual effort to cloud the moods of everyone in England for centuries.

*

Godwin and I became intimate over the following months. I would awake with Frances, write a line or two, drop it into his box in the morning and return to my writing desk. Frances would play in the sitting room with Marguerite, whose English had become near-fluent. I attended dinner parties at Joseph's once more, dined with Mrs Hays and attempted to keep my soul and body together through conversations with friends and evenings with Godwin.

On a Thursday evening in late November, I found Godwin waiting for me and Frances outside my apartment. As I opened the door, he said hello to Marguerite and gestured for her to take Frances up the stairs. I nodded and said goodnight to them both and as we sat on the sofa together, he kissed me gently and ran his fingers along my neck.

"Chez moi," he said in a whisper. "Shall we return to my apartment and philosophise the world once they are asleep?" I giggled as my heart pounded against the walls of its cage. Pausing for a moment, I contemplated his proposition. I tried to remember when I had bled last and nodded in assurance. Live in the present.

"You express yourself in the politest of terms." He kissed my forehead as we rested on the sofa for a while longer. "Did you read your essays today?" I shuffled back into the sofas seat and lay my head on his lap. He stroked my hair in a mindless fashion as we mused over our days and past week.

"You know I respect your independence of character Mary?" he asked.

I retrieved his hand from my head and kissed it gently. "Of course, and I do you. My heard and heart are too torn to be enveloped and suffocated in your affections. I would make friend with folly if I were to repeat the sentiments from the last few years."

"We love freely or not at all. That must be decided tonight or we shall forever part."

As we ascended the stairs to check on Marguerite and Frances, I assured myself there were no highway men, or rough seas and stranded isles to contend with. No guillotines or beheadings. I was safe, for this evening at least, to familiarise myself with his heart and body and the pleasures we would taste together. I kissed Frances goodnight and whispered to Marguerite I would see her in the morning. A grin washed over her face and she mouthed the words be safe as I closed the door behind me.

Godwin and I walked to his apartment, strolling hand in hand and arm in arm. I let my body relax into the wistful feeling of uncertainty, the feeling of being human, one would say. Entering his apartment and admitting us into his room, Godwin undressed me immediately. My heart set ablaze with fire and cracked the ice which had formed solid around it, swirling and spinning itself into a frenzy.

"Shall I, inspire you with my desires?" he brushed my lips with his finger as he turned me around and untied the bows from my dress. "Or," he breathed down my neck, "shall I find pleasure in every crevice of you?" He grasped my hair in one hand and pulled my head to his lips.

"Kiss me won't you?" I stroked my fingers through his hair as he lifted me onto his bed; his warm eyes pouring over my body. "What is the matter?" He knelt beside the bed and intertwined his fingers with mine. My mind wandered from the feeling of his lips against my skin to the thought of nature and pleasure of our sex, how it made us that we often attain happiness only by way of pain. I tried to force my mind to abandon its senses to pleasure; shuffling my weight to relax into the cotton.

"Your mind keeps you its prisoner Mary, I can see it in your eyes and feel it in your hands." He caressed my knee with his lips. "Breathe." Godwin rose above me and met my eyes with a grin. Glacing down he considered my breasts and lowered himself back down to kiss them softly. A few moments passed and he undressed himself and joined me fully on the bed.

"That felt lovely," I said. "Why did you stop?" He kissed my forehead and he pulled me up to the pillows so we lay next to each other in comfort amongst his linen.

"I want to promise you something, before we philosophise any further." He stared down at his body for a few moments and exhaled. "I do not need or want a woman to be, devoted to me and I know you do not want that either. Marriage, does need not happen in our instance. I crave independence and mutual understanding. Are you content with that?" I studied his words in my mind for a minute and stroked his bare shoulder, his skin warm and prickled with small bumps.

"This desire to marry makes mere animals of my sex. We marry and act as such children may be expected to act. We dress, paint, and nickname God's creatures." I rested my head further into his pillow and stared at the ceiling. "We render ourselves insignificant objects of desire."

"I desire you," he kissed the tips of my fingers. My heart pounded again. My body burning against the warmth of him.

"You understand me though?" I hesitated for a mere moment.

He laughed cooly and smiled. "I understand you Mary, what troubles you?"

"We are taken out of our sphere of duties, and made ridiculous and useless when the short lived bloom of beauty is over. And do not even start me on why girls be told to resemble angels when they are young and beautiful for in this respect it is their persons, not their virtues, that procure them this homage." William's eyes followed my hands as I expressed my rage against the situation of my sex towards the ceiling.

"And what if we need to marry?" I turned to face him as my heart stopped for a beat. Paris. The embassy. Frances. I gulped and shivered away the thought of what it would mean for my girl.

"Why would we ever marry? If you fancy a woman taught only to please, you need to find yourself some other." He kissed me again and rested his hand on my chest.

"Oh. Is that so?" he said in a playful tone and we drifted into an embrace. His body on top of mine and together we moved in rhythmic order as one. He caressed me on my neck and pressed my hands into the sheets again, pushing down until my body fired drunken sensations through my veins. I closed my eyes and saw nothing. Not a memory, not a flash of an idea, want or desire; my mind followed my body and gave into the feelings of pleasure I thought I had closed off from ever feeling again.I sunk into my heart's torrent of delights as we made love.

St. Pancras Church Middlesex
London 29th March 1797

"I cannot bring myself to wound your heart Mary," said William. "However objected I am to marriage, if it is necessary to you to protect the one you carry then so be it. I do not want you to suffer more and endure more troubles on my behalf." William lent against the doorway to the kitchen and stirred a small cup of tea. "What shall you wear?"

"You talk as though it happens tomorrow." William raised his eyebrows and smiled as he sipped. The light from the sun soaked morning cast an ethereal glow into the kitchen. We talked for a moment more and upon finishing his tea, he placed himself beside me at the wooden table. The kitchen was meagre, only the necessary things, I told myself, but it was ample for myself and Frances.

"Mary, we can be married tomorrow or next year or never. It is your choice."

"I only want to give him, our William, the best chance at life he can." I rubbed my stomach and felt those familiar twitches of life.

"Papa?" called Frances.

"Yes dear one what is it? Oooh you are so tall now, look at you." William picked Frances up from the floor and placed her on his lap. Her gentle eyes widened at my face.

"Mama, papa?" Frances began to play with my hair. I stared at William who was now fixated with the little one.

"Your mumma and papa shall walk into a beautiful church, not too far from here and, together we exchange words and then—"

"And then we kiss!" William tickled Frances and kissed me on the forehead. "Let us marry then. We shall go next week. I shall enquire with Marshall and Johnson."

"No one else, not even Mary."

"Not even Mary," nodded William. "It is decided then."

"It is decided," I said, and an unforced smile found itself on my face. But as I looked towards Frances my heart knew what this meant for her. My unfortunate girl.

*

"You are late," said Joseph, smiling.

"The world shall continue if I am late or not," I said laughing as we walked through the church's iron gates. Arms together, we took deep breaths in as Joseph opened the heavy wooden church doors to St. Pancras Church, a white knight amongst a garden of leafy trees.

"It is rather smaller than I remember," I said. Another breath. Joseph gripped my arm tight and nodded.

The morning light dispersed through the high windows and danced across William's face, who smiled at the sight of us both. The stone was cool underneath my shoes and the six rows of wooden chairs were empty except for Marshall and the clerk of the church.

As we approached William, his smile widened. "You look beautiful," he said, nodding to Joseph who had placed himself beside the clerk of the church William's friend. Another breath.

"Dearly beloved," said the vicar. "We are gathered here today to join this man and this woman in holy matrimony. William Godwin, do you take this woman to be your wife, to live together in holy matrimony, to love her, to honour her, to comfort her, and to keep her in sickness and in health, forsaking all others, for as long as you both shall live?"

"I do," said William.

"Mary Wollstonecraft, do you take this man to be your husband, to live together in holy matrimony, to love him, to honour him, to comfort him, and to keep him in sickness and in health, forsaking all others, for as long as you both shall live?"

"I do."

The vicar joined our hands together and smiled at us. "Repeat after me."

"I, William Godwin, take you Mary Wollstonecraft, to be my wife, to have and to hold from this day forward, for better, for worse, for richer, for poorer, in sickness and in health, to love and to cherish, till death do us part." Another breath.

The vicar nodded at me and I stared into William's eyes. "I, Mary Wollstonecraft, take you William Godwin, to be my husband, to have and to hold from this day forward, for better, for worse, for richer, for poorer, in sickness and in health, to love and to cherish, till death do us part."

Joseph stood and gave the ring to William "I give you this ring as a token and pledge of our constant faith and abiding love."

"By virtue of the authority vested in me, I now pronounce you husband and wife." I glanced at Joseph who nodded with his friendly smile. "You may kiss the bride." William kissed me and our two guests and the clerk clapped in unison.

After thanking Vicar Champneys and his clerk, the four of us returned to the morning outside the church and strolled amongst the trees and graveyard.

Joseph found a small spot to rest beneath one of the trees and patted the seat beside me. As we sat together in silence for a few moments, I let the wind carry unsaid words between us. "It is peaceful I—"

"I was trying to—"

"You first," I laughed. He shifted in his chair and turned to face me. I had looked upon his face many a times but this time his features appeared relaxed. His shoulders, less upright than usual; his countenance and expression appeared soft.

"I was trying to find some particular time to ask you but I have yet the chance."

"Mm?"

"Your life has been hard with, Imlay and Frances. Scandinavia, France. Losing Olympe and your friends in the salons." I focused on the breeze in the trees above us as I remembered her face. What colour were her eyes? How did she smile? "Have you found whatever it is you were looking for?" I furrowed my brow.

"I do not quite understand what you mean?"

"One would assume someone who travels countries and leaves her friends is either running from something or looking for something." I let his words sit in my chest for a small while.

"I...I am sorry I left you here in London."

"I need no apology Mary I am a grown man," Joseph

coughed a few times into his handkerchief. "An old one at that." I picked several leaves off his jacket that had fallen and returned them the wind.

"After everything with Henry and Sophia I could not bear to stay here and face the judgement and embarrassment. My head longed to stay here but my heart too shamed to stay. I thought if I moved to France I would find peace."

"He forgave you in the end," Joseph tapped the edge of the seat. "Find peace in the middle of the war?" I smiled at the thought of how stupid it sounded aloud. "You did not answer my question." We both looked over to William and Marshall who had found a seat for themselves on the other side of the graveyard.

"This time it will be different."

"How so?"

"I think I require my own space and independence. I want to be loved and my heart riveted, but it is not necessary for him to be always at my elbow, nor I at his. I want him to love me for who I am. My mind is half-stupid, constantly at worry, but I think I have found peace in his. He is not childish, or in need of grand things of me. He does not make me feel smaller, in fact I postulate he quite adds to my joy." The largest smile I had ever witnessed appeared across Joseph's face. He turned to face me a little more and held my hands together between his.

"Finally Mary." I furrowed my brow. "Finally your heart understands."

"You have convinced me of something I once thought impossible Joseph."

"Is that so?" he replied.

"The heart is treacherous, and I am thankful for this friendship between persons of different sexes."

"Do you remember when we returned from the north?" Joseph relaxed back into the bench and soaked in the view even further, the precipice of summer gracing the air around us. "Scandalous I tell you. We could have married you know, that would really have perpetuated the rumours. Imagine the books we'd sell."

"I do think we would render each other completely mad if we were to ever marry Joseph. Godforbid you live that long to outlive him." I nodded to William who caught my gaze and nodded to the two of us. "Humour me and do so will you?"

London Wednesday 30th August 1797

I have no doubt of seeing the animal today, but must wait for Mrs Blenkinsop to guess the hour. I have sent for her. Pray send me the newspaper. I wish I had a novel or some book of sheer amusement to excite curiosity and while away the time. Have you anything of the kind?
M

"Mrs Blenkinsop tells me everything is in a fair way and there is no fear of the event being put off till another day. For the present she thinks I shall not be immediately free from my load. I am very well. Call before dinner time unless you receive another message from me."
M

"My dear girl, are you done writing? You will be delivering soon." There is too much to write.

"Soon," I said, not removing my gaze from the page.

"Mm," she said, I could hear the humorous judgement in her tone. "You will never stop will you?" I shook my head. "A letter?" I nodded. "To Godwin? He is downstairs girl."

"No," I said, feeling my stomach. "To the little one. And Godwin's departed for lunch."

"How do you-"

"He helps me eat if he is here and he is not, so he is not back yet." Mrs Blenkinsop smiled again and finished tidying the blankets.

"Rest when you can, he will be here soon."

3pm August 30th, 1797

Mrs Blenkinsop tells me I am in the most natural state that promises me a safe delivery, but I must have a little patience.
M

11.27pm, the same evening

"Mary you need to push," said Mrs Blenkinsop. "Now."

"I cannot, oh it hurts." She took perfect hold of my legs and held them down so I could not move.

"Mary you need to breathe dear woman for Heaven's sake. Breathe." I took air in and out. One, two, three. "Push, Mary push." A bellowing, inhumane scream lurched from my lungs. "Mary." With a final push, I exerted any remaining effort and the screaming monster left my body, gulping and screaming at the world it had been pushed into.

"William!" I said, as tears poured from my eyes. "Our dear William." Mrs Blenkinsop held the small creature high, cut its cord and wrapped it in a small blanket. "Water I need water please."

"Mary, my dear girl, it is not your William." Blenkinsop turned its small body to face me. A girl.

"Send for Godwin please," my body ached as I tried to sit. After several minutes of preparing the room, the midwife opened the door and Godwin entered.

"How is our William?" he said, placing himself on the end of our bed. I shook my head.

"It is a girl," I said.

"Our Mary?" he said smiling, and I nodded in reply.

He grabbed my hand and kissed it. Mrs Blenkinsop, standing in the corner of the darkened room smiled, acknowledging the many hours we had spent together.

"There shall be two Mary Wollstonecraft's to contend with then," he said as we laughed together. "She is wonderful. You are wonderful." He smiled the familiar and rare smile I so loved of his. One of those smiles which has a quality of eternal reassurance with it. One that says, I see you. It understood you as far as you wanted to be understood. I had only come across it once before in my life; my heart panged at the thought of her buried in the cemetery in Lisbon.

"Now, get some rest. I shall see you in the morning. I have been told to leave you at peace," he whispered, kissing my forehead before he stood. "I shall be in my study if she requires anything." Mrs Blenkinsop nodded and attended my bedside.

"Now he's gone, is there anything you need my dear girl?" she smiled at me again as we passed the little one between our arms.

"Water please and maybe a cool towel? I am warm." As I lay my head on the sweat-soaked pillow, I could hear Mary's small noises. So sweet and small, just like her sister was.

"A towel and anything else?"

"No, that is all thank you," I said, turning over. The pain in my stomach continued to rage in a violent temper. "A new stomach perhaps?" Mrs Blenkinsop laughed cooly and closed the door.

Thursday, August 31st, 1797

"Send for the hospital," quipped Godwin at the end of my bed. "There is a Dr Fordyce there and a Dr Poignant. Westminster Lying-in Hospital do you understand? Do not stop for anyone, do you understand?" the midwife's assistant rushed out of the room.

"Mr Godwin it shall be okay," said Mrs Blenkinsop.

"Mary darling, how are you feeling?" I tried to open my eyes.

"Warm," I replied, closing my eyes again.

Friday September 1st, 1797

"Mary can you hear me?" a familiar voice said from my bedside. "Dr Poignant is here with me."

"Dr Fordyce?"

"Yes Mary. We are here, we are going to take a look at a few things okay?" I tried to nod but my body could only produce a small groan. Voices fussed over me. My body turned and turned again. A cool instrument against my legs. Pain. Sharp pain.

"Apologies," said a voice unfamiliar. A hand held my hand. William.

Sunday, September 3rd, 1797

"Oh my dearest Mary, you look better than I expected," said another familiar voice. "Oh, where is Basil? Tell him he needs to hurry. Mary, oh congratulations Mary, she is a delight! A delight my dear Mary." Mary Hayes rubbed my arm as though she were removing dirt. "Heaven's forbid he hurry, Basil hurry would you?"

"I shall be up in a minute Mary," a faded voice said from the parlour below. Though the pain was not as bad today, my body ached for sleep.

"I need to go to Kensington today," said William. "Dr Fordyce saw you this morning, and he thinks you are on the mend my dear girl." I effort'd a small smile, though, somewhere in my body something still ached. "You be good to her won't you? Tell her the stories of your travels won't you?"

"Oh shall I ever," said Mary. "We climbed up the tallest cliffs and mountains. Oh and there were goats, have you ever laid eyes on one? You have seen a goat haven't you Mary? "Oh, it was truly magnificent..." My eyes closed as our friend recounted her travels.

Wednesday, September 6th, 1797

"Oh, Godwin, I am in Heaven," I said, letting the laudanum course its way through my veins like lightening rippling through a tree; soaking into the roots and depths of my body.

"You mean, my dear, your physical sensations are somewhat easier. There shall be no going to heaven right now, the world needs you here. I need you here."

"That shall do for now. Second dose," said Dr Carlisle.

"Mr Godwin, a Miss Paine is downstairs, she has arrived with Mr Fenwick and a Mr Dyson," said the midwife's assistant whose name I could not remember. William fussed my hair out of my eyes. The blurry outline of his figure instilled comfort in me I thought I had lost.

"I will be back in a moment, wait here," said Godwin. I do not think it quite possible I should go anywhere soon. A small laugh escaped from my mouth.

"Sir before you go," said Dr Carlisle. "I think a wine diet

might be perhaps the way to go this evening if this does not do its job."

"Wine?"

"Wine," replied Dr Carlisle. "I cannot give her more of this dreadful stuff as I do not want to hurt her." I could hear William adjust his weight on the floorboards.

"Whatever you say, I shall send Mr Dyson and Mrs Fenwick to fetch some more amicable wine than we have."

A few minutes, or hours later, I could not tell, Godwin returned to my bedside.

"Darling, Joseph sends news for you. He is north and will not be back for a few days. He will visit when you are better." His warm hands intertwined with mine. He had writer's skin, like mine, soft and delicate.

"Mary, you will be better," his voice cracked. "Here have some more wine."

"More?" I uttered, shifting my legs underneath the blankets. "Godwin?" I needed air. "Window."

"Window? Oh, you want the window open, of course, here." As he opened the window, the summer breeze danced its way in, pushing its way through the curtains. The house cracked and breathed at the cool air as small noises of strangers talking from the street below drifted in.

"What are they saying?" I asked.

"Who?" replied Godwin.

"People."

"Oh. Uh," he paused for a moment as he listened out the window. "Well, a gentleman is talking about the weather."

"How English," I smiled. "Tell me more."

"There is another gentleman, a brash looking man. Maybe about thirty. He appears to be quite perturbed." I closed my eyes again as the air from outside filled my sleepy lungs.

"Mary?" his voice much closer than before. "You are going to make it, aren't you?" I moved my hand and pressed his hands together.

Thursday 7th September 1797

The pain subsided enough I could sit upright. By mid-morning, the entire party of our friends had gathered in our room. Montagu, Marshall, Dyson, Fenwick, Dr Carlisle, Dr Fordyce and Godwin stood at the end of my bed.

"Where is Fanniken?" her small head poked out from behind Godwin at the utterance of her name.

"Go see your mumma," said Dr Carlisle as Frances walked to my beside.

"Hello my little one," I kissed her forehead as she tried to climb on the bed. "You are getting heavy!" I said, the group laughing as Godwin tried to wrangle the small monster off me.

"Kiss for mama?" she blew a small kiss to me in the air.

"Mama hungry?" asked Frances. "Apple? She extended her hand towards me, offering a small sliver of apple.

"Not quite my dear one, maybe tomorrow I shall join you and papa for dinner." William handed her to a servant I did not quite recognise, and she disappeared downstairs. "Thank you all for being here."

"We wouldn't have it any other way," said Basil.

"You are quite right Mr Montagu," said Godwin. "They are all here to help you."

"Tell me," I said. "What is occurring in the world? Have I missed anything?"

Basil let out a small laugh as he adjusted his collar. "Well," he said. "Napoleon plans to launch an invasion on England."

"Oh," once I laughed, everyone of our friends joined in unison. "After a revolution and starting a war with us they want to invade us?"

"Correct," said Basil. "Ambitious one he is."

"And a count of appurtenant countries," added Dyson, who had settled himself against the door frame. Together they were a painting. Varying in statures, not one of them alike in age, height, manner or make, but all were friends. One man's absence was unbearable for my heart to accept.

Godwin shook his head and would not look at me. "Joseph is stranded up north. I tried Mary."

"Those roads be terrible." I half smiled and wiped down my blankets. Unsaid words floated behind their eyes. "The weather is strange this time of year." Godwin's eyes shot to me and we smiled together.

"Come, let her rest some more," said Dr Carlisle. "We will see you tomorrow Mary." One by one, they each bowed and left the room, leaving behind Godwin.

"Do you mind if I dine with them this evening?"

"Of course not my darling." My heart fluttered in my chest, but this time it was not for love; it was a foreign pain I could not name. My feet ached from not stepping foot on the ground in days. I let my chest rise and fall as Godwin walked to my bedside once again.

"Goodnight my love," he said.

Friday afternoon, 8th September, 1797

"I did not know what bodily pain was before this," I said to no one in particular. I could feel the weight of someone on my bed and the sounds of breathing. William most likely.

The pain was unrelenting, a persistent ache that radiated through my body.

The laudanum failed me.

I was numbed by the wine.

"She is shaking," a voice said. "The whole bed is shaking." Godwin.

"Decided mortification is what it is," said one voice. "Something is dying from inside of 'uh, most likely to do with the birth Mr Godwin."

"Can you remove it?" said Godwin.

"It will kill her."

"She is dying god damn it. Mary." Godwin shifted closer to me, I could feel his breath on my cheek. A teardrop fell onto my face, yet I could not wipe his tears away. A heaviness weighed on my eyes.

"There's a spot for you at the table downstairs Mary... Mary there's supper and your favourite wine, cheese, some blackberries."

"Do not lay a cloth for me," I whispered.

"Mary..." his warm hands pressed against my shoulders and shook me. I could not move. "Oh what have I done..." the weight of his head pressed against me. I wish I could comfort him.

Sunday, 10th September, 1797

"I know what you are thinking of..." I whispered in reply. "I trust you to take care of them."

"One in a million of persons in her state might recover," said Dr Carlisle from a corner of the room. There was hope in his voice before. Not now. They dare not tell me; you do not tell a dying man he is dying.

"Not one person in a million has her good constitution of mind and body," replied William, squeezing my hand and kissing it.

Sleep.

Peace.

"I cannot open my eyes," I whispered.

"Keep them closed then my love and sleep. I shall be here when you wake up. And so will Frances and Mary."

As heaviness took hold of my body, I nodded, my eyelids growing heavier with each passing second.

William gripped my hand as I drifted into my infinite dream.

London Monday 11th September 1797

"Sir, she requested this be left for you to send to Johnson," Godwin's servant handed him a stack of parchments at the breakfast table.

"It's for her Frances." Returning his spoon to the table, he leapt from his seat.

"Where is she?"

"In the parlour, shall I retrieve her?" he nodded and after a few minutes, the bereaved philosopher and Frances walked together to a small park, the small patches of sunlight illuminating the benches.

"Frances?" said William, placing her on his lap.

"Yes papa?"

"This is from..." William placed the parchments back within his coat. Godwin's chest expanded until he could not hold his tears any longer and after a few moments, he let his body collapse onto the bench. He shook his head and wiped away his tears.

"Papa, why crying?" Godwin pulled a small handkerchief from his pocket and dotted his tears away.

"Your mama is...your mama is gone little one." Frances stared at Wiliam who had pulled her into his chest as he cried into the arms of her little girl.

Number 72, St. Paul's Churchyard London
Wednesday 13th September 1797

Fuseli.

One who loved you, & whom I respected, is no more.
Mrs Godwin died on Sunday.

J Johnson.

Number 72, St. Paul's Churchyard London
Wednesday 13th September 1797

I arrived in London three days too late. It is something that will pain me forever, that I could not see her and tell her that I loved her so dearly as a friend. But I can recount for you the final hours of Mary's life so below.

My dearest friend Godwin, the philosopher, had fallen asleep in his study. But by 6 o'clock in the evening, a sobbing servant had entered his room. Not wanting to know whether she were alive or had expired, he ascended up the dark stairs of their Polygon home and into her shadowed room.

She was then almost insensible, but recognised him and tried to smile. He remained on his knees by her bedside for over an hour and a half, then his Mary, our Mary, died, resigning her struggle for life as she had some while since resigned her struggle for happiness.

Clinging to his principles to stay his anguish, he crept downstairs, went to his desk, and filled in the entry in his diary; he had never missed a day—he would not miss this. He could not, however, bring himself to write she was dead, and the only blank in the diary follows the date of:

10. Su. —— 20 minutes before 8 —— —— —

Number 72, St. Paul's Churchyard London
Wednesday 13th September 1797

Mary Wollstonecraft's, my dearest friend's remains were deposited, on the fifteenth of September, at ten o'clock in the morning, in the churchyard of the parish church of St. Pancras, Middlesex. A few of the persons she most esteemed, attended the ceremony; and a plain monument now rests underneath the trees, by some of her friends, with the following inscription:

MARY WOLLSTONECRAFT GODWIN
AUTHOR OF
A VINDICATION
OF THE RIGHTS OF WOMAN.
BORN, XXVII APRIL MDCCLIX.
DIED, X SEPTEMBER MDCCXCVII

Mary Wollstonecraft Godwin possessed, in a degree superior to any other person I ever knew, a mind full of strength and intuition. She was often right in her philosophy. Mary would adopt one opinion and reject another. She reasoned little but was sound in her determinations. The light of a life friend was lent to the world for too little of a time and is now extinguished forever.